THE
HIDDEN
PEOPLE

Also by Alison Littlewood

A Cold Season
Path of Needles
The Unquiet House
A Cold Silence

THE
HIDDEN
PEOPLE

ALISON
LITTLEWOOD

Jo Fletcher

New York • London

Jo Fletcher Books
An imprint of Quercus
New York • London

ISBN 978-1-68144-293-8

Library of Congress Control Number: 2016953283

Distributed in the United States and Canada by
Hachette Book Group
1290 Avenue of the Americas
New York, NY 10104

Manufactured in the United States

10 9 8 7 6 5 4 3 2 1

www.quercus.com

For my mother

Come away, O, human child!
To the woods and waters wild
With a fairy hand in hand,
For the world's more full of weeping
Than you can understand.

William Butler Yeats

Why did they bring me here to make me
Not quite bad and not quite good,
Why, unless They're wicked, do They want, in spite,
to take me
Back to Their wet, wild wood?

Charlotte Mary Mew

Chapter One

It was at the Great Exhibition that I first saw my cousin, and even then I could not but think of it as a convergence, not merely of the great new powers of industry and machines with those of hill and tree, but of different times. Here was the future, loud and brash and busy, and here all the idle repose and gawping of the past, drawn to this place to marvel upon its arrival. The year was 1851, and that was utterly apt, for the apex of the century had been crested and we were now rushing headlong towards the next at a pace that must surely increase a thousandfold before its end.

I can still recall my first words to young Lizzie, as I already thought of her then, though I blush at the memory. I can only apologise for being what I was: young and rather callow and a little too pleased with myself. I was tall, dressed in a new silk top hat and floral waistcoat, and sporting, best of all in my own eyes, my first real moustache. I smiled down at the shy creature, under the gaze of my father and her own, and said, "How do you find this, the Great Exhibition of the Works of Industry of all Nations?"

Under the modest and rather worn brim of her bonnet, her plump lip twitched. A single blonde curl bobbed prettily. I should say that Lizzie—or Elizabeth Thurlston, as she was then—was my rural cousin, a denizen of the fair lands far to the north of our capital, and she had come up to London by train with so many others to admire all the wonders within the Crystal Palace. We had timed our own visit accordingly, though it had entailed a reorganisation of our plans so that we could attend on a one-shilling day, rather than our appointed Friday, when the charge was increased to two shillings and sixpence. It was especially crowded; the roads had been all but blocked with omnibuses, cabs, private broughams and flies. Of course we did not mention it when we met them beneath the great elm tree which stood near the Prince of Wales Gate. I was not, I hope, so irredeemably without good qualities as that.

"I 'aven't seen it yet, Cousin," she replied, her voice as gentle as the bounds of propriety could command, although with the unfortunate trace of Yorkshire in her vowels.

Still, I couldn't help but recollect that whereas my mother had married well, her sister was said by all accounts to have married somewhat low, and as such I had never had the pleasure of making the acquaintance of my cousin until this very day. And yet the great progress of the iron rail had been so rapid that such meetings must surely have become rather commonplace. It was said that half the population would make their pilgrimage to see the Great Exhibition before its end, though afterwards I discovered that the nearer number would be a third; still a remarkable total.

I glanced up at the towering elm which marked our meeting place. Outside, the day was of mixed character. Spears of bright light occasionally found their way between lowering grey clouds, so that it was unclear whether rain or sunshine would come to dominate. The tree filtered it all, casting a cooling shadow across our faces. It had been said that the opponents of the exhibition—for such did exist, if it can be imagined—had fought most bitterly against the felling of Hyde Park's ancient trees to permit the construction of the Crystal Palace. Not wishing to let anything impede their progress, the committee had duly made some alteration in their design, and as a result the trees themselves had been enclosed within a barrel-vaulted transept, held aloft by soaring arms of iron; a feature which I now felt had come to be the glory of the whole.

My father, at his most expansive, exchanged some pleasantry with his brother-in-law and indicated the way forward into the exhibition. The commotion of it already rang in our ears: the rhythmic thrumming of cotton manufacture, of steam-driven machinery and marine engines; the clatter of hydraulic presses and the rattle of the latest Jacquard looms. It was wonderful and it was fearful, and I tried to peer beneath Lizzie's bonnet once more, thinking of a sudden that I should very much like to see the expression in her eyes.

My father broke in upon my thoughts with a sharp, "Take Lizzie's arm, Albie," and I had no time to cast a remonstrative glance at his use of the diminutive form of my Christian name before her little hand—somewhat browned by days spent out of doors—slipped around my left elbow. I had no further opportunity to spy upon her features as we processed together side by side into the bustle and the noise, surrounded not only by the heady sound of industry, but the endless murmuring of a thousand human conversations.

We wandered at liberty and without design, through the exhibits of the colonies and other nations, before returning to the western side of the structure, where was housed all the progress and pride that our own fine country could offer. I forget what it was of which we spoke. We watched the inexplicable operations of piston and cog, smiled over splendid silks, tapestries and exquisite china and gasped at the magnificent Koh-i-Noor diamond. We stood apart whilst her father pressed through the crowds of men dressed in their smock-frocks to see a noisy flax-crushing machine and a mechanical reaper. Then all the latest medical and scientific apparatus was spread before us, as well as the accomplishments of modern horology in the form of intricate watches and clocks, their numerous ticks and springs giving way all at once to the midday chimes.

Lizzie raised her chin to me, and I saw the delight in her nut-brown eyes before my father cried out, "Look! Let us see whether we shall have a storm."

It was then that I was introduced to a most curious exhibit: that of the Tempest Prognosticator.

We waited for a school of charity girls, bedecked in wide white collars and straw bonnets, to move aside before we gathered around it. At first, it was unclear what it was we were gazing upon. Concentric rings of what appeared to be brass surrounded a central pillar turned from shining ebony or some other dark wood, culminating in a device a little like a crown, a little like a bell.

"A barometer," my father pronounced. "Most ingenious! Science and the powers of animal instinct, working in harmony . . ."

Animal instinct? I knew not of what he spoke. I found my attention already wandering a little, for Lizzie had begun to trace a ring around the exhibit, running one finger along the rail, and when she saw me watching, a little smile almost mischievous in nature crossed her lips. Then she leaned in, her eyes narrowing, and she wrinkled her nose.

I found myself peering more closely to see what had disturbed her countenance, and then I did and I recoiled. At the base of the instrument, arranged in a circle, were twelve bottles, and in each bottle, if I did not mistake myself, was a leech, each vile curled form pressed against the glass.

I turned to my father. I do not know if I managed to keep the disgust from my face, but if I did not he gave no sign of noticing.

"Leeches have a singular talent, besides their medical advantages," he proclaimed. "They have a certain sensitivity to electrical conditions in the atmosphere. When a coming storm is detected, they endeavour to climb out of their prisons, a motion that is sensed by these small hammers—there!—causing them to strike the bell. The more agitated they become, the worse the storm and the more the bell shall strike." He laughed. "But the jury is motionless and the bell is silent. Thus, we shall have no storm!"

He never suspected how very wrong he was, and yet no one else spoke. We merely contemplated the strange, almost alchemical-seeming invention, and my father smiled as if he had dreamed it up himself.

After a time I found I did not know where to look and so instead I read the information which accompanied the exhibit. I noticed with a start that its creator was named, of all things, Dr. Merry-weather; but I had no wit to make a humorous remark upon it, for I could not help but think of what must be entailed in the care of such an instrument. Clocks must be wound after all, and this, too, must surely place certain demands upon its owner. I imagined a maid polishing the glass, oiling the shining metal, brushing dust from the smooth wood. And what then? Would the possessor of such a thing have to take each leech, freeing it however momentarily from its confinement, and in order to preserve its life, press each in turn against his skin? The thought reduced me almost to gloom, a most unaccustomed state for my then self, and presently we moved on and I hardly know where it was we went or what we looked upon. I only know that Lizzie's arm was in mine once more, and that she was quite unaffected; as I suppose she should have been, being a child almost of nature herself.

At last we came to a crystal fountain, and its liquid tones sang away my melancholy. It was situated by another great elm, or per-haps the same one, my senses and my memory being, by then, entirely dazzled. Lizzie did not appear to notice. She chattered away about how they would break their journey, since rail hadn't yet come to Halfoak, and I became a little confused, thinking at first she said *our folk*; and then I understood, but she was already speculating that maybe one day it would, and then she could get about quite easily. And there she stopped as a new sound impinged upon our senses.

One of the exhibited organs, a device intended, I believe, for the Queen's Procession, had begun to ring out, accompanying the tinkling of the fountain with a new tune, one I instantly recognised. It had been published some few years before and was already quite familiar. I had barely named the melody in my mind when Lizzie slipped her hand from my arm, clutched both instead in front of her, drew in a deep breath and began to sing.

All things bright and beautiful,
All creatures great and small,
All things wise and wonderful,
The Lord God made them all.

As she sang, her voice suddenly rising strong and pure above it all, the sunlight speared through the crystal of the roof, through the great boughs of the tree, and laid its dappling upon her, a finer lace than any the exhibition could offer. I realised that conversations had quieted, that people around us had stopped to listen just as if Lizzie were an exhibit herself, made not of wood or iron or glass but of flesh and blood. She was an angel; she was a bird. I watched her as she sang of all God's creatures, of flowers and glowing colours and of tiny wings; of the greenwood and the meadow, the sunset and the morning. She sang with her eyes closed, as if conscious of no one, the small coarseness in her speech quite untraceable in her song.

The rich man in his castle,
The poor man at his gate,
God made them high and lowly
And ordered their estate.

How apposite it was! And then her song was done and the tones of the organ faded away, and I realised that everything around me was just as it had been: the machinery, the busyness, all the rushing progress of our age. Time had started again, and I shook my head at my own muddle-headedness as she rejoined our small party.

I could not think of what to say, and yet I felt I should speak. Such, I believe, is ever the impetuosity of youth.

"Just as our good queen has named herself Victoria," I said, "choosing to forgo her first given name, Alexandrina, and instead named herself—why, I think you should rather be a Linnet than a Lizzie!"

I felt my father's eyes upon my face and I let out a small spurt of laughter along with my words.

The lady did not reply; she merely dipped in a rather artless yet charming curtsy.

Her father laughed too, and I only realised then how little I had heard him speak when he barked out in rough tones, "'Appen she should make it Vicky, then, and you shall be Vicky and Albie!"

I knew by the white press of my father's lips the extent of his disapprobation and horror at such a suggestion. I do not know if our relatives from the north ever knew it, but he was a still pool whose waters ran deep, and I could sense the anger simmering within him, even if his voice remained low. With an even greater excess of the politeness that ever characterised his conversation he wished them well for the long journey that was ahead of them. He told them of our pressing engagements and the demands of the City, and on both our parts, he took our leave.

I nodded at Mr. Thurlston and shook his hand and had time only to press Lizzie's palm in mine before we were hurrying away; before I had even time to gather myself or properly say good-bye. It was only then, as we left through the high and shining doors and put the palace of crystal behind us, threading through the bustle towards the grey rooftops beyond, that it even occurred to me to remember that our good queen, besides choosing the name by which she should be known, had elected to marry her own first cousin.

And yet my father had no cause for either fear or anger. I did not see Lizzie again, not for many a year; and even then, it was not for some time after she was dead.

Chapter Two

The irony is not lost upon me that I barely heard Lizzie spoken of again until 1862, a little more than ten years later, the year after Prince Albert had died. So much pomp and wealth and importance, and still they could not prevent his passing; the typhoid took him the previous December, as it had taken so many others. Queen Victoria was of course plunged into the deepest mourning, for theirs was ever said to be a union of love and not simply one of convenience or state.

Our once-happy queen now wore black, was surrounded by black, and her very heart was said to have fallen into darkness. It was rumoured that she preserved his rooms just as they had been while he breathed; that hot water was brought each morning as if he were about to rise from his slumber and wash his face; that his linen was refreshed each day, as if she were endeavouring to make it appear that nothing had changed when in reality, everything had.

I was sitting at dinner with my father, his hair now quite grey, and Helena, my wife of the last eighteen months. She was dressed with her usual neatness in a watered silk, her raven-dark hair swept back from her high, clear forehead, adorned by a lace cap and with two neat little ringlets about her ears. She was pale of complexion, sweet of lip, and her brown eyes were always calm, reflective of her even temper. She was what Father called a sensible female, and he was right to say so, for she had been known to steer my course if ever it became uncertain. She had a visage of which the words of Lord Byron might have been written: *She walks in beauty, like the night.* And yet she knew at once if the haberdasher tried to cheat her by so much as an inch or the housekeeper helped herself to the tea.

My mother had never known her, having died of an ailment of the heart some years previous to Helena becoming Mrs. Albert Mirralls. Our Yorkshire relatives were on my mother's side of the family, though some illness had kept them from the occasion of her funeral, and after that unhappy event I had scarcely heard them referred to again; so it came as something of a surprise when Father suddenly leaned forward and said, "Do you remember your cousin Elizabeth?"

I had so much thought of my cousin of the north as "young Lizzie" that for a moment I did not know of whom he spoke. Then I remembered, and I flushed. "Certainly."

"Well, a most singular thing has happened to her, my boy. You remember I told you of her marriage to a cordwainer—a shoemaker in Halfoak—James Higgs was his name, I believe."

I agreed that he had indeed told me of such a thing, perhaps two or three years since, although I still recalled my feelings upon hearing that pretty little Elizabeth Thurlston had consented to become plain Lizzie Higgs.

"Well, it appears that a quite horrible occurrence has taken place, and you must not be shocked to hear us speak of it, my dear. But possibly you should prefer to leave the room?" This last was addressed to my wife, but she demurred, insisting in her gentle tones that she would stay. She ever had a way with my father—her own parent was Mr. Sherborne, a trader in possession of some repute, substantial means, and perhaps as importantly in my father's eyes, no living sons.

"Well, what do you think! She has passed away, poor thing. It is quite, quite terrible."

Now that he had not laid eyes on her for many a year, he sounded utterly contrite at her fate, but I did not reflect upon that. I found that a lump had risen to my throat and stayed there, and the sight of my father's face, struggling as I knew he was to find words when words usually came so easily to him had filled me with apprehension.

He turned and looked at me, his eyes shining momentarily as the gaslight flickered and hissed. "He has killed her, Albie."

He had not called me Albie in many a year, but I did not think of that either. I frowned. "Who? Who has—who would—?"

"Her husband."

"What? Father, how could such a thing be? It must be false. No one would ever—"

My wife reached across the table, placing her cool hand on my own where it had curled into a fist.

"It appears that he was suffering under some delusion, my boy. Perhaps he was prone to it; I do not know his family. And those in the country—well, sometimes their thoughts run in unfortunate grooves. Unfortunate, indeed."

"Whatever do you mean?" My voice was taut with anger, my words blunt. At one time my father would have taken a strap to me for such a thing, but now he only sighed.

"I am told he thought she is—or had been, rather, stolen away by the fairies."

My mouth fell open. It was Helena who spoke into the silence left by my astonishment. "The fairies?"

My father raised his hands in front of him, staring at them for a moment as if the answer was suspended in the air between them, and let them fall once more. "It is apparently rather common where they come from. People believe all manner of things. Elves churn the butter; witches charm milk away from the cows; trolls populate the bridges and the woods. Why, when I was a boy, my own mother told me of a place called Runswick Bay, where a hob in a cave could cure the whooping cough, if he was persuaded with just the right charm." He paused. "And sometimes, they say, the fairies take a fancy to a newborn babe or a lady of comely features—" here he glanced at me, ever so briefly, "and steal them away, leaving one of their own in their stead. Wearing a semblance of the one who is stolen, naturally." A note of contempt stole, at last, into his voice.

For a moment, I could not think how we had begun. I only pictured my cousin, stirred by the sound of a hundred clocks striking the hour all about her; the delight that was in her eyes. The delight that was in mine, when I heard her sing, in her beautiful voice, of beautiful things.

I shook my head. "But, Father—how do we proceed from fairies to uxoricide? The killing of one's own wife—of little Lizzie—? Both are surely naught but fancies. It cannot be so."

He cast a glance in my direction. "She was no longer a child," he reminded me. "And fancies—sometimes, it seems, they can run too free, to the harm of all. James—or Jem, as I believe he was known—thought his wife stolen away and a changeling left in her stead. To one superstition is joined another: that various charms will effect to chase away a changeling, when the real wife or child must be returned. Such was his belief." He paused. "Perhaps, after all, we must pity him, rather than—"

"Pity? *Pity!*" For a moment I could only repeat the word. "If what you say is true, sir, we must—" Once more I felt Helena's hand on my arm.

My father rubbed his eyes. "One such charm entailed the holding of an afflicted person over the fire."

His voice was so low, it was a moment before I could absorb his words. I could not speak but words crowded in upon my mind: words and images too, and some of those images were terrible, and they stopped my breath.

"She was burned, Albie." He met my eye at last. Now he only sounded weary; weary to the bone. "He held her over the fire and she was consumed by it."

Helena made a choked sound; her hand left mine and went to her throat. I rose to my feet. I could not listen; I could not think.

"Not possible," I said. "Not possible!" I slammed my hand down upon the table. This couldn't be. My cousin was a child. She was all artlessness and innocence, a shy smile on plump lips; delighted, nut-brown eyes. She was an angel; she was a bird. She was a sudden pure voice, and I heard it; I swear, in that moment, I did, returned as if to mock me.

> *He made their glowing colours,*
> *He made their tiny wings . . .*

She was my Linnet. I had pictured her as a sylvan maid dancing in some green meadow, and perhaps now she was; perhaps she was.

We spoke for a time of how awful it was, but I barely listened to the pronouncements of my father or the softer exclamations of my wife. I felt as if my blood were heated within my veins. It was like something from a savage land, or a history book, or one of the wilder romances that ladies liked to read. It surely wasn't anything that could happen to a real person, let alone a relation, however distant in geography or condition of life; let alone my little Lizzie. I kept staring into the fireplace as if it could enlighten me, but it was cold. All about us was solid and dependable and just as it had always been: the gleaming mahogany; the heavily dressed mantle, with its velvet covering and fringe; the *objets de vertu*, each set upon its little circle of lace; an ancient needlepoint bearing the words from scripture: *Teach me what is good*. I could rest upon none of it.

At last, Helena endeavoured to turn the conversation to brighter things, though with little success. We were a taciturn party and the hour was yet early when we retired to our rooms. I think that even then something was beginning to stir within me, an intimation that this incident would not let me go so easily.

I met my father's eye once more as we said our good nights, and I knew in that look that what had taken place would haunt him too. However, it did not strike me until afterwards that there was more than sorrow in his expression. Inconceivable as it might appear, I think an idea had started to grow within him that should never have taken root and yet which I could not bring myself to tear asunder; that if he had not taken our leave of my cousin that day, in the palace of crystal, everything might have been different. That in some distant and peculiar way, the terrible thing that had befallen young Lizzie was entirely his fault.

Chapter Three

The clock set into the old church tower was as curious a thing as I had seen, perhaps even since my cousin and I had glanced at each other from the opposite sides of a display case wherein stood the Tempest Prognosticator. There was no tempest now. Halfoak was drowsy with sunshine, making the old stone of its houses glow with golden light. The church at the heart of the village was built low to the ground, nestling like some wood mouse settling into its burrow. The tower was only a little taller than the rest of the structure, pockmarked with age and seen through a skein of floating pollen as if through a veil. Behind the church wall were glimpses of the final resting place of the flock to which it had ministered throughout the years. In front of it was the village green on which I stood, and behind me was an inn of ancient construction.

Upon the green itself stood the tree which I knew at once must have given the village its name. A tall, raw, twisted thing, the oak was greened over with a canopy of leaves, and yet it stood upon only half a trunk. The damaged section was blasted, the wood charred and dead where it must have been struck by lightning. It had not been forgotten though, for coloured ribbons trailed from the living branches, soiled and limp, the remnants of some past Mayday celebration to welcome in the summer, perhaps, or maybe simply as a remembrance of how the village had come to be called Halfoak.

It was the clock set into the church tower which most caught my eye, however. It had a plain white face, perfectly ordinary, as far as that goes. The hands were of black iron, or so it appeared, and were also perfectly ordinary, other than the fact that they were too many in number. The hour hand was shorter, as is usual; the other two were a little longer, and the same length.

I blinked again. I realised I had heard of such things before, but I had believed them long vanished from the world. I almost heard a voice, excited and chattering: *The railways 'aven't come yet, not to 'Alfoak, but mebbe one day soon . . .*

Well, it had come here now, or within ten miles at least, and here was its witness: one of its minute hands showed Railway Time, otherwise known as London Time, marching across the land, set by the great Observatory at Greenwich and relayed across the nation by electric telegraph; whilst the other showed local time, that ordination originally fixed by use of a sundial, which even now I could spy set into the wall of the church, its gnomon and part of its dial plate quite rusted away. It had been some years since stationmasters were armed with almanacs and schedules listing all the differences so that passengers could be apprised of the necessary corrections to their watches as they travelled across the land. I looked at my own pocket watch now, and found, with equal parts of annoyance and amusement, that it had stopped at around midday.

The time in Halfoak was either twenty-three minutes past five, or about that number until six o'clock; or perhaps both at once. Standing in the heart of the sleepy village, I bethought it a good thing that the clock was not required to tell the year, though the very configuration of its timepiece suggested somewhen in the past. I decided I should assume local time to be the one trailing, and I tried not to smile. At least I was not to catch a train by it; not yet, at any rate.

I almost felt I had dragged the modern day into the heart of the riding along with my bag containing changes of clothes and some sundry items, which I had set down gratefully by the serving hatch of the Three Horseshoes a short time previously. I introduced myself and enquired if they had a room. It had felt like an age since I had alighted from the train at Kelthorpe, the nearest town, and hired a carrier to bring me the rest of the way by cart, since there was not a pony and trap to be found. I was now in the wilds indeed, somewhere close to the border between the south and west ridings, and I still felt rattled by the jolting journey; the springless cart was a far distant relation of the smooth and efficient hansom cab of the City. It was in some part due to my discomfiture that upon entering the inn I had walked into the taproom rather than the parlour, and yet it was there I had found my host, a Harry Widdop, according to the enquiries I had made.

"We's got two," said the fellow, a suitably stout and ruddy-faced man with his shirt sleeves rolled about his elbows. "Which does tha want?" And he glared at me as if all my future happiness hung upon my answer.

I explained that I had not had the good fortune to visit the region previously and that being the case I had no preference; which one would he recommend? At which he eyed me with suspicion, his eyebrows drawing down into a frown, his sandy mutton-chop whiskers bristling, and he slammed down the tankard he was engaged in polishing. He disappeared from view and I just had time to reflect that what these Yorkshire fellows lacked in volubility was more than amply compensated by their forcefulness of speech when he reappeared from a doorway to one side of the hatch. He gave a little toss of his head, which I assumed was an instruction to follow him from the public area into his domain.

The door gave entry into a narrow passage. Widdop stopped only to choose, at length and with some forethought, a key from a peg on the wall, leaving an identical key hanging at its side. He led the way along the passage and up a narrow and creaking stair of bare and somewhat worn wooden risers and proceeded along a corridor carpeted in some long-faded pattern which ended in a white-painted door. He pushed it open—there was a keyhole, but the door was not locked—and brought me into a surprisingly bright and airy chamber with a well-curtained bed, a washstand and a dresser backed by a much-speckled mirror. The window stood slightly open, admitting a soft breeze smelling of summer meadows, but he crossed the room and abruptly pulled it closed. I was engaged in thinking that I should open it again the moment he quit me when he sharply pulled the curtains across, covering glass and shutters alike, and plunged us both into shadow.

I endeavoured to keep the surprise from my expression, but I must have met his gaze somewhat stupidly for he pronounced, "If tha should want ter shut out t' moon. 'S unlucky to look upon it, wi' t' moon up high."

I nodded, as if I had the first inkling of what he spoke, and he told me his terms—which were most reasonable—and, after pressing the key into my palm, left me alone in my new abode.

The first thing I did, of course, was to cross the room, the boards beneath my feet surely announcing my every step to anyone below, and open the window. Off to the side were a collection of outhouses and the inn's stables, but beyond them was a glory of rippling golden corn and flower-spotted meadows, culminating in the deeper hues of woodland. I could smell the new growth, the muskier smell of horse and from somewhere not too far away, the more chemical scent of washing. Still, it was all most idyllic, with only the distant forms of labourers in the fields to show that this was not the scene of some Elysian repose but a land required to nurture its occupants.

I concluded that my room must face east and that upon the morrow, should I see the hour, I would be treated to a fine sunrise—or perhaps, remembering the landlord's words—I should first see the moonrise. I wondered if his other room must be at the opposite end of the inn, thus being unlikely to see either, having the church to cover the sunset from view, and I considered it my good fortune that his hand had not strayed to the other key on the peg.

I did not wish to wait upon that celestial occurrence, however, nor even to unpack the bag which I had placed at the foot of the bed. Quite aside from the need to begin the mission on which I had come I was eager to be in the fresh air, which smelled so wonderfully clean after all the yellow fogs and smoky fumes of London, so it was little time indeed before I descended the stairs once more, exchanging a nod with the landlord as I passed through the inn. I stepped outside, and from thence it was but a short step to the front of the church where I lingered, Railway Time and local time alike ticking away the minutes whilst sunlight bathed the nape of my neck.

I turned my back upon it, somewhat reluctantly now that the moment had come, looking along the road to where almost the last homely cottage stood and towards the hill that rose to the north of the village. It was a landmark which must have been visible for miles about: no mountain, but it stood proud of the rolling pastoral slopes which surrounded it like an island jutting from the sea. It was notable both for its stature and also for its peculiarity of shape. Only a little taller than it was wide, the hill was quite round, culminating in a flattened top that made it look like nothing so much as an upturned pudding—no doubt the genesis of its name: Pudding Pye Hill. On closer examination I could see the top was not entirely flat, however: a narrow protrusion like a tombstone adorned its summit. This was, I had been informed, a tumulus or barrow, so it was indeed a grave or some other ceremonial place of ancient times. The only other natural irregularity upon the surface of the hill was the jutting crown of a small grove of trees. From this distance it appeared to me like nothing so much as a gathering of local gossips, bending towards each other to catch some choice morsel of news.

That reminded me of why I had come, and my mood faded. I shifted my gaze down the hillside. About halfway up—*neither up nor down*, I thought, the words of the old rhyme coming to me— stood a single cottage. There was no sign of habitation, rather a general air of abandonment, though that might simply have been my fancy.

Dust rose around me as I walked towards it, catching in the back of my throat. The ground was parched, rutted with old cartwheel tracks now set hard, and yet before I reached the foot of the hill I found a little brook sunk into a channel in the earth. Its banks were almost choked with long grasses and its bed with watercress, but it sung merrily along, revealing glimpses of shining brown pebbles between the shifting green. Its clarity and coolness made the day's heat press upon me with greater intensity, and I longed to slake my thirst, even to rinse my face in the sharp, cold water.

Naturally I did no such indecorous thing, but stepped across a little arched stone bridge, quite charming in its rusticity, and stopped for a moment to wonder what my cousin's thoughts must have been upon the realisation that this would be her marital home. I could not imagine, but was flooded instead with a wave of anger that threatened to sweep me away. How could she have tied herself to such a blackguard? Did she have no intimation of his character? I remembered her shy glance, her clear voice rising so beautifully above the tinkling of the crystal fountain. She was an innocent! There was a fineness in her, and for a moment I stopped, unable to go on, overwhelmed by the thought of so sweet a dove being caged in such a manner.

I took a deep breath and went on, reminding myself that though she had possessed some delicacy, she had spent her days surrounded by those who had none, and that despite her City relations, she had few prospects to lift her aloft. I fought down a pang against my father at that, for how had I been better? I had barely thought of her, not for years. I had entered into my own more felicitous union, under the approving gaze of my parent, and had spared little thought, let alone a sovereign, for my poor dear cousin of the north.

Yet here I was, brought here by some impulse that had bewildered not only my own mind but my father's and that of my own dear, sensible wife. My head was mazy with sunlight, my step uncertain. Still, at least the thought of her misfortune and our failure to lend her any assistance had smoothed my way: we were the only family who remained to her, and my father had silently agreed to my visiting with a view to seeing if there was anything I could do. And that made the matter of leaving my employment a simple one, for I was currently a clerk in my father's business, working in turn at each lowly position in order to learn everything that could possibly make me of most use to him; in time, and when he decided it, I would rise to greater heights of responsibility. My father being somewhat harder upon family than those without connection to him, he had not yet seen fit to offer such advancement.

I shook the thought of such clockwork occupations from me and went on, leaning into the slope as it grew steeper of a sudden. The little path was dry and clean and edged with emerald tufts of grass, dotted with bright daisies. I did not stop until I reached the neatly constructed gate, where I glanced up and saw the cottage, and the reality was so distant from the picture I had built of it that for a moment I thought I was looking upon a vision.

It was in every way charming: a low, stone structure nestled into the hillside with a roof half covered in moss and twining ivy. It had a somnolent air, its windows being half shuttered like eyes just beginning to close, and it came to me then that they should have been closed properly—and then I realised the shutters had not been made fast to mark my cousin's demise because her husband was a villain, and there must be none who cared for her enough to carry out even that small service. I recalled the place as I had expected to find it: a hovel, crumbling and dismal and cold, reflecting the heart of the one who had brought her to this pass.

Swallowing down my anger once more I opened the gate, glancing at the garden to see a profusion of colours just inside the wall— *God made their glowing colours*—and peas in want of picking, their weight pulling at their stakes.

No smoke rose from the chimney. No rattle of pans or happy cries came from within. No birds sang. All was as still as if I were in the heart of a forest, until I stirred and walked up to the door, every nerve concentrated upon listening, as if by doing so I could conjure her from the air.

All things bright and beautiful . . .

And then something at once choking and bitter impinged upon my senses and my hand shot to my mouth. It was the smell of charring, of some unpleasant meal left too long on the stove: of something gone bad. I coughed it away, but I already knew that it would not leave me, that smell; it was beyond the power of anything to freshen. I stumbled back from the door, imagining what the air must be inside, the miasma trapped therein like some lurking beast. I caught a glimpse through a half-closed shutter as I turned away of a silent hearth, grey with unswept ashes, and then the house was behind me and instead I saw the whole of Halfoak spread below, the image of bucolic peace and calm, and I stumbled from that too and hurried away from it all, up the hill.

Gradually I began to slow as I realised how the nature of the hillside was changing. More of those bright-eyed daisies peeped from the verdure, and all about me were dandelion clocks, nature's own timepieces, their heads so laden and gauzy that as I went higher they began to take to the air, floating past me and hurrying onwards, as if carried on a matter of some urgency. I remembered a game I used to play in the park with my mother, so long ago, blowing away the seeds and counting: *one . . . two . . . three . . .* The total was said to tell the hour of the day, and now here were hundreds of airborne hours and minutes rushing away all about me.

The sight was calming and my breathing steadied as I went on towards the summit. I found myself drifting for a time and I remember only fragmented images: the rough old back of the tumulus rising before me, the wide vista spread below, an open sky dotted with white scudding cloudlets. And I remember laying my hat upon the bank and leaning back against it, letting time float away while I stared into that blameless and peerless blue.

When I rose to my feet, the sky was deepening from the colour of forget-me-nots to that of periwinkle, a deeper purpling above promising the onset of evening. My limbs felt light; it was as if I had slept a night and a day away instead of resting for a matter of moments. Quite refreshed, I decided I would make my descent a little further around the hillside, thus avoiding the sight of that sad empty cottage, and I made my object the little stand of oaks. I could just make them out, the leaves dancing in the light breeze, and as I went I saw that the hill was not perfectly round after all; the grove was set into a little ledge, as if someone had taken a spoon to the Pudding Pye and set to.

I began to see that my progress was not to be so easy after all. The ground had not at first appeared treacherous, but it was made irregular in every direction by unruly tussocks and pocked with rabbit holes that threatened to turn my ankles. The flora grew wilder as I went, wiry brambles gaining thicker stems until they became a thorny wilderness, armed with inch-long daggers that tore at my legs. They soon gave way to dark mounds of growth, thick and matted. There was a warm musty scent that reminded me unpleasantly of what I had sensed—or imagined—about the cottage door. Gorse bushes grew amongst it all, their unruly sharp twigs leavened by flashes of brilliant yellow.

I took a more circuitous route, beginning to regret my choice of destination; the back of my neck was hotter than ever and I was forced to bat away the cloud of midges which were moving with me. Then a path opened before me: there was a clear way after all, carpeted in a gentle grassy sward. I stepped along it, seeing the grove ahead like some promised land, and was of a sudden reminded of the aisle of a church edged on each side by silent pews: an aisle created by nature, the air heavy and somnolent, laced with only the censer of musky flowers and nature's hymn of the soft murmur of bees.

In another moment I emerged into a little clearing. The oaks stood tall and stately about me, whispering their secrets, and before them was a grassy dell with a darker circle marked upon it, caused by some variety of fungi, I guessed, continually spreading outwards from the centre to find fresh sustenance; though I had not before seen such a thing, I had heard them referred to as fairy rings.

The ledge upon which the trees stood narrowed as it cut into the hill until it was lost in shadows. I found myself drawn inwards, walking beneath the twisting branches as if I could process right into the mound, until the ledge culminated in a darkened cleft, shadowed and obscured by grey rocks jutting from the green. Then I saw something odd amidst the grass. I narrowed my eyes. It looked like nothing so much as a short black handle, bound about with twine darkened at its mid-point, perhaps with the sweat of a man's hand. I went nearer and bent to examine it more closely. It was sticking into the ground a small distance from the cleft in the rock. I could just see the brighter shine of a blade disappearing into the earth. I was reaching out to grasp it, half bewildered, when an urgent call cut into the air behind me.

"Nay—tha mustn't! Dun't touch it!"

I whirled about and saw a woman in a simple cotton dress and white pinafore, her head covered by a plain straw bonnet. She was perhaps in her thirties, and she held the hand of a small child; its other was pressed to its face as it sucked its thumb. With dark hair tousled in a tumble of curls and face tanned like a nut, it took me a moment to identify the child as a boy.

My startlement, I think, surpassed their own, but my next reaction was to wonder at her effrontery. "Why ever not?" I asked.

She looked askance in the direction of the cottage and leaned in, as if from such a distance she could whisper in my ear. "'E put it there!" she said. "'Im!"

Before I could reply she continued, "It's to bring 'er 'ome." She spoke as if this would explain all: her sudden appearance, her odd pronouncements. "It'll keep t' door open, till she comes back!"

"Who ever do you mean, madam?"

She rolled her eyes. "Yon. Lizbeth Higgs. An't tha 'eard of 'er? Fairies took 'er an' put that enchanted stock in 'er place. 'Er 'usband, 'e burned it up, see? An' 'e put that bit o' bright metal there so as to keep t' gate open. Otherwise it only opens yance every seven year. This way they'll 'after give 'er back, see? T' fairies will. An' then everyone'll see 'er, an' they'll 'after let 'im loose."

I concluded that I was conversing with a madwoman, infected with the same nonsensical superstition which had hastened my cousin's death, and I pressed my lips tightly closed.

"I spied yer up yon." She was obviously not to be deterred. "Up on t' barrer. Tha mustn't sleep there. It belongs ter t' good folk, din't tha know? Kip up yon and you'll wake silly; they'll steal your soul clean away. I came up ter warn yer." She took a step closer, affecting nothing but concern, and I softened towards her a little. I glanced at her boy, still silent, still with his thumb in his mouth. He stared back at me with eyes as black and bright as sloes.

"Not from these parts, are yer? Else tha wun't a come." She glanced around, drawing her light shawl more tightly about her neck. "I dun't like it mesel'. I'm off back now. I saw yer and I've teld yer, an' that's me Christian duty, and it's done. I'd not be 'ere after sunset for nubbody's silver, an' that's the truth on it. I'll bid yer good day, sir."

Her unexpected politeness rattled me more than all her odd words and prompted me into saying, "Forgive me. You meant well, I'm sure. Lizzie—Elizabeth Higgs was my cousin."

At this she looked really quite startled. She took a step back, dragging her silent child with her and gazed about as if made newly nervous. "'Er cousin?" Her expression gave way to a glare as equal parts of disbelief, astonishment and suspicion fought for command of her features. At last, all gave way to a kind of pity. "Why then, sir," she said, "that bein' the case . . ."

I waited, wondering what fantastical utterance would follow upon all that had preceded, and then she took my breath and made my mouth fall open in what, in other circumstances, might have been a quite comical fashion.

"You'll be wantin' ter see 'er then," she said.

Chapter Four

I could scarcely keep up with what happened next. The good lady, who gave her name as Mary Gomersal, marched me once more down the hill and across the stream, along the dusty road and back the way I had come. The child dragged at her heels and spoke not at all. I myself began to feel like a naughty child being led homewards as the door of the Three Horseshoes beckoned and we entered the dark. It took a moment to see that its taproom was now the abode of two old gaffers, the dominoes and scattered pennies on their table leaving little room for two frothing pints of beer.

The landlord appeared somewhat surprised to see Mrs. Gomersal and her child, particularly, perhaps, because of the presence of a lady in his taproom, but she went towards him directly and said, "This 'ere gennleman's come to see *'er.*"

His eyebrows shot upwards in imitation of a pantomime clown. "I knows it! 'E's stopping 'ere."

By this time my head was spinning with heat and fatigue and lack of sustenance. Mrs. Gomersal turned to me and narrowed her eyes. "Tha's seen 'er already?"

I could only shake my head.

"Tha knows 'e's 'er cousin, then?" The good lady addressed the landlord once more.

The effect of this statement was dramatic; his eyebrows this time sinking as a frown gained mastery of his features. He leaned in towards me, staring as at some hitherto unknown and unsuspected creature. "'Er cousin? Why, yer din't say—I din't connect—I mean, I'm sorry, sir. I shall show 'er to thee at once. I thowt—I thowt yer was nobbut a gazer."

Such, I supposed, must account to some degree for his bluntness at our first meeting, though a certain brusqueness of manner seemed natural to the fellow. He reached behind the bar and fetched more keys, this time a whole fistful, from which he selected one. Then he stared at it as if a thought had struck him.

"Come now," said Mrs. Gomersal, "No more delay. 'E mun see 'er at once."

The landlord cast one further look at me—this time one of reproach, as if it were my fault he had not connected my name with that of my cousin—before leading the way back outside into the still-bright evening. "I give 'im t' best room," he muttered, "and even warned 'im not ter look on 'er when t' moon were full. Bad luck, that."

I realised he was speaking to Mrs. Gomersal, who had followed us, still with the strange little elf-child in tow. I wondered briefly if she were awaiting some coin and my hand went to my pocket, but then she bustled ahead of us as if to show us the way. I still felt dazed. I had assumed my cousin to have been buried at once and had entertained no expectation of seeing her; I had come only to seek some remembrance perhaps, possibly even a likeness, adorned with a lace handkerchief or a lock of her hair.

They directed me around the side of the building, the landlord holding open a wicket for me to pass through, and I recognised the outhouses I had spied from my window: the back of the stables, a bay mare nodding over the door of one of the stalls; a workshop; a coal shed; a brew house; a privy. Around a corner there was a smaller rectangle of yard with a pump at its centre, and judging by the damp sheets that twitched idly in the breeze, a wash house.

"We couldn't 'ave 'er in t' back," Widdop explained. "Crowner din't like it, but soon as 'e came for the inquest, 'e unnerstood." His voice had fallen quiet and a little low, so that for a moment I did not take in the words. I preferred not to dwell on what his tone portended. This odd outing had already taken on the nature of a dream, and I knew not how I had come to be here, or what I would do next. I looked down at the cobbles and saw they bore the traces of soapy water. The hems of my trousers were darkened; I had not noticed it before.

"They're usin' t' yard, while she's in there," said my host, then hastily added, "It's no bother."

We ducked beneath the line of washing and I saw a washtub and dolly peg in the yard, the tub still full of greyish water. Set into the wall of the outbuilding behind them was a single plain door and a darkened window, which appeared to have paper pressed against the inside of the glass. He went up to the door and turned the key, then stood aside.

"I'll wait," he said. "While yer pay yer respects, like."

Mrs. Gomersal nodded as if that were the right thing, folding her arms. As soon as she let go of her child's hand he slumped and sat cross-legged at her feet. All three of them looked at me expectantly and I looked back, and then I turned and stared instead at the door. I knew not what lay upon the other side, but I suddenly did not want to see it.

I swallowed hard, realising that my throat was dry as sand. I could not imagine what this place had to do with my cousin. I had wanted to see where she had lived, and now I had seen it. I had wanted to understand what her story had been; to reconcile myself to the way it had ended. I realised that it had all felt like a story to me, and with good reason—such things did not really happen, not in these days. It was a dream of a tale: far too gone in fantasy for any book.

But I was here, and it was no story. Instead there was a door, as plain and blank as thousands of others like it, and yet I found myself reluctant to take a step towards it.

They were waiting for me, however, and so I forced myself to move. At once, my gorge rose. There was just the suggestion of a scent on the air: the same stench I fancied I had detected outside the cottage on the hill. I swallowed, and at once wished I had not. It was the kind of smell that told on the stomach as well as the nostrils, and I knew I would not be rid of it, not all that evening; possibly not even thereafter.

I reached out with a hand that no longer felt like my own and pushed the door open a crack. Then I pushed it wider, and without looking around again at the eyes that watched my progress, I stepped inside.

I blinked to accustom my vision to the shadows, and began to make out particular forms. There was another dolly tub and some draining slats, a bittle and pin abandoned in a dusty corner, a clothes airer and pulley and a large mangle, too heavy to move, all sitting there silent and unused. The windows were indeed covered with thick layers of old newspaper and in the dim light it was difficult to make anything out. Then I realised that what I had at first taken for a mound of laundry upon a table was in fact something else. All at once I saw feet; and from thence, the rough outline of two legs, a torso with arms crossed at its chest; two shoulders; a head, the whole covered with what appeared to be white muslin, barely disguising a rather less respectful piece of oilcloth. Another step, and it was obvious that here was the source of the foulness that had seeped from the door. *She should have been buried at once,* was my only thought. *Why did my father not tell me of this?*

Here was reality, and it was more than my mind could hold. I stopped and gazed upon the pitiful object that had been my cousin; that had been Elizabeth. *Linnet,* I whispered her name under my breath, and the thought of her brought me to myself. I could almost feel the pressure of her hand taking my left arm as I walked slowly towards what remained. The oilcloth was not seemly. No candle burned for her. The windows being covered—that was as it should be, but *oilcloth*? I railed against it. Then the idea entered my mind that the poor creature was not even coffined, and my bewilderment gave way to a dull anger.

I kept moving until I stood at her side, as if she had become the exhibit in some sorry show. I reached out and touched the covering, and in the next moment, I had reached out and drawn it back.

I knew at once why the oilcloth had been chosen. Freed of its prison, the vile odour that had been trapped within spilled freely into the room, assaulting my senses so that at first I did not even see the monstrous thing beneath, thinking its darkness only more cloth. I staggered away from the mephitic onslaught, batting my hands against it as if it could be stopped. I choked, bending double and retching painfully, though I expelled only a thin fluid. Yes, here was reality in all its bitterness and pain, a surfeit of it.

I straightened once more and I could not stop my eyes from stealing towards the horror that lay there: the charred, cracked skin; cheekbones gleaming through shreds of burned flesh and black cinders; rivers of crimson wending through their desolate landscape. The effect of each individual atrocity combined to render the features unrecognisable to my eye, and I was grateful for it. Not only the ravages of fire but those of time had made their assault upon this thing that had once been human, yet had been treated as so much less.

The worst thing—the thing that would return to me night after night, making me sit bolt-upright in my bed, gasping for breath and staring wide-eyed into the dark—was the way the skin had shrunk back from the teeth, which were oddly perfect, even and white, forming a bright grin that stood out purely from the corruption all around.

There came a sound—a high, sharp sound, from under the cloth that still covered much of the sorry object. I reached out and drew it back a little further and saw that a Bible had been placed on her breast, and upon that, a plate of what appeared to be salt. I was trying to imagine what relic of paganism had made them do such a thing—was it to keep evil spirits away?—when the source of the sound was released and a large black fly, fattened on who knew what, darted towards me.

I tugged the cloth upward once more, no longer caring how the body was covered, only wishing that it was, but the oilcloth no longer fit. I let out some inarticulate sound, a child's sob, and a distant voice called out—I do not know what it said, though it was full of concern. I tugged hard on the cloth, pulling it over the awful skull with its thin covering crusted and peeling, and I realised that a few scraps of hair remained; it was brittle, strands of it crumbling at my touch, and then I saw a flash of a finer, paler hue at the nape of the neck.

The room darkened and I turned to see a shadow filling the doorway. Quicker than thought, I pulled a small knife from my pocket and cut a lock from the poor head of what had once been my cousin and slipped it out of sight once more before hands came to help me straighten the oilcloth. The landlord worked with his eyes narrowed, one sleeve pressed across his nose and mouth. Without ceremony, without even looking at her again, he grasped my elbow and pulled me towards the door with no more formality than if I were a horse. I did not object—I was glad to step into the light, though now I was being impelled away, I had to turn and look. I wish to the Lord who made me that I had not, for I saw that the Bible had slipped from her breast and was now lying half open upon the floor amidst a spill of salt, its pages crumpled, as if she herself had thrown it aside.

I turned from the sight, already aware that—God forgive me— were a hundred Bibles thrown into the dust, they could not have tempted me to step for a second time into that terrible place.

I leaned back against the wall of the wash house, trying not to think of the poor creature at my back, yet able to do nothing else. I felt the lowering sun on my face; I think I cried. After a time, the landlord assisted me inside the inn. His helper and her child were nowhere to be seen, and I did not recall when they took their leave of us. I found myself sitting at a table in the taproom, a glass of brandy and water at my elbow. He set meat before me, though I could not eat a morsel.

I sat there whilst the windows darkened to indigo and then nothing but blackness. The settles around the walls of the room began to fill with labourers from the fields and I was soon surrounded by living chatter and gruff exclamations and laughter. Every so often,

I looked up; was it my fancy that several eyes at once darted away from mine? I cared not.

After a time, some wag started up a country tune. I could not see who began, as his rough voice was soon joined by others:

> *As I walked out one sweet mornin'*
> *Across the fields so early*
> *O there I met with a bonny maid*
> *As bright as any fairy.*
> *"Where are you going, sweet maid?" said I*
> *As by the hand I caught her.*
> *"I'm going home, kind sir," she said*
> *"I'm nowt but the weaver's daughter."*

I bestirred myself and saw through the throng my host, Widdop, at his customary place at the hatch, polishing a glass. He was accompanied now by a cherry-cheeked maid I assumed to be his daughter. The girl was about Linnet—*Lizzie's*—age when we first met, and I found I could not look at her.

In a moment, Widdop had set down his glass and was at my side. His expression was half of worry, half apology, as if he had been quite deliberate in the trouble he had caused; and it occurred to me that perhaps he had, that there might have been some mischief in it. After all, of warning of what I should find in their outhouse they had given me none.

He spoke to me, his voice lowered so that it could not be heard by the boisterous crew. "Forgive t' table," he said. "We'd 'ave put you in t' parlour, sir, only, well, this were nearer—"

I waved his concern away; it was of no consequence. All I could see before me was that sad object, lying alone and cold in the wash house.

"You'll be wantin' t' keys, then, I suppose, sir?" he said. "To t' cottage?"

"Of course I shall not," I replied at once. I hadn't even thought of it. The question of the property, of what should happen to it or to whom it belonged, had never entered my mind—then it struck me, quite forcibly, that a great many things had not.

He nodded as if it were what he had expected, his expression one of palpable relief. And yet he held in his hand a key. He held it out and I stared at it. After a moment, for want of any alternative, I took it.

"I'm actin' as agent for it, sir," he said, "just at t' minute. Rent's paid up for a month in advance. 'E were doin' all reet, were Jem Higgs. Harvest money, you see—lots of 'em buy new boots wi' it." He shook his head, as if he had realised something sad: "They'll not see 'em now, I reckon."

I did not reply and after a little reflection he continued, "'E paid rent to t' young squire, Edmund Calthorn, but after what 'appened— the old squire, 'e said it were best that key were kept near. Didn't like t' constable always callin' for it. 'E isn't in t' best 'ealth, 'is wife's taken up wi' 'is care, an' 'is son in't up to much, if I may set it out plain, sir. So I said I'd take it forra bit." He stared down at it now, much as I had a moment ago. "I don't rightly know what to do wi' it now, sir. No one'll sort it, an' it's still full o' their things, an' no one knows if 'er 'usband—if 'e's coming back again."

"I shall not require it, I am sure."

"A good thing, sir," he said, stirring himself, although he did not take back the key. "It's not a good 'ouse, or a lucky 'ouse, neither. Not even afore this. They say you can 'ear 'em up there on a night, dancin', like, playin' their unnatural music. That's not a good thing to 'ear, sir. Not right it in't, an' that's a fact."

I did not reply to this remarkable statement, but merely thanked him for his pains before making my retreat, hurrying up the narrow stair and along the corridor and thence gratefully into my room. I was glad to close the door behind me and to be alone once more, and was just drawing the curtains of my bed, ready to hide myself away inside them and think of nothing at all, when a breath of a sweet breeze caressed my cheek and I realised that the window was still open.

I crossed to it, the steady creak of the floorboards mingling with the sounds of revelry penetrating the room from below, and I paused a moment, caught by the peace of the scene without. Everything was still; all was silent. The fields lay silvered under a sky brimming with stars. The sweetness of the air was indescribably lovely. I looked down and made out the dark hulk of the wash house, covering its awful secret—but this place was full of secrets, was it not? The thought of the man my cousin had married passed before me. I wondered what manner of creature he had been, and how he managed to conceal what he was—how had he persuaded her, an innocent, to join herself to him?

I shook my head and, raising my eyes once more to the heavens, saw that a brilliant moon had risen. I bethought myself of the landlord's warning and smiled for what felt like the first time in a long, dreary age. Whatever had happened here, Halfoak was beautiful—*bright and beautiful*, and the Lord God had, after all, made it all. I whispered the words of the hymn under my breath as I pulled the casement closed and turned from it, feeling a little clearer.

I realised I was still holding the small silver key in my hand. I slipped it into my pocket, feeling for a moment the slightest touch of the pale hair I had placed there.

> *He gave us eyes to see them*
> *And lips that we might tell . . .*

I could almost imagine a sweet voice joining my own, soaring effortlessly above it, as clear as mine was hoarse; as powerful as mine was whispered. The idea of it was a comfort. That was Lizzie; that had been my Linnet, alive and on the brink of her life, full of pureness and joy in having that life, and that *thing*—that thing I had seen in the outhouse, I suddenly knew, as surely as I knew the shape of my own hands, could not possibly ever have been my cousin.

Chapter Five

"She must be buried at once." That was my first address to my host when I took a seat at breakfast upon the morrow. My appetite had returned, but I could not allow myself to think of freshly laid eggs before the matter was in some way settled. "What arrangements have been made for her?"

His eyebrows performed their little dance. "Well, none yet, sir. I'd supposed t' parish would 'ave ter bury 'er—"

"The parish?" I interjected, "Nonsense. There must be someone she called her own who could take care of matters."

He frowned. "None, sir. 'Er mother's gone, years back, and 'er father went afore 'er. She'd only got 'er 'usband, sir, an' . . ."

He had no need to finish his sentence.

"She really had no one else?" I thought of my little Linnet with her dainty form and shy looks, cast alone into such a world, into such a fate. It was often said that city folk were all the poorer for not knowing their closest neighbour, whilst in the country everyone knew everybody, that they all helped one another. I shook my head. "None at all? Then I shall do it." I had never before carried out such a task, but I knew my father could not be spared, even if he were willing to come to Halfoak. The idea was strange, taking such a thing upon my own shoulders, and my right hand strayed to the pocket wherein lay that lock of my poor cousin's hair. "Yes, of course I shall. I must see about it at once."

Widdop nodded as if this was what he had hoped; I thought I detected relief in his features. No doubt he would be glad to have the use of his wash house once more. "Then you'll be wantin' t' ca'penter, sir."

"The carpenter?"

"For t' coffin, an' that."

"Ah. Of course."

"Now t' crowner's done wi' 'er."

"The crown—The coroner. Yes." Reality was crowding in once more. The idea of someone examining that blackened form, of placing it in a wooden box . . .

I swallowed hard, no longer sure I felt hungry. "And, I suppose, I must see the undertaker."

"Undertaker's t' ca'penter, sir."

"I beg your pardon?"

"Aye. Years now—says 'e does t' box, mun as well do t' rest of it an' all."

"Ah—I see," I said, though I didn't, not really. I nodded my head in what I hoped was a knowing fashion.

"Well, folk'll be right glad on it, sir. An' to think I thowt tha'd come from t' papers—or from a waxwork or some such thing, come to take a likeness an' make a show o' what went on. I'm sorry for it."

I waved his words away. "Perhaps you could inform people in the village," I said, "that the funeral will take place most urgently. There should be memorial cards, of course—though there can be no mask or photograph—and other such matters, all with due regard to degrees of kin, though I scarcely see how—"

He shook his head, taking a moment to reply. "They'll not fuss about none o' that," he said in a low voice, and he shifted his feet as though suddenly eager to be gone. He muttered something about bringing my breakfast.

He returned in due course with a dish laden with eggs and bread and dripping and fried kidneys and I set to, famished once again, pausing only briefly to wonder why it was that he suddenly did not seem able to look me squarely in the eye.

It was odd walking towards the sleeping church once more, thinking how soon it must be woken to ring the last knell for my poor cousin, and yet it was a relief to think of being rid of that black thing in the wash house. It was something I could barely connect with her at all; I longed for it to be gone, as the whole village must, so that I could think of her once again as rivalling the birds in their endless song of summer.

My daze of yesterday had passed. I quickly settled matters with the carpenter, who promised to set about making arrangements to have the body measured before returning to his workshop to begin work forthwith. I had also sent a boy over to the next village with a telegram, informing my family that there were affairs to settle which might occupy me for several days yet. This was becoming a most perplexing situation, raising all manner of questions in my mind, but the most pressing thing was to give to my cousin the peace she deserved after all that she had suffered.

The church door opened to my hand with a gentle creak. The wood had weathered to the utmost smoothness, and the smell of the interior of the church was all of comfort: dust and time and the pages of what must be the oldest book of all, along with the faintest hint of beeswax. All inside was quiet, save for an almost inaudible rustling that might have been the movement of mice. I passed through the porch, with its stone benches worn to a dip at their centre, and found the church quite empty. I cast my eyes over the double row of dark pews, imagining them darker still with the villagers all dressed in the colour of mourning, and realised there was someone here after all: a girl of fourteen or fifteen, her hair caught back under a cap, was on her hands and knees. A sudsy cloth in front of her revealed her purpose. She caught my eye and stood at once, dropping into an awkward curtsy, though she did not speak a word.

I asked after the whereabouts of the parson, whereupon she gave an eager nod and led me back out of the church door, around to the side and through the graveyard with its greened and leaning stones. The peacefulness of it all was a salve to the heart. The idea of my cousin finding at last such a resting place comforted me—and then it served to remind me that we would also need the services of a gravedigger. Before I could start to fret over how long it should all take or speculate over whether that gentleman would also be the carpenter, the silent girl stopped in front of me and pointed towards a little wooden gate set into the farthest wall, from whence came the sound of somewhat forced whistling.

I thanked her, approaching the gate and leaning over it prior to opening it only to find myself almost nose to nose with a white-haired fellow in spectacles, engaged in securing runner beans around a pole. He was in his shirt-sleeves and he blinked at me myopically, his lips still pursed, though now no sound emerged. I made my apologies, introduced myself and apprised him that I sought the parson, upon which his demeanour warmed.

"Come in—do!" he said, hastening to open the gate, which he did with three sharp tugs. I stepped from the graveyard directly into the garden, which I saw was half covered in some lush blossom foaming across the lawn; from the corner of my eye it appeared to be half in the thrall of winter, in spite of the heat of the day.

He recovered his flat-topped felt hat from its place on the wall and mopped his forehead with a handkerchief as he led the way into the house, calling to the maid to bring us tea with bread and butter. This raised such a storm of a clatter I feared for his china, but, unconcerned, he led me into a small parlour with a view of a narrow lane bordered by a hedge liberally festooned with honeysuckle. He turned his back upon it and bade me to sit, before saying, "Forgive my appearance. It is an evil, you know, of such a small living."

I was uncertain what reply I should make, and so I merely nodded and had instead begun to tell him the purpose of my visit when he held up a hand to stem my words, nodding his head sagely, as if he knew everything already.

"The day after tomorrow," he pronounced.

"Ah—sir, I had hoped that everything might be in readiness tomorrow," I began. "The condition—the advanced state of—of decomposition, sir, is such—"

"The day after tomorrow will be quite sufficient," he intoned, "and will allow for all the necessary preparations."

I wondered whether the tone he used, which was somewhat grey and listless, was the same in which he would make his sermons. "The carpenter is already at work—"

He nodded again as if he had heard it all once, twice, thrice before. "We must not progress with unseemly haste," he said. "The young lady in question must have all due care paid her at this time."

"Of course she must—but she has lain there, in the wash house, for a week already. It's—" *It's an abomination* is what I wished to say, and yet I did not.

There were more nods, as if he were in full agreement. "You will find Widdop, the landlord, most eager to assist in any way you require. The carpenter also. And Mary Gomersal, the widow of a local man, is quite able, in her small way; a little midwifery, as well as the laying out of the dead."

The laying out of the dead. I imagined the woman I had met, cowering about the wash house doorway, trying to clean the charred thing I had seen; her cloth rasping away the layers of burnt skin . . .

I closed my eyes. I opened them to see the parson leaning back in his chair, contemplating the ceiling.

"I—I have met her," I faltered. "Mrs. Gomersal, I mean." I recounted our odd meeting on Pudding Pye Hill and the parson stirred then, as if he were angry, but just at that moment the door opened and in came our tea and bread and butter, borne on a tray the dimensions of a moderately sized table. It was followed into the room by a red-faced buxom woman taking short, noisy breaths. We fell silent as she laid it all out and bustled away again without ever once glancing at either of us.

I felt a hand close about my wrist and I started and looked up to see the parson leaning towards me, his eyes staring most earnestly into mine. "What you have to know," he said, "is that they're riddled with superstition and nonsense. Riddled! Have a care not to listen overmuch; simply tell them what you need of them." He let me go and settled back once more. "That is what I recommend. Ha!"

Again, I did not know how to reply.

"Their beliefs have only the barest tincture of holy writ," he continued. "There is little wonder that God chose to smite the tree at the heart of the village with lightning. It reeks of sulphur, and they are little more than heathens!"

"You have heard their tales, then? That my cousin was stolen away by the fairies?" I threw a trace of mockery into my voice so that he should know at once I would have nothing to do with such outlandishness.

He leaned forward once more, this time fairly hissing into my face, a light burning in his eyes, "Fairies and elves? Brownies and goblins? Do you know what they are in reality?"

Nothing, I thought. *Nothing is what they are.* But I contented myself with merely shaking my head.

"Devils, sir! Devils and demons, sent to lead good men astray. Fairies? There is no such creature. All are children of Lilith; they are nothing of Pan. These fellows think them things of nature, but they are none! Only emissaries of Satan himself, aye, of old Mister Splitfoot as they call him, and by their split feet shall ye know them. Look into their eyes and you shall see no soul! If they seek to steal humans away, it is only to pay their tithe to Hell! They are come to enchant and to enrapture and whisper in ears that are eager to listen, and as for those who seek them out—those who go looking to find evil—why, they shall find it, sir, and only harm shall come to them!"

Before I could even consider that his sermons might be more lively than I had heretofore imagined, he slammed down his palm for emphasis, unfortunately catching the edge of the tray. The teapot slopped; the cups jumped on their saucers and the thinly sliced bread greedily drank the tea which spilled upon it. I stared down at the darkening edges.

"Such was her husband," he said, "and see what came of it, God have mercy upon his soul!"

To that I had no answer, and it came to me that it was odd to hear the man spoken of at all, let alone in such a way. Indeed, I could barely recall any other person even mentioning him to me— in my mind he was some shadowy, faceless creature, something a little less than human who had emerged from darkness only to commit this terrible deed before melting into formlessness once more the moment I ceased to think of him.

Mercy upon his soul? An image rose before me, a white grin in a blackened visage, and I passed a hand across my eyes.

The parson did not appear to notice my distress. "The day after tomorrow, then," he said, and poured out the tea as if nothing untoward had happened, then passed me a cup, the saucer still swimming in what had already been spilled.

Chapter Six

Harry Widdop wore an almost sombre expression beneath his sandy brows, appearing as sage a fellow as the parson had been earlier. "Friday," he said, shaking his head as if all meaning in the world was compressed into the word. "Unlucky day, that."

I sighed. I thought for a moment of asking him to elaborate, but decided against it. I merely repeated the word—"Friday"—and he shook his head once more, as if that were all that needed to be said.

Despite his misgivings, he agreed that the inn was the best place for refreshments after the service, and that he could provide whatever was necessary. For a moment I had considered whether it would be best to throw open the cottage so that her friends and neighbours could bid her farewell in her own dwelling place, then decided I could not bear to do so. I had determined that the unhappy house at the edge of the village could remain in its present state a little longer, and I was so lost in imagining it settling further into its nook on the hillside, its garden being overtaken by dandelions and creeping vines, that it took me by surprise when he said, "'As she a frock?"

I blinked. I could not, for a moment, fathom his meaning.

"For the layin' out," he said.

I stared at his seamed face, my eyes opening wide as I tried to comprehend his words, and then I understood. If my cousin had a frock—well, surely everything she had was still in that cottage, shut up close with its acrid scent and its bad memories.

"You've got t' key," he said, as if reading my mind.

I caught my breath. "I have. And a day at liberty tomorrow, but really, I should prefer—" I took another deep breath, which failed to quite settle me. "Really, it would be better if a woman could go— an individual who would understand her needs. I am happy to lend them the key, you know, if there is anybody you could recommend. Mrs. Gomersal, perhaps?"

It was Mr. Widdop's turn to draw in a breath; his was a sustained draught that whistled between his teeth. "She'll not go in there," he said slowly. "Not many will, not now. Not many would afore, truth be told—it's an unlucky place, bein' so near t' top o' that 'ill. It's not right; we allus said it, 'round 'ere, but she would 'ave it, all t' same."

An unlucky day; an unlucky place. I found myself remembering the parson's words about superstition and nonsense, and fought to smother the outward signs of my irritation. It appeared that the landlord did have limits to his usefulness after all, and I would have to go myself—and then it crowded in upon me that it was right somehow, that I, her only relative to stand by her, should be the one to minister to her final needs. Thus I found myself agreeing to the errand and I tried not to think of it as I dined, retiring soon afterwards to my room.

The view from my window was lit once more by the moon's silvery witch-light. The fields lay still, not a bird or a branch moving, and the sight answered something deep within myself. I realised I did not feel the lack of all the London evening sounds: the hails of tract-sellers; the constant rumble of carriages and cabs; the step and chatter of passers-by; the tormenting of a Jew's harp or tin whistle for coin; the bustle of those hurrying to lectures and recitations; the chiming of doorbells and churches. All the hurry-scurry of the City was far distant; everything was peace.

Eventually, I shifted my gaze from the scene without to my own hazy reflection in the glass, nothing but a shadow amid shadows. I lifted my hands and let them fall, the answering movement clarifying what was my outline and what was the trace of the line of trees in the distance. Beneath it were the more regular hunched shapes of the quiet outhouses and their single lonely occupant. *Soon*, I thought. She would have company soon, beneath the ground, in a quiet grave open to rain and sunshine alike and grieved by neither. There were worse things, perhaps. At least then she could forget, although I would endeavour to ensure that she would not be forgotten.

After a time, all the homely sounds of the inn began to impinge on my consciousness. There was the scrape of a chair; the rumble of laughter at some morsel of gossip or a local joke; a cry for more drink. And then, strident and somehow merry and sad all at once, there rose the higher, piercing tones of a fiddle.

I listened to it for a time, though I did not recognise any of the tunes it played. I know not how long it was until I slept, but the music followed me into my dreams.

Chapter Seven

I had first to see to the completion of various other matters regarding the funeral the next day, so that the sun was already beginning to decline from its zenith as I set out upon my task and walked along the now almost familiar lane. I was learning to think of it in local terms, thus it was "along t' big road" I went, in the direction of "t' little road," my steps quite steady so as not to betray my innermost thoughts. My hand strayed so often to the key in my pocket, where I felt also the touch of my cousin's hair, that if I had found it not I would most sorely have felt its lack.

It may have been an impression lent by the fresh clean air and the perfect sunlight but I had the sense that I was doing the correct thing; that in fact all was right with the world. Something dreadful had happened, interrupting the course of days with its outrage, but calm had returned, along with the natural order of things. God was surely in His heaven, smiling down with the sunlight that warmed me as I went. I realised I had never known a day of tempest in the countryside; all was sunny and beautiful before me, and I found that I could almost forget the purpose for which I had come.

I crossed the little bridge and the softly running waters beneath it and set foot upon the track that led upwards on its singular course to my cousin's door. I had learned from the landlord that many about these parts called it the Reeling Road; though I knew not why, for it did not reel at all; its course was straight and true. There was no need or opportunity to linger or stray, and almost I wished there were.

The sun grew hotter and the air thicker as I pointed my steps upwards. It reminded me of dreams in which running became at once imperative and impossible, the limbs slowed as if mired in the blackest treacle.

All too soon there was the gate before me, standing a little ajar, and I tried to remember if I had left it that way. My spirit quailed inside me. All was too quiet, too isolated, too *ordinary*. It took only a few steps to reach the door and I found I was holding my breath as I drew out the key, reluctant to breathe in any of that awful stench. When I did taste the air, I found only the sweetness of honeysuckle and at the edge of my hearing there was sound after all: the somnolent murmur of bees.

I turned the key in the lock. I expected it to stick meanly, some badly made, cheap thing, but it turned true and I heard a sharp *snick*.

I bowed my head a moment, thinking of the fair curls that had hung down from my cousin's cap, and then I reached out and turned the handle. The door opened smoothly without creak or jarring. Inside were stone flags, softly gleaming—perhaps from my cousin's own hand—leading away to a back door, that entrance being guarded by a little mat of oilcloth. The sight of that at first raised unpleasant images in my mind, but this one was neatly cut and placed and had been polished to a sheen like marble.

There were two doors set midway along the passage. To the left, I knew from my glimpse of what felt an age ago, was the parlour. The one to the right was unknown to me. Between them and the back door was a staircase and it occurred to me that I could simply go up and find my cousin's wardrobe, take what I needed without ever entering another room. And then I told myself I may as well see it all, and I turned to the left and opened the door to the parlour.

As soon as I did, the smell of burning rushed upon me, more strongly than ever. The first thing I saw was the hearth with its spill of cinders; before it was a rag rug, much spotted with sparks from the fire. The fire irons hung neatly on their stand, all save the poker, which was lying upon the hearthstones. A lamp standing on the floor under the hood-end had been knocked awry and was tilted against the edge of the grate. I stood for a while, staring into the empty fire, as if it could whisper all its secrets. I suddenly longed, strongly and painfully, to know the truth, however dreadful, of the last days of my cousin's life. I shook my head. Could any good be the result of such delving? I had come here to gain some sense of her life. I had come to say good-bye.

I turned about the room. Without knowledge of what had happened in this place, all appeared in almost perfect order. I had expected to find a meanly appointed hovel, but here all was comfort. The table might not have the high mahogany gleam of the one in my father's house, but it was respectably polished and solidly built. There were some wooden chairs, ill-matching, but serviceable, and a little faded sofa. In one corner, a preserved fox in a glass case endlessly watched the room, its foot set upon a stuffed mouse. The mirror was wider than it was tall, the ceilings being lamentably low, and it hung opposite the fire rather than above it. I noticed that it had not been covered after the sad event.

Over the fire was a plain shelf bearing a framed engraving of a landscape, a few Staffordshireware plates, a Bible, a prayer book and a card whereon was printed the text: *The Lord giveth and the Lord taketh away.* I stepped closer, staring at it, and only then noticed that a clock stood next to it. It was not ticking; the hands were not moving. Here, time had been stopped, as it should have been. Someone had paid my cousin that little attention at least, even if they had neglected to cover the mirror and shutter the windows. The clock read a little before midnight.

I let my gaze fall to the floor. It was sullied with footprints and little clods of earth, as might be expected after all the tramplings of the constable and others who had been drawn to this place after its occupant had so precipitately left it.

I turned from the sight and towards the windows. The shutters were half open, as I had seen them before, perhaps to shield the contents from the full heat of the sun. I left them for now, though they should have been decently closed upon this scene of grief. I would do it upon leaving; after the funeral let anyone else open them who would.

The walls were of thick stone, and suddenly an image lay before me: a view of London as revealed to me from the train, a terraced kingdom, all colour leached by distance and covered by a constant grey pall. The houses had been identical to my eye, row upon row of pattern-book homes built of brick which was in places so rotten that smoke was escaping sideways from the chimneys.

The cottage spoke of decency and solidity, and yet . . . and yet. He had killed her, my Linnet. How could such a monster have resided within such a home? But I remembered what the landlord had said: that this was an unlucky house, that none would even enter it. That might have been the only reason my cousin's husband had taken it: because none other would have it. It had been tainted from the start. And if the cottage was comfortable, if it was homely, that was no doubt the work of her hand, not his.

I shook my head. What had happened was abominable and could not belong in any place, no matter what silly ideas had grown up around this one. Superstition must be put down for the good of all. I looked around once more, this time thinking as a rational man. All was just so, save the poker and the lamp. Yet here were other things: a greenish stain on the edge of the rug. A little china jug of something left on the table, smelling at once sweet and sour, though still more pleasant than the burnt air of the room.

I longed suddenly to throw open the shutters and disperse the air, but custom would not allow it; it would be improper until the funeral was over. And for the funeral, a gown—*a frock*—was needed. I turned my back on the room and the glimpse I could see of a kitchen beyond it, and returned to the hall. Despite all my intentions of rationalism, relief washed over me; I was an intruder expelled from that room, and all the better for it.

There was still one more intrusion to make. I climbed the stairs, hearing the wood creak and resettle. I wondered how many times my cousin had taken just such a course, bearing a candle to light her to bed, never imagining how her life would be curtailed just yards from where she stood. I found at the top of the stair two bedrooms, to my surprise; both had slanting ceilings and were uncarpeted, and both were equipped with washstands and ewers. One bed was hung with red curtains, the other half-curtained in blue. The latter had a lighter, more feminine appearance, and a glimpse into the wardrobe proved me correct; its shelves were full of light colours, of fabrics more delicate and fine than I would have expected of a village cordwainer's wife. Puzzled, I ran a finger over them, detecting the faintest scent of rose petals, only then realising what I was doing and pulling away, feeling more than ever an intruder. Yet who would perform this service for her if I did not?

I had thought of something in plain white, but instead I found myself unfolding a dress of fine, pretty fabric, trimmed with organdie and with a broad white ribbon at the waist. There was a little bonnet with flowers in a matching colour. Gloves of white kid I placed into my pocket, feeling their softness like skin against my fingers. A memory rose then, of a great clamour of sound: the hissing of a steam engine, the rhythmic rattle of a Jacquard lace machine, the tinkling of a crystal fountain, the high purity of a song. I hung my head, blinded for a moment. I hardly knew how I had come to be here, far distant from my own life and all the people I knew, so surrounded by strangeness I might have been in a foreign land.

A sudden rapping disturbed my reverie. I half expected to see a bird flapping against the windowpane, but there was only the blue sky, God's own sky, curving above it all. I did not know if I could have imagined the sound. It had been like a knock, though it came from up here rather than below. Then I whirled as I heard a soft scuffling coming from the landing.

I hurried to the door and looked out, but there was nothing to be seen. Was it a mouse?

Another rapping came from the other bedroom and I stared at the closed door. Had I left it shut? I could not be sure. I stepped forward and pushed it open with my foot, still holding my cousin's dress, suddenly sick at heart as to what I might see, but the room was just as still and quiet as it had been before.

I shook my head. There was no sound save that of my own breathing, and that was too loud and ragged for a grown man. I reminded myself that the house was old and that it was settling around me, adjusting to my sudden presence; that was all.

I turned and made my way back down the stair, eager to be gone. I drew the front door closed behind me, draped the dress over one arm and turned the key. Only then did I recollect that I had not closed the shutters, and yet I found myself so reluctant to re-enter the cottage that I persuaded myself in an instant that it could not possibly matter.

But there was still another room into which I had not looked. Slowly, as if some unseen force were drawing me towards it, I went to the window and peered in. I know not what I expected to find, but it was not what I saw: the opposite wall was lined with shelves crammed full with the moulds of men's feet. I blinked, and realised they were lasts, some with new leather being formed upon them, all neatly labelled with little squares of cardboard, each no doubt bearing the name of somebody from the village. He had been a cordwainer, had he not? And here was his workshop. I peered around the shutters, my discomfort at being there quite forgotten in my curiosity. There were tools hanging from pegs on the right-hand wall: awls, broad knives, files and implements for which I had no name. A gleaming stack of shoe-buckles sat upon another shelf next to coils of waxed cord. Bowls full of brass sprigs and hobnails sat upon a bench and a paste-pot with its brush jutting from it stood by ready to be applied. There was a pile of tongues, all cut out and ready to be stitched into pairs of boots no doubt paid for by the harvest money that Widdop had spoken of. And in one corner there were sheets of hide, soaking in some unknown substance.

I could not help but think of stories I had heard of the fairies, coming out at night to stitch with their fine needles and tap with their little hammers, carrying out the shoemaker's art in far more delicate fashion than man's hand could ever accomplish. Perhaps James Higgs had chosen this cottage for that very purpose; such ideas could not but enhance his industry with a kind of glamour, if tales of the good folk were put about. And then I looked down at the floor and saw no fine pair of fairy-stitched shoes but a pair of rough labourer's boots, sturdy and strong for tending the fields, and I upbraided myself for falling into such a reverie. I reminded myself of the man who owned such a workshop and what he had done, and the strangeness of my position returned to me: here I was, a stranger to both of them all these long years, peering in at a little corner of their lives. No, of *his* life—and this whilst I bore his wife's funeral gown in my arms.

But surely the man deserved no consideration from anyone; it was he who was the intruder now: an intruder upon a sane and rational world. I turned my back on the possessions from which he had rightly been separated and walked out through the gate. I was about to turn down the path and make my way from the hill when instead I glanced up towards the summit.

I froze. A lady was standing there, a short distance away, upon the path that led to the barrow. Her figure was tall and her bearing erect, and her back was turned to me so that I could not see her face. Her dress was gleaming white, almost dazzling in the sun, and a neat bonnet, equally brilliant, entirely hid her hair from view.

I opened my mouth to greet her, but words had left me. I expected every moment that she would turn and I would see her face and an odd reluctance stole over me so that I thought of simply stealing away from her. I was not sure her face was anything I wished to see. An image of the fireplace rose before me, followed by that of a cracked and blackened visage, a body abandoned in a village wash house, and a strange fear took hold of me. What if she should turn as I was trying to leave? What if she started after me, more quickly than ever I could run? In my mind her step was light and airy; she might reach out and grasp my shoulder before I even knew that she followed.

I gritted my teeth, reminding myself that I was not such an ignorant creature as to be afraid, and I walked towards her. The lady, like a being glimpsed within a dream, slowly began to turn. The sun's light was momentarily dimmed by the passing of some cloud and I saw then that her hair was dark and that her cheek was pale, and as I watched her lips parted into a welcoming smile.

I caught my breath, and then I heard her voice: "Albie—I knew it would be you!"

It was my wife. *My wife*, standing there on the golden path with the sunlight glancing brightly from her bonnet and her dress—and yet I did not know how she had come to be there; indeed, I doubted the evidence of my eyes.

"Will you not speak?" Her smile, so open, began to fade from her lips.

"I—"

"My dear, are you well? You have turned quite pale."

I knew that I had to make some reply and so I assured her that I was quite well.

"Are you not pleased to see me? I enquired after you at the inn. They said that you would be here. Such a pretty place, is it not?" Her glance wavered over the cottage and then back towards me. Her eyes narrowed as she fixed upon what I carried, draped across my arms like a—*like a body*, I thought, and suddenly I could not rid myself of the image.

"I tried the cottage first, since that is where I was directed. My dear, did you not hear my knock?"

I frowned. The rapping I had heard could certainly have been a knock upon the door, and yet it had not sounded so: rather, it had seemed to come from the bedrooms, or even the air itself. But then, I was a stranger to the house; perhaps it possessed odd echoes of which I knew nothing.

I roused myself at last and said, "But, Helena—how came you to be here?"

Her smile had entirely fled her lips. "Why, for you, of course. I came here for you. I sent a telegram . . ."

"But I have not received one—I have had no time to receive one, not here, let alone to tell you—"

"Tell me what, Albie?"

To tell you not to come, is what I had been about to say, and she knew it. I fell silent. I no longer knew what to say; indeed, my head was swimming most alarmingly. It must have been the shock of seeing her, and the heat; it could be nothing to do with the strange notions that had taken up residence in my mind; my imagination was my own and if it were beset by a thousand odd ideas, I would surely not be overwhelmed by it.

"I am sorry, my dear." I forced a smile. "I am happy to see you, of course—I am merely surprised at your being here. Did my father have no objection to your making the journey?"

"I can manage your father, Albie." Helena smiled, but I did not; I did not doubt that she could, but I also knew my father to sometimes display a good humour he did not feel. I doubted he had consented to the matter quite so easily as she was making out. It had been an impetuous decision, not at all like her, but there was nothing to be done about it now.

"Come, take my arm and we shall walk back to the village," I said. "Isn't it charming? And the air is so pleasant, after the City." I turned a little towards her and she stared at my arm. No; she was staring downwards and I realised she was still focused upon what I held: another woman's pretty dress, laid out, like—

No. I would not think of it. Instead, as I folded the garment to hold more easily beneath my other arm, I quickly explained its purpose, and her eyes softened at last, her expression giving way from irritation to concern.

"Oh, Albie!" she said, "I can see things have been difficult for you. It is good that I came."

Somehow I could not bring myself to voice agreement. It felt rather as if some new disturbance had come and that the air was reacting somehow, re-forming itself around us. But Helena put her hand on my arm and despite my headache, we made our way steadily homewards, or at least, back towards the village. I told her of all that had passed, though I did of course spare her the more lurid particulars of the spectre lying within the inn's wash house, in the place of my fair cousin.

It was no time at all before we were entering the inn together, and my good host immediately abandoned his position by the casks to greet us both, but mainly, I think, to see what item of clothing I had brought. The moment he laid eyes on it, his countenance fell.

"Is it all right?" I asked, surprised.

"Aye—it's right enough, I s'pose."

"Whatever is it? It looks fine enough—it is a quite delicate material, and with a clean white trim, you see here—" I felt Helena's gaze on my face at my sudden interest in feminine dress, but I did not meet her eye. I still could not imagine what was wrong.

Then he said, "Aye, it'll do. Prob'ly dun't mean owt, anyroad. It's just, wi' it bein' green an' all—"

"Is green unlucky?"

He snorted. "It's not that—it would be if she were getting wed in it. But it'll 'ardly matter for owt now, will it? It's just—well, it's not right. It's *their* colour, in't it?"

He gloomily pondered the gown, rubbing his whiskers in a musing fashion, and I could do nothing but stare at him. I felt my cheeks redden. But of course, it was "their" colour. How could I not have thought of it? Even if I did not believe in such creatures—and of course, I did not—I should have known that.

I crushed it in my hands as if I could banish it from sight. "I could fetch another," I said, as I realised too that I had forgotten about inner wear: linens, stockings, a corset, everything that was proper. How had I been so foolish?

"It'll serve," he said. "Mary were tellin' us, she dun't think she can get 'er dressed right, not really. She might 'ave to cut the frock, lay it on t' top, like."

"And it will be a closed coffin, will it not?" Helena's voice was crisp and clear, all brisk enquiry without a hint of dismay. We both looked up at her as if she had awoken us.

"Aye," he said, at the same time as I murmured, "Yes."

"There then," the landlord said, taking the offending article from me and moving away. "I'll gerrit sorted."

I sat for a while with my wife, giving brief answers to her queries about the village and its inhabitants and the funeral, as far as I was able to concentrate through the fog of my thoughts. I told her of the "ca'penter" who was also an undertaker, of the strident parson and his ranting, of Mary Gomersal and her elfin child, feeling all the time at some distance, as if I were still standing in another place; caught, perhaps, on a sunny hillside. But the thing that was uppermost, that refused to be banished from my mind, was to wonder how I ever could have been so foolish as to see that my cousin was sent to her grave wearing the colour of the fairies.

Chapter Eight

Whether it was an unlucky day or not, upon the Friday everything went amiss. From the beginning, Helena arose pale and cross from our bed. She rubbed at her eyes, complaining most bitterly about the lateness of the hubbub that had come from downstairs, though I confess I had not noticed it—I had slept quite soundly, and that, she told me with a hand to her forehead, had made it worse, disturbing her further with my noisy exhalations. The bed was lumpen, and she proclaimed it most likely infested, becoming all the more incensed when I observed that if it was, I had been entirely unconscious of it.

Helena had previously professed her disinclination to wear any article that was darker than grey—but such a grey! She had brought with her a pale watered silk, but it had such an unseemly shine that it surely would not do for a funeral, let alone for mourning, and I said as much.

"Mourning!" she exclaimed, as if it were a ridiculous idea. "For a distant relative of my husband's—and one I never once met?—why, that would not call for even *ordinary* mourning. And you know, Albie, that I cannot bear the smell of dye, even if there had been time to blacken my good silk. Why, anyone of any breeding would decry such a thing as a silly affectation, if not absolute nonsense."

I could see there was no use in remonstrating, and of course she had not her full wardrobe at her disposal so even had she been inclined, there was little chance of her now producing a sombre-coloured crape or even a bombazine.

I then ventured to suggest that, as a lady, perhaps she had better not attend the funeral—after all, I reminded her, our own dear queen had not seen fit to attend that ceremony for Prince Albert—but she gave me such a sharp look as to instantly quell my words. Her vehemence quite surprised me; Helena had always been so level, one might even say a little too reserved. An image rose before me of my father effecting our introduction, he talking too much in the most jovial tones he could muster, and Helena's low responses. We had been at dinner with a number of acquaintances and I particularly recalled the high, tinkling chatter of the other women around us, arrayed in their brightest and most gaudily frilled and quilled dresses. Science had lately risen to new heights when it came to the extraction of the most brilliant dyes from such dull matter as coal-tar, and all were racing to outdo one another in dazzling the eye with their violets and fuchsines and garnets. Helena had followed no such fashion, no doubt to the opprobrium of the ladies, but to my father's undoubted approval. Her gown had been of a soft, quiet shade of blue-grey and it had struck me that evening that she was like some calm island in the midst of noisily crashing waters that only broke harmlessly upon her tranquil shores.

Break upon her. I shook my head at that thought, reminding myself that I had known it to be a fine thing, and her a fine woman, from the moment I was thrown together in her company. Helena was a lady of simple elegance, all that any man of reason could desire, and now I told myself that I should have the good sense to capitulate to her wishes.

She bustled about the room, gathering together my black arm-band, my hat with its crape trim and my black gloves—and yet there too things went awry, for she could not find the right one.

She searched the wardrobe and cupboards, decrying the roughness of the wood and the meanness of our accommodation, and at
last she ran her hands down the pockets of my frock-coat, whereupon she let out an exclamation. In the next moment she had
slipped her fingers inside and withdrew them again, only for her
triumph to give way to confusion as she stared at the little lock of
golden hair in her hand.

She stared at me, the shining strands bright against her own dark
hair, but already I thought I could detect the scent of charring,
borne by that curl and now creeping through the room towards us.

"Your cousin's?" she asked.

I gave my affirmation and when she spoke again her voice was
the model of politeness, though it shook a little. "How often," she
asked, "had you seen her in your life?"

"Just once, Helena. As I told you."

She looked down once more at the pitiful lock of hair, her
expression one of disdain, possibly even disgust. "Do you intend to
have it made up as a keepsake?"

"I—I hadn't thought of what to do, my dear. I suppose I merely
wished to have the possibility. Do you think I should?"

Her eyes shone with a sudden fierceness as she crossed the room
to the washstand and cast the thing into one of the china dishes. She
turned her back upon it—and me—rubbing her fingers together as
if to rid herself of the touch of something tainted.

Tainted. The word rose to my mind, and it brought anger with it.
My cousin had been an innocent, duped into a bad marriage with
a worse man, and she had not deserved what had befallen her. And
now all the countryside was alight with tales of little folk and devils,
just as if her fate were one to relish for the entertainment it afforded.

Well, today they could have entertainment enough: my poor
cousin would be laid to rest at last, and there would be an end of it.

I had begun my own preparations, donning my funeral attire
then taking up my hat and smoothing down the crape, conscious of
my wife's eyes upon my face, when I heard the sound of hooves in
the yard outside.

I went to the window and stared down. Widdop had informed me that the village would expect a walking funeral, with pallbearers alone, but I had insisted that my cousin should have a hearse and coach, and the carpenter-undertaker had assured me he would take care of it all. It would still be a simple affair in comparison to a London funeral, of course, in part because of the necessity for all to be expedited swiftly, but also because it seemed to me to be more fitting: a modest funeral for a modest girl in a modest village. Now here was our hearse: nothing but a cart hung about in black ribbon, more suited to some rather sombre Mayday parade, with three boys sitting in the back of it, no doubt to assist him in carrying the sad object into the church. Their cloaks looked as if they were last dyed the colour of despondency many years before. Our "coach" followed. At least the horse drawing the "hearse" was properly black, if an inelegant, sway-backed creature. Ours was chestnut with a dark sheet thrown over it, as if such a tawdry thing could address the lack of sable.

My wife, leaning at the window next to me, gave a burst of dry laughter. "No plumes, I see."

My irritation returned. "Of course there are no plumes—we are not in the City."

"I am perfectly aware of it," she answered drily.

In the yard, the landlord was greeting the undertaker and his lads; he went to the wash house door, turned the key in the lock and pushed it open; the space filled with shadows and I turned away from the window. After closing my eyes a moment in due solemnity, I led the way outside.

When we emerged, the little gathering had moved to the front of the inn and the coffin had already been settled on the cart. I was glad to see that it at least had been draped in a fine black velvet cloth. Widdop's daughter emerged from the inn bearing a tray weighed down with bread, cheese and beer, and the lads set to with obvious relish. The parson had declined to attend on me before the service, or at the high tea to be given after it; I tried to swallow my resentment as I looked across to the church and saw that although the peals had begun, he was not even to be found standing at the door.

The undertaker turned to us, still clutching a piece of bread and butter, and ran his gaze up and down our figures. He hastened at once to the "coach" and returned with his mouth full and his arms overflowing with crape. "Lucky I brought these," he said in muffled tones, and shook them out straight: two more rough cloaks, such as those worn by his lads.

Helena stiffened beside me. She caught her breath, ready to throw out some sharp remonstrance at this countryman who deigned to think he could correct her choice of dress, but I took her arm.

"That will not be necessary, thank you," I said, and I led her towards the coach and handed her into it. The man turned to stare after us, shrugging his shoulders; thankfully, he chose instead to swallow down his bread rather than speak. I asked after the other pallbearers—there should surely have been six, at the least—but he made some excuse about the others having been called to the harvest.

We made a small procession, but I hoped it would suffice; I had not thought a larger fitting for such a rural setting. The church, after all, stood within our view, and in a matter of moments we were at the door. The boys and the undertaker handled the rough coffin between them with only a modicum of fuss over the pall, and it was not until we were taking our seats in the first row of pews that I realised we had seen no one else. The parson made his appearance at last, moving to stand at the front of the church, his hands folded in front of him.

The pealing of bells stopped abruptly and we sat and waited in silence. I looked around at the brightly coloured windows, the pews, the pulpit with the Good Book open upon it, and I thought of what I could not see: the spire, and clock and all its workings somewhere above us: the clock with its white face and its several iron hands. Perhaps we were in the wrong time after all and soon the peal would ring again and the doors would open and all of my cousin's neighbours and friends would be there. They could not all continue in the fields, not on such a day; they would fill the seats around us, ready to join together to bid her farewell, to sorrow over the terrible thing that had been done to her—to show that they too felt her death keenly, both a misfortune and an injustice.

The parson cleared his throat as Helena leaned towards me and whispered, "Did you hire no mourners? No feathermen or mutes?"

"Of course I did not," I whispered back. "Such artifice is for the City. I thought . . ."

But I did not say what I had thought: that we should see an outpouring not paid for but spontaneous and heartfelt and fitting for the memory of a simple country girl as innocent and clean as spring water. I abhorred the practice amongst the genteel classes of sending their empty carriages to mourn at the lychgate, as hollow as the sentiment they were meant to express. Surely here there could be no requirement for professional mourners, those black crocodiles with their false tears; there would be no more need for them in the country than there was for wax flowers. But now, looking around the empty church, it struck me that I might have done my cousin a disservice. Had these rural denizens stayed away in protest at the simplicity of the funeral, the lack of gloves and weepers and feathers?

Helena's whisper came again. "Did you have invitations sent out?"

"There was no time for such—the landlord took care of it all."

She gave a little toss of her head, but there was no more time for words or to compose myself or to collect my mind into the correct mood of solemnity because the parson had stepped forward. Without even looking at us, he began, and I quickly realised my earlier surmise had been accurate after all. He started to drone in dirge-like tones as if he were speaking to the air or the walls rather than the small group seated before him.

I stared down at my hands. I could not concentrate upon his words. All I could think of was, *what had I done wrong?* For surely something had gone amiss. I had known that Widdop himself would be absent, kept busy by the inn and the preparations for our refreshments—but where was everybody else? Had he failed to inform the villagers? Surely there must have been some mistake? They had been told the wrong time or the wrong day—a more auspicious one, perhaps. I should have taken it all into my own hands—but then, I did not know who were my cousin's especial acquaintances and friends. I rubbed my eyes. Everything was a blur. Words floated around me, and then I realised that Helena was tapping my shoulder, that she was standing.

"We shall sing a hymn," the parson intoned. "'All Things Bright and Beautiful.'"

Of course: I had chosen it myself. I had pictured the gathering, all our voices joining as one in some poor semblance of my cousin's song, and now here we were, two of us and the undertaker's boys, them trying hard not to snigger as our voices wavered, failing utterly to fill the church with our song.

And such a hymn it was. I had not before thought upon its length. We stumbled onward, verse after verse, my wife's voice becoming quieter and quieter, the parson's little more than a dry rasp, until I could hear only my own thin tones. I sang more loudly, deliberately, trying to overcome the deficiency as I stared at the sad object in front of us, at the dust tumbling through the air and settling upon the coffin's pall, and I thought of its contents: a young girl turned to ash, her skin cracked and blackened, her white teeth, her soft green dress, and I wondered what on earth she could possibly be thinking about it all.

Finally, with a *How great is God Almighty, who has made all things well*, it was over and I could sink gratefully into my seat. I realised only when Helena leaned over and wiped my cheek that it had become quite damp.

I felt then it must surely all be over, but another trial awaited: my last farewell to my cousin, which took place at the graveside. As a member of the fairer sex Helena naturally awaited my return and as I went on alone, peace came over me at last. There was the little graveyard, quiet and still all around me. I cast a little dirt onto the coffin, though thankfully I saw none of it; I could see only Lizzie's face peeping from below her bonnet, the brightness of life shining from her eyes. I did not even look at the parson as he said his final droning words. I did not look into Helena's face as I met her once more and we did not speak as we made our way back towards the inn.

To my surprise, the undertaker and his boys declined our offer of refreshment, and for a moment the retreating clop of hooves on the lane was the only sound. Inside, I was not sure what I expected to see—red faces, perhaps, burning with their shame, but what we saw was nothing; not even our landlord was anywhere to be found. I heard some slight noise coming from the parlour—the snuggery, he had called it—where our tea was to be laid, and I led Helena in that direction. There we found Widdop laying out crockery and silver at a small table, perfectly unperturbed. Another table bore cold veal, stuffed chine, pork pies, potted meats, bread and butter and boiled eggs, glasses of porter and a steaming pot of tea. In quantity it was little more than a handful of people would require, and I stared at it for long after he stood back to allow us to be seated.

"Where, sir, is the rest?" I asked.

He shifted uncomfortably.

"You did tell them—you did invite them, as I asked?"

"Aye, sir, I did."

"And yet . . . ?"

He cleared his throat. "Everyone's that busy, sir, in t' fields, an' that. I knew they—if there's nowt else, sir . . ."

Helena's hand closed on my arm and squeezed hard. "Thank you," she said, betraying no emotion in her low, clear voice, and the landlord made his retreat. She poured out the tea and filled our plates before settling herself before the repast. After a moment I sat also, but I could not eat. Helena picked at the food. Neither of us had anything to say.

When for a time we had sat and stared quite stupidly, she drew a deep sigh. "Shall we retire to our room, my dear? Or go for a walk? Taking some air might—"

I turned to look at her. "I shall wait," I said. "There has been some error, I am quite sure. A young lady has died in the most horrific circumstance, and the least her neighbours could do is pay their respects. To fail to do so would surely be the most impertinent neglect."

She nodded; she could hardly do otherwise. After a time she went over to a rack in the corner where were displayed some periodicals and idly leafed through them, tut-tutting over the seed catalogues and issues of *Farm, Field and Fireside* before finally returning with a single uncut newspaper. She perused it as best she could, though I believe she could scarcely have taken in a word, such was the promptitude with which she abandoned it once more.

No one came. I rose; I looked into the taproom. I tried to remember when I had seen the place so entirely empty and realised that I never had.

The teapot emptied. The landlord did not return. I stood and paced.

"My dear, this is most trying," Helena said. "I really must—in my—I must return to our room. I need to rest a little."

My brow clouded at her words; I could not think when she had become so unfeeling. But I merely nodded and saw her to the door. She swept her skirts—her pale grey, shining skirts—through it and did not look back.

I sat there alone for a while, then I stood and went to the window. The lane was empty and the day was wearing on; it had become a little dull. Eventually I left the parlour and took a seat in the public bar. A box of dominoes had been abandoned on a settle and I laid them out, lining up the edges of each tile with a sharp *click*.

After a time, the landlord's daughter came in. She asked if there was any other thing they could provide and I told her there was not. Shortly afterwards, I heard her clearing away the plates in the snuggery. Still no one came; there was no boisterous talk, no pouring of ale, no fiddle.

A mistake, I told myself. *It was all a mistake.*

I fetched the newspaper Helena had abandoned and read it, focusing upon each word in turn until the light began to fail, and still no one came, and I do not remember a single line of what I read. The landlord came back and I watched him bustling about, running a cloth around the serving hatch, tidying the rows of gleaming pots, glasses, jugs and bottles on the shelves in the room behind.

"It is quiet, this evening," I said.

"Aye, sir."

"Why is that, do you think?"

"No reason. 'Appen folk are tired. Lot o' work, this time o' year."

"And yet, it has been so busy of late—you must be happy to have such business."

"Aye, sir."

"Odd, is it not, that none at all have come today?"

He slowly raised his head. "'Appen."

"But you knew that they would not do so. The supper—it was meant for two, was it not?"

More slowly he said, "'Appen."

"So where are they?"

He appeared alarmed at so blunt a question and I myself felt the rudeness of my glare, though I could not bring myself to soften it. I do not think that I expected a response, or perhaps I expected only to hear something vague about the attractions of a working man's own hearth, but that was not his reply.

"There's a house on t' lane," he said softly. "As you go south out o' t' village. They calls it t' beer house, though there in't a sign. There's a chap brews a bit, an 'e keeps a room—t' farm folk some-times drink in there, see, so as not to meet wi' t' young squire when 'e's in t' inn. They can be a rafflin' lot and 'e dun't allus approve o' their ways. You unnerstand?"

I did understand, all too clearly, though I thought the squire had little to do with it; not this evening, at any rate.

I stood without another word and left the inn.

The beer house was quite simple to find. It stood a matter of moments beyond the crossroads, a short walk from the Three Horseshoes, and the rising moon lit my way along the rutted lane. I heard the place before I noticed it. It was a moderately propor-tioned brick house with shabbily painted shutters, nothing more

than a decent-sized worker's home. I would not have known it at
all had it not been for the merry sound of a fiddle drifting into
the cool night air and the rough shouts of encouragement that
underlined its chorus. I felt my feet falling into time with its tune
as I walked towards the door. I did not know what I should do or
say. I lifted a hand to knock and let it fall again, listening to the
numerous voices within, and then I turned the handle and pushed
it open.

The music grew louder at once, accompanied by unruly voices,
which rose in song:

> *I can kiss but I can't wed you all,*
> *But I would if I could, great and small,*
> *I long for to cuddle you all,*
> *For you see I'm a beautiful boy*
> *Aye, you see I'm a beautiful boy.*

The passage was narrow, distorting the sounds so that although
loud, the song appeared to be coming from a great distance. The
house was somewhat shabby; it had once been got up with cut
paper, but this now hung loose and torn at the corners. I walked
down the passage to an open doorway, following the clamour.

The heat of their bodies, heavily worked and tightly pressed in
together, hit me at once. I could smell their sweat and their beer-
addled breath. The fiddle's high notes floated above the bass rumble
of their chatter, wherein no words could be distinguished.

They were working men, in working men's dress; their rough
trousers bore the stain of the fields despite being buttoned at the
bottom against the mud, and some still had gaiters of sacking tied
about their knees. Dirt and powdery chaff had spilled from their
boots, soiling the floor. Some wore drab fustian waistcoats over
their shirts, in shades that put me in mind of the poorhouse. Others
were in their shirt-sleeves, indifferently clean mufflers at their necks,
and some wore smocks yellowed with careless washing, or perhaps
the lack thereof. Their faces were apple-cheeked and shining and

their smiles were all the same, though their eyes, in that moment, appeared entirely devoid of expression.

I stared as, one by one, they felt my presence and turned to face me, stopping their idle chatter. The fiddle music rose once, twice, and then faltered and was silent.

I did not speak; I had no need of words. They knew their own shame; they had shunned her. They had shunned my cousin just as if every last one of them really thought her a fairy or some other hobgoblin creature and my real cousin vanished into the air. Or perhaps it was as the parson said: as if she were a devil, as if she were the one who had sinned rather than the brutish man who had killed her.

Another moment and I had stepped out again at the door and was walking quickly away. I did not stop until I reached the cross-roads, when I realised that the moon had risen over Pudding Pye Hill. It was almost full and I could see the shape of that prominence quite clearly against a sky that was brilliant with stars, but I could not see my cousin's cottage. No lights shone through the chinks in its shutters. Perhaps they never would again. The injustice returned to me anew, and with it, the shadowy form of the man who had wrought it.

I looked about me at the crossroads, at the lanes leading away into the dark and the fingerpost that marked their directions. This might have been a place where a gallows once stood. Perhaps one should again; but then, they had taken the murderer away, to a town large enough to hold him. He would face the judgment of man; then he would be sent to face that of a higher power still.

I found myself trembling with rage at the thought of him. At least now he could not steal my cousin's rest, though he might yet disturb mine.

I walked on and did not look up again until I was in my room at the inn. I closed the door and saw that Helena was watching me from her place in an upright chair. I wondered if she had been sitting there since retiring; her cheeks were wan and there were shadows in her eyes. She rose to her feet and reached out her hands towards me. "My dear," she said, and I went into her embrace, relieved that the differences between us had somehow been resolved. After a few moments she raised her head. "At least, my love, we may go home now." She smiled; her eyes shone. A dimple furrowed one pale cheek.

I drew away from her. "My dear, of course I cannot."

"But why?"

"Why—you need ask me why? After the way they have treated her?"

Her eyes glared into mine with renewed intensity. "She is dead, Husband. She is buried. What need have we to stay longer?"

"They shunned her—after what has happened!"

"And what can we do? What can *you* do, Albie?"

"Nothing! I do not know, but I know that I cannot turn my back on her with all the others. They think her a fairy, Helena. They must! Or what reason could they have for their actions? Either they are mad, and I must know the depth of their madness, or there is something else; some other reason . . ."

"Albie, you are being ridiculous! A terrible thing has happened, it is true. But she is gone and he will be hanged and there is nothing left for you here. Why should you stay—what is she to you, that you would?" Her eyes glistened, not with tears, but with anger.

"It is common decency, Helena. Someone must stand by her—do you not see? I must *know*. I must *understand*."

"We cannot stay here!" She actually stamped her foot. "I cannot stay in this awful inn—in this room! Albie—"

"Then I will set you on your way, Helena. I did not ask you to come here. You must return home; indeed, I really think it best. But—perhaps you are right . . ."

For a moment, she did not speak. I think she could not. She drew in a great gasping breath, and then she straightened. "My place is at your side. I am your *wife*."

"Helena, it is better that you go. Who will manage everything at home for my father? And perhaps it is right that I should be alone."

"I will not go. I shall not! You are wrong to ask it."

I shook my head, lost in frustration, half turning away. And then, almost without my volition—as if the words had been waiting there all along—I said, "Very well. I absolutely cannot go home as yet, and you insist you will remain. But you are quite correct: there is absolutely no possibility that we can remain in this place." I crossed to the window and stared out. I could not see the moon, though the world was bathed in its silvery light. "We must find somewhere else to stay."

Chapter Nine

We removed the next morning to my cousin's cottage. It was not until I turned the key in the lock that it occurred to me that this was the last thing I had ever considered I would do. To stay in the place where such terrible things had happened . . . yet now it felt a proper outward sign of standing alongside my cousin, to say, *I am with her and you are wrong and ignorant, and if not entirely wicked, then foolish.*

My wife knew none of this; she simply stood back and waited as I pushed open the door, steeling myself against the smell which must surely rise again from the cottage's interior—but there was nothing, only the faint hint of polish. Now the funeral was done, we could throw the shutters wide open and let God's light in onto the scene of all that had occurred. Something inside me lifted in response; it felt like the correct thing to do, the *good* thing to do, and I set about it at once, beginning with the parlour.

From thence, through the glass, I could see the road to the village: a white road now, so brightly did it shine in the sunlight, which was beaming down more strongly than ever. Bees lifted heavily from the nodding heads of foxgloves just beyond the glass, then settled once more. All was harmony.

I turned and realised Helena was standing in the doorway to the kitchen. She withdrew and smiled. "It is all so clean and neat," she exclaimed. "I had not expected it to be so tidy."

She was right; I had tried not to look at the empty hearth, but I did now, and found the spill of cinders was no longer in evidence; it had been neatly swept, as had the floor. The lamp, its glass chimney polished and sparkling, had been replaced upon the table, which was now covered by a thick chenille mat with a tasselled fringe.

I walked over to Helena. The kitchen's plain brick floor was clean, the open range, though cold, recently blackleaded, and a deal table looked freshly scrubbed. The scullery area was small but just as orderly, with pans, scoured and polished, arrayed on a dresser, along with several coppers. A roasting jack, surely intended for use before the open fire in the parlour, was set back against the wall. I walked into the room, feeling as if I were stepping into the heart of Lizzie's domain. There was nothing out of place; every surface shone.

I opened another door and found a small pantry and larder combined, set into the north side of the cottage for coolness, with only a small window, just enough to let in the light. It was cast further into dimness by an elderberry tree planted outside, no doubt to keep away the flies. I could see how smartly my cousin had kept everything: the floor here was of tile and the larder shelves of wood, slate and stone, each for their various purposes, were arranged with neat rows of pickles and preserves, flour and sugar. There were baskets on the floor for vegetables. Opposite them, pantry shelves were stocked with cups, dishes and some china and glassware. Another, smaller door was set into the far wall and I opened it to find a store that must fill the space under the stairs. Here were mops, buckets and beaters, a coal-scuttle, kindling and a cinder sifter, all in their place and ready for use. There were supplies of carbolic soap and borax, laundry blue, insect powder and other such things; a tray of candle ends and a snuffer; and a box of oddments, including an old pair of scissors and what appeared to be an ancient and rusted pair of iron shears.

"It is odd, is it not?"

I frowned and entered the kitchen once more. "Why, my dear? There is nothing to suggest my cousin a slovenly housekeeper, though she may have been reduced in circumstance."

"No! That is not what I meant." It was Helena's turn to frown. "There is nothing here spoiled—there is no meat hanging on the hooks, no mouldy bread, no eggs, no foul milk in the jug. Whatever does it mean?"

It took me a moment to understand her, but she was right. My cousin had not gone off on a journey, preparing everything for her absence; her husband had not willingly left the house, but had gone in company with the constable. Both their lives had been suddenly curtailed, each by other hands than their own, and so surely the larder should have been full of rotting things; the scullery sink could have been filled with sooty pans a-soak in greasy water; beetles might have taken up residence in the ceiling corners and dust settled upon the floor. Instead all looked as if it was intended to be so, the house closed up as if awaiting the arrival at any moment of its family.

"Someone from the village must have come in, that's all," I said. "A maid, perhaps." And yet the landlord's words echoed in my mind: *It's not a good 'ouse, or a lucky 'ouse, neither.* Had my cousin even had a maid?

"Well, that is exactly what we shall need: a maid, Albie, at least for the very short time we shall be staying here." My wife wrinkled her nose.

I sighed. It was just like her to think of such matters. "I shall enquire in the village," I said, "but for now, let us settle ourselves. If you really wish to stay here, of course. There will be none of the elegancies to which you are accustomed, Helena—there is only one parlour; there is no musical instrument. There will be no creams or blancmanges or any of the things you are used to—"

"Well, we must have tea, at least." She did not meet my eye, but instead pulled a face, looking about the room. "We must light the range, I suppose. How—interesting."

It was only then that I realised my wife had never before done such a thing herself. I had not thought of it; my father was fortunate enough to keep a parlour maid and a cook as well as a housemaid. Helena was more accustomed to learning watercolours and the piano than the work of a household. I thought of Lizzie's neat and shining dishes and pushed the thought from my mind: of course my wife was unused to such things; it had never been her expectation. And yet this would be the first house in which we would reside together, even if it was, as she said, for only a short time; our first establishment of our own.

I said that I would see about some water, and I went through to the back door. The key was in the lock; I turned it and went out, almost tripping over a boot-scraper, to be greeted at once by the sound of birdsong. I had thought that all in the countryside would be silent after the rattle and clatter of London, but it was not. To the birds' calls were joined the busy humming of insects; from somewhere came the lonely call of a cuckoo.

I was relieved to see that the cottage had its own pump; we should not have to haul water up the hill. There was also a little outhouse and, in the far corner, a privy, all grown about with fragrant jasmine and honeysuckle. In the garden between was a gooseberry bush, along with red- and whitecurrant bushes, all heavy with fruit. Peas and runner beans were rampaging over their stakes. There were abundant herbs; I identified mint, marjoram and thyme, but the rest were a mystery.

When I finally turned to go inside, I noticed for the first time a little date stone set above the door. I drew myself up and peered at it, but no matter how I tilted my head, I could not make out the year; the figures were misshapen, appearing to have melted in the heat rather than succumbed to wind or rain.

I found Helena all impatience. She had discovered the store and was exclaiming over the heaviness of the coal-scuttle and the inconvenience of the tinder, which was nothing but dried gorse; it had scratched her fingers. I helped her with it, picturing my father's face at the idea of such a thing. But Helena was right: she was unused to arduous household tasks, so we must have a maid, or at least a charwoman for the rough work. I had not any idea of where we should find one, and yet someone must have been here: the hearth, after all, had been swept. The scattering of ash I had seen on my first visit was gone; the little china jug with its mysterious contents had entirely disappeared.

So short a time after leaving I found myself once more at the Three Horseshoes and in conversation with the landlord. I had already enquired about the primary purpose of my visit, which was the hiring of a horse. The shillings I passed to him lightened his somewhat dour countenance, shadowed perhaps by the loss of his lodger, though his manner was helpful, even deferential, as if he wished to make up for his shortcomings in the matter of my cousin's funeral.

Before I should lose the advantage of his current helpfulness I turned to the subject so dear to my wife's heart, but at this his face closed up at once. He drew in a breath that whistled across his teeth. "Dun't know about that, sir. None'll go up there, see. I did war—I told thee. I can speak to t' farms, ask them to call on you fer your orders, like   milk, an' such, but that's it. I'm not sure I could even get a girl up there once a week, to 'elp with t' washin' an' the like—I reckon they'd spook at it."

"But that's nonsense," I blurted. "Someone has been there already—and quite alone, presumably! Why, the place has been made neater than a new pin."

At this, he started; I might even have said that his cheek paled. "That cannot be right, sir, beggin' your pardon."

"And yet it is. Someone else must have a key—possibly my cousin's maid? Or Mrs. Gomersal? Someone has most certainly been there since—" I left that sentence unfinished.

He shifted his feet. "Sir, there's no mistake. That key were put into my 'and for safekeeping by t' owd squire, an' that's because 'e lives over towards Kelthorpe, at Throstle Grange. 'E din't want no visits from t' constable an' such, an' 'e din't want to be troubled comin' over 'ere, not bein' poorly an' all. 'E wanted it kept 'ereabouts, like I told you afore. It's t' only key I know of. There's nubbody else been in that 'ouse since it 'appened, an' no mistake." He paused. "Not since t' police theirselves went over it nohow, an' they dun't clean up nothin', an' that's a fact."

"But the hearth has been swept," I protested, "I saw it myself. And the smell is different . . ."

Again, I caught myself, and was startled when he grasped me by the shirt-sleeve and drew me to him, leaning in and speaking most earnestly.

"Sir, I'd 'ave a care, beggin' your pardon. That 'ouse—it's a wrong 'un. Up there—there's strange matters, on that there 'ill. I shan't go there meself, not nohow." He took a deep breath. "That's where *they* live, see? That's where they dance, under t' moon. Tha mustn't listen to 'em. Tha mustn't partake of owt they leave yer." At this I pulled away, but still there was no brooking the man. "But I'll tell yer summat else fer nowt. If they's tidied and cleaned up, like they was said to do in years gone by—you mun thank 'em forrit, sir. Leave 'em a little water on t' 'earthstone. Or pour 'em a little milk onto t' 'illside. They'll be content wi' that, sir. They'll not turn on yer then."

I silenced him with a hand and said, "Sir, I am astonished. Must I be thus addressed—have I fallen, without my knowledge, into Bedlam? You talk of myths and stories, nothing more. You seem a sensible man, sir—a practical man. You cannot truly believe—why, you are having a joke, at our expense! And I with my wife to keep—"

"Aye, an' I'd keep 'er close, an' all!"

"How dare you!"

"Beggin' yer pardon, I meant no 'arm, only to 'elp. But—gah!" He shook his head. "There's none so deaf as them as'll not listen, an' that's the truth on it. I know such things are passed, sir. Some say as t' railways 'ave chased 'em all away—that the world's changed, an' we all know better now. Well, mebbe it 'as an' mebbe it an't. I dun't profess mesel' wise in such matters. But I do know this place, sir, an' I know I cannot 'elp believin' in what I know to be true."

He spoke this last right into my face, so that I felt the spray of his spittle; his eyes were aflame. I could do nought but stare at him in dismay. I *was* in Bedlam. There could be no doubt that he at least believed himself sincere, though I knew not what reply I could make to his madness. After a moment, I gathered myself. "So this is what they think—the villagers? They stayed away from my cousin's funeral because their minds were deceived, as your own, with this devilish superstition—they really believe her stolen away by the fairies?"

He straightened himself at that as if he were at last recollecting himself. I could only hope that my words had made him ashamed of the crazed notion that had taken possession of his senses. I remembered then something that had been said to me and attempted to press home my advantage. "The parson, you know, is in full agreement that fairies and goblins do not exist. He says that your creatures of the hill are nothing but devils and demons, come to torment the simple and fool their minds—to lead them astray—even down to the very depths from which they came!"

My speech served only to revive his intensity of feeling. "Aye," he said, "Aye!" He leaned in close once more, meeting my look with his own shining eyes. "But 'e still believes in 'em, dun't 'e!"

I was struck speechless by this undeniably logical, if outrageous, riposte. There was little else for me to do but shake my head over the stubborn ignorance in which I had found myself mired, to take to my horse—the bay mare I had seen peaceably nodding in its stall—and to set out upon my journey.

We clopped along, hooves raising dust from the rutted lane, the dry smell of it secondary only to the musky scent of the mare and the almost cloying floral notes rising from a froth of wild carrot along the verges that shone so brightly in the sun it hurt my eyes to look upon it. It was so bright, and indeed so beautiful, that I found my mind wandering gratefully from my errand, even whilst the rocking gait of the mare carried me steadily towards it with almost the regularity of a machine.

After a time I saw men working in the fields, hacking at their crop with scythes and raking it out into lines, tasks that were entirely mysterious to me. There were women there too, wearing capacious bonnets which covered the backs of their necks so that only their hands would be browned with their labour. Children worked at their sides, too industrious, too young or too poor to attend school. The sight made me rein in the mare and gaze at the scene as a corresponding image appeared to me of clerks flooding into the City, clinging to omnibuses and thronging the streets at the clock's command. Here, where the church clock bore two minute hands, they surely had need of none. They would go to the fields at sunrise and cease when darkness fell. Outwardly, too, they were different; here, the workers wore pale cottons which shone back the light of the sun, and I felt suddenly the stark contrast of my own night colours; what a crow I was in comparison! Dark wools were a requirement in the City, where such pale tones would quickly be ruined by the coal smuts which were all about. Here, things were of necessity different. Materials so strongly dyed would quickly fade in light such as this; smart blacks would soon turn to rust. And there was another difference, of course: for even a peasant in the country was likely to live far longer than a city man.

I tipped my hat and wiped my forehead with my pocket handkerchief, realising I appeared half faded already with the dust that clung to my clothing. The mare, as if in full knowledge that my period of reflection was over, started again at her steady pace. Shortly afterwards the road widened and I made out most plainly the frozen imprints of footsteps and of hooves as well as the ridges thrown up by cartwheels, all speaking of animals being driven to market and village folk going to make their purchases. I had spied nothing but an occasional waggonette in the distance; I never drew any closer before they vanished in at some gate or other. There had not been a single hawker, peddler, cheapjack or farmer's wife with a willow basket swinging on her arm. The road did not look familiar to me, although I must have been brought this way from Kelthorpe. Had I simply not noted which way I had come? There had been no landmark I recognised for some time, nor a waystone or fingerpost. I drew the horse to a halt once more and it stood and waited patiently, shifting its haunches, and for a moment I did nothing. Then I realised, with a start, that I was not alone. I became sensible of the presence of an old man sitting almost in the hedgerow, clutching a half-devoured plum, its bright yellow flesh all a-drip with juice. His beard was red as a fox and his eyes were darkly twinkling and fixed on me, though he said nothing. He simply nodded, as if that expressed everything he needed to say, his face alight with some barely concealed amusement.

"Good day, sir," I said. "Can you tell me if I am on the right road to Kelthorpe?"

The words must have been wasted as I said them, for however could I have gone amiss? The road was straight and true, marked by its market drovings and other business.

"Oh yes," he replied, his voice as merry as his expression. "Oh yes, you are on the right road indeed!" And the little fellow rose to his feet and pushed his way through a rent in the hawthorn. I stood in the stirrups, peering after him, but I saw him not.

I knew not whether to nod at his reassurance or shake my head over the singularity of its expression as I nudged the horse into resuming its steady motion. This time I did not stop until the town of Kelthorpe was all around me. I had had little opportunity, when I had passed through it previously, to make any examination of the place. Now I saw that it had its own little church, the doors thrown open and lined with flowers. There was an inn, and on the far side of a square, a series of pens that must accommodate its market; the generosity of their provision made me grateful indeed that it was not a livestock day. The faint whiff of singed hooves suggested a farrier not far distant, and that of hides indicated a sadler. There were several small shops; a baker's boy emerged from a nearby doorway, setting out on his rounds. There was also a pleasant green with a well and chained bucket, a little bench and a rather curious jutting of stone that might once have been the base of a buttercross; possibly a remnant of the Dark Ages now fallen into ruin. I could not see the railway station from this vantage, though I knew it must lie behind the taller, grander structure, no doubt constructed for some civic purpose, which took up most of one side of the square.

I found someone to feed and water the horse at the inn and the sleepiness of Halfoak returned to me more keenly at the sight of the ostlers briskly rubbing down a pair of post-horses and the rows of occupied stalls. I wondered if Halfoak had once had such business. The greater number of its stables were empty, so perhaps the horses were at work in the fields; or perhaps Mr. Widdop's fortunes were somewhat in decline. I remembered the revelry that had sounded from below my room in the Three Horseshoes and pursed my lips.

After several hours in the saddle my steps felt uncertain and I was grateful that the way was short. The inn's potboy directed me to the tall building I had spied earlier, and despite all the pronouncements of ill-luck I had heard since I started my sojourn to the country, I fell in with the object of my quest before I even reached the door. I hailed him and introduced myself. "I apologise that I sent no telegram or letter," I said. "Such things seem to take no little time in this part of the world and I thought it more efficient to simply call upon you and hope you will be able to receive my enquiries."

The constable straightened. I would even say he puffed himself up, unfortunately making it more obvious where his blue uniform was missing a button. He was a little shorter than I, and tending towards stoutness. His beard was neatly trimmed, however, and his manner at least spoke of some little pride in his profession. He did not smile. I took the impression he rarely did, but possibly that was an asset to him, in making his countrymen think him a shrewd fellow.

He greeted me politely enough, introducing himself as Constable John Barraclough, and said that he would be happy to accommodate me whilst he took his luncheon, if I had no objection. Upon my stating that I had none, he led me not towards the quiet building but towards the inn, and I quickly recognised that I would be expected to stand him in refreshment. My first intimation of the man must perforce be adjusted; frequenting the local hostelry was not to be expected of any constable, even in such remote parts, where discipline was surely still a requisite of his occupation. It appeared that here, as in Halfoak, everything followed its own well-worn path, regardless of the world around it.

He ordered fried ox tongue and udder with bread for us both, and cider, which I hoped at least might make the man more voluble. We were soon ensconced in a booth of old dark wood, which made us feel quite private; whether we were so, however, was another matter, and I found myself asking my questions in a lowered tone. He asked a few of his own, examining me upon what my interest in the case should be. I informed him that I was Elizabeth Higgs' cousin, that I was dwelling in her cottage and that I had arranged her funeral.

At last he was satisfied, and he frowned and stared down at the table before continuing in the manner of a schoolmaster, "You are correct, sir, in your surmise about the husband's superstition; or at least, in what he says is his superstition, which may be one and the same but may not, if you catch my meaning. He believed the lady to be a changeling: a shadow left by the fairies. His strange supposition began, it is said, a little after Midsummer Eve—Saint John's Eve, that is, June twenty-third. Many places give the night over to church and prayer; in Halfoak, they are said to cling to the old ways more than most, and largely spend it in singing and dancing, despite the disapprobation of the parson. They still light fires too, bone fires and wake fires, the biggest being up on Pudding Pye Hill; now, that is a place with a somewhat evil reputation, as you will have heard. Like many places with barrows and such upon them, it is said to be a fairy hill, and the folk make their dwelling within it, in a land where it is always summer; and summer is the time of an increase in their influence on our world."

I recalled the landlord's words about the unlucky place, and affirmed that I was aware of such, though I had not before heard it spoken of in such clear detail.

"Well, Midsummer Eve is one of the times when the fairies are said to be abroad," said the fellow, breaking off as our plates were delivered and waiting until we were alone once more. "It is a night of revelry for them too, but also a night when they are inclined to steal away with newly married ladies. Mrs. Higgs did not satisfy on that count, of course, unless it was that she had remained childless; but she did fulfil upon another. They say that those who are most beautiful have more of an attraction to the fair folk. There's a saying in these parts: 'What's bred in t' blood will out in t' bone.' Thus they think the fair are close to the fairies, and are in particular danger from their attentions." He took a large bite of bread and chewed ruminatively.

"But to what purpose?" I exclaimed. "Even if such things should exist—which of course they do not—why on earth would they do such a thing? And how?"

He sighed, as if making such an explanation were a tedious matter; as if he should have to explain to a child why the world is round. "The good folk, as they call them—mainly from fear, I think— the quiet ones, the hidden people—they're fading, you see?" His voice dropped in volume, as though even now one of them might be listening at a chink in the wood. "Their race is weak. And so they take changelings—human children, or women who can bear them, to strengthen their lines. And in their place they leave one of their own, worn-out and old, bewitched to look like the one they're meant to replace, though of course they do not thrive; they soon sicken and die. Or they leave a stock of wood, similarly enchanted, and with similar outcome. These changelings can be identified by their weaknesses, or some disfigurement, or by a sweet temper turning of a sudden into querulous and unnatural ways. They might refuse to speak or eat. A child might become a milksop or a squalling affliction. A good wife may be transformed into a shrew. There are many ways of telling." He nodded, as if he really were a schoolmaster giving instruction in a perplexing and obscure new skill.

"Such happened to Mrs. Higgs, or so her husband said it happened. And so he used fire to drive her away. He remains quite insistent that she will come back to him again; that she will return to the perilous hilltop from whence she was stolen. I was there when he was arrested, and I'll tell you this." He paused, though he scarcely needed to ensure he had my rapt attention. "The man was entirely beside himself when he was taken away, though curiously, it was not because we had him for her murder. He said the reason was that it deprived him of the opportunity to meet with her again on the hill, and to show to the world his wife was come home again, as whole and healthful as before."

"But she has not come back," I whispered. I recollected another recent encounter upon the hill, and Mrs. Gomersal and her tumble of warnings. What was it she had said about the blade stuck into the earth? That it would "keep t' door open." Did she too believe that my cousin would one day walk through it?

Constable Barraclough did not notice my distraction. "No," he replied, "and she shall not come back. It is all a remnant of a bygone age, made of phantoms and moonlight; though he might make a go of it in his defence, all the same."

"Whatever do you mean? Why, he shall hang!"

My expostulation gave way to silence between us and in the pause I heeded the soft tap of footsteps outside the booth, followed by their surcease.

"Ah—well, maybe he shall, and maybe he shan't," the constable said, regardless. "He has been sent up for the Assizes, and it shall be for them to decide. But he has this in his favour: that he says they tried to cure her before the night she was burned—aye, and not just once either, but several times. He said he gave her physic and charms and such, all before he resorted to fire. We looked into the matter and there are others who speak for him. I should say no more about it, only to add: the lawmen will argue theirselves blue that his particular kind of madness was as real as daylight, at least to him. He'd borne a good character until then, and there's some already thinks his hand was governed by a type of mania. It may yet carry with the judge."

"But it cannot!" I could not keep the vehemence from my voice. "It is merely further proof, is it not, that he tortured my cousin before he sent her to her grave?" I could not conceal the depths of my shock at the notion. I had considered Jem Higgs as already belonging to the past. That he might fight his judgment, or try in some deceitful way to use events in his favour had never occurred to me. If he had intended it, surely he would have claimed her skirts had merely been set afire while she tended the hearth, and it was far too late for that. But to prevaricate, to try to evade true justice—why, a gentleman could never do such a thing . . . but then, as I reminded myself, a gentleman he was not.

"I do not say it is right, sir. Only that it is." The constable eyed me mildly as he took another large bite from his bread and spoke around it. "But why do you not see him yourself? You could visit him, ask him your questions."

That further wrapped me in silence. I experienced the same sense of strangeness as when Mrs. Gomersal had announced to me that I might see my cousin. The whole affair had so far taken on the nature of a tale in a storybook that the very idea came as a shock; Jem Higgs had been little more to me than one of the parson's demons and devils, or some sly-faced pantomime villain cackling behind a mask. I could hardly think of him as flesh and blood, as someone I might actually stand in front of and look in the eye. And yet I had peered in at his window and seen the tools he had handled every day. I would perhaps, this very night, be sleeping in his bed. I passed a hand across my eyes.

The constable cleared his throat. "It is something of a step, I'll be bound. He is not in Kelthorpe, of course; we have no detention room here. It's a quiet place, with quiet folk. There is a little vagrancy, or men falling asleep whilst driving a cart; and always a few tenants who think they can eat the rabbits off their fields; but I've never before seen the like of this. I cannot be sure I should wish to see the fellow, if I were in your place. But there is something I might ask. Since you are lodging at the cottage, could I require that you are vigilant as to the whereabouts of a journal?"

"A journal?" I blinked.

"Higgs was most insistent that his wife kept such a thing. He said he'd had his doubts, quite natural doubts, as to the correctness of his surmise about her nature, whether it be fairy or human; but that he one day happened upon her journal and read a portion of it. Within it he found certain proofs of her character and became quite decided on the matter of what must be done. Search was made, however, and no journal was to be found."

"Of course not. If he says it contains proofs that she was a fairy, it reveals such a thing to be impossible! He is merely attempting to make himself appear more lost in madness, which you say is his whole defence. I have seen no such article. I doubt there is any to be found."

"As you say." He gave a slight bow, or perhaps only ducked his head to fall to his meat the more readily. He said few further words on the matter. As for myself, I ate little. The bread was dry in my mouth; it tasted of nothing at all.

I sat and pondered on Constable Barraclough's words for a time after he had departed. They whirled in my head, disjointed ideas that would not connect in any meaningful way. *They're fading, you see? And so they take changelings—human children, or women who can bear them.* It all felt like a dream that would blow away with the morning. I was haunted by the wild images he had conjured, mainly of villagers dancing wantonly around their bone fires and wake fires, discarding items of dress and making terrible cries as they went. Yet in my mind's eye there were other, quieter folk watching them from the shadows: people with red hair and dark twinkling eyes. I sighed, rousing myself—and something he had said came back to me like an echo: *Physic and charms and such.*

I stood, made certain new enquiries for information, and walked out once more into the sunshine. I had been directed to a sturdy brick house that stood in a wide garden upon a street a little removed from the square. The door was answered promptly to my knock by a maid in a clean white cap who informed me that the master of the house was out at present. She directed me into a small morning room where I could wait.

I surveyed the overstuffed chairs with their pattern of blowsy flowers; the mantel with its flat-backed china shepherdess; the polished occasional tables, each crowded with vases and ornaments and knicknackery, all set upon little needlework doilies. Everything spoke of domestic felicity, which came as a comfort in its way, and perhaps such was its intended effect upon those who found themselves its occupants. I was almost nodding in my seat when I heard a voice in the passage.

Shortly afterward, the owner of the voice entered the room. He was a tall, gangling gentleman wearing a neat jacket a little worn about the cuffs and a well-starched shirt. His dark brown hair was blown awry and his cheeks were pink with exertion. He excused his appearance, having come, he said, from a nasty case of consumption, and he thrust out his hand to shake my own, introducing himself as Doctor Newberry.

His smile faded as I informed him of my business in that place, to be replaced by a look of frank puzzlement when I asked what light he might be able to throw upon my cousin's circumstances prior to her death.

"I beg your pardon," he said, putting up a hand to rub his cheek, "but I am afraid I have no intelligence to give. I was called upon by an acquaintance of Mr. Higgs, but I said to him what I would say to anyone: that there was no treatment I could provide without seeing the husband at the very least, even if it was inconvenient to visit the lady, but the husband did not come."

"He did not?" I was as bewildered as he. *Physic and charms and such.* If Higgs had truly been concerned for his wife's wellbeing, must he not have seen a doctor? And yet here was the doctor, the only one for miles, according to the innkeeper, and Higgs had never seen him. The defendant's case was surely blown to pieces, and all for the sake of a single question!

I had begun to think the constable a simpleton, when he added, "Of course, it is quite possible it would not be myself to whom they would refer. As nonsensical as it is, they cling to their old ways in that village, and in many others hereabout. The medical profession is not yet as well-regarded as it ought to be. Why, the most beleaguered labourer, about to take his last breath, would rather throw his fate before the quack than a trained professional. It is most trying.

But as I mentioned, I would only treat the lady if I had seen the husband, and I venture to add that my decision was quite correct. I really cannot regret it."

It had already occurred to me that here was a man who might possibly have been of some assistance to my cousin and had done nothing. I wondered if I should be angry, but then I recalled my own family's remove from all that had passed. We were her nearest connections and we had done nothing; why should it surprise me that no other man had?

It was with a sense of renewed sadness that I took my leave of Doctor Newberry. I reflected that at least, upon my return, my hearth would not be empty or friendless. It would be lit by the soft glances of my wife, and I was glad of it as I took once more to horseback, this time impatient at the mare's unhurried pace as I made my way back to Halfoak.

Chapter Ten

Strange to say, it was with a degree of relief that I left the greater bustle of Kelthorpe behind me and reached once more the quiet lane through the village. I could smell the cut hay and sweet flowers, and all about me was birdsong; swifts looped and dived through the air above my head. Still, despite my earlier haste, after I had returned the horse and crossed the little bridge that led to Pudding Pye Hill, I had begun to feel the easement of walking upon my fatigued limbs and I resolved to stroll a little longer. The warmth of the day was leavened by a cooling breeze as the sun lowered and so I strode on up the hill and turned to take in the panorama.

Everything was thrown into a rosy hue, the sky smeared into the most fabulous tones of orange and apricot and the whole land-scape hung with long shadows, though it was difficult to make out what cast them. It was a most apposite moment to clear my mind and contemplate the perfect wonder of God's creation, and I found myself wandering further, without design, to the summit of what some thereabouts claimed was a fairy hill.

I felt lighter as I went, as if I could cast away the weight of all that had passed and feel only the beauty of everything growing around me, being renewed and replaced as everything upon this earth was renewed and replaced. I found my steps wending not towards the old hoary barrow but around the top of the hill and towards the little grove of oak trees. I could just see their crowns, silvering and darkening as the breeze turned them this way and that, and I thought of the good folk, named out of some sense of fear or misplaced respect, carrying out their revels beneath my feet in a *land where it is always summer*. I smiled, thinking of that. I could not imagine it being anything other than summer here, so perfectly mild and soft was the air; so scented the breeze with nectar and sap.

After a time I found my mind wandering. I simply walked wherever my steps led, letting the dandelion seeds settle on my clothes, and I listened to the hum of bees, the tick of crickets and the sighing of the oaks. I walked through other flowers I could not name, and it put me in mind of when I was young, walking with my mother in some pleasure garden. In some distant time, before I was born, she had lived in the country, before removing to the City with so many others; and she had recited strange names to me, searching for lady's mantle and sweet cicely, bellflower and yellow archangel, though we never had been able to find them. So little had flourished in the City; outside the parks even the trees struggled for existence, for little would thrive save for the plane trees, which resisted the effects of the greasy coating lent to each leaf by factory fumes and coal dust. Now I looked upon strange forms, petals of purple and pink and yellow, and wondered if they corresponded in any wise to the names she had once told me.

I was distracted from my reverie by a motion in the grass; I peered down to see the tip of each blade tipped with gold, and there it was: little eyes, staring back at me. Then they blinked and in the next moment a butterfly lifted from the verdure and fluttered away. I turned to follow its flight and was blinded by the evening's last flush of sunlight when a figure rose before me.

It was like the last time, but this lady was golden: golden and slender and lovely. Her hair was touched by the sunlight as if she

were aflame. I could not see her face but I had the impression of a
wonderful luminosity about her skin, and her form was so fine the
light seemed to shine through her. I stopped like a man spellbound
and my breath caught in my throat. I think my mouth fell open. She
was here after all, and I almost spoke her name—*Linnet*—and my
hand went to my pocket, wherein had lain the lock of her hair; but
I found it empty.

She turned her head and at once her skin coarsened, becoming
opaque once more, her eyes resolved into their own earthy brown
and I saw that it was my wife who stood there, and once again I had
not recognised her.

She met my fixed gaze and at the sight of it her own expression,
which had been full of wonder, hardened. Her face was now quite
as it had always been, and yet her eye was cold: a shiver shook me
at the sight.

She flung out her hand. I could not make out what she intended
by it, lest it be an expression of repudiation, and then I became
conscious of a great silence between us, and I realised that I had
been humming all along the hymn that had become so fond to
my memory.

"My dear," I said, recovering myself, "I am so glad to see you.
How came you to be in this place?"

"And you, my love," she replied after a pause. "Why, I have been
trapped indoors all day. I saw the sunset from the window and longed
to view it without interruption." She turned and looked about her,
pointing through the brake of gorse towards the oaks and the circle
in the grass beneath them. "This is a singular place."

"It is." I found myself wanting to tell her of all the warnings I
had heard: to avoid the hill at sunset and stay away from where the
fairies dwelt, but I swallowed them back, knowing not why I should
even think of saying them aloud. They were all nonsense, tales told
to frighten children. There was no reason why she should not walk
in this place, to take the air and enjoy the vistas it provided.

She took a few steps nearer the oak trees and the odd cleft behind
them. Then she exclaimed and she walked a little faster through the

clearing. I put out a hand as if to stop her, then let it fall as she cried, "Look! There is a knife of some kind, set into the ground."

She bent, ready to pull it free, and in a moment I was at her side. I reached out and touched her shoulder; it was hard and unyielding. "Pray, do not do that."

She stiffened further. "Why on earth should I not?"

I forced a casual smile. "My cousin's husband set it there. He thought—he thought it would enable her to return to this place, that it would hold open some kind of door into the land of the fairies."

She looked into my eyes for what felt like a long time. Her expression gave no intimation of her feelings, but when she spoke again her voice was laden with contempt. "Superstition?"

I frowned, pulling myself taller. "No," I said, "evidence." And it struck me almost at once that it *was* evidence, though not in my cousin's favour; it might be another element to strengthen her husband's defence. And yet I could not help but feel some measure of relief, as we made our way from the hillside to the enclosing walls of the little cottage, that the knife he had put there so carefully was still firmly in its place.

Chapter Eleven

That evening we ate slices of ham and cheese with bread that Helena told me had been sent from the village. She did not say who had come, though I assumed that my erstwhile landlord had been as good as his word. He was proving an odd mixture of usefulness and almost wilful confusion, though it did not prevent me from devouring the meal; I had been able to eat little at the inn.

As we ate I told Helena something of what I had discovered earlier in the day, though I soon gave it up. She had said she felt chill upon our return, though I scarcely knew how that could be possible on so clement an evening; still, I laid a fire for her in the parlour and now we baked before it. Her face gleamed as she stared steadily into the flames. She did not speak and the light flickered across her features, making it difficult to read her expression; it gave it the appearance of changing moment to moment and I found I did not like to watch. I fell to staring into the fire as well, listening to its hiss and spit. Its dancing merely conjured more fearful images still, and yet I could not look away from them.

I banished the thought of what had happened upon this very hearth, but I failed to settle on anything more cheerful. I could not help but wonder if this was how things would be between us: bound not in mutual chatter but in brooding silence and oppression of spirits.

After a time, I found that it was not entirely silent after all. In spite of the closed shutters and drawn curtains I began to hear snatches of music from the village below; the fiddler must have resumed his playing at the inn. It was odd that it could be heard at such a distance, but such must be the strange acoustics of the valley.

And then I noticed a china jug on the floor just by the hearth, and I started, thinking of the one I had seen there before, but this one was different. I rose to see what it held, remembering Widdop's words about thanking the fairies with an offering of water. There was no water in it, however; the jug contained nothing but the slight residue of a greenish fluid. Upon peering into it I discerned a smell, a little like milk but rather stronger, so that I almost did not like it.

Helena's voice came from over my shoulder. "Oh—that! It was brought by your Mrs. Gomersal. 'Beastlings', she called it, which it seems is the first milk taken from a cow after it has calved. Quite charming, I am sure. She said it was to be poured onto the ground on the hill, for your little folk—" Here my wife laughed. "It is some kind of offering, I think. But I found I rather liked the taste."

I stared at her. "You drank it?"

She gave a smile, made strange by the irregularity of the light. "I did."

I peered once more into the jug. The scent was already fainter, yet there was something about it that was invigorating; with the sound of the fiddle drifting from the village I felt energy course through me. I did not wish to return to my seat and remain idle, so I took the jug into the kitchen and put it aside for washing. Our plates had been left there too; the neatness of my cousin's kitchen was already in disarray. I reminded myself that Helena was unused to keeping her own establishment; it would hardly be reasonable to expect all to be in order.

When I returned to the parlour, my wife was standing by the window with her back to the room. She had drawn back the curtains and partly opened the shutters. I went to see what it was she looked upon, and she shrank away from me. I did not remark on it, but gazed out. The light of the waxing moon had made the night gleam. I made out the little cluster of houses at the start of the village, along with the tower of the church with its strange double clock. Around it, fields stretched away in every direction and the white road wound through it all. It was so beautiful I could not speak. I realised that, indeed, all sound had stilled, even that of the oddly drifting music.

I twisted my head and saw the curve of Helena's beautiful cheek. I could not help it; I bent and kissed her neck. She turned to me. Her eyes were dark and soft, and slowly, her lips stretched into a smile. I could see the form of it quite clearly, and yet somehow I could not read what it meant.

"Goodnight, my love," she said, turning away. "I find I do not like the fire after all. You have the room to the right hand of the landing."

"We are not to share a room?"

"It is a warm night, my dear, and I am restless. I fear I should keep you awake." She turned to the fire and, taking up her shawl and wrapping the end of it around her fist, she grasped the iron poker, prodding the coals into pieces that quickly flared and would as quickly die. She stabbed at it vigorously, as if she would extinguish it all at once.

I did not comment upon her change of heart about the temperature. I simply bade her to sleep well and soon enough after I followed her up the stairs.

The risers creaked underfoot, despite my endeavours to step quietly. I entered the bedroom, staring around at the unfamiliar furniture; there was no table or chair, no chiffonier, and I noticed the ware was mismatched—what I had first taken for a ewer was just a cracked earthenware jug. I examined the bed, thankfully finding all in order, though the sheet was rather worn and had been sewn side to middle to make it serviceable once again. I set out my shaving brush and razor, noticing that the mirror on its stand had been

clothed in little lace curtains and tied with a bow, and I thought of
Lizzie slaving over the fancywork.

Despite the heat of the day the coverings were cool and I lay
there, waiting for my body to warm them, dwelling upon the point
that this was our first night in a home that we shared with no one
else. The doors between us felt as if they were miles distant; I disliked the sense of being alone, though my wife's words had been
quite reasonable. Still, even with nothing to disturb me, sleep was
impossibly remote.

I pushed the bedclothes aside and set my feet upon the floorboards. I thought I could distinguish some sound lacing the evening
air once again, and something in me wanted to hear it more clearly.
I crossed to the window and gently eased the shutters open before
putting my face close to the glass, so that my breath misted against it.

This window overlooked the back of the cottage and I could just
see the wall that encircled the garden. Beyond that, the hillside rose
away towards the barrow. The bounties of the garden, at this hour,
were turned to a blank darkness and I could make out little of it.
From somewhere amongst the shadows came the soft hooting of an
owl. I shuddered; the bird was ever said to be of ill-omen, showing
its ominous nature in shunning the light of day for night, but surely
such a notion was as outmoded as the idea of little folk dancing on
the hillside. And then all thought was forgotten because I could
hear that music again, and in another moment I had pushed open
the window.

Sweet, cool air rushed in, rich with the scent of leaf and flower
and musk, so heady that it made me long to rush outside and walk
among it. And the fiddle rose, its melody twisting and crying and
yearning, so rapid and light it sounded like another instrument altogether from the one I had previously heard. It was so beautiful, so
full of life that my blood was invigorated and I found myself tapping
my foot against the floor. I was unfamiliar with the air it played, but
it was like quicksilver, like lightning dancing across the sky; it made
even a steady man such as I wish to cast aside all thought of decorum
and dance.

I realised I was smiling, until it occurred to me to wonder what I must look like, should anyone be able to see me leaning out of the window and grinning like a madman, and I straightened my demeanour. I shook my head as if I could free myself of the infectious rhythm of the instrument, and yet all that I could think of was: *the Reeling Road—ah, it is aptly named after all!*

I pulled the window to, and just as if I had rejected the call of the music utterly, it was suddenly cut off. I felt bereft and tried widening the gap, but no; it had quite abandoned me. Feeling newly despondent, I slipped into bed, but I soon cast off the bedsheets once more. After such a moment of lightness, they were too hot and heavy to be borne. I turned and turned again. It was as if I had taken some intoxicating potation; my limbs were light, my head spinning, though all about me remained solid and earthbound and drear.

I no longer wondered that Helena had chosen to sleep alone. It was fortunate that she had. The change in our locality and circumstance, the heat of the sun, the long journeys we had both undertaken—there was little wonder that the result was an infuriating restlessness. Helena must have felt it too; it was no doubt the cause of her feeling chill earlier in the evening. I wondered if she was sleeping now, or if she too was leaning out of the window, listening to night noises and being carried away by silly fancies. But of course she was not. Hers was a sensible and soothing nature and I was grateful for it, in that instant, more than ever. I wished for her to be with me, breathing coolly and quietly at my side. I turned and looked at the pillow next to mine. No indentation marred its white surface and I found myself unaccountably angry; I seized it and hurled it from the bed.

I tried to sleep, but could not. All the events of recent days kept rushing through my mind, and little wonder. Wild tales were no inducement to peace or rest or the unreachable release of sleep.

I sat up. I lay down. I shifted my attitude on the bed. I got up. I exchanged my pillow for the one I had cast aside, but all was to no effect. My limbs were heavy as lead one moment, light and restive the next, wanting only to move, to rid themselves of this awful energy that coursed through my veins. I stared up at the bed hangings and scowled at everything around me. And then a memory came: a light step, the slight pressure of fingers taking my arm, a quiet voice in my ear, and I remembered the words, though they were not the ones she had spoken. Instead, they were my father's words: *Look! Let us see whether we shall have a storm.*

I sat bolt upright, rubbing at my hair. I did not know what hour of the night it was and I did not wish to look; it could make no difference. It was not as if I were in London, bound by the hands of time to be seated at a desk until they declared I could go home again.

I covered my eyes as all emotions crowded in upon me at once. They did not even feel quite like my own, or not all of them did, such was the disorder of my mind. And then, exhausted at last, I lay down and I must have slept for a time, for I had the strangest of dreams: of dancing, not wildly but in stately fashion and full of grace; a beautiful woman, appearing from the sunlight on a hillside; then darker visions of doors that remained open, when in truth, they would have been much better closed.

I opened my eyes. My forehead, nay, my whole body was running with sweat, so that I thought at once of fever, yet I felt quite calm, almost myself again. I did not return once more to slumber, but stood, and still in my nightshirt, I made my way downstairs.

The quality of the light had led me to think it morning, but the corners were still laden with shadows and I could see but little. I entered the parlour, where only a thin grey light penetrated the room, outlining its barely familiar shapes. The fire had long since died; no heat remained in its coals. I crossed the room anyway, stepping tentatively across the stone floor, and put out my hands and found the chair in which I had sat the preceding evening. I was occupied in sinking into it when I froze utterly.

Two eyes stared at me from across the room.

My own eyes widened. I did not blink; I dared not close them for a moment. The eyes were bright little glints in the dimness and they glared at me quite steadily, without flinching or looking away.

They stood but a few inches above the floor, and they were undeniably real, and present, and watching me. *The beastlings*, I thought.
They have come for the beastlings, but they are all drunk! I turned towards
the door as if even now Helena might be coming downstairs, all
unsuspecting that the hidden people had come for their revenge.

I stirred myself, rushing to the window, reaching out and dragging the curtain wider. I forced myself to stifle my own startled
laugh.

It was the fox—the red fox in its glass case, its black eyes dead and
fixed and staring.

My heart raced in my chest even whilst I smiled at my own
foolishness. I was assuring myself that it was merely the lateness of
the hour and sleeplessness and odd dreams that had so infected my
thoughts when a noise started outside the window.

I jumped; a chill crept across my skin. Then I realised what it
was, and yet somehow, though natural, it felt stranger by far than
it had before. The birdsong, the gentle birdsong that had been the
music of my days here had begun again, but suddenly and without
warning and with not the faintest trace of music in it. What had
once been harmonious was now discordant, an intrusion on the
sane human world. It was as if all the various species were singing
at once, their notes tumbling over one another, vying to make the
most jarring cries. There were sharp, high snips that made me think
of shining scissors; shrill wails which surely must have been of panic;
wild, uncontrolled whistles; a harsh guttural croak that sounded to
my ear like mad laughter, and all was overlaid by the long, shivering
call of the owl, the bird of ill-omen. And the idea seized my night-
bound and stirred imagination that they were singing for me, nay,
that they were mocking me as I stood, still and silent, trying not to
disturb the air any further by drawing a single breath.

The cacophony went on; I know not how long it lasted, as the
fox watched and I stood staring at nothing, and when I thought
it impossible for it to become louder still, they met the challenge,
raising each other to bolder cries and lewd calls. I closed my eyes. I
had a memory. I was ten or eleven, travelling back with my father

from some late visit. We were traversing some of the less respectable
streets of the West End just at the spilling-out of costermongers and
other lowly characters from the cheap and disreputable entertainments of the penny gaffs. One young fellow tossed his hat into the
air. Another glanced up as we passed and when he saw me watching
he opened his lips in a lascivious grin and turned to the girl next
to him, whose cheeks were rouged like a Frenchwoman's, and he
grasped her thin skirts in his fist. In the next instant he pulled them
upward, petticoats and all, and I glimpsed her mottled white thigh;
heard a shriek that spoke at once of indignation and delight—and
then my father had reached out and pulled down the blind of the
brougham and the sounds had been dampened as if it had been a
door of iron.

I opened my eyes. For a moment the jumble of sounds continued, and then, just as suddenly, it stopped.

I realised without surprise, as if it was what I had expected to see,
that Helena was standing on the other side of the room. A shawl
was loose about her neck, her dark hair twisted upon it in a dark
stream. She pulled her nightgown more tightly about her, as if she
were cold.

"My dear," she said, "I somehow knew you would be awake."

I made to reply, but knew not what to say.

"Then I will tell you something. I thought there would be a better time, but I cannot wait longer." She smiled, though it did not
speak of pleasure. "But you know, do you not—can you not guess?
You know already why it is that I came."

I did not answer. I did not even move. It was as if there were a
stranger standing there, speaking some foreign tongue.

"Come," she said, "you *do* know. You know all—you have seen
it!" Her eyes shone brightly. "You are to be a father, my dear!"

I stared at her and she looked back at me. I do not know how
long we stood there, but I feel quite sure that as we did the light
outside the cottage increased, for her skin began to pale, taking on
an almost unnatural shine as if it were not soft and yielding but as
alabaster, and her eyes turned hard and cold as ice.

She turned on her heel and went out of the door. I heard her step once more upon the stair. She did not stamp; she did not hurry. The door to her room opened and closed again behind her. I felt as if I had dreamed her words. I could not order my thoughts, which crowded and tumbled upon each other.

At length I came to myself, called out her name and hurried after her. I stood at her door, and I remember speaking, a torrent of words, though I do not know what I said. I did not go in but knocked softly at her door, as if I were some acquaintance come to pay a call.

She did not open it; no sound at all emerged from the chamber. The birds were singing once more, though the awful din of earlier had relented into something sweet and pleasant that spoke of the dawning of another beautiful summer's day; of harmony, of everything made into sweet concord; so that I hardly knew whether I had dreamed all that had passed before, or why it had troubled me so.

Chapter Twelve

When our little household rose properly later in the morning, I went and kissed my wife and held her hand and led her to a chair. I told her how happy I truly was. We would need to set up our own establishment, of course, and remove from my father's house, and I told her how I had anticipated, even longed for such an occasion.

And yet here we were, in our own little cottage—for now, at least—and she remained pale and silent. I bade her to stay where she was and in my own clumsy way I took her part and cut bread for our breakfast, spreading it with butter, noting that the kitchen was falling yet further into disarray; but she proclaimed herself bilious and refused to eat. I partook of it myself and although it was good bread made of good flour, it was quite dry in my mouth.

Presently Helena proclaimed herself too ill to attend church, which news gave me a little start for the days had rather flowed into one and I confess I had not thought of it being the Sabbath. At that moment the distant bells began to chime, calling one and all to service. I pictured the villagers, most of them strangers to me, all taking their accustomed places. I remembered the way they had not troubled to attend my cousin's funeral and I decided it could not matter if I missed a sermon in circumstances such as these.

We sat and reached for some occupation. Helena took out a book she had brought with her and I offered to read aloud from the Bible that I had discovered on the shelf, but my wife was unforthcoming. As she turned the pages, I peered at her little bound volume. It was nothing more than a novel, but I could not bring myself to protest. I felt most keenly my odd reaction to the news of her condition, and endeavoured now to be solicitous, filling the range with coal and setting the kettle to boil for tea. I could feel its heat even through the closed door and I reflected it was an evil of the little cottage that it should be positioned so near the parlour; though I supposed that it had been placed as far as possible from the larder, and indeed, that winter would put another aspect upon it entirely. What an inconvenience it must have been to Lizzie that her husband had taken such a fine room for his workshop! I positioned myself upon the farthest cushion of the sofa whilst Helena protested that she preferred her chair, and she perched ladylike upon its edge, intent upon her book.

A little afterward, I announced that I would go out. Something had been occupying my thoughts and I wished to enquire into it, even if it were a Sunday. At that, Helena rose to her feet. "I am not an invalid," she announced, as if I had done her some terrible wrong. "A little air would freshen me wonderfully."

Thus we walked arm in arm down the little path towards the village. When we reached the bridge over its babbling stream Helena hesitated, gripping my arm more tightly, so that I almost felt I was pulling her across. When I asked if she felt faint, however, her lips pursed into a thin white line, and I made no further enquiry.

I had hoped that the service would have ended and I saw that my surmise was correct when we started along the lane and I saw that we were not alone. Ahead of us, wearing a neat print dress and beribboned bonnet, was Mrs. Gomersal. Her impish child, running about at her heels, turned to stare at us. He had been plucking flowers by the stream and he clutched a straggling bunch of yellow kingcups to his chest.

Helena walked on ahead, smiling at the boy. "What a lovely child," she exclaimed, and he stared blankly back, a line of spittle running down his chin. "And who are you, little master?"

"'E's all right," said the mother, which led to a bemused nod from Helena. She did not realise the woman had thought her London "who" a Yorkshire "how." And then Mrs. Gomersal said, "Good day," and bobbed an almost imperceptible curtsy.

My wife continued in her feminine chatter, ascertaining that the boy was seven years old and a little slow, his mother answering most of the questions on his behalf. She proclaimed him "a good lad for all that," and said that he was not alone but had two elder sisters who were "getting t' dinner on."

"And do you go to school?" my wife enquired.

"'E does most times, ma'am," his mother said. "There was a time t' squire's wife got up a Sunday school an' taught a bit o' readin', but that's fallen by-the-by. An' there's a dame school, but there's none such now, not at 'arvest, an' everyone all so busy in t' fields."

The waif nodded, suddenly eager, and he began to shred the flowers he held, letting flakes of gold fall to the ground. "Cleanliness, godliness and spellin'," he chanted, as if by the result of much drilling, though his words were ill-formed. I realised it was the first time I had heard him speak and I opened my mouth to ask in which subject he excelled, before I bit the words back. Perhaps it was better so, for his mother gazed down at him as fondly and proudly as if she had raised a prodigy.

Mrs. Gomersal turned to Helena. "Did you see to t' bis'lings?" she asked, nodding as if in anticipation of the answer.

"Oh—very helpful, thank you," was the response, and Mrs. Gomersal appeared quite content with that, until the child suddenly piped:

"She drank it." And he pointed, directly and impertinently, at my wife's stomach.

Helena's smile faded and she drew her wrapper around herself as if she could hide her figure from his staring. Mrs. Gomersal grasped the child's arm and shook him. She met my wife's eye and made as if to speak, but it was her turn to reconsider her words and she merely nodded after all.

I made some comment upon the fineness of the day, such ever being a means of smoothing over any difficulty, and she said, "Well, I'll not keep yer from it." And she turned, only staying when I motioned for her to stop.

"Mrs. Gomersal, I was hoping you could help me with a little information," I said. I had meant to walk on to the inn and ask Mr. Widdop my question, but it struck me that this meeting could be fortuitous; she knew of midwifery and such matters, did she not? Perhaps she would be the better subject. "It transpires that my cousin was ill for some time before her—before what happened, and I was hoping to discover something about it, though I am not sure who was her medical man. Would you possibly know anything of it?"

At that she gave me a frank, unblinking stare, almost as if she thought she were being played for a fool, but after a moment she answered softly, "Aye, sir. I knows, as any round 'ere'll tell you."

"Then perhaps you could direct me to the gentleman?"

She stood for a while, thoughts flitting across her features, then she composed herself and said, "I'll do better'n that, sir. I'll take you to 'em. It's a bit on a walk, an' I'll 'ave ter get straight back fo' t' dinner, but they'll ne'er see thee otherwise. I'll get 'em ter talk to thee, but I'll tell yer this, sir: it in't no gennleman."

I longed to question her further on the matter, but her face closed up tight and I decided I should not, at least while my wife was present. I turned to Helena and pressed her quietly to return to the house, and was astonished when she threw my hands off her own. "I shall do no such thing," she said, loudly enough for Mrs. Gomersal to hear. I gave her a questioning look, but I had no wish to make a scene and so the four of us set out together.

Almost at once we turned aside from the lane and our guide stepped neatly across a little stone stile set into the wall that I had never before noticed. I turned once more to Helena to press on her the need to go home, if only to preserve her skirts, but in the next moment she was following. Grateful she had left her crinoline in

London, I handed her over the stile, then looked about. We stood in a wide field that appeared to have been left fallow for some time: the ground was a little uneven, and grown up like a meadow. A narrow, trodden-down path led along one side of it.

"The leys," Mrs. Gomersal informed us, and pointed towards a little knot of sheep at the far side of the field nibbling at the clover. She led the way alongside the hedgerow of thick and tangled blackthorn, a profusion of white mouse-ear and pink campion, according to our guide, spilling from under it. She pointed out these and various other grasses and wildflowers as we went, so that her voice became like a litany: *shepherd's purse, corncockle, meadow cat's-tail, self-heal, crested dog's-tail, toadflax, enchanter's nightshade, yellow rattle, lady's bedstraw, fox-tail.*

We made our way in this fashion towards the farthest end of the field, which culminated in a little tangled stand of trees. I somehow felt misgivings at the sight of it and began to wish we had never set out, but it was now too late. Mrs. Gomersal's child lagged behind us, snatching at the colourful petals, not heeding his mother's commands to "step short." My wife's hems rustled and snagged, but I could see by her expression that she would not go back without seeing this to its end. Possibly she wished to know, because of her condition, whatever medical man might be found in the vicinity. She complained neither of the distance nor the heat, only striding along in a most determined fashion.

Finally we stood beneath a mixed stand of trees—alder, hawthorn and elm trees, I was informed, that was both deeper and more shadowy than it had at first appeared, and I realised that what I had taken for a tangle of undergrowth was in reality a rough shack darkened with age and tumbled about with ivy and moss. It possessed a forlorn, abandoned air, and my wife echoed my own thoughts when she said simply, "Here?"

I spluttered. "What is this—the home of some hedge-doctor? A quack?"

Mrs. Gomersal hesitated. "Well, they call 'em a cow-doctor, but I think that's just for form, sir, if tha takes me meaning. So as not t' upset t' squire or t' parson nor owt. It's—"

She spoke no further for at that moment a rickety wooden door flew open, crashing back so hard that the whole structure shook, and in the next instant the most extraordinary being was striding towards us. It was not a gentleman, as our guide had warned us; it was not even a man. It was a tall, broad female wearing a tucked-up dress under an apron stained with blood. Her sleeves were rolled up and as she came she wiped something—flour or dust—from arms that were as brawny and tanned as a sailor's. Her visage was rather square, with a high blocky forehead, a determined chin and an angular nose, her countenance made yet more singular by the cloth patch which entirely concealed her left eye. Her right was the most brilliant of greens, and it shone vividly as she turned it upon one of us and then the next; or rather, upon me and my wife, for she glanced at Mrs. Gomersal only once, and at the child not at all.

"It's Mother Draycross, t' wise woman," Mrs. Gomersal said in a voice little more than a whisper, "though some calls 'er Mother Crow. She's one o' the cunning folk." Then she said, more loudly, "'E's 'ere to consult."

I did not think to correct her in her pronouncement for we were already being beckoned inside. At this, however, Helena demurred at last, not refraining from wrinkling her nose in distaste. Softly, and most determinedly, she stated that she would remain where she was. Duly, it was with Mrs. Gomersal alone that I steeled myself and entered the shack, removing my hat and ducking beneath the low door.

The mean abode had been dingy outside and it was cramped within; indeed, there was only a single room. A thin straw pallet lay pushed against one crumbling wall whilst on the other was a tiny grate with a blackened pot hanging over it. A piece of wood balanced on two stones served as a table upon which stood a clay bowl, a pestle and mortar, an almanac and what appeared to be a pharmacopoeia, with next to it a single rough wooden chair. The ceiling was more occupied than the floor, for it was hung thickly with bundles of herbs and dried flowers and mysteriously folded papers.

A peculiar grating sound drew my attention towards the corner and I realised that was not all: there was a large cage of woven hazel twigs and within it was a rather fine black bird. My first thought was that this must be the reason for her being named "crow," but although the creature's feathers were of the deepest sable, it had rather unusual eyes; they were not black, but entirely yellow. The "wise" woman saw the way my gaze tended and she hastened towards it and threw over the cage a dirty and much-faded cloth.

Mrs. Gomersal spoke in a whisper that surely must have carried to Mother Draycross as well as to me. "She'll not 'ave anyone lookin', not till she knows what tha comes for. It's got powers, see, that bird. It'll draw out t' jaundice just by glarin' at yer wi' its yellow eyes. She'll not 'ave yer cured for nowt."

I sighed at the nonsense she spoke. I had expected the quack-doctor to be something suited to a poor man's purse, but I could not bring myself to believe that anyone would subject themselves to whatever ministrations this woman could provide. She was slovenly and unclean—surely her cures would only make a sick man sicker. And yet if I wished to know what had happened to little Lizzie, I knew I must refrain from showing my disgust. As I looked away from the cage, I noticed something else that was curious.

A rough shelf lined the back wall above the woman's pallet. Arrayed along it was a peculiar and arcane collection of bottles: some containing herbs or seeds; others with ancient flowers floating in murky fluid; some with less wholesome contents resembling human hair and fingernails. There was also a much discoloured and stained clay pipe.

Mrs. Gomersal had begun once again her litany: "Violets," she whispered. "Mistletoe—that's for whooping cough. Groundsel. Henbane—that's for madness. Celandine—that'll clear t' worms from an 'oss. Agrimony leaves, rose-hips, lobelia, pudding grass."

The old woman made an irritated sound that shushed the recital, but I was unconcerned. The thing that was of more interest to me stood upon the end of the shelf and I needed no explanation of what lay within it. A plain glass bottle, larger than the rest and somewhat dirty, contained the curled, wet bodies of leeches, awaiting any patient who might have need of them. I grimaced. At least here was something of the medical practitioner's art, but Mrs. Gomersal, seeing the direction of my gaze and not quelled by the lady of the house, poured in at my ear, "They tells 'er t' weather. 'Tis set fine, is it not?" And she spluttered with heedless laughter.

I did not listen for the sloven's response, but inwardly I was aghast. Did the cunning woman already know what science had so recently discovered? It surely could not be. I composed my expression and turned towards her, but she was not looking; she had crouched over a rough wooden box placed upon the floor and her hands were hidden inside it. From its unknown innards came a loud rattling as of pebbles or other objects striking together.

"She's failproof," said Mrs. Gomersal, as if I had asked. "Aye, sir, that she is! A seventh child of a seventh child. There's power in that, an' no mistake."

I could not bring myself to appear impressed. The hag in the filthy apron had straightened, having retrieved something from the box and concealed it within her right hand. It was impressed upon me once more how ugly was her visage, and I could not help but wonder, somewhat cruelly, why it was that if her talents were so "failproof," she had been unable to cure her own blindness.

Mother Draycross drew in a sharp breath, sounding akin to indignation, or perhaps amusement, and she smiled, revealing cracked, browned teeth. Then she spoke in a portentous tone, her voice oddly deep, much more so than I had expected. It was rich also, almost like honey, although she had her share in the same uncouth accent as the villagers. "I'll tell thee where me eye went," she said, and she glared at me so intently with the other that I suppressed a shiver.

I reminded myself that she could not have read my mind; it was an obvious thought to occur to anyone upon seeing her for the first time so it had taken very little skill to happen upon it.

But she began her tale. "Some use iron goggles to spy on t' fair folk. Not me. I'm t' seventh daughter of a seventh daughter, and I've

seen 'em from me cradle. An' I'm a chime-child; I were borned as
t' church bells rang, an' thanks to that, I can see sperrits an' all. I can
see off t' evil eye; I can cast charms; I can tell t' future, or some on
it. An' I can find lost things," she said leaning towards me as if this
was why I had come.

"Failproof," interjected Mrs. Gomersal, but no one paid her any
attention.

"If I'd only 'ad red 'air," the crone went on, "I'd 'ave been com-
plete. As it is, we see through a glass darkly."

I started a little at this, uncomfortably reminded that I had
missed divine service and it was as if she had turned it to mockery. I frowned, but she gave me no opportunity to protest, and I
confess that I was beginning to find her fascinating. Yet my interest
was tinged with sadness, for surely here was the culmination of that
superstition which had proved fatal for poor Lizzie.

"I lived forra time with t' fairies," she said. "Aye, I went into their
'ill. 'Tis allus summer there, an' there's feastin' and music fit to burn
yer ankles, if only you dun't join in t' dance. Years, it felt like I were
there, though I were wise an' I ate nowt in all t' time that passed. An'
I learned from 'em; 'bout flowers and trees and 'erbs, all that grows
or flies. I was there ten year if it were a day, an' never ate a thing. An'
yet when I come back again, only ten minutes'd gone by, so that no
one ever knew me gone!"

I hardly knew what to say to this—I longed to comment that it
had all come out wonderfully convenient for her and that I must
give her credit for such an expedient; but I could see from the corner of my sight Mrs. Gomersal watching me with sharp eyes, so I bit
my lip. I wished that my guide would depart; I felt almost embar-
rassed by her seeing me in this place. It was not proper. And had
she not informed us that she must see to her dinner? And yet she
stayed. Mother Draycross too kept on staring almost to the point of
pertness, though all the time she was shifting from foot to foot, as if
quite unable to forget her time in the fairy reel.

"All t' time I were able to see them wi' my own good eye," she
said, pointing to the patch she wore. "I never needed no spells for

that. An' then one day they rode out, all followin' their queen, an' I smelled the fire and woods and 'ills an' I knew I 'ad to go 'ome again. That was on account of I never ate owt, see. If I 'ad, I'd a been lost for good. An' I stopped dancin'," and then they knew summat were up.

"So one of 'em, an old 'un, 'air like a fox and twice as cunnin', 'e smiled at me. Smiled!" She nodded, as if soliciting my agreement that this was quite a terrible thing, and I returned her nod in sheer confusion. "An' then he reached out wi' 'is thumb an' finger an' 'e plucked it out: me good eye gone, an' me 'alf blinded, an' 'e just laughed in me face. 'All water is wine,' 'e said, 'An' thine eye is mine!'"

I had a sudden image of a little fellow with a ginger beard sitting in a hedgerow, biting into a juicy plum, and I think I blanched. It was a good tale and she told it well.

"I never saw 'em more," she said, "not like I used to. But there's still ways." She stretched out her right hand and uncurled her fingers. There, lying on her palm, was a piece of crystal: a smooth oval of milky translucence, solid as a hen's egg.

I did not know what I was expected to do or say—this was not a situation I had ever envisaged being in, nor was I ever likely to find myself in such again. I wondered if my wife were listening outside, and what expression might be on her calm, sweet face. I thought of her condition and shifted with discomfort; I must state my business at once and leave as soon as I could.

"Madam, I am here to ask about my cousin, Elizabeth Higgs. Her husband came to you, thinking his wife to be ill, and I wondered how it was that he proceeded with her treatment."

She threw back her head, tossing about her unkempt curls, and fairly cackled. "Ill," she said, "ill, you calls it!" She smiled then, and held out her hand, her left this time, and each line upon her palm was clearly delineated by the dirt ingrained into the skin.

Mrs. Gomersal leaned forward and whispered, as loudly as before, "You mun cross her 'and."

It took a moment for me to realise what she meant. "Ah," I said, and pulled a thruppence from my pocket and laid it upon the woman's avaricious palm.

"No, sir, for this a *golden* fee."

I sighed. I felt I should argue, but could not rouse the energy to do so. I took out instead a half sovereign and set it next to the thruppence, which I went to recover, but was stopped short when the harridan snapped closed her fingers and let out a snake-like hiss.

She slipped both coins into the pocket of her apron, her one eye gleaming with satisfaction at the chink they made.

"Now she'll tell everythin'," Mrs. Gomersal pronounced.

"Aye, I saw 'er 'usband," Mother Draycross said, "an' it were plain that she'd been taken. An 'ouse like that 'un? How could she not! It were foolery from t' start." She went to the shelf as she spoke, idly touching certain objects as if they were her talismans: a tiny bottle with a tinier stopper; a bundle of herbs which gave off a sharp and dusty scent; a little wooden box with something that shifted inside it.

"I made a preparation," she said, "nowt more'n that. The seven cures—a few 'erbs an' such. It's not easy to swaller, nor yet on yer belly, but I said she 'ad ter drink it fer all that. An' I give out certain words to say when she did. It 'ad to be after t' church chimed eleven and afore it struck midnight, an' then 'e'd ter put 'er to bed. After that, she'd be forced to flee up t' chimney afore sunrise, and all 'e need do then were watch for 'er, comin' out o' that gap in the 'ill— the 'ollow 'ill, unnerstand?"

I nodded, biting back my retort that the finest scholar in the land would be hard-pressed to follow the loss of her aitches, but I thought of poor Lizzie and I fell silent.

"An' I made some other stuff," she said, "so that when she come back, great age would not come upon 'er of a sudden—dependin' 'ow much of our time 'ad passed while she'd been dancin' an' carryin' on under that 'ill."

It occurred to me to wonder whether the constable had thought to speak to this woman, for it was now beyond doubt that the crone had had a strong hand in whatever had happened to Cousin Elizabeth; and yet she was clearly not in possession of her senses.

"An 'e reckoned it din't work. I said it must 'ave; that it were 'is own wife sittin' at 'is 'earth, but 'e 'ad none on it. I said to make sure at least, so I made 'im some stronger stuff an' a stronger charm. This time 'e'd to ask in t' name o' God who she was, an' she'd be forced to tell 'im. An' 'e still reckoned it weren't 'er."

"And then what?"

She focused upon my face, suddenly wary. The gravity of my tone had perhaps reminded her that a woman was dead, and that woman was my cousin.

"I din't tell 'im to roast 'er," she said. "I only said: iron an' fire, them's t' only way, if the 'erbs dun't do owt. I told 'im, put summat iron ower t' door an' it stops 'em passin' through—"

"—that's 'ow the Three 'Orseshoes got its name," Mrs. Gomersal interjected in a soft voice, and I started; I had almost forgotten she still lingered. "Three doors they 'ave, an' each one wi' an' 'orseshoe ower t' top on it, to stop witches an' flay-boggles an' fairies an' such."

I frowned. Had I ever noticed such an article upon entering the inn? I did not think I had. Even if I had simply overlooked it, such may have been the way of things long ago; only an old, isolated spinster, loose in her mind and no doubt her morals, could possibly lend them any credence now. And yet my cousin's husband had visited her, and he had listened, too.

Mother Draycross continued, "An' fire—if tha can scare 'er wi' it—t' fairy'll flee away, quick as lightning. They can't abide fire, see, since it's a secret o' Heaven. Then they 'ave to give t' real wife back. Or in 'er case, 'appen it forced 'er to show 'erself for what she was—nobbut a stock o' wood—an' we all know what to do wi' one o' them."

"Are you saying you *instructed* him to burn my cousin?" I could no longer hold in my anger.

"I did no such thing—I teld yer that!" She pursed up her lips so tightly her whole visage turned to a mass of wrinkles. "I'll show yer," she said, sounding almost indignant. "I'll show yer t' truth—you'll see 'em for yoursen, an' then you'll know." She reached out and pinched the edge of my sleeve between her finger and thumb and I had to keep myself from pulling away. She stepped backwards, still tugging on my clothing so that I was compelled to follow her to the window.

She held something up—the crystal egg she had shown to me earlier—and peered at it with her good eye, or her bad one, as she had named it. The rather lovely object caught the light, becoming for a moment a ball of brilliance in her hand.

"I'll warn yer," she said, "they say the folk are beautiful, an' beautiful they are, as far as it goes. But once you unnerstand—once you truly *see* 'em for what they are—why, they're ugly as sin!"

She leaned forward and peered through the crystal as if to demonstrate, then she turned her back to the window and drew me towards her by the shoulders, though I could barely conceal my disgust. Despite the fragrant herbs hanging all about us, I could smell her, the foulness of a person long unwashed, all her emanations and exhalations, and I longed suddenly for the sweet, clean air of Halfoak. But she had piqued my curiosity; what man could resist the promise of such proofs? And Mrs. Gomersal was watching with such intensity that I could almost feel the expectation spreading from her side of the room to mine. I suddenly wanted to look, if only to see what trickery Mother Draycross would attempt.

"If you're to borrow t' second sight," she said, "you mun stand thus." She tugged at my clothing once more. "Your left foot goes unner my right one, so—that's it." She stepped quite deliberately onto my boot, covering the highly polished leather with her own dirty rag-wrapped foot.

"Then my 'and goes on your 'ead."

That was too far. I opened my mouth to object, but it was too late; she had already reached out as she said the words and her bony fingers were delving through my hair, her digits surprisingly strong, until I felt them probing my scalp. It was horribly intimate. She leered into my face with her one piercing eye and I looked away.

"That's it," she said in triumph. "Now, look ower my right shoulder an' you'll see!"

With her free hand, she pressed the crystal into mine. The egg was perfectly smooth and cool and without conscious thought I found myself wrapping my fingers around the pleasing weight—but I suddenly did not wish to peer through it. It was not so much that I feared what I might see; rather I felt the resemblance to a ritual, something pagan and wicked—and upon a Sabbath day, and moreover, one on which I had neglected my duty of attending church. The parson's words suddenly returned to me: *As for those who seek them out—those who go looking to find evil—why, they shall find it, sir, and only harm shall come to them!*

Now here I was, in a mean and filthy hut, pressed up close to this malodorous hag, and I scarcely knew how I had progressed from thence to this.

I raised my hand and held the crystal before my eye. Gnarled and twisted trees masked the view of the golden cultivated fields beyond the deep wood; here, all was wildness. Fungi of brilliant yellow spilled from fallen branches half drowned in ivy. Shadows lay deep upon it all, and yet I could see flowers too, gleams of pink and white. As I watched, the sun speared down through a gap in the canopy, lighting a drift of pollen and setting everything a-glimmer; I saw dandelion seeds floating in their hundreds all about. The sight was calming and lovely and I took a deep breath as if to taste the air.

"See—you see!" Mother Draycross cackled. "There, atwixt that dead tree and t' fairy butter!"

"Of course I do not," I replied, lowering the crystal. "It is all nonsense. I see the trees and the flowers and the sunshine—there is nothing more."

She scowled, at last stepping off my foot, and snatched the crystal away. "Blind!" she exclaimed.

I caught my breath, thinking at first she meant it as some curse, but then she said: "I've only one eye left but I see more'n you ever will." And she laughed, an awful dry sound. "You'll not see for lookin'—you was born under t' wrong planet, after all!"

"Oh," Mrs. Gomersal interjected, "that's bad. It'll not work then, not for nothin'."

I threw up my hands in derision. "Well, that is most convenient, is it not?"

"It's bad luck is what it is," Mrs. Gomersal pressed on.

Bad luck had followed me here, too? I bit back the urge to laugh in her face. An unlucky house; an unlucky hill? Truly, everything hereabouts was said to be so—and meanwhile no one had anything of sense to say about what had occurred, apart from "the fairies did it," whatever that meant.

Mother Draycross seized my arm again, hard, and it came to me that her fingers were like the claws of a bird.

"Tha'll not see, but tha can 'ear," she said. "Block up all t' chinks in that 'ouse, all of 'em—windows, doors, key'oles, all. Wait up until midnight an' then you'll 'ear summat, but dun't look out. Aye, you'll 'ear 'em!"

She peered into my face, all earnestness. I pulled away from her and she stepped back as if affronted before turning towards the window once more. Almost idly, she raised the crystal to her eye, ignoring my presence entirely.

Then she let out an odd sound: a spurt of surprised laughter. She leaned nearer the glass, squinting into the crystal, and she fairly hooted. She slapped her thigh as her laughter gained impetus until she was all but rocking with it.

I protested her lack of decorum, but she affected not to even hear me. I could see every cracked, yellowed and blackened tooth in her mouth as she laughed and laughed, tears spilling onto her cheeks until I realised they were pouring from beneath her eye shade as well as from her "bad" green eye.

Then I saw what it was had so amused the crone.

There, through the window, standing in the wood, was my own sweet wife. She had meandered beneath the trees, making her way among the fallen branches, picking the flowers which grew there. As I watched she drew her wrapper a little more closely about her shoulders as if she felt a chill. She bent to examine the yellow fungi— the "fairy butter," I assumed—before straightening and smoothing one hand against her stomach.

"How dare you!" I cried, though my fury was such that I could barely form the words. There was nothing in Helena's carriage or deportment to invite this woman's mirth, nothing amiss in her attire or her actions: she was as perfectly composed, as calm and serene as she always was.

At last I could stand it no longer. I turned on my heel and stalked from the dwelling.

It came as a blessed relief to be once more in the open. I breathed deeply of the woody air as the twittering of birdsong washed over me. I heard Mrs. Gomersal following behind me, though I did not turn to acknowledge her. I only watched Helena as she came around the corner of the shack, her oval face quite cool and collected, her lips twisted into an expression of scorn and her eyes like two chips of ice.

Chapter Thirteen

Helena remained taciturn, her demeanour clouded, as we made our way across the leys to the village. There Mrs. Gomersal left us and it was not until afterwards that it occurred to me that unlike her witch-friend, she had never demanded payment for her assistance.

Once we were alone, I opened my mouth to enquire of Helena if she had overheard the dreadful "wise" woman's cackling, but I caught myself, deciding that I should not chance bringing it to her attention if she had not already been sensible of it. And so we walked in silence towards the little cottage that had for a spell become our home.

I could not think what I should do about Mother Draycross. She had ill-advised Jem Higgs, that was certain, but it was after all he who had chosen to listen. Surely any man of sense would abhor any "wisdom" a deranged old woman such as she could provide? The largest part of the blame must thus remain with whoever was foolish enough to do so. And yet with the advantage of the growing distance between us, I could almost bring myself to pity her. The shack was so poor that she must all but freeze in even the mildest of winters. She appeared to have no means of earning her bread, save for her proficiency in spinning wild tales of the efficacy of her charms and her ability to discover lost things. Some would say she deserved kindness rather than punishment, this uncomely woman who was quite probably simple as well as impecunious. I doubted she could read her pharmacopoeia; it was most likely placed there to impress visitors. Without her little pretence of magic, she could have no recourse to other means of living save to throw herself upon the parish.

Then I recalled the touch of her fingers in my hair, the smell of her, and I grimaced. I recollected her mocking laughter when she peered out of the window at my wife and I pushed away all thought of pity. In that moment, I wanted only to drag her before the magistrate and have her thrown into the most miserable of cells.

I turned to see Helena's sweet face. Her profile was as lovely as ever, her cheek a gentle pale curve. She did not meet my look. She was staring up at the cottage and I followed her gaze. From this distance walls and windows were almost hidden behind a profusion of flowers and it struck me afresh what an idyll it could make, what a setting for domestic felicity, with its occupants bound by mutual love and respect.

Perhaps such would be the lot of Helena and I upon our return to London, for I was determined that we would now remove from my father's house and create our own haven. Our residence must of necessity be more modest than she had been used to—we would have only a maid of all work rather than my father's several servants—but surely it would suit us. Helena's elegance and refinement, her skill at fancywork, would ensure that it was all fitted up beautifully. I was just anticipating her pleasure at choosing or making all the little items we should need—indeed, my imagination had her stitching a little white bonnet for our child—when she drew a heavy sigh.

"My dear, are you quite well?"

She cast a cold glance towards me, removed her hand from my arm and grasped her skirts as if to demonstrate how dreadfully heavy and cumbersome they were, how unsuitable for the heat of the day, and then she turned and marched ahead up the slope. When she reached the gate she slammed it back as if its very construction was hateful to her and batted at her dress as if by doing so she could save it from the greenery along the overgrown path.

I caught up with her in time to hand her over the threshold. We were met by the trapped aroma of the previous evening's fire, and I pushed away the sudden image that rose before me: a pale grin shining in a blackened visage.

I encouraged Helena to take a seat and rest herself.

We had left the grate uncleaned, the hearth unswept and she saw me staring into the cinders. "It is far too hot for a fire, Albie."

I turned to her. She had taken up her book once more and was fanning herself with it.

"I will make us some tea," I said. "You shall soon feel better." I forestalled her irritated protest. "You do not need to rouse yourself, my dear—your condition—I shall take care of all. Pray, do not stir."

I had started to make my way into the kitchen when I heard a noisy rattling and turned to see Helena struggling to master the hasp to open the casement. I went to help her, pushing the window wide, but my assistance served only to make her more angry and she pointedly returned to her chair and sat there once more, her back perfectly straight, holding up her book. I saw that it was *Wuthering Heights* by Ellis Bell, although I had heard this was in fact a pseudonymous name, designed to protect the respectability of the writer. I had also heard reports of its lurid depictions of rural life—indeed, of *Yorkshire* life—and the smile I had forced to my lips faded.

I did not wish to speak of it at that moment and instead I set a kettle to heat. I wondered what my father would think, and decided I did not care. I had ever been a dutiful son, and he had cared for me in return, but the time had come to start making my own way.

I stood back and stared at the range, remembering laying last night's fire, taking sheets of paper and stuffing them inside before adding the kindling and the coal. Constable Barraclough's words returned to me: *Could I request that you are vigilant as to the whereabouts of a journal?*

I could not imagine why, if such a thing had existed, it would have been burned, but the idea had taken hold and I leaned in to the grate, the heat searing my face, tightening my skin. Was that how it had felt as her husband held her before the hearth?

I shook my head; I would not allow my thoughts to wander this path. Instead, leaving the kettle, which would take an age to boil, I went through to the store where my cousin had kept her dusters and brushes and beaters, along with the coal scuttle and kindling. There was a little box of papers, some of them already twisted neatly into spills, and I sifted through them. I found only old newspapers, their ink smudging my fingers, and an occasional household receipt.

I sighed and started to retrace my steps, only realising upon passing back through the pantry that something had been disturbed. The little jug which Mary Gomersal had presented to Helena filled with her "bis'lings" was no longer stacked neatly alongside the other crockery; it had been smashed into a hundred pieces upon the floor.

I stared at it, and all the events of the day passed before me. I could not rid myself of the woman's presence even here—and now I would need to make reparation to her when I could. I swept the pieces into the corner and returned to the kitchen to set out bread and butter, ham and cheese, though I was already growing weary of such simple fare. I contrasted it with the grand dinners at my father's house, all the several removes served in huge decorated dishes, the silverware that was not thinned with scouring. I sighed once more. I did not wish us to be driven back to the inn, our tails between our legs, to take our meals in their parlour, but I felt a stranger to these domestic matters.

I stopped what I was doing and set down my knife. I *was* a stranger to such matters, and so would her husband have been. His domain lay to the other side of the passage where all the accoutrements of his trade were neatly filed; he too would barely have known what transpired here.

I turned to the coppers and the pans and checked that nothing had been concealed within, glancing briefly at the door. Helena would think me as mad as Mother Draycross if she saw, but of my wife there was no sign; I could not hear so much as the turning of a page. I examined every place a journal might have been concealed, making a thorough search of the store and then the larder and shelves of the pantry, feeling among the jars of flour and rice, tapioca and oatmeal. There was nothing, yet where could be better for a wife to conceal a journal from her husband? I stretched upward, running my hand along the topmost shelf, and my fingers dislodged an unseen object. I grasped it at once, stopping it from rocking, and brought it down. It was a small china jug—I had seen it before, when I first entered this lodging, but not here; then it had been on the hearth, and there had been something inside it. I tilted it towards me and saw the green residue of crushed and unrecognisable herbs. I lifted it to my nose, turning towards the dim light from the little window, and almost dropped it when I saw my wife standing in front of me.

She clasped her hands before her. She did not blink. "What is it you seek, Husband?"

Her inflexion was such that I knew not if she was referring to the object I was holding or to my behaviour; I could not help but flinch, but then I straightened. Sometimes a question is only a question, and Helena must have been tired from our exertions; that must surely be the cause of her querulous tone.

"I am looking for matches, my dear," I informed her.

She nodded, as if that were what she had expected to hear—as if that were the *lie* she had expected to hear—and she left, her skirts sweeping behind her.

I stared at the empty doorway as the coolness of the pantry swept over me. Yet it was not so very cold as I felt and I pushed another uncomfortable thought aside: that the only chill was in my wife's look, and that it had spread from her to me. But she had come after me, following me all the way to Yorkshire—there must be something in that. All else was supposition, or more likely, the product of my inflamed imagination. After the ministrations of Mother Draycross, there could be little wonder if my thoughts were running wild. It was as if I rather than my wife were the one taking silly notions from a flighty novel. In a way, perhaps I had, I thought suddenly: surrounded by such deplorable ignorance, by folk whose lives were governed by superstition, I had been laid siege to by such ideas. I realised I must have a care that they did not begin to obscure my own perceptions. I could not allow such fanciful ideas to take on the garment of reason. Why, the way I was dwelling upon them, they could almost seem natural in this forsaken place; almost to have root in reality.

I found myself thinking of the railway, beating down all such nonsense before it, the rushing heart of its engines bearing it—and the world along with it—towards a more glorious and rational future. Yet it still had to be admitted that it was easier to be a man of sense in the City than in this half-enchanted land.

I forced a smile onto my face, replaced the jug at the back of the shelf and took the tray with our simple meal into the parlour. My thoughts of the railway might have spilled from my imagination and into the house; the heat from the range had spread from the kitchen and filled the room, despite the open window. Helena was sitting as she had before, as if she had never stirred, her posture as flawless and upright as always. She did not raise her eyes from her book, but her expression was one of exhausted forbearance, as if to say, "You have brought me to this. Now see how I suffer!"

"Will you take something, my dear?"

She flicked over a page and I could not but feel the sound was somewhat contemptuous. I set down the tray and said, "Come. It will make you feel better."

"Being at home would make me feel better. It would make us both feel better, would it not?"

I sighed. "Helena—"

"I am not hungry."

"Come, you must eat a little. There is not only you to think of—"

"I know it! Do you think I do not?" She pushed herself up, her eyes flashing as her cheeks reddened.

"You are over-exciting yourself, my dear," I said, willing my voice to remain calm. "Pray, try to regain some composure. Perhaps your novel is a trifle evocative for one of your delicate—"

"Ha!"

I fell silent. I had never before seen such an expression on her sweet face. I had never seen her so out of temper, all her cool equanimity quite evaporated. I gathered myself before I spoke. "I am sorry, my dear, that you are so sadly unlike yourself. So—" *Changed*, is what I had wanted to say, but I found I could not form the word. "So troubled." I went to her side and bent, and she looked at me as I lifted the book from her hands. She let me take it, her eyes widening as if awaiting some explanation, but I made none. Instead I examined the cover. "Really, I do not think it suitable, my dear."

She let out a sharp cry and snatched for it, and when I held it higher, she cried, "It is mine! Return it at once."

"Helena, my dear, I really think it for the best. Later, perhaps."

She pushed herself up from her seat and stood before me, her face contorted with rage. "You think I can bear this place, this . . . *this!*" She gestured at everything around her, encompassing the little room, the hearth, the cottage—the whole village. "You think I can stand to be here without some means of escape, if only into the realm of the imagination?"

"Escape!" I echoed the words, and I confess I let out a spurt of laughter. I opened the book with an incredulous expression. "Where to, my dear? To *Yorkshire?*"

"How dare you! You bring me here, to this awful place, chasing some lost, forgotten—no, *not* forgotten—"

"Helena, please be calm. You made the journey of your own accord. I did attempt to reason with you. Perhaps it would be better, after all, if you were to return."

"And leave you here, to chase some—some lost dream? Why, you did not even know her. You did not even know what she was!"

My mouth fell open; I knew not which of her wild statements had shocked me the most. "Helena," I could only say, "you are not yourself—"

She drew herself taller. "I am indeed," she said. "I am exactly who I have always been."

"And who is that, pray?" I interjected, though she continued as if I had not.

"You, however, have dragged me out here, chasing some little hoyden with no breeding and no sense and one who by all accounts had no morals, either! And this—this is the reason you tear me from our comfortable home?"

I seized her arm. "Helena, stop! This does not become you. You must compose yourself at once."

She did not speak. I saw her wince and I forced myself to loosen my grip. "Helena—"

"Remove your hand. Albie, you did not even *know* her."

"And you did, I suppose?"

"No, I did not, but—"

"No." I found myself breathing heavily. The blood suffused my cheeks. The breeze from the open window touched them and I glanced at the shifting curtains. At least here, in this place of ill-omen, there would be no passers-by to eavesdrop upon us.

"I heard things," she said, her voice sullen.

"Helena, pray do not continue. I think it best if you go to your room for a time and rest. And we should both have something to eat."

"At the inn." She was undeterred. "I heard men talking through the walls. Coarse men. They said that your cousin was no better than she should have been. They said she—"

"Stop—for shame, Helena! I asked you once. Such men cannot be listened to; no good could ever come of it."

"One said he thought her pretty, and another answered that it might have been better if she were not. And then a third said that she was not fairy-struck but *fairly* struck . . ."

"Helena!"

"And now *I* am here, and you will not even look at me. You will not even hear my words."

"You are changed, Helena," I said. "Sadly changed." She did not reply. "My cousin is dead, and not just dead: she is *murdered*. She is the victim of stupidity and cruelty, and now you side with those who stood by and allowed it, those who cut her funeral. Are you then leagued with the rest? Do you not think I should have taken her part? Do you not think that someone should stand friend to her?"

Her eyes flashed. "Yes, Albie, she *is* dead. She is quite gone— unless you count the hair you kept in your pocket!"

Once more I had to breathe deeply. "Think of what you are saying, my dear. I met my cousin once—*once*—and you are right, Helena; I never knew her as well as I might have done. But I heard her sing, and I conversed with her, and I can assure you that she was not coarse; she was not a—a hoyden, as you have said. She was a sweet country girl, innocent—" I held up a hand to prevent Helena's interruption. "You are correct that I did not know her, not as I *should*, but I know the gap she has left behind her, and I cannot leave it that way. Someone must bear witness. Someone must know what happened, and understand, or there is nothing left at all, do you not see?" At that I turned and looked into the fire, at the cold hearth, as if I could read there everything.

Helena moved away from me. She raised a hand, as if the fire were burning and she must shield herself from its flames, and then she sank to her knees in front of the glass case, in front of the fox, its black eyes gleaming.

I went to her and placed my hands on her shoulders to steady her. "My dear, please. Let us not have any distance between us."

She pulled free and stared into the glass case most intently before tilting her head to one side, as if she were listening.

"You need to rest," I said firmly. "The day has overwhelmed your endurance. You must not upset your constitution, especially now."

But Helena did not rise; she showed no sign at all of having heard me, but instead opened her lips and began to sing.

> *As I walked out one sweet morning*
> *Across the fields so early*
> *O there I met with a bonny maid*
> *As bright as any fairy . . .*
> *"Where are you going, sweet maid?" said I*

At these words, her voice changed, becoming lower, more insistent; more cruel. I drew away, staring down at her. In that moment, I felt I barely knew my wife at all. "Helena, where did you learn that song?"

She half turned her head. Her lip curled, an expression I had never before seen on her face.

"Why, Husband, my new neighbours taught me."

"I do not think that you know what you say."

"I do not think that you know what you do."

"I think you must be ill."

She stood, quite suddenly, her back straight, her countenance preternaturally calm. Her hair had come loose of its pins and strands floated about her head. Her eyes, though, were fierce, and involuntarily I stepped away from her.

"I see her," she said. "Why, Albie, I see everything. Can *you* not? You are right: she is so very pretty, with her white cheek turned towards you. What a pity that she does not smile."

"Whatever do you mean?"

"She stands at your side, my dear—that is her place, is it not? She is there now, see? She reaches for your arm."

I snatched my hand to my chest and looked at where she stared. Of course there was nothing there. I heard the words Mother Draycross had spoken earlier: *I've only one eye left but I see more'n you ever will.* I wondered what planet my wife had been born under; what she might have seen, had she looked through the crystal egg.

But Helena had not finished. "I wish you well of each other. She has come back for you, for no one covered the mirror at her death and her soul went into it. Yes! She has returned even from the grave, but oh—pah! The *stink* of her!"

I realised there *was* a smell: the mustiness of unwashed clothes; the musk of unknown herbs and potions; the sourness of an extinguished fire. I almost felt the pressure of the wise woman's fingers in my hair. And I heard her then, that awful mocking laughter as she looked upon my wife through her crystal, and I shook my head and said without thought, "Was it you she saw, Helena? Or the one you carry?"

The laughter went on, echoing in my mind, but it was not the harridan's merriment I heard; it was my wife's, until she stopped abruptly and stared at me, her eyes as cold and bleak as a grave. Then she spun on her heel and left the room. She slammed the door behind her.

I took a step backwards, felt the chair behind my knees and sank onto it. I held up my hands before my face; they were shaking. Now that I was alone, it did not seem possible we could have spoken such words to each other. I let out my own thin laugh, wavering and tremulous, and rather wished that I had not allowed it to escape from my lips.

Escape. Had she really said that? But surely she could not have meant it.

I looked about, realising that at some juncture—though I knew not when—I had set down her book. I found it at my side, closed once more, my wife's place in it quite lost. I took it up and randomly turned its pages: *He opened the mysteries of the Fairy Cave,* I read. *I want to see where the goblin-hunter rises in the marsh, and to hear about the fairishes, as you call them.*

I flicked through the pages more rapidly and saw, *show him what you are, imp of Satan.* I shook my head as words leaped at me from the page: *she must have been a changeling—wicked little soul!*

I closed the book with a sharp snap. I had done well to take it from her. I raised my arm as if to throw the thing into the grate, ready for burning, then felt cool air caressing my cheek and paused. I turned towards the window. Outside, the sky was the colour of flame. It was already sunset.

The food was still spread upon the table, but I was no longer hungry. I did not know what I should do. I closed the window, pulling it tightly into its frame, and found myself staring at the little gap where the sashes met: a chink that had not been sealed.

I took up the book once more, staring down at its plain cover. Almost without thought, I opened it and ripped out a page, crumpling it before stuffing it into the gap between the sashes. My hands were still shaking, but I did not care. It was not enough; more pages were needed, and I kept tearing them free until the gap was closed.

Block up all t' chinks, she had said.

I caught up Helena's shawl where it lay over the back of the chair and went into the passage, the book tucked under my arm. I stuffed the garment into the gap under the front door and tore more pages loose, pushing them into the crack around it and then one more into the keyhole.

You'll 'ear summat, but dun't look out.

I wondered if Helena could hear me, if she had guessed what I was doing, but I could detect no movement from her. I went around the cottage, moving like a man in a dream—and perhaps I was. Upon returning to the parlour, I eyed the chimney. I had no way to block it up, but the hidden people disliked flames, did they not?

I retrieved a Lucifer and some spills from the store and set the fire. Something prevented me from burning Helena's book, but I held the little flame to an old newspaper and watched it spread to the dried gorse I had heaped above it and from thence to the coals. Nothing remained to be done but pace the room, staring alternately into the fire and into the blank eyes of the preserved fox, and all the while, my thoughts were beyond any earthly power to contain: I thought of the flames caressing my cousin's face; I thought of how it must have felt as the soft skin of her cheeks tightened and then cracked.

She has come back for you.

Helena had had no right to say such a thing; she had no right even to speak of her. I threw what remained of the book aside and sat in front of the fire without lighting the lamp as the food spoiled upon the table, the edges of the bread stiffening and curling in the heat.

I could not recognise myself in my actions. I knew that Mother Draycross was mad; I knew that no one would come, but still I waited as the seconds flowed by around me. I checked my pocket watch. I had wound it and now it marked the minutes and hours correctly, but what time? I could not recall if I had set it to local time or Railway Time. Whichever it was, I watched the flow of it in the flames' consumption of the coal, its greedy heart causing the black forms to gleam redly, lending all an unnatural hue. When my watch showed the hour to be hastening towards midnight, I piled more coal upon the fire, feeding its hunger, stoking the flames even higher—I could not block up the chimney so this must be enough. And all the time I worked, it was as if I stood outside myself as well as within. I could see all and understand nothing; it was as if my very thoughts were aflame.

She is there now, see?

I turned and looked into the mirror, but I saw nothing save a blank gleaming. I focused upon my pocket watch: a watch with only a single minute hand. Perhaps I had not, in the end, set it to any particular time. Halfoak had consumed me after all; here, surely iron hands could bind no one? The labour of men was governed by the rising and setting of the sun, by the turning of the seasons and the phases of the moon. They needed no instrument to order their lives, so why should the fair folk be any different?

And then it turned to midnight.

I listened intently, hearing not the creak of a floorboard nor the hoot of an owl nor the settling of the house—and then the fire gave a single sharp *snap* and I jumped as if I had awakened, and I smiled at my own foolish credulity.

Then I did hear something. I was not certain what had caused it, though I thought at once of a gentle breeze soughing through new-grown leaves in springtime. It was not an external sound, however; it came from directly overhead. And then came the softer tread of a step upon the stair.

Helena, I thought at once, and quailed at the thought of what she must think to see her precious pages stuffed into the cracks around the door, and yet I rushed to meet her, eager to be reconciled and at peace once more.

But I found nothing there; the passage was empty. No one stood upon the stair. A soft tapping drew my attention to the entrance to the cottage and the paper twisted into the keyhole gave a quiver. It was as if something was pushing it loose from the other side. A sudden fear took me and I slammed my hand flat against it, keeping it in place, and even as I did so I told myself that it was the wind, though the day had been still save for the gentle warm draughts of summer. Now I thought I detected the sound of a stronger breeze turning about the cottage and the sudden rattle of shutters confirmed me in my surmise.

I returned to the parlour where the fire, as if stirred by a sudden blast, leaped and writhed like a startled snake. I began to secure the shutters, but was distracted by a noise over my head, not the creaking of floorboards under my wife's step but lighter, quicker taps, as if tiny feet were skipping across the floor above.

I followed the sound with my eyes, as if my unblinking stare could penetrate the ceiling, and then a great rattling began outside and I fancied I could feel the force of it. I felt now as if I was one of the little folk myself, for it was like the approach of a giant's booming footsteps, shuddering the floor and the walls alike. I put my hand to my chest, almost believing I could feel the resonance of the sound in my ribs, and the whole cottage suddenly shook. I crouched down to the floor as tiny fragments of plaster started raining from the ceiling; it was as if the giant had come and was shaking the little home in his monstrous fist, making the sashes and shutters and doors rattle.

I rushed to the window to release the catches, to stop that awful uproar, when an urgent whisper sounded at my ear: *You'll 'ear summat, but dun't look out.*

I snatched back my hand. Outside, the wind had grown yet higher; now it was tempestuous; it moaned; it howled. And then a new noise came from behind me and I slowly turned.

The fire was dancing and writhing high in gleeful revelry. In the next instant it shrank, leaving only glowing coals like eyes, and then I heard a soft rushing as it almost blew out. There came a soft pattering; fragments of stone fell from the chimney, as if shaken loose by the brushing of a sweep or the wings of a trapped bird.

I went to it, bending low to peer as far beneath the hood as I could without being singed if the fire were to suddenly leap up once more, but all was dark; I could see no cause. I am not certain I had truly expected to. There was nothing there, but for a little pot of salt set upon a ledge, no doubt to keep it always dry. My heart beat rapidly, like that of a man in a fever; my forehead was burning and running with sweat. Then a loud bang came from the bedroom and I took to my heels, my lips forming the shape of my wife's name.

I rushed up the stairs, but upon reaching the landing I knew that the clamour was coming not from the room she had chosen but from my own. The arrhythmic banging of wood upon wood made me think of a branch being blown against the window and yet I knew there was no tree so tall in my cousin's garden. I threw open the door, only then recollecting that I had done nothing to seal the chinks upstairs. I had not thought of it; indeed, I do not think I had even been rational. And I discovered now that I had not sealed up this room at all, for the window was standing wide open.

I glanced about the chamber to see what might have entered it—a bird, perhaps? Surely it must only be a bird . . . but there was nothing, only the curtains twitching at the window, drawn out into the moonlight by the soft night air.

Another loud rap drew my gaze to the wall. I could see no cause for the sound, and then I did for it came again, and I realised that something had entered the room after all; the wind itself must have found its way behind the walls to lift a section of loose panelling before letting it fall back once more. For a moment it had looked as if something were trying to escape from behind the boards, but I cautioned myself, harshly and belatedly, for my foolishness as I crossed the room. First I closed the window, softly, though it was surely too late to preserve Helena's rest—if she had managed to find any sleep—and then I went to examine the defective panel.

If not for the commotion, I should never have noticed anything, but as I pulled the wooden piece aside, all of a sudden, a sense of inevitability seized me, as if I already knew what I would find. And

indeed, I slipped my fingers into the gap and withdrew them holding Lizzie's journal.

I stared at it. The book had a scuffed black cover, greyed with
dust. Nothing was printed thereupon, but I knew what it was all the
same. I could sense it, the knowledge as clear to me as the touch of
her little hand had once been upon my arm; as bright as the gaze
of her nut-brown eyes, the shine of her golden hair. I almost fancied
I heard her chiming laugh, and as it faded I realised that all other
sound had quieted too.

I stared at it, but I could not open it, not then. I told myself that
I could not countenance the disappointment if I discovered only
some old ledger of household accounts; some ancient thing that may
never have been hers at all.

Except I knew it was her journal.

Eventually I straightened and glanced at the door. There had
been no sound from Helena's room; nothing at all to disturb me.
I slipped the journal under my pillow and then I went downstairs,
treading softly, to be greeted by the sight of Helena's shawl forced
roughly into the crack beneath the door. It had the appearance
of the work of a madman, and I retrieved it, endeavouring to pull
out the creases. I took the papers from around the door and from
the keyhole and straightened those too, until I had recovered all the
pages of my wife's book. My shame grew as I worked. How could I
have behaved so? How could I have taken fright at some little tempest? The hillside surely offered no shelter from such; it was only to
be expected.

I found the parlour in equal disarray, though the fire at least had
died to a glowing smoulder. I recalled my fright at the debris falling
from the chimney, as if such a thing were not also a natural occurrence. How simple I was! And yet I was tired and the day had been
long; perchance the recent strains upon my mind had overpowered
me for a moment?

I reordered the pages of the novel, placing them in their correct
sequence and within the covers, though nothing fitted as it once
had. Strange phrases snagged at my eyes as I did so, although this

time I affected not to see them, and then I caught: *I suppose that she wanted to get another proof that the place was haunted, at my expense. Well, it is—swarming with ghosts and goblins!*

I closed my eyes. Helena had been so angry, but she must forgive me—she must know I was trying to do what was right, for family and for decency. We must both do our best to remain creatures of sense, even whilst immersed in uncultivated ideas; even in the midst of such a strange place, with its stranger folk.

Good folk. Quiet folk. Hidden folk . . .

I sighed, wondering if I had done aright by taking my wife's book from her. Now no choice remained to me; I could not return the novel to her in such a tattered condition.

I went into my room, taking the book with me so that it should remain out of her sight, and I leaned back upon my bed, still holding the sadly mutilated thing. *Wuthering.* That was the name for turbulent, blustering winds, was it not? Perhaps I had conjured them by my disarrangement of its pages.

I set it down on the bedsheet, annoyed at my own irrationality, aware that I was only deferring the moment when I should open another book; when I would run my fingertips across the pages of the journal.

Without looking, I felt beneath my pillow for the other. For an awful moment I thought it gone; but no, there was the edge of the worn cover, and then the whole of it was in my hands. The leather felt as if it were accustomed to the touch of skin. The pages were frayed at their edges by much use. I wondered if Lizzie had always found it necessary to conceal it in such a fashion—she had only been married for a few years, after all; had they been such strangers to one another? And yet he had known of this book, somehow. I imagined him stealing upon her as she wrote, Lizzie lifting her bright eyes to him with surprise and dismay. Had it been so? Was her concealment the reflection of what a brute he was, the sign of her understanding of her mistake?

How the constable would like to know of this! I found myself bending over it as if to conceal it still. It had been *hers* and now it was in my hand, as if put there by Providence. She evidently had not wished for it to be found and she certainly would not wish for her husband to use it in his defence; that notion brought only horror with it. What would happen then? Would the man return here, taking possession of the home she had kept, but without her in it? It was unthinkable.

He said he'd had his doubts, quite natural doubts, as to the correctness of his surmise about her nature, whether it be fairy or human; but that he one day happened upon her journal . . .

What nonsense. What awful slander those words had been. But of course her husband would claim he had proofs; he would desire only to blacken her memory to ease his own dreadful fate. I remembered what Helena had said earlier that evening—so long ago, it felt—about what she had claimed to overhear at the Three Horseshoes. I had thought her merely carried along by a passion, almost to delirium; but perhaps she really had heard some wicked story. If she had, it was surely only deeper proof of what a scoundrel he was.

I pushed all thought of him aside; he did not belong here, alongside this memorial of her, preserved by her own hand; and gently, with one finger, I opened the journal. It felt as if I were opening her heart.

I began to read the page at which it opened, with only some little difficulty over the handwriting.

Mary told me she heard the prince is dead, but I don't know if it's true. She didn't seem right sure herself. Jem's cousin reckons nowt of it, but then he says our prince'll be feasting with the fairies and I think he's just stirring it. I think it's true he's dead, and it's right sad. I said to them all that Albert were right handsome, any one would say so, and Jem just gave me one of his looks.

I don't care. I never saw him, but every one says he were right tall and dashing. I went to London once too and I might have seen him then, if I had been more lucky.

Then it minded me of someone else I met once, who put my arm in his, and I thought he might wish to make a wife of me, but he did not . . .

I closed the book on my lap. All was now quiet. There was not the faintest breeze blowing, not a single tap of wood on wood, and yet I fancied I could hear the sounds of the previous evening, a distant song, made mournful—if not dismal—by the slowness of the air. I could barely make out the tune, or perhaps my memory was faulty, and in any event, I replaced it in my mind with another:

All things bright and beautiful . . .

I let out a long sigh, almost a moan, and I bowed my head. *Oh, Lizzie*, I thought. *Oh, Lizzie.*

Chapter Fourteen

I awoke the following morning to the bright sound of chirruping in the garden. I pushed the sheets back from my face, for they were too hot and heavy. I felt leaden enough from lack of slumber even without the addition of their weight. I thought to sleep some more, but still the sound went on, a cheerful refrain to my dark remembrances, and I finally forced myself out of bed and went to look out.

The garden was thriving in the heat; in fact, to my eye it had run almost entirely wild. Spires of lupins vied for the sun with foxgloves, whilst a hardy vine of some sort had found a way through everything. I recognised roses, pinks and marigolds planted along the edges of the paths, a profusion of colour, but a creeping weed had taken root in their midst and its tendrils had wound their way amongst it all. Negotiating the profusion, clinging to strands surely too light and new to bear its weight, was a blackbird. Its beak flashed yellow as it pecked; its eye was a dark liquid shine that reminded me of something, though I could not think of what.

Beyond the garden wall was the hillside, its brilliant verdure outshining the multitudinous colours about the cottage. It was fleeced with hundreds more of those dandelion clocks; there appeared to be no end of them. I remembered the children's game, where we had used them to count the hours, and now here they were still, just as they had been when I was a boy at my mother's knee. The memory made me feel quite melancholy; I knew not why.

I finished my ablutions, dressed and went downstairs, glad that I had returned the cottage to at least a semblance of normality. It was a pity that I had been so caught up in the influence of night and ruined my wife's novel; but it could not matter. Helena would be more herself this morning, just as I was; I felt certain of it.

My wife was not yet downstairs and I wondered if she too had slept badly after our argument. Our untouched repast of yester-eve was still spread upon the table, the cheese dried, the bread curled. I cleared it away and cut a little fresh bread, nibbling on it as I waited for Helena to rise. As I did, I surveyed the vista: the little village of Halfoak dozing in the sun. I could not but wonder what lay beneath its calm surface and bethought me that perhaps Lizzie's journal would tell me. I had hidden it away once more in my room and I was anxious to open it again.

I thought he might wish to make a wife of me, but he did not.

I sighed. Poor Lizzie. But of course, I could never have married her. Helena had struck nearer the mark than she could possibly comprehend: no, I had not known my cousin; years of neglect and separation had seen to that. But I should have done something. I had not realised how she had looked up to me, how she had clung to the memory of our little meeting. The thought of her fruitless pining hardened my resolve.

I went into the kitchen and set more bread and butter upon a plate, prepared a ewer of water and carried them upstairs. I tapped gently on my wife's door with the ewer and called out to her, but there came no reply; she must still be in slumber. I would wake her with a kiss, and our bitterness would be behind us. I put down the plate while I opened the door, then picked it up once more before I walked in.

My greeting failed on my lips. Helena stood with her back to me, facing the open window. Her posture was stiff and she did not turn as I placed the ewer on her washstand, noting the disarray of her brushes and accoutrements, which was not like my wife; she had always been so neat. Helena remained at the window, her head tilted back slightly. She must be staring up at the sky, or perhaps Pudding Pye Hill.

"Helena, I have brought a little bread and butter. Are you feeling refreshed, my dear?"

I waited for an answer, but there came none. I could not see her face, and for an awful moment I thought I heard the un-restrained, mocking laughter of Mother Draycross; I remembered all the wild talk of changelings and I found I did not want to see. I didn't want to *know*.

I shook such silly thoughts away and went to her side. Her cheek was pale, her demeanour solemn. "My dear, you don't look well. You must eat something."

"I cannot eat." Her voice was dull, a monotone without expression or warmth.

I reached out with my free hand and touched her arm and at that, she caught her breath. Her lip twitched, but still she did not meet my eye; she only resumed her former watching, staring out unblinking at the hillside. I found myself wondering what had so caught her attention and I peered out too, but there was nothing: only the flowers nodding gently in a faint breeze, and the blackbird, digging its beak into some fleshy morsel it had discovered.

"I will wait downstairs for you if you wish, Helena, but pray, do take something, my dear. It will make you feel more yourself."

"I cannot eat." She spoke in the same dull tone as before, words without emotion.

"Helena, let us not quarrel. What is it that ails you?"

She would not acknowledge the question; she did not even show that she had heard. I looked into her face a moment longer and then I turned and left the room. I was outwardly calm, but inside, my blood was rising. She had said such things—dreadful things—in her frenzy. How could she now spurn my overtures in such a provoking fashion? I had taken on the role of the peacemaker and yet was being met with nothing but rebuff.

I stopped dead on the landing.

These changelings can be identified by their weaknesses, or some disfigurement, or by a sweet temper turning of a sudden into querulous and unnatural ways. They might refuse to speak or eat. A good wife may be transformed into a shrew.

I shook my head in rejection of my wife's actions, my own thoughts, the constable's words, the new day that awaited. I returned to my own room, closed the door firmly behind me and removed the journal from its hiding place. I began to read the earliest pages. The entries bore no dates and the simple modes of expression needed a little deciphering, but soon I started to draw some sense from the words.

Jem got a hare yester-night, from one of the men at the Horseshoes. I didn't ask, though he promised at least it were took in the day, not in the dark. Even that rabble would not risk that. I skinned it and roasted it with a bit of rosemerry. We ate it all, and it were fine. It was as if we were just wed again, for a bit. Then he got that look in his eye, and it were even more like. Happen we should have a third along to join us soon, God willing. Jem goes on about it enough. Maybe this time . . .

I shook my head, this time in irritation. This was not what I sought. Last night my selections had been serendipitous, as if the book had opened at something meant for me to read. Now it resisted. I tried another.

Mary killed her pig and she gave me some of the scrattlings and a leg. We shall not starve today. I can smell it sizzling. Jem's still working at the Grange so he doesn't know yet. He is fitting them all up there and he says it shall be a relief when he has done it, for certain. And then he shall make boots for Mary's bairn, so we shall last a bit. It is a blessing the rent is so low, though he never does think to be grateful to me for thinking of this place.

Meat and boots and petty local matters. For such a book, discovered in such a way, to repay me thus! I tutted over it and riffled through the pages, wondering if it would all be the same, more of their meals and the uneventful passing of their days. I had only some small gratitude that although she may have neglected in life to pronounce her aitches, she had not forgotten to write them. But this was merely the dull observation of a dull life; why had she nothing of import to say?

I realised I was crumpling the pages in my frustration and I smoothed them down. There had been some urgent reason her husband had wanted this book to be found. But he might never even have read it; his claim might have been nothing more than a bluff. Its existence could be purely a matter of coincidence, his insistence an invention to save his worthless neck from the rope.

I closed it and stared at its dried, cracked cover, but what I saw was my cousin's face: her own cracked and blackened skin, that awful smile shining through it. I shuddered, feeling for a moment as if a chill presence had passed through the room. Perhaps it had; perhaps my cousin had been drawn here by the way that I had judged her.

But I believed in ghosts no more than I did in fairies: they were all the product of overheated and unregulated imaginations. However, in one sense, I was correct: I should judge neither my cousin's clumsy modes of expression nor the affairs of which she had written, for these were private matters, never intended for my eyes, nor perhaps for anyone's. Besides, she had been forced by circumstance to live among coarse creatures so I should not be surprised at a little vulgarity of expression, some slight provincialism in her speech. And yet it was so long ago that I had seen her, the actual flesh and blood of her, that her image was fading. It was almost as if she had come to be not quite real to me.

I turned to a later section of the journal. To judge by the thinness of the written pages that followed, it could not have been long before her death. Her hand was more than usually wild.

I said no to him again tonight and he was having none of it. He said I would take it and like it, and I said there was nowt wrong with me, only a chill and nothing a bit of kindness wouldn't fix. He wouldn't have none of that neither and then there was a knock on the door. He says go and see who it is, wife, only he said wife like it meant summat else. And I didn't move so he went to see and they came in and stood there as if they didn't even know who I was.

Then he says tha shall take it like it or not, and he had it in a jug, and it stunk. I knew it was what she had given to him because he started to say daft words, about wings and flowers and charms, and meadows and water, and I don't know what else. Then he said in the name of God I had to say me own true name, and I said it. And then he said I had to drink it and I would not. I don't know what she puts in that stuff, but its fowl and I said I would not have it, not in my own house with my own husband, and he did nowt but laugh. The others didn't though. One of them got a hold of my shoulders and shoved me down, and held me on the floor, and I said it hurt but they didn't care. The other went and grabbed my hair, right at back of my neck, and I started to cry then since I didn't think they would have done that, helping just as if owt they said even made any sense. All the time, they would not even say nowt to me nor look at me. It were like I was nothing.

Jem pushed the jug into my mouth then, bashed it in he did and cut my lip, all swole up it is, and he poured stuff down my throat, and I had to swallow it but I choked and he said in the name of God, tell me you are my true wife, just tell me for God's sake what is your name, and I told him I would not, and I never ever would.

I stared down at the rough scrawl. I could sense her terror and her dismay, not just in her words or how they ran on so rapidly, but in the way she had scratched them into the paper. My eyes stung at the cruelty that had been inflicted upon her, and yet a more terrible notion had risen to the uppermost of my mind: what if the constable should see this? Would he take this cruelty for the "proof" of which he had spoken? Here was her husband, attempting his "cure," and here was Lizzie, by her own admission, refusing to state in the name of God that she was indeed his wife. And yet, was that truly unnatural? There was a more rational interpretation:

she must have long regretted entering into matrimony with such a villain. It would be terrible indeed if Lizzie's attempt to unburden herself of her cares and anxieties within these mean pages led to Jem Higgs' escape. Such a thing must never happen. My cousin must have justice and he must pay for his actions. The journal must never fall into the wrong hands or be made the instrument of his release.

I flicked through the pages, the words blurring before me, catching only a word here, a phrase there:

He said I were a fairy, but I think he was only angry at me. He . . .

I hid my new bonnet. I think perhaps I should not keep it, but then why should I not have such a thing . . .

And then:

He filled up every cranny and crevice in the house, even the keyhole.

I blinked and read more.

He filled up every cranny and crevice in the house, even the keyhole. He said Mother Crow had told him he would not see owt because he were blinded, but he might be able to hear summat if he filled up every last chink and listened. He said fairies would come then and tell him owt he wanted to know. And then he said it would be all up with me, and I would not hide nowt from him ever again. I followed him when he stuffed rags under the door and round the windows, up stairs and down, and I laughed at him all the while and told him he was being ignorant.

I closed the book and held it closed, as if it should open of its own accord and accuse me. I was justly chastised, I knew that, and yet knowing did not lessen its sting. I pressed my eyes closed and heard the echo of a woman's mocking laughter, though I could no longer be sure it came from Mother Draycross.

It impressed upon me further that her husband, that wicked brutish creature, had at least not been so dull as to forget the upstairs windows. I told myself it did not signify; it was only that I had possessed greater sense than he; yet somehow, it merely served to drive deeper how stupid I had been, how lost in the mire of superstition.

Another thought came swift upon it, this time a more rational observation. *They*, she had written, and I had not been oblivious to the word when Constable Barraclough had used it. *He says they tried to cure her before the night she was burned—aye, and not just once either, but several times.* I had thought then that he had meant my cousin's husband and some medical man; of course I saw now that he had not.

They would not even say nowt to me nor look at me.

I wondered what Jem Higgs was thinking of at this very moment. I hoped he felt despair. I hoped he felt isolated. I hoped he believed the whole world was ranked against him. He had acted cruelly; he had killed his wife—but he had not been alone, not the way my poor Lizzie had been. Not the way that I felt now.

But I was more determined than ever: I would have the truth. *Lizzie* would have it. And everybody would know who had helped to send a poor innocent creature to her terrible death.

Chapter Fifteen

I left the cottage not long after I had again concealed the journal. I did not tell Helena that I was leaving, and nor did she emerge from her room. I supposed if I left her alone, she might eat something at last, and perhaps, upon my return, she might be restored to her own sweet self.

The day was once again the picture of summer's glory. What need had man, I wondered as I stepped out, to invent a land of ever-present summer beneath a hill? How could there be a summer away from the open presence of the sun, that now brightened all things, chasing spooks and scares away and exposing everything for what it truly was? But, I chastised myself, perhaps I was being uncharitable, for life in Halfoak must perforce be a trial in the winter, when damp stole through floor and thatch, and freezing blasts found their way around doors and down chimneys. How limbs must ache then, about their out-of-doors toil—how fingers must swell! Then there would be every need to invent tales of lasting sunshine. They would stuff their shirts with newspapers for warmth, instead of rolling up their sleeves and mopping their brows. No, despite the slight discomfort afforded by the heat, I was fortunate that my visit here had coincided with what appeared to be an unsurpassed and endless summer.

I had no time to marvel at the day's beauties. I had set myself a task, and I would see it completed before the day was over. I made my way to the inn, glancing upward as I reached the door to spy a heavy old iron horseshoe nailed above the lintel. I tossed my head, the better to examine it as I stepped across the threshold and into the taproom, directly into the view of the landlord standing at his hatch. He greeted me with a nod, but at the sight of my expression, his demeanour darkened.

"What can I do for thee today, sir?" His tone was cautious and I noted that he did not proffer refreshment, drink or anything else. That my purpose was otherwise must have been evident to his eye.

The taproom was empty save for an old gaffer in one corner, his face pitted with smallpox and his eyes misted, his fingers playing with a set of dominoes, much as I once had. He set one down with a sharp *click*.

I went closer, to address Widdop without being heard. "I need a little information," I said, and to ease any concern, "nothing you might not tell anyone who were to pass through the village."

"Is that so?"

"I wish to know who was closest to Jem Higgs in the world—his mother, his father? Did he have a brother?"

He raised his eyebrows ruminatively as he took down a tankard from a hook and began to run a cloth over it, although it was already polished to a high gleam. "Well, now. His mother's passed, o' course. His father, now: 'e's passed too. Then there were one brother, gone to Barnsley to be a farrier's lad. The younger 'un's gone to an aunt ower Selby way—she's owd now by all accounts, seventy-odd, hearing's gone."

"How old is the boy?"

He sniffed. "Eleven or so."

"Too young."

"For what, sir?"

"To be of service. What of other relatives—close relatives?"

"There's none closer'n mother and father and brothers, sir, beg-gin' your pardon."

"I meant in distance, not in degree of kin. Who is closest to him *here*?"

"Here, sir? Why, 'e's not even 'ere hisself."

"I know that." I had to force down my exasperation. "There must be someone. Who were his friends—or special customers, perhaps?"

"Well, 'e worked for t' squire a-times, sir, but none o' the likes o' Jem Higgs'd be close to t' squire."

"The labourers, then. Was there no one who would help him in a strait? None who would help him take care of his wife?"

"Take care of 'er, sir?"

"Someone who would nurse her when she was ill. For she was ill, was she not? So the story is told."

"Oh—aye, sir. Well, we all looks atter each other in these parts, sir. No one'd say no to that. But I don't know of anyone sayin' aye neither, if you takes my meanin'."

My eyes narrowed. "You are saying that he had no friends? Not one?" I thought of the gatherings I had heard in the taproom of an evening, the raucous clang and clatter of companionable and none too sober men. There must surely have been someone prepared to offer aid to the rascal to whom my cousin had joined herself. I wondered if I would see it when I looked into their eyes: their cru-elty; the way they had grabbed her shoulder and forced her to the floor; the way they had held her hair. It occurred to me then to wonder if they might even have enjoyed it: these were rough men, after all, engaged in rough work.

"I dun't rightly know of any, sir."

Click. Another domino was set in place behind me.

"You are hiding something, I am certain of it. Come, now, it can be of little concern to you—and it might be important."

He stopped his polishing and set down the tankard, hard, upon the bar. "Now, sir, I'll not be talked to in that way, not for nowt. T' constable's spoken to who 'e wanted spoken to, an' there's an end on it."

I flung my hands into the air with a sound of disgust. "I shall find them," I said, "if I have to speak to every man in the parish."

"Aye, well, that's as mebbe. If tha's nowt more important to be doin'."

Click.

"I beg your pardon? Whatever do you mean by that?"

"Only what I says. Tha's got affairs to watch ower closer to 'ome, I'll warrant. That place in't agreein' wi' you, sir, if I may speak open-like, an' anyone can see it. P'raps you'd be best off goin' back where you came from."

Click.

I stared at him in a fury, and yet he had spoken the words softly, almost with kindness, and it came upon me of a sudden that he actually had my interests at heart. Such foolishness! As if I, a City man, a resolute and rational creature, could really be affected by this little place. I had succumbed to certain emotions, it was true, but I could rise above it still, and would; and in spite of all, I would carry out my duty to family and—and to God. Yes, to God!

I leaned in towards him and spoke lower. "I have no need of you," I said. "Hide them, if you will. All will be revealed. The truth will be told, with you or without."

He looked at me, running his fingers across his whiskers, an expression somewhat akin to wonderment stealing across his features. He had not foreseen that I should be so determined. Well, now he knew.

He settled on meeting my eyes at last, blazing in their sockets, I had no doubt, and I turned on my heel and walked to the door, accompanied by a sound that rang out with new vigour. *Click. Click. Click.*

It did not prove difficult to locate Mrs. Gomersal's residence. I enquired of a stout matron of mature years who was sitting outside her cottage, her needle flashing as she sewed, and she directed me to a house set into a little lane near the green, tucked back into a garden filled to the brim with sunshine. There the lady herself sat upon the step, much as my guide had been. She was engaged upon weaving, her deft fingers sending stems of straw this way and that, forming a neat little mat. A girl of ten or eleven sat with her, set upon the same task, and the youngest, her odd little elfin boy, was at their feet, doing nothing in particular but teasing a small black cat with a blade of grass.

"Good day, Mrs. Gomersal," I called to her.

She started, then set her work aside. She called out to the girl, "Flora, watch 'im!" before coming to the gate. She returned my greeting politely enough, though she glanced over her shoulder with concern, as if wondering whether she should have sent the children inside.

First, I made apology for the breaking of her jug, and I withdrew some coins to recompense her for its loss, but she waved them away. "Prob'ly for t' best," she said, providing no clue as to whether she had disliked the jug, or if this were some new superstition about its contents.

I prevailed upon her to take something, before saying, "I have a question for you, Mrs. Gomersal, if you would permit me. The answering will be quite simple, I think." I made my enquiry again, about what friends Jem Higgs must have had, to help him administer his "cures." "I do not suppose that Mrs. Draycross emerged from her shack to attend my cousin herself. Her husband must have had some connections in this world, at least until he did what he did."

"Oh—well, aye, sir. We're all friends here, sir. No one partic'lar."

My heart sank. Were the villagers all to be so taciturn upon the subject? "Has the constable already asked about such matters? I am not the constable, Mrs. Gomersal."

"No, sir. O' course you in't." She gave me a worried look.

"But this is a police matter, all the same. If anybody were found to be concealing anything, madam, I fear it should go very ill with them. This is a matter of the utmost seriousness. I wish merely to uncover the truth. I am not the law; I do not have to act as the law would. But I must know who helped Jem Higgs, and if someone hinders instead of helps me, why, then, I should bring the law down on their heads. Do you understand me?"

A look passed across her face, so swiftly I was not certain it was fear, and I felt a pang of guilt; I did not know why I had addressed her so harshly. Perhaps it was the heat of the sun, not just the knowledge of the indignities my cousin had suffered. She was in her grave and could not speak for herself, though her blood could cry from the ground, as the Good Book put it. Her lovely voice was silenced now for ever, and yet I heard it still.

Mrs. Gomersal stared down at her boots and I was surprised to see that tears had dampened her eyelashes. "I'm sorry forrit, sir," she said, in a low voice that would not carry to her children where they sat upon the step. The girl had returned to her occupation; the boy was watching us, his eyes shadowed by his long, curling hair. "I'm right sorry for what 'appened to 'er. You do know it, don't you? She were a neighbour to me."

I recalled Lizzie's diary entry about the pig; about Mary's generosity. "I do, Mrs. Gomersal." I suddenly wished I could take back all that I had said, and the way that I had said it, but something stopped my apology in my throat.

She took a breath and spoke with renewed determination. "Thomas Aikin, sir. And Yedder Dottrell. They're Jem Higgs' cousins—well, not rightly cousins, though they called each other such, but some sorter relatives, if you catch my drift. Thick as thieves, they was."

I frowned. "Yedder?"

"It's not a given name; that's William. But 'e's biddable as a yedder, an' never a fixed idea of 'is own. I dun't rightly think 'e's ever called owt else." She realised my confusion. "A yedder's weaved through a stake to make a fence or bind an 'edge, you see. It bends this way an' that, whichsoever way it's turned."

It did not surprise me to hear this of the man who called Jem Higgs his friend. "And where should I find them?" I could not keep the eagerness from my voice.

"They'll be workin' on Squire Calthorn's land, sir. They're 'is men. Or 'appen you'd catch 'em at t' inn." She looked relieved to be telling me the truth, then appeared of a sudden to recall something. Her hand shot to her mouth and her eyes became unfocused, as if her thoughts had taken her vision far away.

"What is it?"

"It's nowt, sir. Nuthin' at all."

"It's clearly something." I tried to see the object of her gaze, but there was only the sky, little scuds of cloud scurrying across the vast blue, the sun a bright white eye forcing me to lower my eyes.

"It's—I dun't rightly know, sir."

"Mrs. Gomersal, please." I was losing patience.

"It's just—it's t' full moon tonight, sir. I just recalled it. It's—not a good time to be out atter dark, lookin' for no one. You don't know what you'll find. Anyway, they'll not be at t' inn tonight. Best look for 'em tomorrer, sir. Aye, that's for t' best."

My patience was all but lost. I took a deep breath. "I'll not be bound by superstitions, Mrs. Gomersal. All such things should have been forgotten years ago, and it is a great pity for my cousin that they were not. Why, such tales—it is barbarism of the worst kind!"

She pursed her lips. "It is not indeed!" she said. "Them who lives 'ere—them who *sees*—they know better, an' them as won't listen, they'll take their chances. Anyway, it in't no use you lookin' tonight, right or not, 'cos you won't find 'em!"

"Why? Shall they not be on this earth—shall they vanish into the moonlight?" I cried in indignation.

"Aye—'appen they will! Who knows? They'll be up there, see!" She jabbed a finger towards Pudding Pye Hill. "They'll be up there watchin', since they want to 'elp, not cause problems—because they want to see 'er again!"

She gathered herself and continued in a quieter voice. "It's tonight, you see. Tonight's the night o' the full moon—o' the dance." She finished triumphantly. "It's tonight that Lizzie Higgs will be a-comin' back!"

Chapter Sixteen

I sat in the little parlour, taking in its still silence. The sun was fast sinking, but Helena had not deigned to come down for supper. I had eaten little myself, and cleared up as best I could. I had seen my wife after paying my visits, but she had closed her eyes against me; her cheek was wan from spending so long indoors. I asked her to eat a little, and she did, although she accepted only a few morsels, looking as if she would rather cast them upon the ground. She did take some milk, however, and then she had remained, devoid of expression or animation, like a child's carven peg-doll.

I gave up trying to coax her. She had not smiled at me, not once, but she was not accustomed to be thus and I hoped her anger would have dissipated by the morrow. Perhaps then, I could put the constable's words from my mind. *Querulous. Unnatural. Shrew.* They were not good words, and yet I could not keep their echo from my ears.

The time had almost come. I did not want to be seen by anyone, walking up the path to the summit of Pudding Pye Hill at night. I wished to approach quietly, to see what I could and hear what I may. I had not asked Mrs. Gomersal the hour of the cousins' vigil, but I had realised I had no need for her to tell me. It would surely be midnight, the witching hour in all such bugbear tales of phantoms and goblins; I was confident it must be so. Perhaps I was increasing my understanding of the village folk.

Good folk. Hidden folk.

Well, all sensible folk would no doubt be abed at this hour. It was a little before eleven. I hoped the sky would not be cloudy. In the City, the streets were rarely empty; whether it was the cabs bowling young bucks and swells homeward from their sordid entertainments, the jakesmen going about their noisome toil or the knocker-ups calling men to their labour, there was always some business to be done, and gaslights burning to show them their way. Here there was no such thing, and no paved paths to walk upon. Little wonder, then, that the country folk attached such import to the movements of the moon. Without it, the night to them would be as a foreign country.

But I needed reminding that I was not in London. I went to the window and was grateful that there would indeed be light to see by, though I was surprised at its extent. The world was limned in silver, every object casting its own deep shadow. I could not see the moon from my vantage, but I saw its effects. The sky was full of stars, brighter than I had ever seen them in the City, and I wished I could name their constellations. For a moment, I imagined myriad lines between them, weaving each point into the finest net.

This was the night when the fairies would ride, their revels spilling out upon the sward, and if my cousin really was to return, if such a thing could possibly occur, how on earth could anybody make sure to steal her back? On a night such as this, it was almost possible to believe that magic was not far distant; that a strange world could indeed exist within the hill, where even time passed differently. I remembered the wise woman's words about her ten years there which had passed as only as many minutes in the corporeal world. A picture rose to my mind of little Lizzie as she had been when I met her, younger then and more innocent, the vision so clear to me that I expected almost to see her again as she was then. I gave a wistful smile. Dreams and recollections; nothing more, and I must not dwell upon them. I must harden my resolve, since I would have sterner things to face before long: two rough yokels, unprepared and perhaps unwilling to tell the truth.

The world felt suspended when I stepped out into the night. I saw the moon at once, perfectly full and riding high above the hill's summit, lending its gleam to what appeared an abandoned land. I turned the key in the lock behind me and slipped it into my pocket. I had already concealed the key to the back door beneath the oilcloth mat. I thought it best not to inform Helena of my errand, in deference to her current condition, and I did not want her to mistakenly lock the door herself, thus preventing my return.

The air was still, yet the scent of honeysuckle lingered. The flowers glowed whitely where they grew over the wall, though their indistinct forms were distorted, reminding me of some peculiar fungi. I turned to the pale path, flinching at the passing shadow of some night bird which swooped unseen above me.

I wondered that Mrs. Gomersal had not been more afraid at the idea of the cousins being out of doors at such a late hour, particularly upon her dangerous hill. It was after all long since sunset, although possibly they went armoured by some protection against being stolen away by the little folk or catechised in some charm by Mother Crow. I laughed to myself: perhaps they merely carried an iron horseshoe or a poker. Then I frowned; I might have thought to bring such an object with me, but I carried nothing, not even a lamp to guide my way. I did not wish to turn back now; in any event, a lamp would serve only to draw all eyes to me. I could only hope that I would equally well have no need of a poker.

As I went on, accustoming myself to seeing by moonlight, I realised that the hillside mirrored the heavens above: one powdered with stars, the other with dandelion clocks. There was not a breath of air to stir them now—time had ceased to flow—but there was sound, however, drifts of music which must be rising from the village. The notes were difficult to make out; the airs hung on the very edge of hearing. It felt so very nearly like magic that

I could not wonder that the people of Halfoak thought it a realm of enchantment.

The tripping notes lightened my steps. I heard nothing of the two men whose presence I expected to stumble upon at any moment. In the welcome coolness I made short work of the slope and soon reached the hoary old barrow that capped its summit. Its shape was made plain, cutting out the stars with its black form. I suddenly did not wish to go nearer. I knew at once there was no one here, and yet the ancient place had a presence that I could not name. I knew not why I felt so repulsed; only that it demanded something from me that I could not give. It was as if whatever had happened here through all the ages past, whatever worship had been offered or homage paid, lingered still. This was a land not of the living, but of the dead.

And the cousins were not there. I think I had always known they would not be there.

I turned and began to walk down and around the hill, realising only now that the path was *widdershins*, as no doubt the wise woman would have it, and no doubt she would have made it the greater part of some charm; something, perhaps, to entice the dead.

This was indeed a night for charms. The moonlight touched every blade of grass, each flower, every weed and thorn. It touched the thicket of gorse and caressed the boughs of the oak trees.

A rough voice cut into the night, breaking the spell. "A block-head, am I? Well, so be it. I'm a-goin' ter 'ave a little dance."

I ducked down behind a gorse bush, keeping just short of its sharp stems, though it startled me a little to find that although I was concealed, I could see them quite clearly; one sat upon the ground whilst the other, a graceless ruffian, skipped clumsily away from him. The oaks, in their stillness, were reminiscent of regal figures watching over it all. Behind them, I knew, was the doorway into the hill, marked by its jutting stones and the iron blade thrust into the ground, *keeping it open*, Mrs. Gomersal had said. I could not see it—it was lost in the dark—but I could quite plainly make out the fairy ring inscribed upon the ground.

The oaf stumble-stepped towards it. There was no music now, but he appeared to require none. There was only the spurted laughter of the one seated as he slapped at his thigh and slurped at a stone flask he carried. I wondered how long they had been partaking; some time, I guessed, judging by the exaggerated steps of the other, a slender fellow who bent this way and that as he moved. Was this Yedder? I had no way of knowing, but his long stride was such that he might have been wearing seven-league boots. He began to sing some uncouth country song under his breath as he capered, the pauses emphasising the words at intervals as his feet touched the ground. "*Her eyes . . . are like the little stars . . . that shine so bright . . . above . . . Her cheeks . . . are like the rose blush . . . with her I fell in . . . love . . . Her pretty teeth . . . and golden hair . . . a fairy she'd . . . surpass . . . The pride of all the count-ree . . . is me bonny . . . Yorkshire . . . lass!*"

His companion hooted uncontrollably, rocking onto his back so that I could barely see him at all. Was it their intention to make an entertainment of it? Did they think it a jest? Why, if Cousin Lizzie really could return, she would hardly do so for these ruffians. I almost stepped from my hiding place and accused them then and there, but some quiet inner voice bade me be still.

"Tha dun't want to step in that there circle, tha great daft 'apeth." The seated fellow tossed something into the air—a stone?—and his friend snapped about with mock outrage. He whirled again, upsetting his balance and flapping his arms, resembling for a moment a windmill.

"See, see, they'll not get me," he chanted, and went on in a quick rhythm, "I'm as quick as a hare, as nimble as a deer . . . I'm as cobby as a lop!"

"I'll gi' thee 'cobby,' our Yedder," said the first fellow, who must perforce be Thomas Aikin. "I'll gi' it thee round t' lug-holes, if tha dun't gi' ower." Despite his light words his tone portended alarm, and as the other teetered at the edge of the circle, he cried, "Gerroutofit, will yer!"

The other gave up his capering at once. Somewhat abashed, he approached the furze—for a moment I felt sure he would see me, staring straight at him as I was—but he sank to the ground by his companion without once glancing in my direction. "There in't no fairies'll get me, Tommy."

"Aye, well, 'appen tha's right—what'd they want thee for?" The other's voice had turned gruff. "But watch thasel'. Tha knows what's what. Don't mock it, Yedder. You 'eard it all yersen—you 'eard about that nipper o' Mary Gomersal's, din't yer? Wandered off one day an' never t' same since? They said 'e were up 'ere then."

The other snorted. "Aye, an' they say she were up 'ere an' all, seven year ago."

"Aye, well, that's as mebbe. Just dun't step in that circle, see. I'm askin' yer, Yedder, not now; not at this hour. If tha does, tha dun't know if tha'll ever step out of it again."

They fell silent and there was only the clinking of a flask and noisy swallowing, until, after a while, Yedder said, "Ah well, mebbe tha's got summat. It in't right, is it?"

"What in't?"

"T' weather."

"Oh, aye, t' weather."

"No. It in't right. An' it's allus summer, under there—that's all I'm sayin'." He paused. "We should 'ave 'ad a *bit* o' rain by now."

"Well, we should at that."

"Crop's buggered if it dun't come soon."

Thomas grunted. "There's a reason they call 'em kill-crops, all right. It 'ad ter be done, no questionin' that."

"Aye. No one's sayin' owt else, our Tommy."

They fell silent, and yet those words hung in the air, growing louder in my ears until I thought I would burst with anger.

"'Appen we should close that 'ole." It appeared Yedder could not long remain silent.

"That's not why we came, an' you know it."

"No." I heard Yedder's sigh.

"'E'd not want it closin', neither. 'E wants 'er back an' all, dun't 'e? P'raps 'e'll 'ave luck enough to make it 'appen. 'E'll 'ave ter, else 'e'll swing."

Yedder did not reply but leaned back on his elbows, patting out a rhythm upon the ground. It sounded dry and hollow. "I 'eard an 'ole 'ost on 'em'll come out at midnight. They'll be singin' and dancin', and t' queen of 'em'll be at their 'ead. An' Lizzie 'Iggs will be wi' 'em, ridin' on a white 'oss—that's when we've got ter grab 'old on 'er, then or not at all, else she'll not come back again, not never."

"It'll be all up wi' 'im then." Tommy spoke sombrely, almost in despair.

"So we can't shut that 'ole, then."

"I wish ter God thee'd shut thine, Yedder."

The youth did not take offence at his friend's rebuff. "Aye, well. But I asked me mam what she thought on it and she said—beg pardon, Tommy—but she reckons this is nowt but a right bonny do-dance; she said it in't worth a gnat's fart."

There came back a warning grunt.

"That's just me mam, Tommy; dun't think I don't believe it mesel', like." His words rushed on. "There's t' door; that proves it. Though, some say that 'ole leads straight down to 'Ell—but wherever, it dun't matter, does it, Tommy? Since we'll be a-watchin'."

"Stop yer yammerin', will tha, Yedder."

Tommy's voice would brook no argument. There was something implacable in the man, and for a moment he reminded me of the priest, his intense eyes flashing with certainty and zeal. I had not expected it; I had surmised I would discover men who were acting under the instruction of their friend, if only to enforce the semblance of his mania. I had not expected anything in the way of real belief; I had not thought to find any genuine presentiment that Lizzie might be about to make her return.

They sat and drank a little longer, sinking deeper into the nests they had made on the ground. I did not know what to think or how to act. On a night such as this it was almost possible to believe in anything at all; I could picture with perfect clarity the sylvan host of which they had told, clad in shining gossamer, riding forth from the hill, exulting in the summer and in their

night-revels. Lizzie would be among them, her golden hair glim-
mering in the moonlight, almost fairy-like herself. And how she
would sing! Surely that was why the fairies had wanted her, for
her sweet voice . . .

I rubbed my eyes. I had not slept and I had eaten little. I wished
suddenly for my own bed in the noisy, dirty City, where everything
about me was known and understood.

"I'm goin' ter do it," Yedder said, and he stood, his stick-thin
figure outlined against the grass. The trees shivered in some breeze
I could not feel.

"Tha won't."

"Watch me. I'll close it, an' then they'll not come. I dun't *want*
'em to come, Tommy, not now . . ."

He rushed across the little clearing, his shadow pooling at his
feet, pausing only to skirt around the fairy ring. The moon's face
had turned yellow. I did not know the hour and I doubted they
did either, but he had had his fill of watching. He was a "yedder"
indeed, bending away, shirking his task for fear of the night.

As if hearing my thoughts and agreeing with them, Thomas
leaped to his feet and hurried after his friend. He did not go around
the circle but passed straight through it, leaving a line of flattened
ink-dark footprints in the grass.

"I can see it." Yedder's voice was soft, but it carried quite clearly
to me. I straightened, since they faced away from me, and made
out his now squat, troll-like shape as he bent over a little patch of
ground. He had found the iron knife set there by Jem Higgs' hand,
the one object that was supposed to connect my cousin with this
world. This was nothing to do with what I believed; the man had
his errand, to save Lizzie, and it angered me that he did not respect
her or care enough for her fate to carry it out.

In any event, Tommy had reached him and in the next instant he
had knocked his friend to the ground. They wrestled there together,
their rough words turning to brutish grunts and gasps of exertion.

I wrapped my hands about my mouth to muffle my voice and
called out, "Stop!"

The effect of my cry was immediate: Yedder let out a shriek, while the other staggered to his feet, whirling about with his fists, stumbling in his haste to find the source of the sound. He spun again and ended facing the cleft in the hillside.

I do not know how long he stood there, though it felt an eternity, but then he whirled again and ran straight towards me, on the way grabbing his companion, who was also stupefied. As he did so, I flung myself down among the thorns.

I did not see them pass—my face was pressed into the ground—but I heard them crashing by, their gasping breaths and their cries of fear, until my own heightened emotions turned of a sudden to mirth. I shook with it; I pressed my knuckles hard against my lip to stay my voice, and I remained in that attitude until I heard nothing more, and then a little longer, only then raising my head to the clearing. It was as it had been before, as if all the clumsiness and clamour in the human world could not stir its peace. All was quiet; all was still.

I pushed myself up, brushing grass from my clothing, grimacing as I caught my hands on the clinging thorns. I must look an object of ridicule; I considered myself fortunate that my wife had taken to her bed and that all my acquaintances were a great distance away.

I was not certain of the reason for my crying out as I had. I should have challenged them, demanded to know why they had helped my cousin's husband and not his innocent wife; why they had assisted him in administering his "cure." And yet something within me told me that I had seen what I required to see, that I should have no further satisfaction of such clownish men. I wished only to be alone.

I stood squarely in the little gap forming a gateway between the thorns. The fairy ring was delineated before me, as was the flattened place where the companions had sat. I paused, looking down at it, and then I stepped towards the ring, stopping at its edge. The world was made of silver, the very air suspended. For a moment, I did not even breathe. The silence was the sweetest music of all.

I peered into the trees and saw the thin gleam where the blade kept still its vigil. Behind it, through the pale trunks, was a patch of darkness: a chasm in the world. I took another step, my very movements bearing the imprint of unreality. In a moment I would reach the door; if I wished, I could step through it . . .

And then, at my back and all around me, I felt *something*. The nape of my neck prickled; my spine turned to ice. There were eyes, peering from the dark, watching me. I had no way of knowing it and yet I *did* know it, as certainly as I knew my own name. I turned about, slowly, until I had described a circle. I opened my mouth to hail the watcher, but no sound emerged. I glanced down and saw that my foot was over the edge; I was almost standing in the fairy ring.

I stepped across its border and the spell was broken. The sense of watching eyes was gone in a trice, but at that very moment, a figure appeared beneath the trees.

It was a young lady, wearing white floating muslin beneath a green cape. Golden hair spilled across her shoulders and her tread was so soft and light I had not heard her make her way, along some path unseen, betwixt the thorns. I stood frozen, my heart beating painfully against my ribs. I listened for the music that must follow her, but heard only a single sigh, like a breeze in the oaks. I reached out a hand towards her, though she was not within reach; I was seized with the wonderment of awe; with yearning. I willed myself to approach, to grasp hold of her, to draw her back to the world, but my legs were shaking and I stumbled.

When I straightened she was already running, not towards the hillside but away from it, away from the glade and everything it held. I cried out and forced myself after her, gasping her name. The brake of furze was before me and I began to rend and tear at the tangle, but I succeeded only in rending and tearing my own flesh. I must have missed the way. The growth was dark, unleavened by the moonlight; I was caught in the wilderness of thorns. At least she had fled away from the door into the hillside, I told myself, not towards it; she could not be altogether lost.

I cried out again, this time in frustration, and staggered into an open space, only to realise I was back where I had begun. I ran instead along the clear path and around, already short of breath with exertion and fear, but I was too late. The maiden had vanished into the air and far beyond my grasp. Perhaps I had never even seen her; perhaps she had been conjured, not by magic and moonlight but by my own overheated imagination. What had I expected? I had gone in search of dreams and fancies, and those I had found, in too great an abundance to be borne. And yet all I could think of as I stood there were the words Lizzie had written in her diary. I could see the flash of her nut-brown eyes, the mischief in them; the delight, and yes, the admiration, when she turned them upon me.

And waiting for me at home was nothing but the contempt I knew I would see when I looked into my wife's eyes.

Still, I hurried towards that home, or at least, towards the cottage which had for a time taken its place. The odd sense of being watched did not return, though as I went I thought of foxes and hares and tiny birds hiding in the undergrowth, cataloguing every creature it might possibly have been, save one.

But of course, there were no eyes. The vast, indifferent sky stretched over the land, its sparkling beauty impossibly distant, and I felt a mere speck within the world, one little life among so many. My shadow spilled before me, covering each footfall with darkness, making my descent a treacherous affair, and it was a relief when at last I saw the cottage, even though it was benighted; I had left no candle in the window or lamp burning within to light my way. The garden, despite the myriad colours I knew existed within it, was black and uninviting, the whole aspect one of lonely abandonment.

And then I saw that the door was standing open.

My breath froze in my throat. I roused myself into motion, redoubling my pace. Surely nobody could have come at this ungodly hour? I could see no one within. I slipped a hand into my pocket and found there the cold dull metal of the key.

I began to run.

Chapter Seventeen

Upon reaching the cottage, for all my concern, I was overcome by a strange reluctance to enter. I peered around the door to see the black emptiness of the passage. I breathed my wife's name. The sense of abandonment hung more strongly about the place than ever. I forced myself to reach out and push the door wider, stepping quietly inside. I could dimly see that the back door was shut; I rattled the handle and found it remained locked. I raised a corner of the mat— pushing from my mind the time when I had lifted aside another oilcloth and seen what lay beneath—and I saw the key.

I was unsurprised to find the parlour devoid of any presence and the hearth cold. No one was sitting there in the dark: no one living, and no ghost. In order to be thorough before going upstairs, I quickly looked into the pantry and the storeroom, finding all as it had been. I even opened the door to the workshop and stood on the threshold a moment before turning back to the stairs. I had only been delaying the moment when I must go up them. I set my foot upon the first riser then crept, as silently as I could, up the treads. I placed a hand on Helena's door. I could not bring myself to knock, but instead called her name, very softly, disliking the tremulous note that had stolen into my voice.

No reply came; I had expected none. I pushed open the door and, hearing no further sound, entered the room. The window was thrown open and the half-curtains festooning the bed were shifting in the night-breeze. I did not pause to close the casement, but bent and peered under the bed, for all that I could not account for why I did it; did I really imagine my wife would be hiding there, her eyes gleaming in the dark? Then I went to the door across the landing. My own room was as empty as Helena's.

I leaned against the doorjamb and closed my eyes. Helena might as well have vanished into the air; I had not the first idea where she might have gone.

And yet I must find her. I chastised myself for my inaction and hurried down the stair once more and out of the door. I checked the keyhole, to see if she had perhaps found some other key and left it there, but it was empty; perhaps she had taken it with her, then, although I could not imagine why she had not troubled to close the door.

I set out towards the village, the moon shining down on all. I presumed that Helena could not have passed me on such a night; I wished to feel certain she could not have tended her steps up onto Pudding Pye Hill, but I knew in this I was merely consoling myself. In truth, she might have gone anywhere. I could easily have missed her in the dark, or while I stood watching the oafs from the village—or the other form I had seen. I was quite sure that the female figure had not been Helena: her hair had been golden, not my wife's dark tresses.

I lengthened my stride. I never should have left her. If she had awakened in the night and realised she was alone, what must have been her thoughts? I must find her quickly—if she were to be seen there might be a scandal.

At least it was easy to see my way. The road shone whitely, like some mythical path, and soon I heard the babbling of the little brook, its chatter so bright and cheerful; its voice came to me as mockery through the gloaming. It almost did not belong to this night—but no, it was I who was out of place. Everything else was as it should be: the village a picture of sylvan peace, bewitching and charming. The first houses were dark and quiet and yet unlike the cottage on the hill, they appeared sleeping rather than abandoned.

I trotted across the little bridge, glancing at the darkness beneath as I stepped onto the road and at once turned my ankle in a rut and pitched headlong into the dust.

I pushed myself up, rubbing at my grazed palms and brushing dirt from my clothing, and picked my way less precipitously down the middle of the road, towards the centre of the village, accompanied by the distant fluting call of an owl. The dark expanse of the green opened ahead of me and at its centre, the blasted oak, the dead part of the tree's trunk pale against the living wood. The inn's face was a blank. The stained-glass windows of the church glittered. I hurried by, watching for any sign that another person was abroad, but there was no trace of any soul. Thomas Aikin and Yedder Dottrell must already have closed their doors behind them. I wished I had been able to do the same. I peered over my shoulder, no longer able to see the bridge but thinking of the stream that ran beneath it. Some years before, I had seen an exhibition at the Royal Academy, where a depiction of Ophelia, by John Everett Millais, had commanded my attention utterly. Ophelia had been lying in a stream very much like the one that flowed through Halfoak, garlanded by water-weeds and little flowers. She was supine, her white face blank and staring upward, and I had seen at a glance that all sense had departed her; I could almost hear her sad, mad singing in the final moments before she drowned. I had thought of it long after, and I thought of it now, but this time it was not some stranger's face I saw in the stream but Helena's. The line from *Hamlet* returned to me: *Her clothes spread wide, And mermaid-like awhile they bore her up.*

I had actually started back towards the stream before I banished the notion as impossible. Then came the distant tapping of wooden pails and the soft snort of a horse from the direction of the inn's stables. I started away towards the crossroads, thinking of gibbets and hangings, when I spied a pale shape floating in the dark ahead of me.

I looked first for golden hair, thinking it a spectre conjured from my dreams, then I saw that it was not; her hair was dark—it was Helena, my own dear wife, wandering as if she were lost. I hurried towards her, seeing more each moment: her slight figure, wearing only her nightgown, her hair falling in a tumble about her shoulders. All the windows around us were dark and I heard nothing. Even the beer house was silent.

"Helena!" I whispered.

She whirled and her face, as pale and ghostly as her nightgown, broadened into a smile. "Why, it is you, Albie!"

"Of course it is I. Pray, lower your voice."

"Why, my love? Does it matter to whom I speak?" Her expression at once became solemn and her hand shot to her mouth in mock alarm. "Oh—but I have already danced!"

"*Danced?* Helena, do you not know the hour? And you are out here quite alone—"

She gave a knowing smile, one that I did not like to see. "Oh, no, Albie. Never alone."

"Has anybody seen you?" I caught hold of her arm to lead her back along the road, but she was stiff and unyielding and pulled away from me.

"Why, I told you—I have danced! Two fine young men came along the road and they said that they would dance with me—and so they did! Fine, fine . . ."

"Helena, please!"

She gave a trilling laugh. "They thought me a fairy, Albie. Is that not delicious?"

I thought rapidly. Yedder and Thomas, for I was certain it must be they, had been in their cups and disporting in their foolishness—indeed, probably they had a reputation for it; even Mrs. Gomersal had said Yedder could never be steadfast. And they had gone out at midnight to watch for fairies and their stolen changeling by the full of the moon. Now their lunacy could save us from scandal: they might truly believe they had encountered one of the folk, not on the fairy hill, but here in the village. They had never met my wife and they need never do so. And none knew she was out here, alone and unprotected, and in so fey a condition she barely seemed herself. We would return home; she would sleep and feel better. All would be well.

"We must hurry, my love," I said. "Do you know where you are?"

"Of course, Albie. We are beneath the sky."

"Besides that." I could not keep the irritation from my voice. "What is it you thought you were doing, wandering as you are without even pausing to dress yourself?"

She turned her head slowly towards me. Her cheek gleamed like wax in the silver light; only her eyes and her lips were dark. "Why, I was looking for you, of course, Albie. Isn't that what any wife would do?" Her lip curled, as much in challenge as a smile.

I caught her hand, meaning to pull her along with me, and she winced. She cradled her hand and I took it once more, gently this time, and teased open her fingers. There upon her palm was a strange red mark, double curving lines with roughly square blemishes at intervals between them. Those squares put me in mind of nail-heads and I caught my breath and forced her hand higher, closer to my eyes. Though of course it would not be, it looked as if she had pressed her hand against a heated horseshoe which had burned its impression into her skin.

"What is this?" The words burst from me and there was no sympathy in them, but it was too late for that. I could think only of the ancient iron horseshoes set above the door to the inn, ready to ward away any witch or fairy who should attempt to enter.

"Why, in my searching for you I fell, my dear," Helena replied. "I caught my hand against the gate. Is it bruised?"

"It is not bruised—it is burned."

"That is impossible, my dear. I have not burned it."

"Let me look again."

"Oh, but we must away, my dear. Must we not? It would be dreadful if someone should see us, quite dreadful."

She was correct, of course, so I offered her my arm and we began to walk hurriedly along the road, returning to our little fairy hill. It came as a relief when we crossed the bridge and put Halfoak behind us; this time I did not pause, since there was no need now to stare into the dark below and wonder. We followed the white road—the Reeling Road—upward. We were almost home, away from prying eyes. Soon all would be well and reality would assert itself once more, over my mind and over my wife's. More relief came as we gained the gate and passed through. The door ahead of us was still ajar—I too had neglected to close it. Helena examined it as we neared the threshold, her lovely features marred with scorn.

"Helena, for the sake of our peace, pray, give me the key you used earlier." I did not need it now, but I thought it best to settle the matter before we entered. I did not wish to drag further discord inside with us.

"The key, my love? I have no key."

"You must have, my dear. I locked the door earlier this night, to keep you safe. You have found another—let me have it, and I will take care of everything."

"I said I have none."

"But I locked the door," I reiterated. "How then would you have me believe that you—you got out?" *Escaped* was the word I had thought to use, but it was a bad word and I held my tongue.

"But you see, you could not have locked it, my dear, for I *did* get out."

"I am quite sure that I must have."

"And yet the door stands open."

I stared at her. I did not know how she could speak so, how she could be so intractable, but I did not press her further. I handed her inside, pausing only to turn my little key in the lock once more. It clicked quite distinctly, and when I tried the handle, I found it locked. I told myself that I could not have turned it properly when I left for the hillside, though I could not see how I had failed to do so.

I turned from the door and saw the hem of Helena's nightdress trailing up the stair. Her door opened and closed and there was silence.

I sighed. I did not wish to speak to her, and I did not wish to retire just then. The strangeness of the evening, my fear at finding her gone, even the bright fizzling starlight, had heated my blood and I knew I would not sleep. I went instead into the parlour and sat there, staring into the dark grate, as images rose before my eyes: Lizzie being forced to her knees before a leaping flame, her fine skin beginning to char. What had they done then? Had they been shocked and horrified when she began to burn? Had they tried to save her?

I covered my eyes, but the images remained. I let my head fall back and stared instead at the ceiling. There was no sound from Helena's room, not even the tapping of ewer on washstand or of her brush being set down. There was no tumultuous wind or rattling of windowpanes. All was still. The quiet folk were quiet, after all. I realised I had not heard Helena close her window, so it must still be open, admitting the night air and the heady scent of flowers. I suddenly knew exactly where she stood at this moment: by that open window, staring out into the dark with longing in her eyes, as if that were where she belonged; as if she would prefer to be out there now, wandering the moonlit paths on the hillside, all alone.

Chapter Eighteen

That night, I dreamed of my wife. I knew that it was her because of the way she smiled at me: as she had used to smile, open and clean and good—I knew it even though her lovely dark hair had faded to the colour of corn which shone brightly about her as she turned and walked away from me. I did not recognise the room in which she stood, but I suddenly knew that this was our home; we had finally removed from my father's residence.

The room was filled with every comfort. China figurines stood in their frozen attitudes upon the mantle and a large glass bell was full of the orange blossom that had been her wedding flowers, reproduced in wax and tied with a white ribbon. I remembered her insistence upon it, the matrimonial fashion set by our good queen. All was as it should be, and I followed her like a man in a fog of happiness.

I entered a strange hallway, its new crimson carpet protected at the centre with pieces of drugget. Helena was just turning at the corner above me and I saw her full crinoline skirts sweeping around the banisters. She was murmuring as she went, her voice low and sweet; I know not what she said but her tone was full of warmth, of love, and I knew that her words were not intended for me. Still the sound drew me onward. The mahogany balustrade was polished and clean under my hand, the carpet deep and soft beneath its covering, and I felt a swell of pride in my home.

The landing was empty. I tried to call my wife's name, but all that emerged was an unintelligible whisper. Her own voice was clear to me again, however, and I followed the sound into the last little room along the passage. Helena was there, her back towards me, bending over something, and when she straightened and turned, I realised with a start that she was holding a baby.

I could not see it properly, only its white cap and gown, but Helena's expression was full of a mother's love; she had a radiance in her eyes I had never seen before. When she saw me watching, her smile broadened, which made me smile back at her, and then she turned a little, revealing the infant's face.

My bones were transformed to ice, but then I made out the tiny closed eyes; the lids, translucent as rose petals; a snub nose; sweet little lips that rose to a perfect Cupid's bow. The child slept soundly in its mother's arms. I could not move. I do not know what I had expected to see, but the relief was sweeter than anything I could have anticipated. I held out my hands towards it and the child opened its eyes a slit.

My smile froze on my lips as it opened its lids fully to reveal eyes as dark and dull as pebbles. They were not a child's eyes; there was no soul in them. They were too large for its face and angled strangely, like a cat's, and the irises were too large, with hardly any whites to be seen. A thousand colours lay within them, like sunlight shining upon oil. *He made their glowing colours*, a voice whispered, and the child cried out, a harsh, ratcheting sound like the call of a crow.

I sat bolt upright, sweat pouring from my face. I was in my own room, in the little cottage halfway up a fairy hill. A breeze touched my skin, blessedly cool, and with a start I saw that the window was once more open and that Helena stood before it, her nightgown shifting about her. Her back was turned, her hair an oily stain.

"Helena?"

She slowly turned. The smile upon her face was not open or clean or good. "Yes, my dear—whom did you expect to see?" She watched my consternation spread across my face.

"Oh, my dear," she said, "what a father you shall make!"

I could only stare as she walked from the room, leaving the window open behind her.

I pushed off my covers and went to it. The moon was sinking; what could still be seen had turned a livid blood-red, masked by trailing threads of cloud. *'S unlucky to look upon it, wi' t' moon up high*, I thought, and I slammed the window into its frame, pulled the shutters closed and dragged the curtain into place before them.

I knew I would not be able to find sleep again. Was my wife ill? I should call upon Doctor Newberry in Kelthorpe, perhaps. Had she taken to sleepwalking—even to talking and laughing in her sleep? If I spoke of this on the morrow, would she even remember—and if she did, would she admit to it? I did not know the answers to any of my questions, and nor did I want to think of it now, not with the unlucky moon seeing everything.

I closed my eyes. I would not have felt so in the City. There, I would have known what to do.

Instead of trying to sleep I lit the lamp and took out Lizzie's journal. It made me feel more capable at once; at least here had been one who had looked up to me. By reading her thoughts, perhaps I could make myself feel worthy of her.

Things that make you a fairy. There's plenty of them round here, if you believe them all. Not making the butter come right. Burning the joint or spilling milk and not cleaning it up right. Having your chickens die. Not being what they want you to be. Not having a baby. They say changelings are barren, as if it's a fact and they know them personal. Having the wrong baby. Don't make me laugh, I said to Jem when he told us that one. Half the village would be fairies at that, not that they say owt, even when they go past their windows with their bellies big and round like the moon. He knew who I meant and

I laughed at that. He didn't, though. He threatened to wipe the smile off me and so I shut my lips, but I don't need to shut it now I can write it down in this book. He gave it to me—that's summat else Jem don't know and he'll not, neither.

Aye, fairies. That's how you know. Hundreds of them, if you could count.

Thing is, I know I'm not the only one. I'm used to that now. But Jem don't see anything, not really, and he don't have to know it, neither. They say there's all kinds of blindness, and it's true.

Whatever I had sought, I had not found it. My sweet cousin's words served merely to underline the distance that had existed between us. And her odd modes of expression left me with an increase of confusion rather than of certainty; could her husband truly have read such a thing and thought it a confession? I flicked through more of it, seeing her notes about housekeeping and the local gossip. There was not enough milk to be had, since it had all been sold in Kelthorpe and sent off by train to the cities; the thatcher had not yet paid Jem for his new leathern gaiters; the squire—young or old, I did not know—was not worth a farthing. There was nothing there that would not be expected.

I skipped ahead a little and a name caught my eye and I began once more to read in earnest.

Cousin Aikin was round here the other night. He says it isn't long now and he didn't look happy about it. I've seen her in the village and I think she's got more like a month to go, but I didn't say anything. It isn't worth it. She's lost her place, of course, though it were him that put it in her, as everyone knows. Jem had me bring out mugs of cider to drink its health, as if it were here now, and as if they even wanted it. It were then that Tommy said summat about changelings and I burst out laughing, and he stopped his drinking and he looked at me and I looked at Jem and he was looking at me too.

So he *had* been in the thick of it: Tommy Aikin and Jem had been co-conspirators even then. It was odd to think that the falsity might first have been mentioned by Aikin instead of Lizzie's husband; had he even known what he was about, planting such a thing in Jem's mind? And then to return when summoned, to put his hands on her and deal out such rough treatment . . .

As if they even wanted it. I closed my eyes and saw again the baby of my dream, waking, seeing the dark shine of its gaze through its half-closed eyelids. I lay back on the pillow. What a terrible thing it was, to put about such fantastical notions.

I drifted for a while, thinking of nothing, and each time I opened my eyes the night had faded a little more, pushed aside by the encroaching dawn. The birds awoke and began their song, no discordance marring it, not today. I could already feel that the day was to be as fine as yesterday and the day before that. All the days of Halfoak, it seemed, were the same. The sun would be rising, a white blaze in the innocent blue, already warming the earth after the rule of night. All greyness would be banished, as would my grey mood. I turned and sat once more upon the bed and found myself reaching, not for Lizzie's book but my wife's.

As I looked at it I pictured Helena reading it: her sweet, oval face, the forehead high and clear; her sudden look; her most unconscious smile. I wondered that I ever could have taken her book from her, and yet with its loose pages and bent corners, I could now scarcely return it. An explanation would be required of me, one I could not readily provide.

I began to read of Catherine, a wayward and quixotic child, a being rather of the wild moor and the wind and the rain than of the hearth, and I soon became quite lost in the odd story. I could understand why the critics had so spurned it, and yet it was compelling and vivid and elemental. Despite all its strangeness it lulled me into a kind of peace, even a trance. It was a comfort to be enveloped in a world where odd things were accepted so calmly, whilst knowing that at any moment I could close the book upon it all. I did not do so; I read on. I had soon reached the part where the father, who had made such a grave error in bringing the goblin child Heathcliff into his home, was nodding in his chair by the fireside whilst his witchling daughter, at his knee, sang him to sleep, when a darkness closed over me and I myself began to nod, though the sun was surely riding higher, ready to dispel any tiredness. And I almost fancied that young Cathy was sitting at the foot of my bed, her face hidden in the midnight tangles of her hair, and that a song had wended its way through my chamber and into my dreams.

> *O there I met with a bonny maid*
> *As bright as any fairy.*

I sat up straighter, rousing myself. I could indeed hear a song; it was not simply my imagination. Helena's voice was drifting from the next room.

I focused on the words before my face, and all the author's comforts turned to horror. For the father, of course, was not sleeping but dead; the little elf he had raised had sung him into the slumber of eternity.

I bestirred myself and leaped to my feet. Before I knew what I was about I rapped three times, sharply, on the wall dividing my wife's room from my own, and her singing stopped at once. I waited for a cry of protest, but none came, and then I jumped myself, for another triple rap had rung out sharply, not from the wall but from the landing. My first thought was that it was Helena, angrily returning my protest, but it could not be—the sound came from somewhere more distant. Then it came again in rapid succession, *bang-bang-bang*, and I realised with a dart of something like shame that someone was knocking at the door.

I hurried down the stair, almost tripping over my own feet, and opened it to find Mrs. Gomersal standing upon the step, her surprise at the suddenness of my appearance hardening at once into something else. I bade her good day and she gave an ill-mannered curtsy. I stood a little taller and began to enquire in a cold voice what it was that I could do for her when she said, "Beggin' yer pardon, sir, but it's delicate."

"Then perhaps you should come inside." I swung the door wider.

"Sir—no, I think I should not." She lowered her voice. "It—it's about your wife, beggin' your pardon, an' no offence meant." Despite her apology her words were spoken without compunction, though she cast a glance over her shoulder as if to ensure that no one was listening. "I saw 'er, sir."

I raised my eyebrows, though inwardly my heart sank. I already knew what she was going to say.

"Sir, flittin' about by moonlight—it's not safe, sir, beggin' yer pardon, and—I saw 'er, sir, drawn to t' crossroads just like any man what ought to be in a gibbet."

"Now wait one moment. I shall not have my wife spoken of in such a way."

"No, o' course not, sir, but I'm not one fer gossip, not me. That's t' reason I'm tellin' thee, see, not no one else. Only it's a bad sign. I saw 'er all in white, an' I saw who she were dancin' wi' an' all. No good will come on it, sir. She—she in't right—I mean, *it* in't right for 'er, bein' 'ere, is it, sir?" She spoke gently, as if to persuade—nay, *manipulate*—a child into agreeing with her.

"I think p'raps she's best taken 'ome. If not—why, who knows what'll 'appen? 'Appen she'll be taken 'ersen, aye, stolen away like t' other were. Best go, sir, wi'out delay. Before it's too late."

I stared in astonishment at such a speech. To be addressed in such outlandish fashion, and by such a person—why, it was scarcely to be borne. And yet I could clearly see the concern written across her features, so I endeavoured to soften my tone. "Madam, this is outrageous—and by your own words, you undo your argument. There is no reason in it; there is nothing scientific or rational. If it were even possible that my wife were stolen away, as you put it, if she were indeed a changeling, how then would it help her to remove her from the place from whence she was stolen? Surely I could not so easily abandon her. Should I not rather do all I can to have her restored to me? What benefit would be gained by fleeing? I should rather administer such cures as I could find . . ."

My voice failed for a creeping dismay had come upon me even as I uttered those words, and it struck me then that so might a different man have said, one who had perhaps uttered the same protest on the same threshold, though about a different woman; one already burned to a cinder.

Some might even have listened to him. Some might even have believed him to be justified.

Mrs. Gomersal gave no indication of what she thought. Her face closed up and her lips pursed. "As you say, sir," she muttered under her breath, and she dropped another small curtsy before turning and marching off through the garden.

I watched her go with no little relief, then I closed the door and turned to see Helena standing at the stair's foot, still dressed in her white nightgown, staring at me unblinkingly.

She did not open her mouth to speak. She only looked upon me a little longer and then she turned and walked back up to her room, her skirts sweeping across the landing, and her door opened and closed quietly and softly, just as if it were an ordinary thing; and as if all that had been said was nothing more than ordinary too.

Chapter Nineteen

I had thought of walking into Halfoak again, but after Mrs. Gomersal's visit I paused at the door, my hat pressed down upon my head and my hand upon the handle, staring down at the keyhole. I could already feel the sun's heat on the other side and I longed to step from the shadows and into brightness, yet I could not bring myself to do so. I pictured walking along the white road, reaching the brilliant verdancy of the village green and feeling eyes everywhere, eyes upon my back, upon my face, all knowing and unspeaking and yet laughing.

I let my hand slip from the door handle, persuading myself that I had other tasks before me. I must ensure that Helena was quite well. I should write a few lines to my father; I had brought with me pen, ink and paper for that purpose. I knew he would not be pleased that I had elected to stay longer in Yorkshire. I could imagine his stern glares towards my desk at his offices, the clerks keeping their heads lowered to their tasks to escape becoming the object of his irritation as the great clock struck out another hour. I decided then and there that I would tell him our happy news; that this above all things would please him enough to bear with my sojourn a little longer.

And then I blinked and stared harder at the keyhole, knowing suddenly that there was something wrong with it. The metal, and the door around it, was laced with little scratches from all the years of locking and unlocking it had endured. Why so many? Did country folk habitually trouble to lock their doors? I imagined the village settling into somnolence, the light fading from the sky, the last strains of a violin dying against the greater darkness, all men retreating at last to their beds. Why should they lock their doors? It did not meet my image of the place; it was something that divided them from the bustle and modernity of the City as surely as the blackness of the night, unleavened by a single gaslight along the road.

Yet here were the signs of it. Was it simply a defect in Jem Higgs' nature to be so suspicious? What was it exactly he had guarded against?

It's not a good 'ouse. Not a lucky 'ouse, neither.

But it was a solid house, a fine house for a man such as he, one he could only afford to rent because other men had spurned it. A fairy house; the den of little folk, if the stories were to be believed. And the men who told such tales—should I even care what they thought of me? How could they prevent me walking along the road with my head held high?

A sound broke into my thoughts: footsteps were approaching the cottage along the Reeling Road. Had Mrs. Gomersal decided to renew her appeals? I threw the door open to see a stranger, a farmer's lad, his face red and his back bent, sweating through his shirt-sleeves in the heat. I thought of sending him around to conduct his business at the back door, but it did not seem worth the trouble. He came panting up to me, leaving the gate swinging. Rustic syllables broke from his mouth, as bluff as they were brief and impossible to decipher, but he thrust a packet towards me and I took it. I gave him a penny for his trouble, presuming that payment for what he had handed over would be requested at some later date, and he turned and went away, revealing a damp line where the shirt clung to his back.

The parcel was unpleasantly warm and pliant. I pulled open the paper a little and stared down at the red mess in my hands. It was calf's liver, deeply purpled, along with a few small chops. The pungent scent of iron assailed my nostrils and I grimaced as I wrapped the things again as best I could. I imagined it on the roasting jack before the fire, the redness turning to black, the surface crackling to reveal fissures of crimson. I stared after the boy, visible now only as a little cloud of dust as he made his way back to the village. I was not sure how he had got along so fast unless it was that I had stood and stared longer than I had believed. Was he afraid of the place, to hurry so in the hot sun? But of course I knew the answer to that.

I pushed the door closed with my heel and deposited the foul package in the kitchen. The contents spilled from it and I left it to bleed upon the table. I passed through the parlour and went up the stairs and into my room. I could think only of opening a book and hiding myself within its pages. It did not appear to signify much which one I read: the true account which sounded so much like fiction, or the fiction which was laced with the true beliefs of the folk I moved among.

I was so happy to-day. I waited and waited for Jem to come in and I could hardly bare to sit still. I did some sewing but I could not do that neither, I just pricked my finger, so I walked up and down the lane instead. At last I saw him and I waved and he saw me but he didn't wave back. I suppose he wondered what was up, but he didn't hurry neither. It was making me cross by then, but then he weren't to know. So I told him all that moaning and wondering can stop now, because he's going to be a papa.

At first he looked moithered and he shook his head as if he didn't know what I was on about. And then he asked, Really? and I said, Yes, really, and he scratched his head.

Haven't tha got more to say than that, I asked him, and he said it was just that Aikin's lass has started with the bairn, and he thought it was that I was on about, and it was my turn to be dazed: did he think I was accusing him of summat? Did he think me daft? We all know whose bairn that is.

And then he sorter smiled, and then it were gone, just like that. There was just that one little bit when he actually looked happy. And then he said, did I get it the same place as her?

I didn't know what to say at first. He'd wanted it so long, going on and on about it, and now I was going to be a mamma, and I'd thought of nowt but sewing little caps and blankets for its bed since I realised.

I got right mad with him then. I said if I had, at least it would be a handsomer bairn than his own, and he looked at me like to throttle me. I've seen him mad, but not this mad. His lip went white and for a while he didn't say owt, and it were like he didn't hear owt I said, but then he looked at me and told me he had found my bonnet. I knew which it was straight off, the one I hid, the one with little green flowers on. And he asked me who I wore it for, since it weren't him, and I said I was saving it for best. And he said where did I get it from, since it wasn't from him, and I said I saved up and got it my self, but I could see he didn't believe me. And I couldn't say nowt then, since I couldn't answer. All I could think to say was, baby or bonnet? Which is most important? And I don't know which he thought, because he didn't answer me either way.

So that were that. I told him, and he were mad anyway. I cried, but I didn't let him see.

I shook my head over the sad words, the loneliness my cousin must surely have felt in her predicament, and then I remembered: changelings were said to be barren, weren't they? But Lizzie had been with child. So if Jem truly believed in fairy-lore, as he claimed, there was no possibility that he could have thought her a changeling! And this matter of the bonnet, somehow wrapped up in shame—someone had given it to her. Was it a sweetheart? I could not believe it of my cousin, and yet I remembered the words written in her own hand that I had earlier read: *I hid my new bonnet. I think perhaps I should not keep it, but then why should I not have such a thing . . .*

It cast her in a new light. *Fairy struck? Fairly struck?* Even so, the acceptance of a gift was not necessarily the emblem of some deeper guilt. The words she had written in her journal had been for herself and her alone, and in them she had shown herself to be Jem Higgs' true wife. At the same stroke, she demonstrated that he had had reason—earthly reason, outside the realm of enchantment—to hate her; perhaps to do violence upon her, perhaps even to wish her dead.

I closed the book, catching the faintest scent of dried petals and dust, and I wondered afresh at his insistence that such a journal existed. His thread of hope was that its revelations might loosen his bonds, but if he had truly seen it before, he had surely not read it all. What I held at this moment in my hands could only draw the noose tighter until it closed for ever upon his miserable neck.

I hurried across the room and concealed the document once more, not beneath my pillow but in the hiding place Lizzie had once chosen for it behind the wainscoting. Then, in a manner more business-like than I had moved for days, I wrote a note to my father, explaining that I had been unavoidably detained in settling my cousin's affairs, and that I would do everything I could for the family, and that further to such matters, he may rejoice in the news that his own would soon be extended. In anticipation of such happiness I closed my brief correspondence, his respectful son, & cetera, & cetera, and signed with an unwonted flourish.

As I cast my eyes over what I had written—finding, indeed, that I could barely remember the words—*joyous occasion*, and *happy addition*, almost feeling other words (*barren; unnatural; fairy; shrew*) being overwritten, I heard the soft tones of my wife rise in a pretty lullaby, and I felt with full force all the weight of my recent neglect. I stood, smiling. My wife, along with my unborn child, occupied the adjacent room. There she was, no doubt full of fond thoughts, imagining in the corner a carven crib; the purity of the white shirts she would sew to encase those tiny limbs; cradling her arms, already sensing there the warm and lovely weight.

I heard the words she sang, and my smile faded from my lips.

> *As I walked out one sweet morning*
> *Across the fields so early . . .*

I hurried to find her, to impress upon her my deepest affection and assurance of our happiness together, so that her song, like my words, may be overwritten. Helena could sing a new song, one of love and gentle motherhood. I would take her in my arms and banish all that the recent days had placed between us. I pushed her door wide and my smile faltered.

> *O there I met with a bonny maid*
> *As bright as any fairy.*

Her voice was sweet, but her expression was not. Her face was drawn and twisted; I had never before seen it so. She looked older, dried-out and harsh, and full of dried-out, harsh thoughts. She held out a hand as she turned towards me and it remained suspended in the air, as if it were clasped in another's; as if she were being led in some dance. Her eyes narrowed as they focused upon mine. She was wearing my cousin's dress, which hung loosely upon her form, the sleeves limp upon her arms where the cotton had worn to thinness, and I realised she had not fastened it.

As if to show me the truth of this she turned again, gracefully spinning on one foot. The other toe struck the floorboards with a dull *clunk* that was surprising in its loudness. I started at it, though she appeared to notice not at all, and I thought of the parson's words as he spat them in my face:

All are children of Lilith; they are nothing of Pan. Only emissaries of Satan himself, aye, of old Mister Splitfoot as they call him, and by their split feet shall ye know them.

She turned again: *clunk.* And again. Her face turned to me and away; turned to me and away, like something glimpsed in a daedalum, a trick I had once seen whereby glancing through slits in a spinning cylinder lent the illusion of animation to certain lifeless images printed within. I recalled, uncomfortably, that "daedalum" was said to mean "wheel of the devil."

My wife resumed her singing.

> *"Where are you going, sweet maid?" said I,*
> *As by the hand I caught her.*

I reached out for her hand, stopping just short of touching her. Her other hand, upheld and twirling sensuously in the air, bore the mark of the iron horseshoe.

She laughed, then, a long trill with cruelty but no sense in it.

> *"I'm going home, kind sir," she said,*
> *"I'm nought but your own aunt's daughter."*

My mouth fell open, she laughed harder and I reached out and grabbed her hand at last. Hers was cold. "Stop it," I said. "Will you cease at once, Helena!"

"Helena, is it?" She bowed, allowing her dark hair to fall across her shoulders, and peered up at me through the tangle in a coquettish manner more suited to a soubrette upon the stage than a wife. It was awful, almost lascivious, and of a sudden I could hear rough cries and rougher music, the raucous calls of costermongers; I saw the unseemly flash of a mottled thigh.

She went on, "Not Helena, my dear. You see, I am changed—quite, quite changed!" She gave another awful peal.

"You are unsettled, my dear. It is your condition, I know, and your—You must go home at once. A physician must attend you." I already knew, however, that none must know of this. No one must see her with her senses thus deranged.

"Oh, but I am home already! I am home, among my own folk, my dear, just as you wanted. I live in her house, I sleep in her bed and now I wear her clothes for you. I wear her shoes, just for you. I *am* her for you, my dear, devoted husband! Why, I can be anyone you like!" She held out a lock of hair. "Do you like this form? You have the notion I can take another, if you wish it, do you not? Is that what you yearn for when you wander the hill at night?"

"You are not her." I barely knew what I said.

"No, I am not! I shall *never* be her." She sighed. "I shall never be her again." There was something in the way she spoke, as if some hidden meaning was intended, but I could not fathom it. My hands shook; I felt like a man in a fever. This was so bizarre, so—*changed*, I could barely believe it to be my wife at all. And after what I had written in my letter to my father . . . he would be so happy; he would believe all was well with the world. I could not send it. I would tear the paper to shreds.

I covered my face. I must do something to stop this, to *know*, though I knew not what I needed to know—and then I pictured myself striding to the top of Pudding Pye Hill and discovering the cool, dark place that lay beyond the oaks. There I would find the cold iron cutting into the ground, casting its spell, keeping the doorway open.

I shook the idea away. My wife's was an infectious madness; I could not be so influenced. Now she cavorted and twirled like a child in the nursery and I wondered, was this how Jem Higgs had seen his own wife—seen her, and allowed the malady to seize hold of his own brain? Had he himself been in his right senses?

And then I *did* know what I must do. I had judged the man, and I was certain I had done so aright, and yet I saw now that just as Yedder Dottrell had skirted the fairy ring, I had skirted the heart of the matter. I must see the man who had killed her face to face: I must stand before him and look into his eyes. I had to see for myself the callousness and the evil within him and know it for what it was. And I must look upon his madness, so that I could understand it, and so that I could recognise it if I saw it again.

Chapter Twenty

It was difficult to describe my feelings as I followed the warden through the narrow doors and into the passageways that twisted in a quite indecipherable fashion through the tall, stern building. There had been little to suggest, from its façade, what lay within; only the sharpened wrought-iron railing, gleaming coldly, gave any clue as to its purpose. The prison was built of grey stone, rendered darker against the insipid sky. A sense of dampness hung about it, which I felt more sharply after the endless warmth of Halfoak.

My visit had involved a rather tiresome train journey, taking me yet deeper into the barbaric north. I had unfortunately failed to gain the corner seat in the compartment and the window had been particularly ill-fitting, admitting an unfortunate influx of smuts and cinders. I had endeavoured to blow them from my frock-coat the moment I alighted, but the smudges remained.

The gaol was situated not far distant from the centre of a rather small city and even deep within those dank walls I could still hear the sounds of its citizens going about their regular business: the rumble of cartwheels and the chatter from a coffee stand, the shouting of a Lucifer-seller, his cries vying with those of a man selling pigs' pettitoes. Such sounds were not unfamiliar to me, and yet I found myself listening for the twitter of birdsong and the steady swishing of scythes cutting down the hay. I suspect my reluctance to immerse myself once again in city ways was in part caused by my errand; I could never have imagined, when I first laid eyes on Lizzie, that her little hand on my arm would lead me to such a place.

Helena had not smiled as I left the cottage and she did not wave a handkerchief in farewell. I wished it had not been so; I wished I had known how to break the silence that had crept between us. I only hoped she would conduct herself well during my absence. I could not abide the thought of her traipsing and dancing through the village, around the green, past that blasted oak. I could not bear the thought of the folk watching; I would not have any of mine gawped upon in such a fashion, to have her beauty and gentility mocked by uncouth ignorance.

I had looked back only once to see her standing at the door, her cool, smooth forehead unlined, her deep, liquid eyes in shadow so that I could not see their expression. At least she had not turned away as soon as I set foot upon the white road—indeed, she had not moved at all. She could have been standing in that place for ever, her straight figure belonging behind the little green gate, and I pushed away the uncomfortable ideas that presented themselves to my mind at the sight of her.

I had not locked the door behind me—indeed, I saw no way that I could do so, even had I any desire to shut my wife in a prison of her own. At least she had been calm, to all outward appearance anyway, when I gave my explanation for leaving her; that I was trying to ascertain the facts of a crime and nothing more. I had not permitted myself to dwell on whether my words were true.

Now the train had swept me from her, along with all the foolish superstitions which riddled the place like worms in wood. I left behind me only a trail of steam—that, and one thing else; a rather unfortunate mishap which I hoped did not bode ill for my journey. We had not long left Kelthorpe when there came a cry of "Fire, fire!" and everyone rushed to press their faces to that rattling window. I turned myself to see a mass of gold: a hay field, and at first I could not know what was the matter, until I saw a plume of smoke rising from one of the ricks. A flying cinder from the train must have landed there, and men were swarming towards it, trying to seize bundles of hay and carry them to safety before the fire could spread, but it had done so already: the hay was dry and desiccated, and caught at once.

I saw no more; it was swiftly behind us. We jounced along and I settled into my seat, reminded uncomfortably of the unease which could exist between progress and country, rationalism and superstition. I reminded myself on which side of the argument I stood, and I found myself thinking of the wise woman who epitomised all that I hated about Halfoak: its ignorance, its reliance on outmoded ideas, a belief in a magic which could never have existed. I wondered how her stupidity could be called "wise." Surely it was only out of some primitive fear of bewitchment or the evil eye; a similar reason for the fairies being called the "good" folk. Should she too not be dragged from her filthy hovel and into the light?

I could almost hear her laughter echoing from the walls about me now, clouding my brain with anger as if she had indeed bewitched me with some curse. I could still see her expression as she looked out of her window at my wife. The idea that she had ever come to exert any degree of control over what had happened to sweet Lizzie was dreadful to me. I wondered if the constable even knew of the beldam's part in this sad affair. Should she too be locked away and awaiting the Assizes? I was not yet ready to consider speaking to him, however. I must see Jem Higgs for myself, and after that, I might know what I should do.

The warden threw open yet another heavy door, which squealed on its hinges as it revealed an ill-lit stairway leading down. It might have been the opening to Hell itself, which was no doubt fitting enough. "Through here," he said, in a voice as roughly formed as the stone steps. I shivered. The walls exuded a cold dampness that penetrated my bones. I could see the rot blackening the brick. This was no modern conception of a gaol, no Panopticon; but some measure of satisfaction came over me that all was so dismal and disheartening.

The broad-shouldered fellow led the way, his bulk almost brushing the irregular walls, ducking as we passed beneath a lintel scarred with indecipherable scratches. The passage tended downward until we turned a corner, like Athenian sacrifices in the labyrinth of the Minotaur, and a row of doors was revealed, each with a small hatch set into it.

The warden jangled his keys on their great iron ring as if he were warning the inmates to silence, and at that moment I did not know what had possessed me to come. I should be at my desk in the City, taking care of some minutiae of a contract or writing in the ledger. I should be sitting beside my wife as she bent over her sewing. I had not informed my father that I had come here; I could not begin to imagine what he would think of the undertaking.

There was to be no halting it now. As the warden led the way to a door just like all of the others, a series of pictures suddenly rose before me: all the possibilities I had ever imagined of my cousin's murderer's face, like photographs capturing only the most miserable ideas and iniquitous of features. There were bullet-shaped skulls and beetling foreheads; dark, sunken eyes; surly mouths; jutting, gallows chins; in short, all the most ignoble examples of physiognomy that could be conjured by a heated mind.

The door opened. A thin figure stood respectfully within, his head bowed, his arms hanging loosely by his sides. He had not yet been convicted, so he did not wear the broad arrow; his grey uniform hung from him in swags cut for a more substantial fellow. His face was hidden from me and I was thanking my Maker for this mercy when he raised his head.

It is universally thought that interior ugliness does not always reveal itself by exterior show, but I could never consider even moderately prepossessing the appearance of the devil who had murdered my cousin. And yet still he revealed a well-shaped face, a straight nose, a fair-set forehead unmarked by care and cheeks that were only slightly hollowed from privation. But it was his eyes that I most desired to see, and I looked into them most intently. They were blue, the exact colour of the morning sky. It struck me that they were too pale, that they betrayed his weakness of character; indeed, his guilt; but I knew if I had met him in some other circumstance I should never have thought it. In truth, I could see no evil in them. His character must therefore be a matter of clever concealment, for I should have thought him simply a man. The imprint of what he had done, if anything were open to view, rested only in his sagging frame, which spoke of quiescent exhaustion. I may not have been able to make out his wickedness, but I saw a man close to dashing all hope away, and I was glad of it.

I examined his little cell. Its contents were few and mean: a narrow pallet took up one side, its straw stuffing poking through holes in the thin sacking; the very sight set me to itching. The farthest corner held a bucket, its ill-fitting lid failing to keep its foetor from my nostrils. A simple shelf held a cup, a jug and a Bible. A tiny window was barred with iron; there was no other ventilation, only a cold exudation rising from the stone floor.

That was all, save for a further bucket, full of twisted strands of unravelled fibres, and beside it, a solid lump of unmatted rope, black with a tarry substance which I now noticed also coated Jem Higgs' fingers: an outward sign perhaps of his black heart. He had been passing his time picking oakum, and I dared hope, thinking upon his crime. He surely deserved worse punishment—the treadmill or the hand-crank—but after his conviction he would instead find his life's surcease at another rope's end.

The warden rasped something about *minutes* as the door clanged closed. I was alone with my cousin's murderer, and I did not know where to begin.

I watched for some sneer to appear on his features, or some other sign of his depravation, but there was nothing, not even curiosity. I opened my mouth, still not sure what I should ask: was he sorry? Did it not try his soul to have ended the life of so sweet a creature? Instead, I blurted, "Did you truly believe your story? Did you honestly think her a changeling?"

At first he only twitched his lips, as if he were unused to their operation and was only now finding their purpose. "I knew she weren't me wife, sir. She wan't the person I wed."

A thousand words struggled to my lips. "She was sweetness itself. She was a bird."

"If you say so." He shrugged.

"I do say so."

He raised his eyebrows as if wondering how I could ever have heard of her, and I was reminded uncomfortably of the years that had passed in which I had never seen her, had barely even thought of her. His features lapsed into a languid exhaustion. "'Appen that's why they wanted 'er. I allus said she 'ad the prettiest voice in 'Alfoak."

"Whatever do you mean?"

"They say the hidden people watch out for the best on us, sir. They only want the lightest and fairest. I reckon it were 'er voice that did for my Lizzie. She were a songbird, all right. I reckon they 'eard 'er singin' and knew she belonged wi' them an' not wi' us."

His words were so close to my own thoughts that I could scarcely believe he had uttered them. And it struck me for the first time that, albeit by marriage alone, I was related to this man. We were kin; cousins even.

He turned to look at me and I had the disconcerting feeling that he was reading my thoughts. "Who are you?"

I drew myself up and informed him that I was the murdered lady's cousin. He merely narrowed his eyes and said, "Tha's got summat of it on you, I can tell. Been to 'Alfoak, 'aven't you?"

I opened my mouth to reply and found I could not. I had not just "been to 'Alfoak"; I was living in his house and sitting by his fire. I had looked into his private rooms; I had seen the spectacle of my wife prancing in his wife's dress.

"I'd watch it, if I was you."

I lifted my head, suddenly feeling as if I were the prisoner and he the warden.

"Look too 'ard, an' you'll fade," he said. "If yer too interested in t' 'idden people, yer won't 'ave nowt left for ordin'ry things. They call it an 'alf-dream. It's like a spell they cast."

I shook my head. This was not to be borne—I was not the one to be questioned. I straightened and said, "Elizabeth gave you cause to hate her, did she not? How long was it since you had decided you wanted her dead? What made you think of concealing your actions with such a fantastical tale—was it your acquaintance, the wise woman?"

It was his turn to be mute.

"Did Elizabeth beg you for mercy when you held her over the fire? As—as she—"

He shifted his head, but instead of the expected defiance, I saw that his eyes were brimming with tears. "It weren't 'er, sir," he whispered. "It couldn't 'a been 'er."

"No, of course it could not. How easy it would be for you if your story could only be true; if you did not burn your wife but merely rid the village of some hobgoblin that had come to haunt it. If she were not even a human being at all, let alone—let alone the very one you had promised to love, to take care of all her days. Be a man! Confess what you did, if not to your gaolers, then tell it to me. I have to hear it. I *need* to hear it!"

"It in't no tale." His voice was rasping and low. "If it were 'er, what 'appened to 'er? What made 'er say the things she did? Why would she—?"

"Why would she what?"

He stared down at the floor, gathering himself. "She weren't me wife, sir. I in't makin' it up. I knew it 'ud be trouble, bein' in that 'ouse, so near that 'illtop. But it were a fine 'ouse, see, a good 'ouse, an' she were a fine lass, our Lizzie. She said she wanted summat better than were in t' village, an' if I wanted a body like 'er fer a wife I 'ad ter gi' it to 'er. An' so I did it, I took it, an—an I'm sorry fer it! Better I'd never clapped eyes on that 'ouse, or on 'er—"

I waited.

"So they took 'er, t' folk did. They must 'ave. An' I knew it were a changeling in 'er stead, on account o' right when she came, I noticed t' mop-stick were missin'."

I blinked.

"They take a stock o' wood, see? An' they spell it to look like t' one they stole. So that's what they must 'ave done. An' I tried all sorts, sir. I tried wards an' charms an' 'erbs an' all I could do to get 'er back again. After that, fire was t' only way. It's all that were left. Aye, an I'll tell yer what, it would 'ave worked, an' all! I should 'ave been there, see, to fetch my real Lizzie back from t' 'ill, when t' moon were full, only they took us off an' wun't let us go."

The silence lay deep. Of course, he must cling to his story; it was all that stood between him and the gallows. It would take a greater skill than mine to see to the bottom of the matter. All I knew for certain was that my cousin was gone, and that there was nothing but a question where she had been: an empty space, something like the memory of a song.

His eyes narrowed. "Tha knows summat," he said. "Tha must 'ave found it."

I started. "Whatever do you mean?"

"Tha knows—about 'er an' 'im."

"Him?"

He turned and spat upon the floor. "Tha said I'd got cause. Well, mebbe I 'ad, but I'm more a man than 'im for all that. It din't matter, see, what she'd done, not ter me. I put 'er to t' fire cos I 'ad ter, an' that was all. But you 'ave to tell 'em."

"Tell them what, pray? Tell whom?"

"Tell 'em where yer found it. 'Er journal."

I pressed my lips together.

"Tha did, din't tha? It's writ all ower yer. 'Ow'd you know, otherwise?" His expression changed, turning to one of pleading. "Tha's got ter tell 'em. Please, sir."

"I did not. I found nothing."

"Yer must 'ave." He almost wailed the words. "It's t' only thing—"

"No."

His eyes narrowed. "I've teld yer nowt but t' truth."

"And I—"

"Aye?"

Blood suffused my cheeks. I turned from him and hurried to the door. I beat twice upon it and the sound rang hollowly along the passage.

"No! Tha can't just go."

Footsteps grew louder in the passage.

"I—I'll prove it to yer!"

I turned to see Higgs crouching like a feral creature, his hands clawing at his face. "Dig 'er up!" he said.

I stared at him.

"It's nowt but a stock o' wood—you'll see!"

"A stock of wood?" I spoke coldly. "I *did* see her, man. I saw what you did. I cut a lock of hair from her poor scorched head—"

A frown crossed his features, but he shook it away. "It'll not work till she's back under t' ground! Aye, dead and buried, as all should think— once she's there, back in t' earth where she came from, she'll turn back into what she is!" He lunged across the cell and grabbed at my sleeve. "I burned t' firewood, sir, an' that's all. Tha'll see! Just dig 'er up—"

The door opened. The warden strode in, saw the prisoner grasping at me, stepped forward and struck him a resounding blow with his stick.

I ducked beneath his arm and as I moved into the passage, I caught a last glimpse of Higgs' pale face, a streak of blood running from his skull. I could still hear the man calling after me, undiminished, "Dig 'er up! It's t' only way—just dig 'er up!"

I heard more thuds of the warden's stick and the voice was quelled at last. The warden locked the door upon his prisoner and turned, straightening his jacket and his countenance. I felt I should calm my own racing heart, but I could not. My cheeks still burned, and I burned inwardly too. Jem Higgs was a murderer, and yet he had forced me into a falsehood. I told myself that it was only to be expected as a sign of his wickedness, that he could force others to wickedness; and yet . . . *and yet.*

I heard his cries as the warden showed me out of the maze, not in reality, but in my mind: *Dig 'er up—dig 'er up!* It was the call of a madman, an incurable. Did he intend to escape the noose, if not by his wild story, then by going to Bedlam? Did he think *me* not in possession of my senses? He surely could not imagine I would consider the notion, even for an instant. Still, it instilled into my mind the most dreadful images. I could see her beneath the ground, shut into her tiny coffin, her body frozen and stiff. I could see her face with its wide white grin, the only part of her that was not just as he said: a blackened stock of wood.

I banished the thought. Jem Higgs was an evil man, steeped in evil deeds, and I should have anticipated that nothing but evil would come of my visit. I should leave the discovery of the truth and the administering of justice to those who were most fitted for it. I should collect my wife and leave Yorkshire for ever, removing once again to my father's high ceilings and calm rooms, the epitome of civilised society so different from everything I had known and seen since I first set eyes on Halfoak.

Chapter Twenty-One

That evening, before retiring to my hotel, I wandered about the cobbled streets. There was no train to Kelthorpe until the next day, the timetable not being quite so regular as could be wished. The stationmaster had merely shrugged when I quizzed him on the matter, as if to say, *What shall I do? For no one wishes to go there*, and I could only nod in a resigned fashion, for I did not entirely wish to go there either.

Now I walked upon a well-paved footway, free of wheel-ruts and the leavings of horses, passed by only shop-boys hurrying about their errands, a sandwich-man carrying boards advertising mustard, a constable whose breath bore no taint of drink and ladies whose bonnets were prettily bedecked with ribbons and frills. The day had continued as grey and dull as ever; even sunset left no trace of rose upon the sky, and I was relieved at the sight of it. It was so calming to be cool! To wander about at leisure without the oppressive sun beating down upon me at every moment. There was only the thought of Helena waiting for me, anxious and alone, to weigh upon my shoulders, and I wore that lightly enough, for the thought had seized hold of me that tomorrow—yes, tomorrow, we would return home to London.

I looked down at the smuts that had irreversibly smeared my coat. Such was the province of the city; I could smell the taint of coal-smoke even now entering my lungs. But here, all was *rational*. The people about me were engaged in the solid and practical requirements of business. Here, men believed only in what was true; what they could see and touch and prove; and as the church bells chimed the hour, I felt glad to be standing within it. Another turn, and a fine chapel came into view: there was its clock, steadily measuring out the days, with its hour-hand and a single minute-hand, thus brooking no confusion. Everything was ordered and in its place, and it acted as a salve upon my heart.

I wandered a little longer before turning towards my lodgings and retiring to my room. The bed was a little hard but comfortable, well-curtained against draughts, and as far as I could ascertain, without any miniature intruders. My head sank into the pillow, which rose in two clouds on either side of my ears, and I listened to the old accustomed sounds of evening: the rumble of wheels on a well-paved road; the rattle of shutters, and not a single tweet of a lark or hoot of an owl.

I listened for them, and found I could barely sleep a wink.

The following morning I was roused early when the maid of all work came to set a fire in the grate. Still half in the land of sleep, I informed her it was an extravagance that would not be required, though the moment she left I realised the room was rather chill after my days of waking under Halfoak's summer skies. It was of no consequence; I would not be lingering long enough for a fire to heat the room.

I broke my fast hastily and took my leave for the station. Before long I was rushing through the world once more, on my way towards the countryside and eager to see my wife, and hoping that the hay-ricks might have been moved a little farther from the rails.

Chapter Twenty-Two

The progress of the horse and cart was sleepy in comparison with the rush of iron and fire and steam; the irregularity of the country lanes made it impossible to rest, as did the ceaseless chasing of my thoughts. I looked out instead at the fields and could not help being a little dismayed by the sight. As I neared Halfoak, all had turned to summer once again, and yet it now had become evident that the picture it offered of bucolic contentment—like to something in a painting—was superficial only.

The carrier had lately informed me that we had reached the "owd squire's lands." The corn harvest had been "fossed to begin," he informed me, too early, before the hay was even in, and I could indeed see men setting about the golden ears with their sickles, followed by women gathering and tying the swathes into bundles, children gleaning what had fallen, and behind them all, partridges pecking at what was left.

Despite the clearness of the sky, each little group appeared half hidden in a mist; I realised the phenomenon was caused not by the heat or insects attracted to their sweat, but by the sheer quantities of chaff which floated about them as they worked. I wondered what it must be like to breathe it in, and soon discovered the answer for myself as we passed through a drift of it; it combined with the white dust thrown up by the horse's steady plod first to dry my tongue, and after a short time to tickle my throat and I started coughing. I noticed then that many of the workers wore cloths about their faces. And I saw too that the crop was not golden, that it had passed beyond golden to a pale withered brown that spoke of friability; it must surely crumble to pieces as quickly as it was gathered in.

"It's too 'ot for owt," the carrier proclaimed over his shoulder. "It's not right, it's not, an' that's a fact."

I made some offering of condolence. So many days I had spent among the country folk, and I had not realised that they might be facing a tragedy more wide-reaching than my own.

It's allus summer, under there—that's all I'm sayin'.

Should 'ave 'ad a bit o' rain.

It'll keep t' door open, till she comes back.

I shook myself to wakefulness as the sudden jolt of the cart announced our arrival. I was once more in Halfoak, standing before its blasted tree and its quiet inn and its church tower with too many hands upon its clock. I was back where it had all begun, and for a moment I did not quite know how I had come to be there.

I counted out the agreed fivepence fare for the carter and alighted, set to walk once more upon the white road to the fairy hill, where I had so short a time ago taken leave of my wife.

It was not long until I stood before the little cottage, so familiar now to my eye, suspended halfway up that oddly shaped prominence. All was peace; the door was safely closed. In another moment I realised that the windows were tightly closed too, in spite of the heat, and that furthermore, the whole *place* felt closed. I knew, before I even looked inside, that the cottage was empty.

I hurried from room to room, calling Helena's name, but she did not reply and the things I saw only increased my confusion. Everything was the image of polished, shining tidiness, as if a small army had been at work in my absence. The larder was gleaming, the shelves newly stocked, a fresh jug of milk standing upon the stone shelf, covered by a little cloth fringed with beads. The range had been swept and black-leaded, the open grate filled with coals. The deal table had been scoured. Outside, bright sheets, half damp, were hung to dry. And yet the cottage was as empty as the day I had first seen it.

I rushed upstairs to the bedroom I had occupied and peered into the loose wainscoting wherein was concealed the journal. The item was still there and I was at once relieved and repelled to see it; I did not touch it, not then. My denial of its existence to the husband of its writer had made of it a distasteful secret.

Helena had left, it seemed. She had packed her portmanteau and apparently taken her leave, so eager to resume her old life that she could not bring herself to await my return. But how had she accomplished such a feat of tidiness, and why would she trouble to do so?

I went into her room. There, upon the little birch washstand were her hairbrush and pins, her toothpowder, her bandoline, smelling sweetly of bergamot and lemon. I went to the wardrobe, and there were her clothes, all neatly folded upon its shelves, her bonnets hanging on the little pegs.

She had not gone. She had not left me. There was no time for relief, however, for the question followed hard upon that realisation: where had she gone?

I returned to the parlour and finally noticed what I should have seen before: a calling card set upon the table. I picked it up and examined it, and could scarcely have felt greater surprise than if it had been left by the fairies. The name neatly printed upon the card was "Calthorn"; it did not need much deduction for me to conjecture that a visit had been paid by none other than the young squire's mother.

My second thought was one of horror: had my wife really gone alone to return the call? When I had last seen her out of doors she had been cavorting in the moonlight . . . but I had found her before simply taking the air upon the hillside; she might have gone there again. And yet I knew that she had not.

I hurried out into the sun once more and started back the way I had come. The heat was more concentrated than before, the sun baking the world, the sky innocent of any cloud. My frock-coat and hat were interminably hot. Perspiration ran freely down my face; my kerchief was soon damp from wiping it away. The dust from the road was more infuriating than ever. My steps began to meander sidelong across the rutted track and I was forced to concentrate to keep to the straightest way. My head swam; my thoughts were muddled. I glanced up to see someone looking back at me. I half-expected a fox-haired little fellow with merry cheeks, but it was a woman, her face darkly shadowed under the brim of her bonnet, standing on the other side of a gate. I prepared to hail her, but she turned and bent once more to her task, attempting to tie a stem of corn around a stook, but it kept breaking, so dry as it was; everything was so dry. This summer, so fine a thing, was turning to a curse. The earth was parched. It was unnatural—it was *abominable*.

I forced my steps onward, my mind wandering, seeing only the ground at my feet. Inwardly I was focused on something else entirely: a thin bright gleam. At first I did not know what it was; at last I saw that it was an iron blade, set into the earth.

It'll keep t' door open, till she comes back.

It must be removed. If the blade was gone, the door would close. The gateway to the land where it was always summer would shut. The heat of it would stop, entombed inside the hollow hill so it could no longer taint our skies. The dreadful burning that had consumed my cousin, that now consumed the place where she had lived, would come at last to an end.

I shook my head, dismissing such ideas. They were false visions conjured by the sun, nothing more. I looked up and saw the squire's residence at last, partially hidden by the undulating field which lay before it. There was a stile set into the stone wall. I took a deep breath, and felt better at once. I climbed over and began to walk across the field. The irregular stubble, all that remained of the cut corn, hissed against my feet, turning my steps and threatening my ankles. Despite the harvest, something still grew among the dried stalks, I noticed: little globular fungi pushed up from the earth, reminding me unpleasantly of scalps half buried in the ground.

I had thought the field empty, but when I looked about me I saw a little gathering of workers settling down to eat their heels of bread and wedges of yellow cheese. My throat felt drier than ever at the sight. They noticed me watching and stared back at me in astonishment; the rumble of impertinent laughter drifted through the syrupy air. I did not heed it. The grand house was coming into view, already close enough to make out that it was not so grand as I had expected. Throstle Grange was spacious enough, without being extravagantly large, and judging by the crumbling garden wall clasped in a death's grip by strands of ivy, it was not in the first state of repair.

I remembered what Widdop had said: that the squire was ill and his wife entirely engaged in his care, and the son too dissolute to manage everything as it should be.

I neared the top of the field, dismayed to find that there was no corresponding stile at this side; indeed, there was no wall, just a hedge of thickset hawthorn, and only a narrow gap leading through it, choked with nettles and the peeking crimson of poppies. I thought once more of the fellow I had glimpsed, his hair red as a fox, laughing as he sucked the juice from a ripe plum—he had vanished into the hedge so easily, so perhaps it was not so thick. And anyway, I could not bring myself to go back around.

I lowered my head and pushed my way in among the thorns, to find the gap narrower even than it had appeared. My hat was lifted from my head by pliant twigs; my hands stung with nettles; a sharp thorn laid a scratch across my forehead. I rubbed it with my handkerchief and it came away bloody. I retrieved my hat, the silk quite ruined, and stumbled into a narrow lane of churned mud now baked solid. It ran along the length of the field and at its end, turned around a corner that led down towards the road to Halfoak. I cursed my luck that I had ever seen the stile. If I had gone on but a little further, the way would have been clear before me. I brushed my frock-coat free of the twigs and thorns, but I could not rid the cloth of the smear of sap.

Ahead of me was a pair of wide wrought-iron gates, which were thrown open. The wall itself was more imposing than it had first appeared and it blocked from view all but the upper storey of the property, which was of brick. Through the opening I could see the entrance, a double doorway painted black and polished to a high gleam, bordered by two stone planters, each with a dead bay tree standing forlorn within it. I stepped forward to see the windows, tall sashes elegantly curtained, and a little more of the yard, which was in sore need of sweeping. Several bantams, prettily barred and speckled, scratched and pecked and dropped their feathers in the dust. A tump of turnips was gracelessly mounded in one corner. Then I forgot my curiosity because the fine black doors swung open and my wife emerged between them.

I heard the sweetness of her voice as she expressed some pleasantry and I saw her smile as she stepped out. She wore a pretty white dress with a blue flower print and a beribboned bonnet, and she looked cool and respectable as she put up her parasol to cast a little shade across her face.

A figure appeared in the doorway behind her, a young man with black hair curling down over his ears. His somewhat aquiline nose only slightly marred his otherwise neat features. He was as broad-shouldered as a labourer and yet his stance was louche; as I watched he placed one hand high on the doorjamb and leaned negligently against it. Rumours of his indolence had led me to expect him to be on the verge of manhood, but he was not; he was in his late twenties, about my own age, and easily at a stage in life to have found some useful purpose.

His lip twisted into something that was half amusement, half leer, and as I watched, he winked at my wife's retreating form.

Blood suffused my features. It must be the squire's son; no servant would lounge in so slovenly a fashion. But Helena did not look back at him. Indeed, she had not moved, but just stood there quite frozen, staring straight at me. Her expression had been overtaken by one of horror—it seemed to me she gazed upon an apparition.

I glanced behind me, her countenance being such that I half imagined some monstrous beast standing at my back, then I looked down at myself and surveyed my own attire: my greened, stained coat, my trousers covered in chaff and dust. I felt a trickle of sweat—or was it blood?—run from beneath my much-scratched hat and settle upon my eyebrow. I sensed all the impropriety of my sudden appearance there and—although how I could possibly evade the notice of Edmund Calthorn, I didn't know—I stepped rapidly aside so that I was hidden behind the gatepost.

A moment later, low words were exchanged and gruff laughter cut into the air, and there came the sound of a door closing. I cursed myself. What had I been thinking? He must have seen me. And why should I be so ashamed that I had taken to skulking behind a gate in such a fashion?

But it was too late to be anything otherwise than what I was: a foolish spectacle, the subject of laughter even from farm labourers.

There came Helena's light step and in another moment her shadow fell across my feet. I did not entirely wish to see her expression, but when I raised my head, her face was as sweet as the day we married—no, sweeter. She showed no sign of noticing my appearance; she simply put out her hand and I roused myself and lent her my arm. Her fingers did not recoil from its dampness.

"Have you come to take me home, Husband?"

I did not know how to answer. My thoughts were as disordered as my appearance. I thought of how I had determined to return to my father's house, to really conduct her home at last, but it seemed such a long way away.

"Be careful the fairies don't steal your tongue, my dear," she said.

An' then he reached out wi' 'is thumb an' finger an' 'e plucked it out!

My arm twitched, but again Helena did not notice anything awry.

"Have you been visiting?" I forced myself at last to make civil enquiry.

"I have, Husband. I *have* been visiting. The squire's mother kindly called upon me this forenoon. She excused her husband and son for not calling upon you first, as was proper; I do not believe they hold to the conventions in Halfoak as in other places. It had come to her attention that I was at the cottage and she was most concerned. She was quite horrified to find me left alone in such a place, and where a young lady's life had so recently ended. She thought it terrible indeed, and bade me to spend some time at the Grange, as early as I might."

I remained silent, but Helena went on, "She offered most kindly to send a gig for me this afternoon, but I insisted upon walking. It is so fine a day, is it not? Everything is so sure underfoot that it is really quite easy. And so I came, only to find her troubled with a rather severe headache. Fortunately her son was at home. He was so attentive!"

"How kind of him."

"Yes. Yes, he is. Very kind."

"And yet—" *That was not what I had heard of him*, I wanted to add, but then, the fellow had conducted himself with propriety; such could not be said for me. I could only imagine his contempt at seeing me in my dishevelled state. I had been brought low—and anyway, who was I to question his kindness? I, who had been absent whilst my wife sat alone.

I realised we were halfway along the road. I could hear bright whistling drifting across the fields. I recognised the tune at once.

As I walked out one sweet morning . . .

"Are you quite well, my dear?" Helena asked.

I told myself that the mocking tone in her voice was merely my own imagining, though I could not bring myself to answer.

We walked on in silence, hearing only the sound of our own steps. Pudding Pye Hill soon came into view, the little path cutting its way up through the green, and I could hear the blissful sound of the trickling brook. Another noise broke into the babble: a sharp giggle, making me start, though in the next moment I saw the cause. A little girl was chasing a magpie along the bridge. It settled directly above the stream and she flapped her arms. It regarded her before taking wing and I heard the whirr of its rapid movement as it departed in a series of black and white flashes.

She lifted her head and sang after it,

> *Tell-pie-tit*
> *Thy tongue'll split*
> *An' ev'ry dog in the town'll get a little bit!*

My initial consternation gave way to amusement at her charming game, but my mood darkened again; I could but hope that Edmund Calthorn were not such a "tell-pie-tit" as to put it about that I was a crazed buffoon.

The girl—I recognised her suddenly as Flora, the child of Mary Gomersal—leaned out over the bridge, spilling more of her wild laughter into the air, and a moment later a second head, its bonnet strings undone, poked up from beneath the bridge to meet her. I caught my breath and almost shouted a warning, but the older girl emerged and scrambled up the banking, her hands filled with dripping watercress.

The younger child's shrill voice rang out once more, "Hurry, hurry! Don't touch t' water! Peggy Greenteeth'll steal you away!"

They ran, squealing with merriment, towards the village. The bright droplets that had spilled behind them turned to dark circles on the road.

" 'Urry up," said Helena. "It's not right far now."

I turned, slowly, to look at her. She merely twisted her head and met my eyes; under her bonnet, hers were shining darkly bright, like a bird's.

"Are you all reet, Albie?"

"I—I—"

"Tha dun't look so good."

"No, I—Helena—"

"What is it, petal?"

She had never called me such before. Had I really heard her speaking that way, as the country folk did?

"It's 'ow yer like it, in't it? In't it what tha came a-searchin' for?"

I suddenly slumped, and her fingers clawed into my arm and she held me steady.

"Helena, whatever do you mean by this? Why are you speaking that way? Pray, stop." I felt the ghost of another hand taking my arm: Lizzie's light touch upon mine.

She stands at your side, my dear—that is her place, is it not? She is there now, see? She reaches for your arm.

I shook my head. "I don't feel . . . Helena, let us go inside."

A shy smile crossed her features, a real one this time, making her look younger. "I 'aven't seen it yet." She paused. "The cottage, that is, love. We in't there yet. Why dun't you tell me, Albie, do you like me new bonnet?" She let go of my arm at last and stood before me, curtsying this way and that so that I could see. My heart froze. Had someone given it to her? Had I not seen it before, many times? I was almost certain I had. What was in my mind, though, was a slim volume tucked into a gap in the wainscoting; a secret volume; a secret gap.

"Well, love? What's tha reckon?"

"I—I like it, my dear."

She tipped her head back, letting out a peal of laughter. It was coarse, uncouth, and I could not bear it, no more than I could bear the roughness of her words. What had been charming on my cousin's lips was execrable coming from Helena's.

"Are yer tellin' me a falsehood, Albie? Come on, now. Tha wun't tell no untruth, would yer?"

I shook my head. Was my wife possessed? How *had* she become so changed? And yet the explanation must be simple, as such things always turned out to be. She must know of the journal—she had found it and read it; she knew that I had concealed it from her. She knew everything, though I knew not how. But she could not, could she? The only person who could possibly have known that was dead: my cousin. If she had indeed been my cousin. If the person standing in front of me was indeed my wife.

I stumbled, and once more she caught me, but I drew away from the touch of her hand. I could not bear it.

"Suit theesen," she said smartly, and walked up the hill ahead of me, her step as elastic as ever, unbowed by the heat or the distance or my distress or anything at all. As she went, the sunlight rested upon her, caressing the line of her cheek, making her curls appear almost golden where they emerged beneath her bonnet at the nape of her neck.

I fell to my knees. I did not feel them strike the ground.

Above me, she opened the gate and walked up the path, though I could not make her out between the lupins and foxgloves nodding their heads over the fence. I did not see her go inside.

I pushed myself up and started after her. What else could I do?

I stumbled at last over the threshold, grateful to be enveloped by cool shadows. A loud clatter rang out from the parlour and I entered to see Helena throwing open the windows. She glanced at me and wafted a hand under her nose as if there were some awful smell. "Pah!" she said. "In't it nasty, that—that *people*-smell!"

I sank wordlessly into a chair while she bustled about me. After a while she pushed a glass of water into my hand. I sniffed at it—it smelled of iron, of hedgerows, of plums, and I did not like it but regardless, I sipped it. Other than that, I could smell nothing at all. The parlour had borne no trace of a scent, though the heavy sweetness of honeysuckle was now drifting inside, and there was something else. *The sap*, I thought, *it's rising*, and I did not know why I thought that. Was that not a matter for spring? My temples throbbed and I squeezed my eyes shut.

When I opened them, I was in my room, lying upon my own bed, and the rest of the house was silent. I had no memory of how I had come to be there, unless it were the hazy recollection of a little hand under my arm, leading me upward.

I let my head fall to the side so that I could see the wainscoting. It looked just as it had before. I wished to examine it more minutely, but I could not move. It was not simply the heaviness of my exhaustion; it was as if some spell had weighted my limbs. I could not even consider moving. I tried to speak, but my lips were still and no sound emerged, not even a whisper.

I let my eyes fall closed, telling myself that it was merely fatigue. I needed to sleep. I need not worry about Helena. I knew that she was somewhere below because I could hear her moving around, putting all in its right place. As sleep came, the thought stole upon me like a certainty: there was no possibility that I could go home now, not with Helena in her condition; not with me in mine.

Chapter Twenty-Three

I was not certain what hour it was when I awoke, for the room lay in half-light, though the curtains were partly drawn over the shutters. It was the light of a dream, and I did indeed feel as if I were still dreaming. At least the dreadful heaviness had passed; in fact, my whole body felt light, as if at any moment I might float into the air.

I could recall only fragmented images from my sleep: an opening—no, a doorway—in a rock, a lady standing within it, her form miniature and perfect and beautiful. She wore a crown and flowing green robes, and she smiled upon me. There was a scent—I do not think I had ever dreamed such before—but so it was, the aromatic sweetness of ripe and lovely fruit, and I was steeped in it; the juice was dripping from my chin, running from my fingers, and I felt its life seeping into me, reaching my very soul. I realised too that there was music; it came to me gradually, as if that were the only way of safely taking in such an intense sensation without being overwhelmed. And such music it was! Such things as dreams are made on, as the Bard had it. And it roused in me such longing, such a wild and terrible yearning, that it took a moment for me to realise that some dim echo of it had followed me into wakefulness.

I slipped from my bed and went to the window, my limbs still too light. The odd glow was coming from the moon. It must now be waning, but its crimson face shone out, adorned by ragged tendrils of cloud. The music grew louder—someone was playing a fiddle. An awful restlessness stole upon me; it was as if I truly had eaten fairy fruit and was now compelled to join the dance. I felt the call of it—nay, the command—in every muscle and sinew and fibre.

I started as something silvery flashed past in the outer gloom, thinking of a stately procession emerging from a dark door; then it was gone. An owl? I blinked, making out the rough outlines of the garden, its black and rotting mounds of tangled abandonment, and I saw another pale shape, surely larger than the first. It shifted as I watched, like some voluminous, billowing gown. And then I realised what it was and I leaned upon the sill. It was the washing; only that. It still hung there, unclaimed. I still did not know how Helena had contrived to do it; her hand had never been turned to such in her life; she surely could not have lifted a single copper of water.

Fairy struck. Fairly struck.

I closed my eyes. Perhaps this was the half-dream Jem Higgs had spoken of. Perhaps he had felt it too, leaning out of this very window. If he had done so on a night like this one, there was little wonder he had succumbed. The moon had the look of wickedness, the garden of decay; no good could come of such a night. It was fit only for necromancy and nefarious deeds. Why, if I were a simpler man, one prone to action without consideration, perhaps I would do as Higgs had commanded me: I would take a spade from the outhouse and travel by the shadows of that witch-light to the graveyard, and I would *dig 'er up!*

I shook my head. I barely knew where my thoughts were coming from. Now I was tapping out some rapid rhythm upon the window-sill with my thumbnail, *Rat-ta-ta-ta-ta-TAT!*, and the music had taken up residence in my feet, my hands, my skull; for I was shifting and nodding and tapping where I stood as if crazed by its calling.

The bed was in disarray, the covers crumpled and sweat-dampened. I did not wish to lie down again, so instead I crept quietly down the stairs, expecting at any moment some dreadful creak to tell of my passing and conjure my wife's presence.

The treads did not creak. Her door did not open. I imagined her in her room, sweetly sleeping—or what if the thing she had become, that awful, mocking, disdainful thing, did not sleep? What if she were merely lying there now, her eyes open and staring at the ceiling until such a time as she must rise again—until daylight woke her? But they were underground creatures, were they not? They hated fire, so surely they should hate the sun too.

I closed my eyes and waited until the wave of dizziness passed, feeling the world turning about me just as it always had. I went into the parlour, again with the image of Helena rising vividly before my eyes. I half expected to see her sitting in her accustomed chair, her back perfectly straight, staring at me.

There was no one. The room was dark, the shutters tightly closed against the night, and as I felt my way across it with my hands held out before my face the thought came to me that I might touch something unexpected at any moment, something warm and pliant, fingers that would grasp my own, and it came as a relief to find only the rough wood of the kitchen door.

The window was smaller in there, and partly shaded by the elderberry tree, but it had no shutters, so the room was brighter than the parlour. The moon's ghostly light spilled across the brick floor, bringing out its ancient roughness in gleams and shadows. I went into the pantry and ran my hands across the topmost shelf, too high for my wife to reach; almost too high for me. At first I thought it empty, but then my fingertip touched the little china jug. I brought it down, and at once I could smell it, pungent and sweet and sharp, and I could see it too, even in the dim light. The darkness of its herbal contents stood out plainly against the pale china, appearing almost black where it coated the bottom.

Returning to the kitchen, I added a few drops of water from a ewer, then took a spoon, careful not to clatter it against the sides, and gently teased the stuff loose. It was thoroughly dried and at first didn't want to come, then pieces began to break away. I crushed and smeared them anew until the substance softened, taking on the consistency of a tincture.

I poured it all into the teapot, took some tea leaves and sprinkled them on top, then gave the whole another stir.

Tomorrow I would make her tea. She would drink it and then we would see what would happen.

I rinsed the china jug and replaced it upon its shelf. I eyed the teapot once more as I left the room. Like every other thing it had been rendered clean and shining, freshly polished. All was gleaming and silent, and I realised that the music which had so caught hold of my senses had fallen silent too.

Chapter Twenty-Four

I passed a hand across my eyes. My head did not ache; my limbs felt like my own once more. I felt as if I had had the deepest and most refreshing sleep, and I lay there for a time, enjoying the sensation and listening to a bird singing. I already knew that this day, like all the other days in Halfoak, would be sweet and warm and beautiful.

And then I remembered how I had awakened earlier; my sight of the red moon. Had I really roused myself in the night? Had I imagined music on the air? Had I—?

I frowned, remembering the little jug, the black residue inside it; the teapot. Had I really done that? Had I prepared such unknown stuff for my wife—something the old crone had concocted in her filthy shack? I pushed myself to my feet, remembering her words as if she spoke at my ear. *The seven cures. It's not easy to swaller.*

No, I imagined it was not. I stood, only now noticing that I was still wearing my begrimed clothing from the day before, but that was of no matter. I hurried to the door, seeing that Helena's remained closed: good. I hurried downstairs, not heeding the drumming of my steps, opened the door to the parlour and rushed inside—to see my wife, her countenance quite calm, and a young woman I did not know.

I stumbled to a halt as both of them looked up, startled. Helena's expression turned to astonishment. "Albie—why—?"

The young woman—no, a girl—stared at me, her eyes wide. She had a head of curls escaping from under her cap, and a somewhat narrow face, the features fine, if dreadfully freckled. She was outfitted as a maid.

"Perhaps a change of dress, Albie?"

I bestirred myself, turning towards my wife as she raised a cup to her lips. "Why, Husband, whatever is the matter? You have gone quite white." She frowned and this time took a deep draught of the liquid. I wanted to rush across the room and dash the cup from her hand, but how could I?

"Why do you stare so, Albie?" She forced into her voice a veneer of cordiality. "Would you like some tea?"

"No, I—do please excuse me." I turned on my heel and closed the door behind me, expecting trills of laughter to follow me up the stair, but there were none; there was no sound at all, only that of my own steps.

Before I tended to my appearance I sat on the bed, quite motionless, while my thoughts raced, quicker than I could piece them together. What on earth could a few herbs matter? It was probably a little rosemary and thyme, seasoned with chanting and nonsense. I tried to remember if I had recognised any of its contents from the odour, or from the way it had felt under the spoon, but nothing came to me. The only thing that did was the wise woman's voice:

It 'ad ter be after t' church chimed eleven and afore it struck midnight, an' then 'e'd ter put 'er to bed. After that, she'd be forced to flee up t' chimney afore sunrise, and all 'e need do then were watch for 'er, comin' out o' that gap in the 'ill—the 'ollow 'ill, unnerstand?

I had not even administered it correctly. There had been words to say too, hadn't there? Some kind of charm. Now I had wasted it. That was what actually rose to the surface of my mind, as if the beldam's mad words could even matter, but beneath it was a deeper worry, something swimming darkly at the bottom of a deep pool.

My gaze went to the wainscoting where I knew the journal was hidden. I wondered if it would hold the answer, and yet I could not bring myself to look at it, not now. It had become a guilty secret: I had told a deliberate untruth about its very existence, and in bitter circumstances I did not care to think on. The constable, I was sure, would view my actions most gravely. And that was not all: I did not wish to remove the journal from its hiding place and read because I was afraid of who might see. The notion would not leave me that some incorporeal creature would be standing at my back, peering over my shoulder, watching everything.

I shook all such phantasms from my mind and prepared to dress. It was clear to me now that I must have been suffering from some heat apoplexy, for why else would I have fallen prey to such odd ideas? A little time spent indoors would soon cure me.

And yet, the parson believed in them too, didn't he? And I had heard the fiddler playing in the darkest hours of the night . . .

So perhaps the tea would have its effect: I would return to the parlour in time to see her fly shrieking up the chimney. And then my own sweet wife would return, full of smiles and approval, her dear hand resting lightly once more upon my arm . . .

Sighing, I carried out my ablutions, changed my clothes and went downstairs to see the strange girl flicking dust from the glass case wherein stood the all-seeing fox. She spoke without turning. "The mistress is indisposed, sir. Said she was goin' back to bed."

I caught my breath. "Did she? But that's—she is not ill? I must go to her at once." My heart was thudding so hard against my ribs that the girl must surely have been able to hear it.

She turned at last, and an odd feeling came to me that I recognised her from somewhere. "She said she din't want to be disturbed, if you please, sir." She dropped an ill-formed curtsy. "She said she'd be all right, sir. She wan't ill, she said so. She said her sleep were disturbed, an' she just wanted to rest a while."

I stared at her until I realised I was making her uncomfortable, then I nodded. I went into the kitchen, saw the teapot and opened the lid, then, glancing over my shoulder to make sure the girl had not followed, I poured away its contents. The liquid looked muddy, but it smelled of nothing but tea.

When I returned to the parlour, she was still there. "May I enquire where you came from?" I asked.

The girl—she was only thirteen or fourteen—dropped into that awkward curtsy again. "Mrs. Calthorn asked me to come, sir. She said I should 'elp wi' t' washin' an' owt else yer needed me for. I came yesterday, an' all."

So that was why the washing was done; this wiry girl had accomplished it all. It was so simple an answer. "And your name?"

"Ivy Gomersal, sir."

"Gomersal?" I could not hide my surprise. I *had* seen her before: she had been gathering watercress at the stream whilst her younger sister, Flora, chased the birds.

Peggy Greenteeth'll steal you away!

All was clear. They even resembled one another, despite the freckles, and yet they were not at all like the youngest child who sat so quietly by his mother's knee, teasing his little grimalkin.

"So, you are in service at Throstle Grange?"

"Aye, sir. Just since this last month or two. They—they needed a new girl, an' me mam said I'd be all right. I've some strength in me bones, an'—well, she said nowt 'ud 'appen to one on 'er girls, an' me wi' a sensible 'ead on me shoulders an' all."

I frowned. "Meaning if you did not, you would not be all right there?"

A rather sly smirk crossed her features; she quickly wiped it from her face. "'Appen."

I remembered the squire's son, his muscular stature, his loose, almost animal posture, his insolent look, and I thought I had no need to ask her meaning.

I can kiss but I can't wed you all,
But I would if I could, great and small . . .

The girl's eyes went to her duster, but I needed to quiz her on another matter; much could be learned from an unguarded tongue. I gave a smile and said, "You would have known the occupants of this cottage, then—Lizzie Higgs?"

She looked almost startled. "A little, sir. I din't come up 'ere much. It's not a lucky—"

"Yes, yes, I know all that. What did you think of her?"

There came that sly look once more, there and gone in a moment. "Oh—well, she were too good for t' likes o' me, sir, even if she did 'ave nowt to call 'er own, an' no fambly to speak of."

I blinked at that, but nothing would be gained by betraying my feelings on the matter. "Did she not?"

"No, sir. I dun't think Mr. Higgs knew 'er fambly right well 'is sen, afore they wed. I 'eard tell there were some she could call 'er own somewhere, but they'd long left these parts. She could 'ave been owt. Or a nowt, if you take me meaning."

"I think I do." I tried not to speak too stiffly.

"Aye, sir. 'E did 'er a favour, that's what I say. An' still she were goin' on at 'im all t' time, by all accounts, wantin' a fine 'ouse like this 'un, an' all 'er pretty frocks an' ribbons an' slippers." Her expression became wistful, as if she had often coveted Lizzie's frocks and ribbons and slippers for herself.

I did not heed the pertness of her speech. "Perhaps she would have given you some of her clothes. She was a sweet girl, was she not?"

"Ha!" The exclamation broke from her before she could stop herself, and her hand shot to her mouth. She saw my astonishment and straightened her features. "Beggin' yer pardon, sir, like I said, she thought she were above the likes of me, poor or not. She were right proud, sir, an' she allus 'eld 'er 'ed very 'igh. They'll not say it, not now she's under, but it's true. An' she wun't listen. Folks tried to tell 'er—I mean—"

"Tried to tell her?"

She dipped her head in confusion. "About 'ow things are, sir, up 'ere. 'Ow there's things you shun't 'ear, an' things you shun't listen to even if tha does. An' shun't tell nowt about, if yer do." She glanced around as if anybody could be eavesdropping on her now, and she pressed her lips tightly closed.

I would get no more from her; she was obviously no more than a jealous child. She did not have the breeding, the connections, the grace of a lady like my cousin, and she could not forget it. I glanced upward, wondering how my wife was sleeping. If she was not, she might have heard our discussion through the shrunken old floorboards. There was no sound from above, however, none at all, and then Ivy's duster began to *whisk, whisk*, and I thought I would eat a little, and then step outside; I found, after all, I wished to take the air.

I resolved to walk up to the summit of Pudding Pye Hill. I was of a mind to see the country around me, all of it laid bare, without myself being seen. I fetched Helena's book from my room and secreted it within my pocket before I set out, thinking that a shady spot under the oak trees would be a capital place to refresh myself with a little reading after the walk.

The heat of the sun had already found its way beneath my hat and into my clothing before I reached the gate. It sapped the energy; there could be little surprise that Helena was fatigued. Without the herbs I had given her, she might be worse yet. Rest was what she needed.

I turned up the hill and strode out despite the almost liquid sunshine. The dandelion clocks lifted from the ground and floated around and before me, sweeping me onward and lifting my spirits. The vista was just as lovely as always, and I found myself thinking again that it was difficult to believe that Lizzie had gone. Up here, above everything, it was impossible to think that any sad event could occur to mar such a lovely place. Even the air cooled a little as I rose higher, providing the marvellous comfort of a breeze, and it was not long before I heard the soft rustle of the oaks whispering to each other across the grove. The place was enchanted, though in no unnatural or sinister way. The air was soft on my cheek and smelled of summer, and as I went the sweet, piercing song of a lark rose into the sky.

Soon another sound began to impinge upon my senses. At first I had no conception of what it might be; I stopped still and listened to the sharp little clicks that sounded like nothing so much as the snapping of tiny fingers: contemptuous, dismissive snapping—and then something leaped at the edge of my vision.

I turned, but saw only the brake of furze. There was nothing else; no one hiding amongst the bushes. Then something else snapped and jumped, and I understood: the gorse was in seed; the withered brown pods had ripened beneath the flowers. They looked as if they had been scorched upon a fire, and in a way perhaps they had, for as the sun beat down upon them another burst open and shot its seeds into the air.

I went on, my steps accompanied by the clicking and spitting, lost in a reverie until I stood beneath the trees, the green circle where fairies were said to dance already behind me. I could not remember if I had walked straight through it or gone around.

I sat beneath a tree on a flat grey stone. Halfoak was hidden by the lip of the grove, but farther in the distance were green pastures flecked with trees and sheep and cows and glittering water. Clouds clung to the horizon, casting their shadows over distant villages and towns, but there were none here; only those of the oaks, shifting at my feet like rapidly passing tides.

I took out Helena's book and resumed where I had left off. Here it felt entirely apposite—it was after all nothing but a story, its intimations of goblins and fairies, of charms and magical songs, feeling like something from a fairy tale.

As I began to read, a new sensation stole over me. The novel was nothing but a wild tale of wild folk. I had wondered if all its talk of foundlings and changelings was in some sense metaphorical, but it felt closer and more real now than ever. Perhaps there was nothing of the fairy tale about it: Heathcliff was untamed, an elemental being who belonged in the land and was of the land, and he should never have walked among ordinary men. He brought with him only jealousy and misery and corruption. Surely the author had never intended him as a human character: the word "changeling" was no mere insult, it was real, for surely, a changeling he truly was! Even the old nurse, Ellen Dean, had wished to put him out on the landing as a child, in the hope that he would disappear into the air by the morrow. It accounted for all the strangeness of the novel, and, indeed, its power.

I shook my head. The writer surely could not have meant it to be so. Heathcliff was but a man, albeit a strange one, shaped by his questionable parenthood and unstable upbringing. I pictured him leaning against a door, his posture louche and his look impertinent. He was not a good man, but he was just a man all the same, and then I reminded myself that I should not waste my time wondering if he was this or if he was that because he was, after all, no more than ink; ink on a page, and I ceased reading and stared out at the world going on beneath me while I remained suspended above it all.

A sound roused me from my stupor—not the sound of snapping fingers coming from the gorse; I had long since ceased noticing that. I shook away my drowsiness, closing the book and slipping it back into my pocket. A voice was murmuring words I could not make out. I stood hastily and slipped beneath the trees, away from the sounds. I did not know how many in Halfoak had seen me in my dishevelment, or indeed heard of it, but I did not wish for anyone to see me now. I had no mind to converse or even bid them good day. I wanted only to be alone.

I had just slipped from the edge of the clearing when the voice rang out, bright and cheerful, and a figure appeared from below me on the hillside. It was Mrs. Gomersal, and a moment later her son came into view also, skipping along and striking at the grass with a switch. I stepped farther out of sight.

She turned to him and held out her hand as if hurrying him along. His eyes were bright with life, and a babble of words spilled from him as he answered her. He sounded quite unlike the boy I had seen heretofore, nothing but an ordinary child, enjoying a walk with his mother on a fine day. I did not know how I had ever thought there was something strange about him.

Then he pulled away from her and went rushing ahead on his stubby legs, shouting "Papa, Papa!" as he stumbled into the fairy ring.

I hid myself behind a tree, an instinct akin to that which had seized me only yesterday at the Grange, though there was no reason why I should hide in such a fashion. I could only hope she had not seen, for it would serve to heap foolishness upon impropriety. I was glad that Helena was not there to witness it.

I straightened, brushing leaf mould from my clothing, meaning to call out to them as I walked back towards the edge of the grove—

And there I stopped, because my view of it was clear, and yet there was no one to be seen.

I frowned, listening. There was only the lark, soaring so high I could not see it as it sang its beautiful song. There were no voices, no footsteps; nothing at all. The fairy ring was empty. I felt as if something should have changed, a tree split asunder by lightning, perhaps, to mark their disappearance. I removed my hat and rubbed my head. *The sun*, I thought. *It was only that.*

I retreated under the trees, wanting to clear my mind, but the shadows did not help; they shifted and whispered all around me. Ahead was the little outcrop of rocks, revealing their faces from inside the hill, and the deeper shadows behind them. I did not want to go further, but I forced myself to do so. Was there really a doorway behind them? I shivered despite the heat of the day and found I could not go another step, so I turned instead, my thoughts whirling, and hurried away from it all. The moment I crossed the fairy ring, turning my back upon it, I felt eyes opening all around and behind me, but I did not heed them.

I did not stop until I reached the path once more and saw the cottage nestled into the hillside below and all was solid and real about me. It was only then that I looked back. Perhaps I should have hailed Mrs. Gomersal and her child.

Putting up a hand to shade my eyes, I searched the hillside for their forms. A few moments afterwards, as if in answer, two dark shapes appeared around the side of the hill and turned, but not towards me. They began the ascent towards the barrow.

My relief was followed at once by puzzlement—where had they been? Where were they going? I could still hear the way Mrs. Gomersal had entreated me not to spend time upon the hillside as clearly as if it were yesterday. I could still see the fear, barely masked, as she said the words, and yet there she walked with her small son, not only fearless but happy. How so? And what could it be that brought her there?

Papa, I thought. Did the child really think his father a fairy? Did he think he would find him inside Pudding Pye Hill? If his mother truly harboured such notions she was more lost to idiocy than I had imagined. But why *was* she there? It was a mystery. For the first time it struck me that her circumstances were altogether mysterious. I could not perceive what means she had of earning her bread. I had seen her weaving, to be sure, but that occupation had borne the impression more of a means of filling her hours rather than keeping her and hers from the poorhouse. It was something to do whilst she sat on the step of her cottage, taking in the sunshine—her well-built, decent cottage. One daughter only lately in service—how could such work furnish them with so pleasant a home? And the boy, sent to school outside the summer months? However should she pay the fees?

I had no way to satisfy my conjectures, so I decided it was none of my concern. I knew how the villagers would explain it; no doubt they would have her in league with the fairies, and them supplying her with fairy gold. But if they had . . . whatever had she done to earn it?

I sighed. I was obviously not yet recovered from my malady. I should return indoors, drink some water, refresh myself. I would lie down, as Helena, my cool, sensible wife, was doing. I had no need to do battle with such thoughts. Once my head was clear and the effects of the sun removed, they would disappear like vapour into the air.

I looked out across the fields before I continued. Men buzzed over them like bees, all untiring busyness and industry amidst the somnolence. It went on as far as I could see; it seemed that everyone in Halfoak was engaged about the harvest save me, and those two.

Chapter Twenty-Five

The shady passage was a welcome respite from the heat outdoors. I gratefully removed my hat. Somewhere within, Ivy was singing. Her voice was not strong but her song was artless and it filled the cottage with a sweetness that made me feel its lack before. I walked into the parlour, smiling, and saw Helena looking back at me from her chair by the window.

She was thin-faced and silent, but she responded when I greeted her and even gave a small smile. Her eyes were dark and a little sunken, and yet she regarded me with such sorrowful sweetness, as if to lament over the distance between us and rejoice in the restoration of peace, that it occasioned much relief on my part. I felt her renewed warmth and it occurred to me that for all her effrontery and nonsense, the wise woman's herbs may have had some auspicious influence. But then, if her fairy cure had taken some effect—what did that imply about my wife?

Even as I thought these things, Helena rose to her feet. She proclaimed herself in need of a little more restful solitude and she left the room, closing the door quietly behind her. I sighed. Of course, the "cure" had done nothing. Even if it had any efficacy, I had had too little of it, and I had altogether lacked the words of the charm.

I shook my head over such fanciful notions, wondering what the parson would think of me, and listened to her step upon the stair. For a moment there was silence, then another snatch of song emerged from the kitchen and Ivy appeared in the doorway, a rag rug draped over one arm, a carpet-beater in the other. She was startled to see me, but at the sight of another human being I felt only a new relief which I altogether failed to conceal.

She gave me a look; I could not tell if it was knowing or innocent. I wondered if she had been speaking with Helena in my absence, and if she had, what they might have said.

But the girl simply bade me good day and informed me that there were chops, with potatoes and cabbage she had dug from the garden, and I realised I could smell it; I felt both famished and yet disinclined to eat. I had to force myself to thank her pleasantly, and said, "We shall soon be spick and span with your help, Ivy. I must thank Mrs. Calthorn for lending you to us for a time."

She seemed surprised. "'Appy to 'elp, sir, I'm sure, but I can't do no more after today. Mrs. Calthorn can't spare me longer. Din't she tell you?"

I was not a little dismayed. I wondered if Helena had known—Mrs. Calthorn must have informed her—but I did not wish Ivy to see that we had spoken so little to one another that she had not passed on such particulars to me.

"'Opefully that's all right, sir, wi' t' mistress feelin' more herself, an' all."

"Of course. Thank you, Ivy."

I expected her to go about her duties, but she simply stood there, the heavy rug still draped over her arm, the beater grasped in her capable fingers, and her eyes unfocused as if she were thinking deeply on some unknown subject, or had passed into the land of dreams. She stirred herself and met my eyes, then looked away.

"What is it, Ivy?" I spoke kindly. If she had something to impart, I had no wish to frighten it from her before she could tell it.

"It's just, I dun't know if I should say, but there is someone in t' village if you still need a lass." She actually blushed. " 'Appen I might get in bother for sayin' owt. But she's a friend o' mine, an—"

"Indeed, I shall ensure you do not. We do have the most pressing need for a maid, as you will have seen." Even as I spoke, I remembered my resolution to remove from this place—but we could not leave yet; not until Helena was entirely recovered.

"Well, sir, it's Essie Aikin, see. She was at t' Grange before me, an'—Well, sir, she lost 'er place, as I 'spect you'll 'ave 'eard, an' I dare say she wun't say no to another. 'Er fambly in't rich, an' she can't stop idle, not no more." She closed her lips firmly together, as if to prevent another word escaping.

"Does she not work in the fields, then?"

"She's not up to it, sir, not yet. It's not long since—" Again, there was that abrupt curtailment; the white-pressed lips and reddened cheeks.

I did not need to press her; I knew at once why the girl had lost her position. I had read of the sorry affair in my cousin's diary. I thought of the impropriety of having such an unprincipled girl under my roof—that must have been the reason, after all, why Widdop had not deigned to mention her to me when I had asked after a maid. Then I bethought of the condition of the kitchen before Ivy had come, unclean and musty, the washing in need of dollying and rinsing and wringing, the fire needing to be swept and laid, the water to be carried from the pump . . . and it occurred to me that Christian forgiveness, after all, was of greater importance than punishment for a girl who had suffered such an unfortunate lapse of judgement.

"Very well," I said at last, "perhaps you could send her to me." There would be a further advantage in such a girl: there would be no complaining of the cottage being unlucky, or of its isolated situation, nor indeed any lingering horror at the more recent disaster that had occurred within. She could have little choice, after all, in the matter of her employment.

"Oh, beggin' your pardon, sir, but I can't do that. Me mother'd fetch me a kelk if she knew I'd even said owt about 'er, let alone spoke to 'er."

"Ah. It's all right, Ivy. In that case, could you tell me where to find the girl?"

"Well, sir, she lives down t' bottom o' the village, past t' beer 'ouse an down t' next road—Dog Lane, it is. 'Er 'ouse dun't 'ave a name or owt, none of 'em do, but it's t' one after t' one wi' all t' roses."

"And her family's name—it is Aikin, you say?"

"That's it, sir." She thought. "'Appen you dun't 'ave to go down there though, sir, if you dun't choose. I s'pose you might see 'er in church tomorrer, if she shows 'er dial, anyroad."

I stared at her until her uncomfortable squirm alerted me to the fact, and then I nodded and let her go about her work. She scurried away like a rabbit to its burrow. I had not realised that another week had passed. Once again it had come as a great surprise to me that the following day was Sunday.

Chapter Twenty-Six

Against my expectation, Helena received my suggestion that we attend church with sober, if not eager, agreement. I had considered it carefully, thinking that it might be an occasion for her to be seen by Yedder and his friend Thomas Aikin, and decided I should not let it stand in the way of what was right. There was little likelihood of them recognising my wife in her Sunday attire as the wild creature they had danced with by moonlight in the lane.

I had mentioned it to her that evening, and she had agreed before firmly closing the door to her room once more. She had not re-emerged; she refused all offers of sustenance. I protested that she was not thinking clearly and that she must eat, but I made my protest to the blank, closed door. Church, at least, was another promising sign that she was feeling somewhat improved.

Now God's sun shone down upon sinner and saint alike and all was harmonious. Helena emerged from her room wearing the same pale grey gown she had worn for Lizzie's funeral, but I pushed that remembrance aside; I had our future to think of and I was determined not to dwell upon the past, not today. Divine service would be refreshing for us both, body and soul. We could think upon our

Creator and the world and our little place within it, and it would be just the thing to restore Helena to herself.

I could not help but speculate upon what might pass for a Sunday service in these parts. The parson had shown himself capable of droning dullness and lightning admonishments; I wondered which he would loose upon the world today. And the congregation—surely they would be capable of all kinds of hoydenism and clownishness? I pictured a seething mass of them in their smock-frocks, all crossing themselves at the name of our Saviour, spitting at the name of the Devil and smiting their breasts at the name of Judas.

As for those who seek them out—those who go looking to find evil—why, they shall find it, sir, and only harm shall come to them!

I sighed. They might do well to spit and cross themselves at such things, if it only helped them remember not to listen to such foolishness.

But the parson hadn't really thought it foolish, had he?

At that moment the distant sound of the church bells rang out, calling all men to worship. I took a deep breath and held out my arm for Helena. She took it, as silently as she had done everything else.

I had hoped that we might fall in with Mrs. Calthorn and her son, possibly even receive an invitation to join them in their pew, since they had shown Helena some kindness—it would not only be hospitable but it would surely remove another difficulty, that of where to sit. Each pew was no doubt rented and paid for, the province of a particular family; doubtless it would have been for generations.

This led me to no little sense of awkwardness as we entered through the old grey door and passed into the shady, stone-smelling narthex. There was much rustling of skirts and the murmur of voices, all rising and mingling in a ceaseless whisper. The squire's mother was already in her place in the most easterly seat of the foremost pew, her head bowed. She looked at no one, and her son, leaning back with his arms spread along the back of the seat, stared only upwards. His posture would have been more suited to a settle in the inn.

Farmers and their wives, labouring men with their boots newly polished, maids, mothers, grand-dames, all were taking their places in some social order of which I could make out nothing. Of course, the wise woman was not present. I had not for a moment thought she would be.

The air remained warm inside the church, despite its stone walls filled with shadows. The parson was ready, standing to one side of the pulpit, his hands clasped. His lips were twisted into a semblance of permanent displeasure in spite of the size of the congregation. I half expected that he would notice us and usher us into a pew, but he did not; he was focused not upon the faces around him but a little above their heads, seeing only the ineffable rather than the earthly.

I handed Helena into a seat a little towards the front of the church, and turned to see a burly farmer, barely smothering his indignation at our imposition. I opened my mouth to make some apology, but he turned away, shaking his head. He squeezed onto another row, making rather a noise about it, to some little sound of protest. I ignored it; surely all men could find a place here without turning the admittance of strangers into a matter of disruption? Where had these people been hiding when the time had come to bury my cousin, one of their own? My hand, unbidden, went to my pocket, where I had been wont to find that little lock of hair, but Helena grasped my fingers before I could, with a wiry clutch that did not speak much of affection. Her own hand remained quite cold.

A whisper came from somewhere behind me. "Aye—that's 'im."

There was something else I could not hear, then, "Thowt 'e would 'ave gone 'ome. Mustn't 'ave owt to do."

"Likes it up there, does 'e? Pokin' about—"

I scowled at their insolence and looked around, but I could not identify the speakers. I did notice Ivy, sitting two rows behind me, and next to her Mrs. Gomersal and her other daughter, but they stared straight ahead. The boy was as blank as ever, and his mother turned his head with her hand, correcting his wandering attention.

There was no young girl with an infant anywhere within the church.

The parson cleared his throat. "Sun and rain," he said. "Rain and sun: both fall alike on a land blessed by God and both are needed, though they may not be welcomed alike. Without God's bounteous gifts the wheat will not grow. Without the rain, it will wither where it stands." He looked about, though his stern eyes fixed on nothing.

"But what of the land that turns its face away—what of the land that pays no heed to God's ways? Why then should we blame the Lord when His people reject His bounty? What should He care if they should choose to take care of their own? It is *God's* judgement if they do not live. It is *God's* judgement if they do not flourish. And they *shall not flourish!*" He slapped his hand down upon the pulpit next to the open Bible, which I do not believe he had once glanced at. I thought of a cup of tea jumping in its saucer, but the sound rang louder and longer, echoing from the rafters, and something stirred up there, an almost inaudible rustling. Helena, next to me, let her head fall back and stared upward. I squeezed her fingers, but it was like touching something inert and an image rose before me: another hand, a cold, blackened hand.

"They shall—not—flourish!" The parson enunciated each word, this time glaring into each face before him, one after the next. In the brief silence, no one moved; no one even breathed. Then came the tap of an idle boot swinging against its seat from somewhere behind me and I knew that it was her child: Mrs. Gomersal's elfin boy. Next to me, Helena let out a breath. I looked at her, startled, not so much because of the volume of the sound but because it had been laced with amusement.

"They shall be unwelcome in God's house."

I shifted uncomfortably. Of all the gathered host, the ones most unwelcome in God's house must have been my wife and me: outsiders, unwelcome; we did not understand the lives being lived around us.

"They shall not lie in consecrated ground," the parson went on, speaking as if one point had led to the other, though his meaning was dark to me. "Exiled!" He thumped the pulpit again and Helena let out a spurt of air, not a sound of alarm but again, thinly veiled amusement. She tried to remove her hand from mine and I endeavoured to hold onto it; then it was gone. I had felt no response, no warmth, no familiarity. It was as if we were not connected in any way at all.

"We shall join our voices in hymn, 'Lord, Ever Bridle My Desires'. We shall remind ourselves of the fruits of temperance and goodness. When we are joined, it must be within God's fold and under His eye and within His love. Then, and only then, we become a family; when we are within the greater family of this village and, greater still, within God's family. Then, and only then, will that family last—when its foundation is built upon a rock!"

I thought I could begin to make out which way his words tended. I could not think why he had chosen today for his execrations; had he too expected the girl to attend? Or was he ever harping upon this? Did he take pleasure in seeking out any hint of unseemliness so that he could delight in reproving it?

"Children are born within that love of a man and a woman, joined in the sacrament of marriage. Within that fold. Then, welcomed and Christened, they are safe within God's family for always. They will never be lost. They will never wander in the wilderness—"

From somewhere behind me, someone shifted; there came a low grunt.

"—they will grow beneath the sun, draw sustenance from the rain, and from the love of both mother and father, and from the love they hold for one another—"

A sharp sound escaped Helena's lips. I stole a glance at her. Her hand was pressed to her mouth, but she was smiling under it. I could see it plainly; anybody could.

"Helena," I whispered, my tone one of warning, but it was of no use. As if in answer, a bark of laughter emerged from her lips, as sudden as a convulsion. It was louder than the parson's voice.

I did not see those around me, but I heard them shifting, turning to look at her; to look at *us*. I saw the eyes staring from the corner of my vision. The parson did not speak. Was he too staring at my wife?

My wife—my dear Helena, my modest, calm, composed Helena, who now let out another peal of coarse laughter.

My eyes opened wider as she rocked in her pew. "Helena!" I did not know what to do. I had never before experienced such a thing. I looked around helplessly, seeing the worst: the shocked eyes watching us, judging us, unblinking with the force of their disapprobation—nay, of their disbelief—and then Helena laughed again, dissolving with it so that tears poured down her cheeks.

I did the only thing I could think of. I grasped her more tightly, my fingers sinking deeply into the flesh of her arm, and I began to pull her towards the end of the pew. Thankfully, no one had been seated next to us; there was none to bar our way.

The parson did not react. As I watched, a ray of sunlight speared through the window at his back, bright as a sudden bolt of lightning, casting his face into darkness. I could no longer see his expression; I did not need to, for it was echoed in the faces all around us. The whole village was staring.

"Pardon me," I said, my voice low but audible enough in the silence following my wife's strange fit. She did not laugh now, but tears still spilled from her eyes; I did not know if they were of sorrow or mirth.

"My wife is ill," I said again. "Pray, excuse us." I half dragged her to her feet, thinking for an awful moment that she would sink to the floor; and then she stood and I put my arm around her and supported her. I did not look back until we reached the door, which I dragged open with one hand. It scraped dreadfully against the stone, underlining our egress, and then we once more stood in the burning heat of the day. I shut it after us, and all sound from within was mercifully cut off.

Helena stared at me as if she did not know what could be the matter, or how she came to be standing there. I grasped her shoulders. It took great effort to refrain from shaking her. I had expected this day to bring examples of ill behaviour; I had not expected them to arise from within my own family. My shame redoubled the heat bearing down upon us from the sky. I did not admonish her as I had intended; I closed my eyes and swayed. I murmured, *Wife*—nothing more than that.

She did not answer until I opened my eyes. She was peering at me just as a student of the sciences might examine a specimen under a microscope, as we had once looked upon the exhibits in the Crystal Palace—

No. No, that had not been Helena—

Her mouth twisted, as if she could see all my thoughts and knew my mistake.

"*Am* I?" she whispered. "Am I your wife, Albie? Do we love one another? Is our child to feel the sun and rain upon its face?"

I did not understand. Sun? Rain? I cared for none of her words; I could see none of it, only this ruined moment, here, now; our disgrace and our shame. I turned from her and began walking towards the cottage, seizing her arm as I did, drawing her along with me. She stumbled and would have fallen but I held her up, kept pulling her with me.

What must they think of us? All had seen, except the girl I had thought to hire as a maid—a girl mired in debauchery—and yet now we were as shamed as anybody. Who would deign to cross our threshold now?

There was no choice left to me. I must take Helena away. We must flee this place and hope this did not follow us all the way to London.

I stopped suddenly. What if it *did* follow us? Worse still, what if Helena behaved in this fashion in the City—before our acquaintances—before my *father*? No, I could not countenance it. I could not permit it. There might be no place remaining for us here, but we surely could not return home. There was no choice left to us at all.

With gratitude, I saw that we had reached the bridge. At least I could be thankful for the isolation of the cottage, which was as peaceful and calm and quiet as it had ever been; there, we should be away from it all. It had become our little haven, a gift from my cousin.

The back of my neck burned. I did not know if it was from the sun—God's sun—or from the thought of the church somewhere behind me, or of those eyes . . .

Helena began to sing, softly, and in a mocking tone. I half expected the folk tune she had sung before, something about a sweet morning and a fairy girl, but it was not:

All things bright and beautiful . . .

I whirled, and this time I *did* shake her, until she could sing no longer; her teeth rattled in her skull. "What do you think, to sing that song?" I demanded. "It is hers—*hers!*"

She stared at me, shocked, at last, as she should have been.

I went on: "It was my cousin's song. Her voice was sweet—yours—"

Her expression hardened. "Mine is not? Is that what you meant, Albie? Ah, little Lizzie, the sweetest little Linnet, her song so much more beautiful than my own."

"It was. *It was!*" I pulled away from her, breathing heavily. The words had spilled from me without thought; it was too late to take them back.

I did not know how she would reply, but for a moment she said nothing. She merely pointed towards the sky. "Do you hear that?"

I realised there was something: a bird's voice, rising into the air. At first all was music, then it gave way to a rough chatter that was almost unpleasant. It went on in that way, richness interspersed with shrillness, until I became conscious once more of Helena's stare.

"There is your linnet, is it not?" she said, and she laughed to see my expression. "How it shrieks!"

My eyes narrowed in fury. I wished to tell her just what I thought: that her actions had made her ugly to me; but I did not say it; I only drew away from her in disgust. Shadows hung about her face like a cloud and I could no longer read what was written there. Had she only been teasing me with some notion of her recovery? I wanted to remonstrate, to question her, to say anything to establish that yes, here was my own dear wife; but not a sound emerged. It was as if my voice had been witched away.

Querulous, I thought. *Unnatural. Shrew.*

Her expression was blank, and yet there was a sense of brooding power all about her, concentrated in her once-beautiful eyes. I did not like the way she stared at me. I felt that she could see my every emotion, my every thought, and it made me unaccountably afraid; yet I could do nothing. For a moment I could not even move. I could not look away, nor hide myself, nor change into something that would please her. I was only what I was; I could not fathom what she had become.

In the next instant she had turned and was hurrying ahead of me, away onto Pudding Pye Hill. I did not go after her. I would not take her arm. I gazed up at the summit. I could just make out the rough outline of the barrow against God's pure blue sky. I do not know how long I stared. I did not know what it was that I should do.

Chapter Twenty-Seven

I knew that Helena would already have retired to her room by the time I reached the cottage. What must she do in there all day—sleep? Consider the world outside her window? Dream? Perhaps she had some other tumultuous novel secreted from me. I stood at the gate, looking in. Outside, all was lovely if tangled abundance. Inside . . .

I did not immediately go in, but meandered around the path. It had once been neatly sprinkled with cinders, which gritted beneath my shoes. The beds, edged with cheap shuttering, were bursting with ripe vegetables—globular onions practically lifted themselves from the ground, whilst runner beans dripped from their stakes. Some of the flowers were almost indecent in their brightness. There was a pungent scent of rotting fruit. Birds hopped and pecked among it all, appearing and disappearing like a cunning parlour trick.

There was a spade set into what I suspected to be a potato patch. The blade was caked with mud, the wooden handle worn smooth and shining: it was clearly accustomed to be used, and I found myself thinking that it should be used again. I could not look away from it.

And then I heard the echo of a murderer's words, running through my mind: *Dig 'er up!*

I shuddered and turned my back upon it, looking instead at the village. It was distant and beautiful, both familiar and yet unknown to me; it was hard to believe we had been so comprehensively shamed there. Everyone save us would still be in church, bowing their heads beneath the parson's onslaught. Whatever had made him so angry? Surely he should set the example of peace in his parish?

But no, not everyone was there. It struck me that the girl so traduced in his sermon did not know what had happened that morning, and further, she might be the only citizen of Halfoak who did not care.

My father's son railed within me against the thought of such a presence under my roof. It would be a daily reminder of their sin, one surely greater than our own. My wife had been taken ill—this beautiful isolation in which we found ourselves was not as conducive to her spirits as it was to my own, and I suddenly felt all the loneliness of our position. She had come here of her own volition, but it was because of me that she stayed, away from society, from family, from all that she knew. Having a young woman about the house, one to whom she needs must set an example, might be just the thing to bring her to her senses. We could then return home with no fear of dragging our shame behind us like unwanted baggage. And to have as that young person one who had recently become a mother, someone with whom she could share in a little of that excitement? It was a capital plan! A girl such as Essie Aikin would surely be grateful for any work we could provide; she might even be persuaded to bring the infant with her now and then, for Helena to coo over. That would surely restore my wife to more natural thoughts and womanly occupations, whilst also serving to distract her from whatever ailed her so.

I decided I should go at once. I could speak to the girl before the congregation emerged from the old grey building at the heart of the village, prove myself a sensible man before anyone could put it about that I was not. It would be arranged to the satisfaction of all before the day was out.

Hope lent a spring to my step and I quickly reached the bottom of the hill, smiling at the sweet babble of the brook, before walking past the church. I hardly spared it a glance other than to note that I could not hear the intemperate shouting of its minister, nor did any song emerge or bell peal. Its silence was almost ominous, as if all within it had vanished into the air. Would that they had!

Accompanied only by the hymns of birdsong and the blessing of God's own sunlight, I soon reached the crossroads, and just beyond it the beer house, also silent now. A narrow opening was marked Dog Lane, the letters carved into a large stone, though barely legible; it was little more than a track, heavily rutted along its centre, too narrow for anything but a handcart.

I walked along it, still hearing nothing but the birds and, now and again, the scraping of insects. The lane was edged on one side by a stone wall thickly overgrown with clinging ferns and nettles; I caught glimpses of fields over its unevenly laid top. On the other side, a tight cluster of little houses had been pushed into whatever space had been available. Walls supported one another; fences leaned; roofs sagged. From somewhere came the odiferous suggestion of a shared privy.

I felt a moment of sympathy for those wretches forced to live in such hovels, and yet even the tiny, irregular patches of garden were full to bursting with colour and life. They were mainly given over to fruit and vegetables, though here and there were bursts of brilliant colour to lend a little cheer, some unknown flowers with neat rings of petals encircling their central, brightly coloured eyes.

Then came a garden where the rows of nurturing plants were almost smothered by roses of all colours: blood-red, pink, white, yellow, apricot, all of their petals burnt brown at the edges by fierce sunlight. The house after it must be the one I sought.

As it came into view I thought it the most dilapidated I had yet seen in the village. Paint peeled from the sills; slates hung awry from the roof; its brickwork was slimed with moss. My heart sank to look upon its dismal visage. The garden gave no relief; it was bare, dry earth, with only a few attenuated weeds, and lying amongst them, a broken fork and a tiny knitted glove.

The windows were open, but I heard no sound, not the shriek of a baby nor the cooing of its mother. I had pictured a neatly dressed girl dandling a child as apple-cheeked as herself, handing the white-clad bundle to my smiling wife—but that image fled. Helena would never touch the progeny from such a home; she would not be soothed by it. Why had I ever imagined she could be comforted by any child other than her own—a false child?

And yet I was here. It would be foolishness itself to leave without trying the door and seeing what opportunities might present themselves. I half pushed, half lifted the gate aside, walked to the door and knocked.

There came a rattling and a rustling, followed by . . . nothing. I raised my fist to knock again, but the door was suddenly dragged open. A girl stood there, not cheerful and apple-cheeked as I had hoped, but narrow of face and pale. Her fair hair was lank and dirty, darkened to the colour of damp straw. Her features might have been considered neat—she had a smooth forehead, a straight nose and rather lovely rosebud lips. Her eyes, a somewhat pretty shade of blue, were dull and lifeless, and the paleness of her cheeks sapped any vitality from her. Her grey dress was shabby, and her apron of doubtful white. Her hands and arms were speckled with flour.

She made a somewhat sad impression, and I could not help but think, *she was pretty, once.*

She made no greeting, and so I spoke. "Good morning. Are you Essie Aikin?"

"Who wants to know?" Her pretty lips tightened into an unprepossessing arrangement and she folded her arms before her.

I was a little taken aback at her rudeness, though by now I should have known to expect no better of the uneducated inhabitants of Halfoak; I should make allowances for lack of schooling and opportunities for betterment. But I did not expect that such a bold, saucy creature would make us even a maid of all work. Still, I said to her, "I came to speak to you on the matter of some employment."

She stared at me before blinking once. She did not appear sensible of my words, and it occurred to me that she was probably exhausted: so recent a mother, open to the ridicule of an unforgiving society, she must barely have slept since her condition had made itself plain. And yet here she was, cooking: she was at least industrious, then.

"Tha'd best come in." She drew back to allow me to pass and all my misgivings returned at the prospect of stepping into the dank little home. After a moment I did so, though I found myself hoping for an instant that no one had seen me.

"My name is Mr. Mirralls," I said. "I am currently residing at th—"

"I know who you are. An' I know where tha's stoppin'." She eyed me sharply. She gave no sign that she was aware of her own ill manners.

I took a deep breath, reminding myself that her situation demanded Christian pity from those who knew better than herself. "We require a maid for the remainder of our stay, though I fear that may be short. The duties are the usual for such a position—cleaning, washing, and a little cooking. I understand that you are in need of useful occupation—"

She screwed her features into a scowl. "That 'ouse—"

"—is unlucky, yes. So I have heard it said, though only from unreasonable superstition, and without any cause to which I could possibly lend any credence." I hardly knew why I persevered. If I could not secure the services of such a one as she, none other would step forward to fill the lack—but it had taken less than a moment to see the condition of the room, which appeared to serve as kitchen and parlour alike. The flimsy deal table was greasy beneath its current covering of flour and dough; the hearth was sooty; a filthy pan full of little tied cloths containing who knew what was set upon the floor as if ready to be set to boil.

"I can offer generous recompense for the short time you would be needed," I went on. "I understand that you have particular circumstances . . ."

Even as I spoke the words, I realised there was no sign of a child: no cradle in the corner; no rattle; no little peg-doll wrapped in cunningly fashioned rags; no soft blanket; no white caps. The baby must be sleeping upstairs, away from the smoke and the busyness of making dinner; or perhaps it was in the care of a relative. "If it becomes difficult, you could bring your young charge with you, as long as—"

Her eyes widened further and her mouth fell open. "Me what?"

"Your charge—surely you know what that means? Your baby, of course."

"Me babby . . . ?"

"Yes—you are Essie Aikin, are you not?"

She made no reply, only stared, until I was the one to look away.

"But it's not 'ere, sir," she said, and I returned my gaze to her face, which was now quite white.

"Not here?"

A tear welled at her eye and her lip quivered. I was altogether mortified, although I did not know what I had done, and furthermore, how it should be undone. I stood there as she wept, until at last I said, "Whatever has happened?"

"Dun't you know, sir?" She looked all around, as if to seek help in every corner of the room. "I thought everyone did. My babby got stole. I 'adn't even named it. It weren't but a few weeks old, an' the fairies come and took it away."

The walls pressed in around me, growing closer moment by moment. I felt as if every strange word, every odd idea, every wild story I had heard since my arrival in Halfoak had followed me here. I had not the slightest clue as to what I should say.

Essie said nothing either; her tears turned to sobbing until her shoulders shook. At last she began to sniff.

"What happened? Pray, tell me."

She wiped at her nose with the back of her wrist, smearing her face. "'E was taken, sir. They left another in 'is place. An' I tried and tried to make 'em give 'im back ter me, my little boy, but—but they din't do it!"

I frowned. "They left another—what, they left you a changeling? What made you think so? However did you know it was not your own child?"

She looked me squarely in the eye. I would have taken it as an impertinence had the circumstances not been so strange. "Does tha think I wouldn't know me own blood, sir?"

I did not know how to answer, but she had not finished. "I saw it, sir, the fairy *thing*. Mary Gomersal 'elped me—she were kind to me. She went to t' wise woman. She made me see what it was."

I remembered the shack, the woman's touch in my hair; my wife, standing in a dead wood in a fall of sunlight and pollen. "So what did you do?" I breathed, feeling that everything hung upon her answer—the past, the future, everything I had seen since I came to Halfoak. She stared at me, and I realised I could find the answer without her; I had held it in my hands.

A sound floated through the open window: whistling. Someone, perhaps more than one, was approaching down the street. Divine service had finished. The villagers were coming home.

I forced myself to reach out and touch the girl's thin shoulder. "I am sorry," I said, and I rushed from the pitiful house, my soul aching in sympathy, but every fibre of me relieved to put the sight of her behind me. I caught a glimpse of Jem's cousin, Thomas Aikin, coming down the lane, Yedder Dottrell at his side, their faces drawn and harried in the light of day. I did not wish to speak to them; I did not wish to have to explain myself, much less for them to know that I had seen them at midnight, waiting by a fairy door, for I would be trespassing on matters that were not my concern. I turned instead in the opposite direction and walked away from them. I did not look back, though the lane ended abruptly in another stone wall adorned with little pink flowers. A stile led into the field beyond and I clambered over it, uncaring of what kind of figure I must cut.

I walked alongside the wall until I saw another stile in the distance. It must let onto the white road, somewhere beyond the inn. I hastened towards it, then stopped dead and stared. There was a scarecrow in the field, its out-thrust arms clad in a green coat, and it wore a red conical cap upon its head. Its eyes, little wizened nuts, shone brightly in its face.

The words the girl had spoken returned to me: *The fairies come and took it away.*

I frowned. Had something fallen into place at last, or had I truly stepped into the land of dreams? I felt that I had been waiting for some kind of revelation; that it was within my grasp—that this, rather than my wife's illness, was the reason I stayed. I had wanted so badly to know the truth of what had happened to Lizzie, but it had never occurred to me to wonder if the fairies had ever done such a thing before.

I started once more across the field, redoubling my haste. I knew now where I must look to discover what I sought. I needed to return to the cottage—I had to finish reading my cousin's journal.

Chapter Twenty-Eight

I burst in at the cottage door, eager to rush upstairs and retrieve the battered old book from its hiding place, but a small thing gave me pause: a soft scraping sound coming from the parlour. I peered into the room to ascertain its source.

Helena was sitting at the table, in front of a feast. She must have laid out everything we had: there was salt pork, cheese, bread, butter; some cold tongue, a few cut radishes from the garden; pots of numerous kinds of preserves. She indicated it with a gesture, as if to say, *See? I am trying.*

"We shall eat together," she said, her voice calm, "and then we shall pack up our belongings. Is it not time that we left this place and went somewhere else? We could return to London. We could be there by tomorrow. We can leave it all behind us. We shall never need to look upon the hill again."

"But Helena . . ." She tilted her head. "Helena, my dear, I cannot eat just now. There is something I need to do—things I need to discover. I cannot possibly leave Halfoak just yet."

She made no reply; she did not protest or weep, though the musculature of her face began to change, becoming more firmly set as all turned to coldness. I had seen such an expression upon her face before; I did not need to look upon it again. I quietly left the room, closing the door behind me, and I ran up the stairs, two at a step.

I pulled back the faulty wainscoting and dragged Lizzie's journal from its nook with eager fingers. I flicked rapidly through the pages. Some I had seen already; then, I had thought them dull, irrelevant to her case, but I sought them out now. I could not read quickly enough. My cousin had not discriminated. She wrote of everything she saw about her: the weather; the doings of her neighbours; Jem's struggles with his business; what they ate for supper. And then I found:

Essie Aikin is with child! That chit! She's knapped, aye, and I know who's it is, an all. I don't know what to think. I suppose I didn't expect anything else from him. Right glad I am I kept that bonnet. Might as well have summat. But such things he said! And all to nothing.

Essie bloody Aikin. She were there in front of his nose, wasn't she, and probably shoving it in his face till he couldn't help himself. He's only a man, after all. The little cat! What a witch she is!

Jem told us about it this morning, before he went into Halfoak to measure up for harvest boots. There he was, going on and on about pay-day pockets and I hardly knew where to look, but I don't think he suspected me of owt. Anyhow, then he said Mrs. Calthorn had noticed Essie's belly swelling and that was it, she was turned off at once. How I laughed! It serves her right. Mrs. Calthorn says there won't be any money for her neither, she should have thought of that, she shouldn't have been such a trollop. Wonder what she'd say if she knew whose it was!

And Jem said that's bad, but what did Essie expect? A palace? Marriage? Don't make me laugh. I reckon she might be getting some of their brass anyroad, but Jem said Edmund Calthorn spends over his means already and he won't get more from his mother, though he's got debts shouting louder than hers. He said he's good for nowt. Well, I reckon he must be good for summat, else Essie's belly wouldn't be getting big, not like mine, but I thought better of saying it. Anyway, he's right, in a way. She shouldn't have expected nowt and nowt is what she's going to get. I wanted to laugh again then, but I didn't.

Still, I'm glad it was only a bonnet and nowt else. Though I could cry when I think on it, in spite of all that.

That had been written months ago; when she resumed it was all dullness once more; just life, going on as it always had. There were more little complaints about her husband—he kept busy in his workshop, never quite gaining enough business or earning enough for her liking, and that made me think of Ivy's words. Had Lizzie truly been haughty? But my cousin had been dainty and delicate; of course she would have kept herself aloof from the likes of Ivy Gomersal. She was surrounded by roughness; little wonder if she craved a bit of finery to lighten her days. And if he could not provide for her comfort, he should not have married her.

If he had not married her, she would still have been alive.

I skipped those pages regarding only the minutiae of day to day, and then I found an entry I had read before, the one where his cousin's lass had "started with the bairn"; the one where Lizzie told of her own impending motherhood. I did not read it again, but moved ahead just a little.

They say that the baby won't even suckle right. It did at first, they say, but now they're all talking about it. It's stopped feeding, as if it don't want human food, that's what they're saying, like it isn't the same baby no more. Sounds to me like Essie don't know what she's doing, but some of them's saying worse than that, and her father's got his earlugs wide open. I said to Jem, I bet he does, him not having two pennies to rub and another mouth to feed, but he got right mad then and I shut up. He'd not have owt to say against her father, not even by me, and that's the truth. Cousins is cousins, he says, like as if they were even cousins at all, and I can laugh but he don't have to listen, not if he don't want to.

I skipped over more of it, about some little matters concerning Jem's business, about pecuniary woes that were not of any moment, and found:

Mary Gomersal said it's true. It's all over Halfoak, though I bet no one's telling the parson, not if they value their earholes. She went to visit—said they couldn't pay for physick so she'd see what she could do. I said nothing to that, though I could have. See, I am learning to hold my tongue, even if Jem'd say summat else.

Yedder told Jem about it in the inn and he told me. Mary Gomersal went and looked all over the bairn, looked for marks, and said she found one, right on its belly. Essie said she'd put the iron scissors under its blanket and the Bible under its crib, and Mary said that weren't any good, she'd warned her before, and it were too late now.

They didn't like that, not at all, but she said it weren't a matter of what they wanted and wished, not now, and they said she looked right hard at Essie at that, which made me laugh.

Mrs. Gomersal picked it up and rocked it, and the bairn burst out roaring and its face went red. She held it near the fire and it went redder still and Mary shook her head over it. She talked to it and said in God's name this and God's name that, but it only cried some more, and she shook her head and said they all had to leave it in the house and go outside.

So they did, and only Mary went up and peered in through the window. And she watched and watched some more, and then she called them over. And what did they see? Yon baby waggling its hands and sucking its toes, smiling, all calm and quiet and happy like, and she said that proved it, because it were only happy when it were nursed by its own, them as none of them could see. She said that's what they do, when every one else goes out the fairies come in, and they take care of their own. She said if she looked side-on she could see the light of them darting all about, and that was proof of what it was.

I didn't say nowt to that. I don't reckon Essie was right happy. She said it'd be all right, and if it wasn't hers she'd take care of it just as if it was, and she cried. It was enough to soften her father anyroad, and Mary Gomersal just shook her head and said she'd get some medicine and sort it out, and she *went away again, still saying Essie's baby were already gone and only she knew how to get it back again.*

And still the man refused to confess! To hang must surely come as a relief—what a monster must he be, to remain here, where he had committed such dreadful deeds? Did he merely fear the torments to come? For surely he would find himself in Hell, and it would be his turn to burn, for ever and ever.

I heard a step upon the stair. I listened to its progress, followed by the door opposite mine opening and closing. At first there was no other noise, but then came the soft sound of someone singing.

> *Look, Lizzie, look, Lizzie,*
> *Down the glen tramp little men.*
> *One hauls a basket,*
> *One bears a plate,*
> *One lugs a golden dish*
> *Of many pounds' weight.*

I secreted the journal beneath my pillow before slipping from the room. I did not knock before entering my wife's.

She lay upon the bed, staring up into the canopy, much as I had a few minutes before. Her face was pale. She suddenly reminded me of the painting of Ophelia, singing her last sweet song to the world and quite, quite mad.

I said her name in a low voice; I felt that more would startle her. She had not acknowledged my presence in the slightest, had not even looked at me. I leaned over her to see that her eyes were glassy; she was focused on nothing; the pupils did not adjust. She only began to sing once more, in a slow and haunting voice:

> *Lizzie, Lizzie, have you tasted*
> *For my sake the fruit forbidden?*
> *Must your light like mine be hidden,*
> *Your young life like mine be wasted,*

Undone in mine undoing,
And ruined in my ruin,
Thirsty, cankered, goblin-ridden?

I was horrified. I drew back, not knowing what I should do. Should I shake her, or snap my fingers before her eyes? Should I call her name until she returned to me? When she had spread our food upon the table for us to eat together I had at least had a glimmer of hope, but it had been snatched away. I wondered if that had been the intention all along: to show me a ray of light that only made the darkness darker. This could not be my wife. This thing possessed her form, but everything she had once been was absent. I knew then, as certainly as I knew myself, that this was not the woman I had married.

I turned and walked—though I should rather call it drifted, my limbs felt so weightless, my mind floating—from the room and down the stairs. I went along the passage and into the parlour and out again, into the kitchen, and from thence into the little space at the back of the house which served as a store cupboard.

There were all the cleaning accoutrements, the brushes and buckets and rags for blacking and scrubbing and dusting, each task with its own tool, just as it should be. I started to go through them, laying each item aside as I inwardly catalogued and discarded it, hardly knowing what I did. And his words came back to me, and I understood what it was I was searching for.

I knew it were a changeling in 'er stead, on account o' right when she came, I noticed t' mop-stick were missin'.

I let out an odd, dry sound. It was only after it left my lips that I recognised it as a sort of laughter.

They take a stock o' wood, see? An' they spell it to look like t' one they stole.

I threw down the last of the sundry items and stayed as I was, staring at the wall, focused upon nothing. I thought of Helena in her room, somewhere over my head. Had she tired of her song or did she sing it still? Had she eaten anything? Was she asleep—*did* she sleep, now? I knew none of the answers, for all I thought I had discovered so much, but in truth, I had discovered nothing at all; nothing that could even matter to me. I think I gave in to a kind of despair. I had uncovered something of the past, but lost my own wife. She had passed beyond my reach; and I had not the first idea of how to get her back again.

Chapter Twenty-Nine

That night I dreamed I walked in the churchyard under a yellow moon. I had no lamp to see by, but I needed none. All was limned in silver, though the shadows were a deeper black than I had ever seen them. When I looked behind me, I saw that my steps had left ink-dark impressions upon the grass. The night was entirely silent and I was alone and I was not afraid.

In the way of dreams, it was only then that I realised I was carrying the spade from the garden over my shoulder.

I walked to the rear of the graveyard, where the newest additions were situated, and I discovered a mound that had no stone; it was too recent for any stone to have yet been cut. There was no marker of the days and months and years which had signalled the beginning and end of her time upon this earth.

I swung the spade from my shoulder and let its impetus make the first cut into the sward. The ground yielded at once, as if capitulating to my actions. I stepped upon it, driving it deeper. The earth was almost black by moonlight and things moved within it, things with slender, skittering legs or tubular, slimy bodies, withing together and fleeing the silver blade as it bit down. I discarded the infill. I went on, my movements regular, almost mechanical, the *bite—step—dig—throw* of it taking on its own rhythm. Soon I was standing in a dark pit and then I stopped, because this time when I stepped on the spade, I heard instead of the scraping of earth the dull knock of wood.

I fell to my knees, not caring how filthy they were, and brushed the dirt from the surface until I uncovered a shining plaque, and then the coffin nails that held everything within: her blackened skin, her singed hair; the green dress I had chosen for her—the answers, perhaps, to the questions that had taken possession of my soul.

I knew not how I freed the nails or how I loosened the lid, but a moment later I was raising it and allowing the silver light to fall upon what lay within. And my breath filled my lungs until they ached. I cried out, though I know not what I said; because Lizzie was within, and she was no stock of wood.

Nor was she a blackened ruin.

Lizzie was fresh and healthful as ever. She was waiting there for me, and she opened her eyes and smiled as if she were glad to see me. She held out her arms and they did not crack or splinter or crumble into ashes. Her fingers sought my own and twined around them, and hers were warm. She sat, shaking back her hair, which was golden and curling, save where one lock was cut a little shorter than the rest.

I smiled back at her and loosed my hand from hers; I slipped it into my pocket and found there the hair I had taken, and I held it up to her own. We laughed together, and for a moment my forehead leaned against hers, and we stayed like that for a while, just looking at the hair, as if it were a sign; as if it were a key.

She was not made of wood. She never had been. She was flesh and blood, and she was beautiful. I wrapped my hands about her arms and helped her to stand. I realised we had not spoken; we had no need of words. I could still hear her lovely voice inside my mind; too sweet to release it into the sullied air for anyone else to hear.

And yet she was *there*. Her hands were in mine once more, and they fitted. They *fitted*.

The smile faded from her lips.

I frowned as her eyes darkened and I opened my mouth to ask what troubled her, but no sound emerged; not because my voice was too fine for this world, but because I could not speak. Shadows were growing all around and I felt eyes watching us, but I did not turn to see them because my gaze was fixed upon her face. There was nowhere else I wanted to look, nothing else I needed to see. And yet something was happening to her.

As I watched, her cheeks began to change. The skin thinned before my eyes, her cheeks sinking, growing hollow, while her eyes shrank into their sockets, and her hair—it was not gold, not any longer; it was silver—

I shook my head, forming the word *no*, but I could not prevent it as lines began to mar her lovely features, carving new fissures through her skin as it coarsened, growing age-spotted; but it did not stop there, for older still she grew, and yet older, until I could not bear it. I clutched at her, pulling her close to my heart, feeling her form withering in my arms.

I do not know how long I stood there, or when I first realised that I was holding nothing but dust.

I awoke, opening my eyes to see the dark canopy over my head, just as it had always been, and I opened my mouth and no sound emerged. What should I say? There was nothing, nothing to say, nothing to be done, and I stared up, my eyes unfocused, not troubling to wipe away the tears that were spilling onto my cheeks.

Chapter Thirty

The next morning I rose to the sound of a lark, the very embodiment of a fresh summer's day, and yet my head was clouded and my whole being weighed down by care. It was a wearisome matter to rise, bring water, wash and dress, and I felt no more awake when I had accomplished these small but necessary matters.

I wished for no more than to open my cousin's journal again, to uncover the secrets of her existence, but there was something I had to do first. I could not continue in this vein, wondering and vexing myself over the most impossible questions. It was as Jem Higgs had said: I was living in a half-dream and something must be done to rouse me from it. I was no longer sure I could claim to be a rational creature. I felt I was closer to Lizzie than any other person; my cousin was looking over my shoulder every moment, following everything that I did; willing me onward.

I went downstairs and found the things I sought. I had glimpsed them in the farthest corner of the storeroom and they were there still: a pair of iron scissors, which I opened into a cross; and some old shears, also of iron, ridden with rust.

I placed the shears on the little ledge over the cottage's front door. The scissors I placed upon the parlour table.

Then I went to prepare something for a hasty meal. I did not wish for us to linger in the house, not today. There were things I needed to see before I could resume my study of my cousin's book. Shortly afterward, I knocked softly upon Helena's door. She opened it immediately, conveying the impression that she had been standing silently on the other side, and I started back, examining her white complexion before speaking. "Helena, my dear, I thought we could take a little air. It would refresh us both wonderfully, I am certain."

She did not speak, but it was of no consequence. She followed me down the stairs. I indicated the table in the parlour, set out with our simple breakfast, the scissors in their place beside the crockery, and she shook her head and stepped away from it. I nodded. It was what I had expected. And then I offered her my arm and prepared to leave the cottage. At once, I felt a drag upon my arm as she stopped quite suddenly.

"What is it, Helena?"

"Nothing, Albie. I merely feel a little faint."

I glanced up at the iron shears, gleaming in the shadowy passage, quite sure my wife—quite sure that *she* had not noticed them.

She pulled on my arm once more, as if she wanted only to go back inside. Her forehead was clammy; her breathing had quickened.

"A little air would be most cleansing," I said, and attempted to draw her forward once more, all the while unsure if I was willing her onward or eager for her to reveal herself. She did neither; just stood there, as if whatever animating spirit enlivened her body had entirely vanished.

"Shall we take a little turn about the garden?" I indicated the way along the passage to the back door of the cottage, which I had earlier unlocked. She nodded a little too eagerly and started towards it, drawing herself taller as we went, and she pulled open the door herself and stepped out, without hesitation, into the sunlight.

We did not perambulate about the garden. We walked straight around the cinder path and towards the gate, as if by mutual consent, and a little later we stood in the lane. I had not thought where to go; I had only wished to see her step over the threshold and had considered nothing beyond it. Now I brooded on her refusal. She had entered the inn, of course, passing beneath the iron wards nailed above its doors, but that seemed so long ago as to be immaterial.

Now Helena tugged on my arm; she had made the decision; she led us upwards. We did not speak or pause until we were standing before the oaken grove, the fairy ring ahead of us.

She looked up and smiled.

"How do you do, my dear?" I asked.

"I feel a little better."

"How so?"

"Why, it is as you said, Albie. The air has revived me wonderfully. Is this not a lovely place?"

"And yet you are so anxious to leave it."

Her lips twitched with mirth or dismissal, I was not certain which. "It is a good thing to come home, is it not?"

I was unable to interpret her expression and I did not know how to answer her. I had the same creeping sense I had felt so often of late, that I had taken the hand of a stranger. I wished I could peer into her thoughts; I wished I could read what lay beneath the surface.

"And where is your home, my dear?"

"Why, with my husband." The words fell carelessly from her lips and she swung away from me as she spoke, wandering into the centre of the fairy ring, and there she stood. I was mindful of another sight I had so recently discovered in this place, and the cry that had rung in my ears: *Papa, Papa!*

I wanted to ask who her husband truly was, and I opened my mouth to speak, but the words surprised me; I had not planned to speak them aloud. "Where are they? Where is Lizzie? My wife—the baby?"

She turned, her forehead creasing, her mouth falling open, and she flattened her palm against her belly. She saw me looking and let it fall. Then her expression closed entirely, her lips snapping shut, her eyes growing dark, and she stalked past me and began to hurry away down the hill once more.

There was nothing for me to do but follow. My hand went to my pocket, feeling into the corners, but whatever it was I sought was no longer to be found.

Below me, Helena had reached the gate. She thrust it wide and strode through it before marching straight in at the front door and I stumbled to a halt and stared at it. She had not hesitated—this time she had walked straight through it, despite its iron guardian, and the words I had read in Lizzie's journal returned to me: *I laughed at him all the while and told him he was being ignorant.*

My heart fluttered within my chest; a terrible lightness pierced me as the world all around me paled and retreated. I put a hand to my head. I was ill, then; that was all this was; and then the moment passed and everything returned, just as it had been before. I took several deep breaths, reminding myself that I needed to eat, that if I did not I too would wither away just as if I was an unnatural child, and I went on, my steps more sure than before.

Helena stood in the parlour, her back straight as a larch, staring steadfastly into the fire. She whirled when she heard my step. "How dare you?" she said. "How dare you question me and torment me so!"

A sudden fury seized hold of me. "Is it torment to be who you are, Helena? Is it torment being required to be what you purport to be—my wife?"

Her face crumpled into ugliness, she curled her hands into fists and tears sprang from her eyes. She let out a cry, a little like a shriek, and I half expected her to burst into flame where she stood. She looked like an elf or a goblin. I took a step back from her, not knowing if I was afraid or disgusted, but she followed me, drawn in my wake.

"Helena"—I forced myself to speak calmly, even coolly—"is it so difficult for you to show that you are indeed who you are? To say, in God's name, that you are the dear, sweet lady I call my own?"

Her mouth fell open in incredulity.

"Will you not say it, Helena? I know it may be seen as an odd thing to ask—and perhaps it is—but it is a simple matter, too, is it not? So small a thing."

"Where is my book?" she suddenly snapped.

"Your book? What does that matter now?"

"My book! You took it from me. I want it, Albie—I need it!" She actually stamped her foot.

"*Need* it?" I could only stare.

"It is mine—my own! And you took it from me. It is quite necessary, I assure you. If I have no means to escape this place, if I cannot even dream, I shall—I shall go quite mad!"

I said, "You wish for that book—that wild, superstitious, *mad* book—in order for it to make you sensible once more? What, do you require some manual to unlock the secrets of the fairies and elementals and all manner of unnatural things—is that what you *need*, Helena, at this moment?"

"More than you!"

I did not know if she meant she needed the book more than I did, or if she needed it more than she required my company, but the end of it was the same. "You shall not have it," I said. "And he who wrote it—"

"*He!*" Her eyes blazed. "You think a *man* wrote it? It was not!" Her voice took on a note of triumph. "It is exquisite; and it was written by a *lady*."

I was shocked into silence. I could not conceive that such wild matter, full of such tumult and such passion, peopled by creations that fairly deserved the appellation of savages, could possibly have sprung from the gentle pen of the milder sex. Helena saw the doubt in my eyes. She leaned back and laughed at it; she laughed into my face.

I turned and snatched up the scissors from the table and thrust them towards her. She jerked aside, holding out her hands so that the cold metal could not touch her.

"Hold them," I commanded, "only that!" and she stared at me before slowly stretching out her hand. She snatched at them and cast them into the fireplace. They were dashed against the wall; the clatter of it still rung in my ears as she rushed headlong from the room. I tried to see her hand as she went by, to see if the touch of iron had burned her, but her fingers were curled tightly into fists and I saw nothing that was conclusive, nothing that could help.

I felt a rush of lightness and turned to lean upon the table, the food blurring before me, and I realised I had eaten nothing. I grabbed at the bread, tearing pieces from the loaf and cramming them into my mouth. I did not know how things had come to this. I did not know what to think or feel or what to do that would be for the best. All around me was in ruin, and I knew not how to restore it.

After a while, the things about me steadied and the strange lightness began to pass. I sat, feeling a little better as the shadows began their slow progress, tracking across the room, marking out the passing of time.

Before long I forced myself to stand and examine the ledge over the front door frame. I half expected the shears to have vanished into the air, but they had not; they lay there still. My wife had passed the test, though it be the test of a madman.

But she was coming in, a little voice spoke in my mind. *She could not go out that way. If you had wished to prevent her ingress, the shears should have been* outside *the door.*

I shook my head. It was nonsense, and I would not think of it, not now, not any longer. I made my way up the stairs and listened a moment. There was no sound, none at all; it was a house of silence. And I walked into my chamber and found Helena standing there, her hair loose as if she had been tearing at it, and I saw that she held my cousin's journal in her hand. She turned when she saw me. Her hand shook. She had bent back the spine; the cover was twisted, as if she had been wringing it like a rag. "Is this what kept you away from me, my husband?"

I held out my hand for it, but she clutched it tighter. "Oh, my dear, all your fondest hopes must have been cast so low. I am sorry for you—quite!"

"Whatever do you mean?" It was an effort to keep my voice from shaking. Anger—nay, rage—was boiling within me. How dare she? It was mine—and now she held it as if she could not bear the touch of its pages upon her fingers, as if she were too fine to be soiled with such matter. Still, she found what she sought and began to read, her high, sing-song tone grating on my nerves:

It minded me of someone else I met once, who put my arm in his, and I thought he might wish to make a wife of me but he did not . . ."

"That is enough!"

"Poor, poor Albie. What you must have felt, to hear your little Lizzie pouring out her feelings for another in its pages. I had no idea you were suffering so."

"It was not—I—she did not speak so of her husband. And it is of no matter, no consequence; that is not why I came to Halfoak."

"Is it not? Is that not her hair upon your dresser, my love? It is a little too pale for my own, unless living in such a place is turning it quite grey." She paused, looking into my face, which must have been stricken. "And of course it was not her husband. That little hussy most likely had a dozen followers. Oh, Albie! You did not think it was you of whom she spoke?" Her eyes widened in wicked delight. "Oh, you goose!"

"Helena—"

She turned the page and read on, her vowels flattened in a dreadful exaggerated semblance of a Yorkshire accent. I was certain my cousin could never have spoken so bluntly. "Ah saw 'im agin yesterneet, ridin' 'is 'orse. 'E was so easy in t' saddle, like as if 'e was borned theer. An' 'e looked on me and tipped 'is 'at an' winked so pretty, ah could not doubt but—"

"Stop—stop it at once!" I leaped towards her and snatched the book from her hands, hearing the crack of its spine, the tearing of paper, and I saw only my wife's white face, so close to mine and yet full of fear, of *horror*, and I gave some inarticulate cry and raised a hand and pushed her from me as hard as I could.

She fell back, her grasping hands catching the bed-curtains and dragging them with her. I tried to catch her, but she landed in a heap on the floor at the side of the bed. I said something—I know not what—some words of apology, of regret, but she squirmed away from me, her face turning from white to crimson in a moment. I could see the darker imprint of my thumb upon her jaw. I pulled the curtains away from her, reaching for her hand, but she snatched it back. "Helena, I am sorry. Please, allow me to assist you."

She opened her mouth and spat at me and I stared at her, completely astonished. Then she pushed herself up, edging around the wall towards the door.

"Pray, Helena—my dear wife—do not be afraid. I did not mean—"

"*I am not your wife*," she said. Her brows were drawn down like thunder. "Is that not what you have wished to hear? Well—it is the truth!"

She turned and fled from the room, not troubling to close the door behind her, and I stared after her, not knowing what I could do or what to say. After a moment, I sat down heavily upon the bed. The journal was in my hands, in a most wretched condition. I started running my hand across its cover, over and over, as if I could undo all the harm it had undergone since it was new.

I opened it and began to read. There was nothing else to be done, and so I immersed myself once more within the life of another.

Jem insisted I went to see the bairn again to-day. He said Tommy Aikin is his friend and the least I could do was bring myself to be a friend to his lass, even if I did think I was better than them. I didn't bother arguing, I just went. I didn't like it much. She still hasn't sorted out Christening the thing, though she said she didn't reckon the parson would do it, and I suppose she's right there. And she still don't have a name for it. She said she'd not found what it is yet, but I reckon if she did want it to be stolen by the fairies, she couldn't have gone about it better.

Tommy wasn't there, he was working, but Mary Gomersal was. The baby was crying and carrying on and Mrs. Gomersal said it was because she'd given it the cure. She says the true bairn will be back by midnight, and if it's not, the fairies will regret it. Then she said she was off, and told me I'd best not upset matters because it was all done and dusted, like she'd just give it a bath or summat.

Anyway Essie said she felt better about it. I told her I'd brought some milk and sugar for if she wanted help feeding it, and she nodded but then she said she didn't see any point till she got her own baby back again. No good feeding one of theirs, she said, and I told her she'd best do it just in case the fairies were mad once they got it back again to see a half-starved creature. That seemed to do the trick and she fed it, though it was a weakling little thing, hardly wanted to sup or sleep or cry or anything, just stared at me with these big blue eyes, till I couldn't help but think it were old, older than the hills, and I hardly knew what to think of the little thing at all.

I reached the bottom of the left-hand page and skipped across to the right, where I caught the latter part of an account of a brawl breaking out in the inn over rough words said to Tommy Aikin. I shook my head in confusion. This didn't follow at all. Even the tone of voice had changed. And then I noticed the furred line between the pages, suggestive of several leaves having been ripped from the journal. I ran my fingertip down the roughened line. I stood and cleared the fallen bed-curtains from the floor, shaking them out to make certain that no papers were concealed in their folds. I searched the floor and under the dresser, but there was nothing. Had Helena secreted them within her clothing? Had she even had the opportunity? How could I tell what she might have done?

I am not your wife. Is that not what you have wished to hear? Well, it is the truth!

I sank down once more. I read on a little further, but I found no mention of the infant: nothing of its cure, nothing of what that had meant. I had no doubt that Mrs. Gomersal's herbs would have failed in their purpose, but what had become of the mite after that?

And then, after I had thought to find no further mention of it, I caught the word "baby," and I read on.

Well there is no baby, not any more.

I caught my breath, forcing myself to continue.

There is no baby, not any more. It flowed out of me and I couldn't stop it, and there was nowt I could do. And now Jem knows I am false because like he says, his wife was with child and I am not; I am barren, and that's a fairy, and that means he can do anything he pleases.

So I said again that I'd tell, and that shut him up a bit. I don't know if I meant it or not; it just doesn't seem right to me and I think summat needs doing but I don't know what and I don't know who I would tell. Parson don't care for owt that isn't in his own backyard and there isn't any constable here, not in Halfoak. The old squire or the young squire both would only be glad, though it's not nice to say and I don't like to think on it. I don't know what possessed me once. But it doesn't matter, not really. There isn't nowt here, nowt being taken care of like it should be taken care of. It's all left to folk to do what they will, and sometimes folk don't do the right thing, and who am I to say it should be different? Still, it rattles Jem's cage when I say it. It sent him mad as a fox put in with the chickens. Still, what's it matter? Nothing is going to bring it back. It isn't going to make me feel any better, though it did just for a minute, when I saw his face. But there's nowt I can really do about making him angry. I cannot breathe without doing that. So it doesn't really make any difference, not now, not to me or any one.

When I read that, though not understanding the half of it, I bent my head and I wept. For my poor cousin to endure such unhappiness, to be thus estranged from her husband, was unutterably sad, and I hated to think of her that way, stuck in this place, all alone, miles from those among her family who would have taken pleasure in helping her—and yet I had not helped her.

There were two lost children in Halfoak. I bowed my head over her book, where she had written those sad words with her own little hand. And I thought of her longing for and crying over someone else, a person she perhaps *had* thrown herself upon for comfort, when he was an unworthy object for her affection; when all the time a better man was thinking of her.

I can kiss but I can't wed you all,
But I would if I could, great and small,
I long for to cuddle you all,
For you see I'm a beautiful boy
Aye, you see I'm a beautiful boy.

I shook the words away. Many a girl in the village had fallen prey to the same infatuation, and doubtless in many other places besides. Who would not admire the son of a landowner, so fine upon his horse? For the man she had written of could only have been Edmund Calthorn. It was a tale that had been told many times before, and in as many places. And in Halfoak there was so little in the way of society; there were so few comparisons to make. How many females, then, must have made him the hero of their imagination, though he was so dissolute a creature?

And I—I had not thought of Lizzie at all. I should have; the guilt written upon my father's face had testified to that. No: I had not thought of her when I should have done so, and then all might have been well. Instead, I had allowed myself to be shaped and influenced by my father. I had taken his choice when it was placed before me, rather than holding tightly to the little hand that had once clung to my arm.

And now she was dead—*dead!* I wept at the thought of it, and I pitied her. Her poor shortened life had ended in misery and fear and the most insufferable pain; it was more than any being should have to endure.

I read on, the words blurring and shifting upon the page, and I realised I had seen this before, that I had caught up with myself; there was nothing more. I had reached the account of them forcing their dreadful physic down her throat.

. . . There was a knock on the door. He says, go and see who it is, wife, only he said wife like it meant summat else. And I didn't move so he went to see and they came in and stood there as if they didn't even know who I was.

Then he says tha shall take it like it or not, and he had it in a jug, and it stunk . . . he said I had to drink it and I would not. I don't know what she puts in that stuff, but its fowl and I said I would not have it, not in my own house with my own husband, and he did nowt but laugh. The others didn't though. One of them got a hold of my shoulders and shoved me down, and held me on the floor, and I said it hurt but they didn't care. The other went and grabbed my hair, right at back of my neck, and I started to cry then since I didn't think they would have done that, helping just as if owt they said even made any sense. All the time, they would not even say nowt to me nor look at me. It were like I was nothing.

I stopped reading and stared into space. I pictured Jem and his uncouth friends, surrounding Lizzie around her own hearthrug, the size of them; their strength. And yet somehow I could not see it at all. It had all gone dark to me. Would Yedder, foolish as he was, pull a woman's hair? Would Tommy? And after all I had seen in Halfoak . . . I shook my head. All I could think of was a little china jug, smashed all to pieces.

Did you see to t' bis'lings?

No. It was not the men of the parish who dealt in herbs and hedge-medicines. I closed my eyes, picturing the scene. There was Lizzie, pleading against their madness—their *ignorance*. There was Jem, an angry husband, slighted by her. And the little jug, held to her lips—

And everything I thought I knew suddenly changed.

Chapter Thirty-One

A short time later I strode down the white road towards the village and Mary Gomersal's neat little cottage. I had not said goodbye to Helena; I did not suppose that she would speak to me. I could not think of her now, and in truth I did not know what I *should* think. Other matters must occupy me, things of a most pressing nature: the reason I had come to Halfoak. I felt the truth was opening to me at last, as a lock yields to an imperfect key only after much pressing.

I soon arrived at her gate and found her much as I had before, her unnatural cub at her heels, playing some unknown game with leaves torn from a mulberry bush, while mother and youngest daughter diligently wove straw with their sun-browned fingers. Mrs. Gomersal looked up at once, as if some sixth sense had informed her of my presence.

She stood and dropped the thing she worked upon, not a mat or a bonnet or some such useful thing but a doll made of corn, some of the ears still bearing grain. The girl had been busy dressing hers in ribbons, scraps of cloth and little flowers. She waved it at me now. "A kern-baby," she said, "for when t' harvest's done an' t' fields are ploughed. They'll plough it into t' ground, see? For luck, for next year's crop."

"Stop yer natterin', Flora." Mrs. Gomersal spoke in a low voice, but in a tone that would not be brooked. "'E dun't want ter listen to thee."

No: I did not want to listen. Nor did I speak.

Mrs. Gomersal bade me good day, in a sweeter but no less uncertain voice. I examined her countenance, trying to read the traces of the past written upon it, but I could not. I tried to picture her presenting her little jug of herbs to my cousin and telling her to drink. Had she really forced it down her throat? Had it been the false "cousins" at all? I could almost see her, standing upon the threshold, ready with her "cure"; her face set and no pity in it at all.

I didn't think they would have done that.

But Halfoak was like that, wasn't it? All the harshness and difficulties of life were here; the lack of forgiveness and the stern judgement; the sin and its fruit, hidden beneath a veil of sunshine and sweetness.

Mrs. Gomersal dropped a curtsy, still waiting for me to speak. "Pray tell me, madam," I said, "why, when I asked you directly who had helped administer certain 'cures' to Elizabeth Higgs, you sent me to enquire of her husband's friends—his 'cousins'? Were you afraid of some reprisal for the part you played in it? Or did you merely take pleasure in distracting and toying with me?"

She took an involuntary step back; the heel of her boot struck the step. She did not look around but snapped at the girl, "Go inside—go inside at once!"

Flora scrambled to her feet, spilling chaff and scraps of fabric from her pinafore. In another moment she was gone. The boy did not move, but continued laying out leaves like playing cards upon the path. He was unconscious of my presence and his mother appeared unconscious of his, as if she did not expect him to heed her.

Her mouth opened and closed. Then she said, "Sir, I only 'elped them as needed it. I only ever try to 'elp, that's what I does."

"Did you help when my cousin was held over the fire? Did you very kindly help with that, Mrs. Gomersal? Or did you merely stand back and watch her burn?"

She shook her head earnestly. "Now, sir—I'll 'ave none o' that."

"You sent me to Jem's cousins, but they were not there when it happened."

"I—no, sir. I'm sorry for it, sir. Only—it were t' way you looked at me, is all."

I swallowed hard. It was what I had expected, yet I had not been certain until she confirmed it. I saw the scene before me once more. *They*, Lizzie had said. *They.*

"It was you. You and—and Ivy." The girl had been in my abode. She had swept the very fire which had consumed Lizzie Higgs. Had the girl no shame? "You knocked her down. You held her hair. And what then? Did you throw lamp oil upon her dress to help the fire along?"

"Not that! Never, sir. I told yer, I'll none on' it. I teld 'im what 'e 'ad to do, an' that's it. It were 'im what did it all."

"Is that how the constable would see it, do you think?"

"Jem'll never blame me." She pulled herself taller. " 'E'll not do that. I told yer, 'er own 'usband did what 'e did, an' 'e'll stand by it. See if 'e dun't! All I did was try an' 'elp 'em all, by God an' t' Bible an' owt else they'll 'ave me swear on!"

"Perhaps you are right," I said. "Perhaps he is not so cowardly as some, to hand over another in their place."

"They would 'ave 'elped if 'e'd asked 'em. Anyone would. They'd 'ave ter. It's t' only way, when the 'idden people get in."

I paused. "That was the reason why you had me see her remains, was it not? You thought to yourself, here comes one who will look into the matter, who will stand by her. And so you sent me in to where she was—why? Did you think it would frighten me from Halfoak before I could even begin to ascertain the truth? Is that the reason for all your warnings about Pudding Pye Hill—about her cottage? To make certain of my leaving it?"

"Sir—sir!" Tears sprung into her eyes. "You speak as if I planned it all—as if I did it all, and not *them*! The 'idden people! As if it was all my design, and not—not to try and fritten them away! You don't know what it's like 'round 'ere, sir. You dun't know what *they're* like!"

I opened my mouth to protest, but at their mention I could not speak. All I could think of was my wife: my wife, who was not as she used to be. Who was now querulous. Unnatural. A shrew. Who was *changed*.

"You must see it, sir. It's plain for all to see what lives 'ere. I did summat because I must. The folk—the *good* folk—they'd take 'alf t' village if they could. We'd all 'ave nobbut cuckoos' nests, an' not a mouthful nor a penny nor a roof on us own, if we give 'em leave. An' they'd drive us mad wi' pretendin' to be the folk we know, the ones we love, sir, an' all the while, they're not—"

At that she threw her apron over her face and wept into it. I did not know what I should say. I waited until she let it fall and uncovered her reddened eyes. Then she turned to her son.

"You see, I know what it's like, sir. See 'im sittin' there at me feet? Aye, look at 'im! See 'is black eyes an' wild hair and wilder ways? You think I'd wish that upon another, sir, when I see it every day an' can 'ardly bear the sight? I were only tryin' to be kind an' spare the lass what I 'ad mesel'. I did what I 'ad ter, sir, an' what the wise woman said I must. Tha's all a body can do, in't it? I din't do nowt wrong, sir, if I din't manage to do nowt right!"

I started. "You say your own child is a changeling?" I was astonished. But she knew the wise woman, did she not? She knew the "cure." Why would she keep such a one under her roof?

She sniffed, then she shook her head. "That's not what I said, sir."

"But—"

"I did not. But 'e's one on 'em, all t' same. I—I fell asleep on the 'ill, sir. Just where I said you should not. That's 'ow I knew, in't it? I fell asleep an' I got took. I slept an' I danced in that sleep, an' that dance—oh, such a dance! Well, when I woke up, I 'ad 'im in my belly, din't I? 'E were in me, an' I'd no choice about it then. I just 'ad to wonder and wonder 'ow much of 'im was me, an' 'ow much was one o' them."

She turned her head and met my gaze. "Do you know 'ow it is, sir, to watch your own, an' love 'em, an' not even know if they are who you think they are, or summat else altogether? I pray you never do, sir. At least—at least it were all right for *them*. They could do what they 'ad to, to get rid on it. There were none o' that for me. I 'ad to keep mine, an' look where that got me. You reckon you 'ave a good place in life, an' you see it all slipping from you, all on it."

I felt a mist coming down across my thoughts; it was as if I were falling into the half-dream of which Jem Higgs had once spoken. "You *consorted* with them, is that what you are saying—that your child is only half a human child?"

Papa, he had said, there in the magical grove on the fairy hill.

She only looked away.

"And why were you there? Why were you walking upon the fairy hill that day?"

She remained mute.

"You warned me that it was dangerous."

"Aye, sir. I could only tell you what I learned by me own mistake." Her voice was barely above a whisper. "I am well punished for it, am I not?"

I glanced at the boy. He was still playing with the leaves, laying them out in a ring, all the stalks converging to a central point. He did not look at us and he did not listen. He was in his own mind, in his own world; intent upon his own simple game and nothing else. I suddenly felt exhausted, beyond my capacity to bear. Perspiration trickled down the back of my neck. I wished that I had never come to Halfoak. Oh, to be in London once again, with all its grey smoke and fog! I wished I were already being swept away from here by a ferocious and unstoppable engine, leaving only burning ricks behind. But there was still something else I must ask.

"So where, pray, is Essie Aikin's baby?"

She started. She evidently had not expected me to know anything of it.

"What happened to it? What did you do?"

She pursed her lips. "Nowt but what we 'ad to. An' that's all I'll say on the matter."

"You will tell me where it is."

"I'll tell you nowt." She screwed up her face in anger. "An I'll thank ye to leave my door. I've entertained thee enough. I've done nowt but what I 'ad to do for me and mine, and it in't none o' yourn. What are we to thee? What's any on it to thee? Tha'd best be goin'. Aye, you should gerroff, before the folk get an' 'old on thee that you can't prise loose. There's nowt for thee 'ere. None'll speak to thee; none'll 'elp thee. We look after us sens around 'ere, cos that's what we 'ave ter do, and none else will."

I met anger with anger. "Do you think so? Why, I have spoken to the mother already, and she would have told me all if I had pressed her; it was only pity that gave me pause. I shall speak to her again."

"Will thee now? Tha will if tha can find 'er."

My eyes widened. "Whatever do you mean?"

She laughed in my face. "Owd Tommy said she'd been upset." Her smile grew broader. "It were you, were it! As if she an't 'ad enough. I said if she couldn't let it rest, 'e should take 'er off for a bit. Aye—she's gone! Off to relatives in t' north, where none can get at 'er. Where none'll upset 'er and frit 'er wi' no questions."

I could only stare. Relatives in the north? Somewhere farther and wilder than this? And yet I could see by the triumph written upon her face that it was true.

Slowly she turned her back on me, spitting sidelong onto her own path before she grasped the boy's ear and dragged him with her. He curled his little hands into fists and beat at her side, but she was implacable. It was not until he was out of sight that I realised the unnatural child had not made a sound of protest at his rough treatment; nor had a single word fallen from his lips.

Nothing remained but to walk away from her cottage and towards Pudding Pye Hill, by turns shaking my head and burning with rage over the woman's brazenness. At least I had gained something of the truth of it. And I should not do as she had so charmingly suggested and leave this place, not now. The eagerness with which she bade me to quit Halfoak had made me the more steadfast in my resolution.

I looked up, the sun blinding me momentarily, and made out the smooth outline of the hill. I froze. It was not quite smooth after all; it was not entirely isolated. As if Mrs. Gomersal's talk had summoned the hidden people to the surface, a dark form was clearly outlined against its edge. I blinked. At first I did not know what it was, and then I realised: it was nothing but a man on horseback, his posture loose and easy. I knew at once who it was.

I shielded my eyes, but could see little better. His form was made indistinct by the light and I could not tell what his business may be. Perhaps he was riding for its own sake; possibly he was surveying all that he would one day inherit. After all, the hill offered a fine view of all his father's lands. So he was not afraid of all the evil rumours and stories that had been put about. I wished suddenly that I had spoken to him when I had seen him that day with Helena, and yet something had prevented me; something besides my own dishevelled appearance.

It still struck me as odd that Mrs. Gomersal had not been afraid of the hill either, at least until her escapade. She had given no satisfactory account of why she liked to wander there in spite of its evil reputation. It was a place to be shunned, was it not? It was not a place of work nor yet of leisure. Even if a man were unafraid, it was odd that anyone would go there by choice. It was a secret place, a midnight place. It occurred to me then how useful would be the tales of its hidden residents to anyone who wished to hide their actions from the everyday tide of humanity. To such a person, its stories would be treasure indeed. To frighten other men away, to keep dark matters safe, away from prying eyes . . . I recollected the words of the antic cousins who had awaited Lizzie's return at the grove:

You 'eard about that nipper o' Mary Gomersal's, din't yer? Wandered off one day an' never t' same since? They said 'e were up 'ere then.

Aye, an' they say she were up 'ere an' all, seven year ago.

So they had known of Mrs. Gomersal's adventures. I wondered if she was like the wise woman, claiming herself wiser by the uncertain virtue of her contact with the fairies. Her tale wrapped her in the finery of their silken mysteries; it lent authority to her bearing and weight to her words.

I watched the squire's son a little longer as he rode about. A pity it was that he was not better employed. His father's illness and his mother's distraction had left an emptiness into which all manner of weeds had been allowed to flourish. Halfoak might not be so backward were it not for such abnegation of duties; but then I remembered the parson's sermonising, his talk of the blasted oak tree, the sign of God's wrath, and I sighed.

It was true that the squire's son appeared to have sprung from the hill itself like a warrior of ancient times—of the same tribe, perhaps, who had buried its people under the barrow. And then he put me in mind of something else, and I wondered that I had not seen it before. With his surly ways and dark locks, he resembled none other than Heathcliff, the subject of my wife's book. And he too was a fairy-like creature, was he not? Appearing at least half elemental, striding about the country, the victim of wild passions and impulses that any civilised being should have long since mastered.

Poor Essie Aikin. What had she been thinking? She surely could not have imagined that Edmund Calthorn would marry her. It was a pity that she had not thought to invent some fairy father; none had shunned Mary Gomersal as they had the silly Aikin girl. No: her tale had saved her. And the boy also; like Heathcliff, he was at least half wild. I had even thought of him as an elf. Did she really imagine he had been born half of some fairy creature? Or was this mysterious being, as Heathcliff had proved to be, merely the creation of a woman?

I stood there I knew not how long, pondering it. Edmund Calthorn passed out of sight; the very air was motionless. Slowly I felt all the presence of summer wrapping itself about me as if to soothe all troubled thoughts away; to make me part of this place. I shook myself like a dog emerging from a dream. Then I turned my steps and pulled myself across a stone stile and entered a field that was full of grass and clover.

Chapter Thirty-Two

For a time there was nothing but the susurration of my steps through the long grass. I remembered the names Mary Gomersal had told me: meadow cat's-tail, fox-tail, dog's-tail. I felt as a man moving through a world of his imagining, letting the fronds brush past my hands. The seeds clung to my clothes, but no use in brushing them away when there were so many. Across the meadow, sheep raised their heads and regarded me before falling to the clover once more. The sun beat down, as it always did in Halfoak, the summer a timeless season that might remain for ever. All was the picture of bucolic peace, and yet that peace could not touch my heart. I felt like a dreamer; I felt like a fool.

I heard the clatter of pots before I made out the rough outline of the wise woman's shack amongst the twisted growth which surrounded it. Even from here, the woodland looked dank. At its edge, the sunshine reached everything; berries hung fat on the hedgerow; birds called to one another and flitted from branch to branch. All spoke of life, quite unlike her den. I could smell it: the rot in the timbers, the mustiness of unwashed clothing, the *uncleanliness* of it all.

Another rattle told of her movements: she was brewing some potion, or making up a magic bottle, something to ward off the evil eye or find a lost trinket or make the corn grow straight, but I cared not. I pushed my way through the clumps of ivy and brambles to the crooked door and knocked.

All sound ceased, as if someone had frozen in surprise. She had not foreseen my coming, then, with all her hedge-magics. There came a blundering and scraping before the door swung wide.

She was wearing her apron, still dreadfully stained, and her hands were again clotted with sticky dough. I peered past her and saw that she was making oatcakes upon the piece of wood which passed for a table. Her single chair was piled with dirty clothing.

There had been no endeavour to tame her hair, which still hung loose and unbrushed. Her cheeks were paler than I had last seen them; I wondered if she had previously reddened them with beet-root juice, as a harlot might.

She stepped back and indicated that I should enter, though she had not spoken, and I remembered her voice; deeper than I had expected and laced with honey.

"I am come to ask you a question," I said.

"Step in," she replied, and her voice was higher than it had been; perhaps she had not yet donned her wise woman's tone as well as her accoutrements.

I went inside, removing my hat as I ducked beneath the papers and bundles of herbs, no longer finding in them some mystery, only the pitiful and dangerous remnants of a belief which should be long dead. She rubbed dough from her hands, picking it from between her fingers with one of the items of dress piled upon the chair. I would have expected no more from such a slattern; but that was by no means the worst of her attributes. I remembered the way I had allowed her to set her foot upon my own; I felt once more the creeping of her fingers through my hair.

"A moment, sir," she said, remembering this time to affect the dramatic lowering of her voice. "I'll ready me crystal. I'm sure the sperrits'll be ready anon." She hurried over to her wooden box and darted a look at me. "You've not forgot the fee, sir? Of gold, if you please."

I drew myself taller, feeling a cobweb or one of her papers brush the top of my head. I paid it no heed. "I shall not pay you a penny," I said. "I am not come for your hocus-pocus or enchantments or any such foolery. I am not one of your peasants who can be blinded by your nonsense. I merely wish to know what enchantment did Mary Gomersal purchase from you in order that she should bewitch Edmund Calthorn?"

Her eyes opened wider. Then she opened her mouth and let out a laugh that was more like the barking of a fox. "Ha! Oh, sir—that's good!" A new light blazed in her eyes—an awakened kind of look, and wary, and yet there was mirth in it too.

"What was it?" I pressed. "A spell? A potion? A bottle? A paper—your herbs?" I batted at one of her hanging bundles and powder floated from it. The scent was of pepper and dust and the passage of time.

"I'll not charge thee," she said, leaning forwards, as if in the companionable sharing of confidences.

I waved her words away. "Tell me at once!"

"Why, sir, it's like this. A woman's 'chantments need no potion, sir. They dun't need no charm. If a lady cannit accomplish *that* by 'ersel', why, she's no lady!" She laughed raucously at the absurdity of calling Mary Gomersal a lady; I did not join in.

"You say she managed such a thing herself?" My tone was indignant. I thought of Mrs. Gomersal, and I thought of the squire's son, with all his insolence and wildness. He was little more than my own age, and all the repugnance of it returned to me. However would she have possessed the audacity without bolstering her brazenness with some charm?

"She wasn't always such!" the beldam said, as if reading my mind. "Seven year an' three childer'll do that to a lass. She were a pitcher, once. Aye, an' besides, 'e's not one to turn it down, whatever wrappin' it comes in. Not where it's freely gi'en!"

I can kiss but I can't wed you all,
But I would if I could, great and small . . .

She laughed again at my expression. "Oh, aye—it's just like a young 'un to think mutton never were grown from a lamb." Her tone was unmoderated by my glare. "But 'e's not one to turn from his meat, is 'e, bein' allus hungerin', an' anyway, 'e 'as to find amusement where he may, dun't 'e? An' there's plenty on it about! 'Sides, there's nowt like one a bit older an' married afore to show 'im t' way!"

Her riotous cackling filled the little shack, ringing from its rafters, rattling her supplies of herbs and noxious liquids and old, old knowledge, and I pushed my way through her hangings and ducked through the doorway, the harsh sound of it following me still, incongruous in the peaceful meadow.

There was no use questioning her further, and no need, for I was beginning to see it all. I retraced my steps through the long grass, looking behind me once to see her standing at the door, watching me go. She had grasped her skirts in both hands and was curtsying to left and right, as if to make a show of her harlotry, and I walked more quickly, straightening my back, trying to conduct myself as a gentleman; and all the while accompanied by the dreadful rough music of her merriment.

Chapter Thirty-Three

I hastened towards my cousin's cottage, feeling I could not reach it quickly enough. The day's light was deepening, the sky turning fiery. The shadows of each blade of grass and stone and flower stretched towards me.

I had been a fool. All the time I had held the secrets of Halfoak in my hand, and what had I done? I had passed over them. My cousin's journal had been telling me everything, just as no doubt she would have wished it to do—*willed* it to do—and yet I had not seen it. I had skipped over the pages, thinking her life nothing, glossing over the most important part of all.

At last the little bridge was ahead of me. The brook's babble did not sound so cheerful as before—perhaps a reflection of what I felt—and I leaned out over it. The water had yielded to the summer at last; its level had sunk and it was fairly choked with weed. If rain did not come it might dry up altogether. The watercress would turn brown and wither, like the crops in the field: all the pretty gold turning drear, crumbling to chaff, so that the harvesters were forced to breathe in the dead stuff that was the ruin of the village.

I did not care for Halfoak now, or what became of its folk. I wanted only to hold my cousin's journal and see, written in her own hand, in ink upon paper, what I already suspected to be true.

Her husband had been right to want so badly for it to be found. He simply had not known the right reason.

I hurried up the path, ignoring the perspiration that gathered beneath my hat and soaked my clothes. And then I saw the place, really *saw* it, and I stopped.

A pall of smoke rose from the chimney. There was nothing strange in that; we had been forced to use the range for water and meat—but what smoke it was! It gathered thickly over the roof, too much of it to readily dissipate into the sluggish air, swathing the tiles with grey, softening the very outline of the building.

I did not stop to wonder; I ran towards the door.

I burst inside to find the parlour an inferno, the fire banked high and blazing, flames licking and darting from it where the chimney would not draw; it hissed and spat like a cat in a corner. Lurid light flickered over the hearthstones and every surface, catching the eyes of the preserved fox, which glared and gleamed, its fur shining more redly than ever. And it glittered from the eyes of my wife. She was in a parlous state of undress. Her gown hung open, revealing her linens, shining whitely in the shifting glare. Her hair was coming undone, some caught up at the nape of her neck, some dangling in her eyes, some flying about her head and limned by the blaze into fiery points. Images flashed before me: the squire's son, riding out upon the hillside; the beldam's awful parody of coquettishness; costermongers spilling from a penny gaff, a flash of mottled skin, their grinning lips, harsh laughter . . .

"I almost fit her dress now," she said. "Do you see?" She twisted this way and that and I started, because I saw what it was that she held in her hand.

Her lip twitched. "What do you think, Albie?" Her voice was calm, as if she were about to ask whether I should prefer milk with my tea. "Shall I add a little more wood to the fire? Another stock, perhaps?"

"Helena—I do not know what this is," I replied, "but you must stop it at once. You must gather your wits."

"Gather my wits, should I?"

"I . . . You are not acting as a rational person. I thought you disliked the fire, did you not? It is too warm. And—Helena, I thought you did not wish to touch the irons . . ."

Raucous laughter spilled from her before she composed herself. She held up her hands. They were wrapped around in white cloth—handkerchiefs—entirely covering her skin. She had not touched the irons, then. But what could it matter? Such thoughts, such ideas, could not apply to us. They *must* not. *A man of reason*, I reminded myself, and I focused on the thing she held in her hand, the thing that mattered more than any other. "Give me the journal, Helena. You cannot conceive how important it has become."

"Oh, but I know, Albie!" She was suddenly furious, her eyes flashing brighter than any flame. Then she gave way; she sagged, looking terribly unhappy.

"I admit to you, Albie, I once thought this house haunted," she said. "I heard things—music, calling to me in the night. It made me wish to dance more than I could bear." Her expression turned to wistfulness. "I thought that it must have been spirits, it was so very beautiful. But then I saw what this place had wrought in you, and I realised: we have no need of ghosts, do we, Albie? What would a ghost do here that we have not already done?"

She swayed, staring down at the journal as if she did not know how it had come to be there. I stepped forward and reached for it, but at the same time she stepped back, a little closer to the fire. I did not know how she could bear the heat. I could feel the skin of my cheeks tightening; it was like standing at a Hell-mouth.

"This house is not haunted, Albie. It is you who are haunted."

I shook my head in confusion.

"Yes! You are haunted, but not by spirits. She has always been here, has she not? She is present constantly; she is in your every thought; she is in your heart. How could I ever displace her? How can I fight?" She glanced down at the journal in her hands. "I cannot remonstrate with her; I cannot push her aside, or beg her to go, or banish her. She will always be here, because you will it so: always present to your mind, if never to your eye!" She did not look at me again. She whirled about and in one movement, hurled the book upon the fire.

I cried out and leaped forward, falling to my knees before the flames. I grasped the tongs and reached after the journal, but they were too short; smoke rose around my hands and between my fingers and I could smell singed hair and overheated flesh. I snatched my hands away and instead grasped the poker, hoping to thrust it between the pages, to catch hold of it in some way and prise it loose, but I dropped the iron with a cry. It was burning hot—it had seared a line clean across my palm. A large blister was rising there, but it did not matter. I grasped my own handker-chief and wrapped it around my fist, preparatory to reaching into the inferno, but even as I stretched towards it, blinking furiously against the sting of smoke, I saw that it was too late, for the pages were blackening, like hair; like skin. The paper was crumbling away, becoming nothing but fragments that floated, wraith-like, up the chimney.

I cried out, feeling as if I were the one turning to ash. It was entirely hopeless. Lizzie's words were already far beyond my reach.

I heard Helena's voice behind me. "You see? Anyone may be burned by iron, my love."

I pushed myself across the stone flags towards her, and once more I was grasping the poker in my fist. I closed my eyes; for a time, I knew only darkness.

When I came to myself I was kneeling once more before the fire, my eyes closed, my shoulders shaking. My cheeks were wet with tears. I was alone in the room. The fire, once so hungry, had spent itself; it had turned grey, already dying.

I rose, ignoring the pain in my knees and hands. Outside the window, twilight had come, though I could still make out the shapes around me without need of a lamp. There was the table; there the chairs; there the old faded settle, all as familiar to me now as if this were my own home.

I turned my back on them and proceeded up the stairs. I went into my room and found all in order, save for the bed-curtains that had been tugged loose and lay still upon the floor; and another book that had been cast aside on my pillow.

I rushed to it and picked it up, but it was not my book: it was my wife's. Mine was quite lost, and the pain of it struck me anew.

I let the pages fall open. Some were loose and drifted to the floor. I let them fall; I had read them already. I turned the pages, letting the words flow before my eyes. I could not make them out; they meant nothing. And then I turned another page and something stilled within me. I read on, not quite believing what it was they told me.

My breath quickened. As if a veil had been torn from my eyes, I saw what I must do.

Chapter Thirty-Four

The sun had quite faded, the last of its light already passed beyond the horizon, but the moon had risen. It was waning but still near full, and its yellow, swollen face lit the path before me almost as clear as day. The whole sky was luminous with stars.

My every step was too loud to my ear and yet at the edges of hearing, there was music: someone was playing the violin, a quick and lively air. I did not pause to wonder at its source; it could have been anywhere—it could have been pouring from the sky or rising from the earth. There was nothing else, no birdsong or distant cry from a cow in the fields or an owl from the glade; all was still, save for my own self.

I wondered if I should be afraid, but I was not. I felt only a kind of numbness that had spread through each limb and into my bones. My heart alone felt heavy. I could not give way to despair. There was something I must do and if I allowed myself to waver I would fail, and if I failed, I would never be able to bring myself to try again.

I went on, alone in the world, until I reached the place I sought. I stared at the ground: a patch of sward a little raised from the grass around it: one that I had seen before and had not thought to *look* at.

I swung the spade from my shoulder and let its blade rest upon the ground. I stood there a while, allowing myself a brief contemplation, bowing my head in respect or apology, or both; and then I seized it and, ignoring the pain in my burned hand, thrust it into the ground.

It would not give, at first. The earth was hardened by days of sunlight and I tried again and again, in vain, until I found the place the grass had previously been cut to permit what lay beneath, and it yielded before the blade.

Beneath it, the soil appeared almost black and images filled my mind. I took deep breaths. My heart thumped against my ribs. My hands were shaking; I did not know what I would be forced to look upon. But I had seen the words in my wife's book, and I had known what to do.

> I got a spade from the tool-house, and began to delve with all my might—it scraped the coffin; I fell to work with my hands; the wood commenced cracking about the screws . . .

Everything had become so clear to me when I had read those words and my course remained clear now—and yet it made me think so vividly of my cousin that when I looked up once more I expected to see the churchyard all about me, the quiet stones, the sleeping church, the dark yews standing sentinel about it; and at my feet, Lizzie's own little grave.

But I was not there; I was not even in Halfoak, not really. I was standing in the grove, the oak trees all about me, their leaves whispering to one another. At my feet was the little patch of ground beneath the trees, a short distance from what Mary Gomersal had told me was a door. Just in front of my spade, pushed partway into the earth, was an iron knife.

I did not pull it from the ground but wrapped my handkerchief more firmly about my damaged hand and resumed my labours, parting the earth and casting the spill aside. The hole grew deeper and more shadowed and I could not readily see into it. I was glad for that, and yet not glad, for how should I know when I found what I sought? There would be no box, I knew that.

I went on, allowing my motions to become mechanical. It was an age and yet too little time until my spade met something that was softer than the earth. I jumped back from it. I cast the spade aside and kneeled, pushing away the dry soil with my hands, both wanting to see and dreading what I sought. At first I did not know that I had found it. The cloth was dry as the earth, but it did not give under my hands and I realised it was *not* earth, and the next thought was relief that it had been wrapped, and that I did not have to see its face. Then horror returned, because I knew I must unfold the cloth and see what was concealed within.

I carefully freed it from the soil and lifted it onto the grass. The once-white cloth was now stained and darkened, the bundle so small and light and pitiful. I reached out, all gentleness, and folded back its wrapping until I had revealed what had lain hidden so long.

I stared upon the tiny hands, still closed into fists. I saw the spine, each vertebra clearly discernible, as if the little creature had tried to curl back into the form wherein it had grown, when it had last been warm and safe and loved. Wisps of hair clung to the peeling scalp. It lay with its face turned inward, and I was grateful. I did not wish to look upon its eyes; I could not bear to see its pain.

I let out a breath and stared into the night, through the trees and towards the stony side of the hill. I remembered what I had seen the night I had last come here at a dark midnight hour: a white form, drifting between the trees. Had I really imagined it, for the slightest moment, to be a fairy? Had I truly thought it had been Lizzie? Of course it had not been. It was Essie Aikin, searching for her lost child. She had buried the changeling, here upon the hill, in exchange for her infant; it should have returned by the light of the moon, but the fairies had cheated her.

Her child had been here in the ground above Halfoak all the time. Essie had done what she had been told: she had battled the changeling, casting her charms and chanting her spells, and none of it had worked; she had not had her baby returned again; it had not emerged, dancing and happy, after joining in some fairy procession. It was *here*, and she had not owned it. She had not even named it.

My thoughts turned to what they had done to it; to what she had been *told* to do to it. What suffering had they inflicted? Suddenly I did not want to know the truth; it was too much for this world. It was too *real*. What had they done? Forced herbs down its infant throat? Had they sung wicked songs to it, made it cry, stuck it with pins? And then what? Held it over the fire, thinking it would shriek its way up the chimney, until, finding that nothing worked, that nothing ever could—had they brought it to this place to conceal what they had done? Or had they simply left it here for the fairies to claim, until its breath failed in its body and they were forced to bury it?

And yet Essie Aikin had come searching for it. She had tormented a creature she had not believed to be her own child—that she did not even think human. She had come, a fond mother, seeking her true child, having done anything—*any* thing—to bring it back to her again. And what had been her thoughts when the fairies broke their pact? Her living child had not returned; all that remained was this pitiful, nameless creature, barely having drawn breath and already becoming a part of the earth.

Chapter Thirty-Five

The next morning I awoke to fresh clean sunlight spilling in at the window. The curtains fluttered against the shutters; I must have opened the casement when I returned the night before, perhaps longing for the freshness of the new day. What had passed had taken on the texture and character of a dream and I wished, more than anything, that it could have been one. When I looked down at my hands, though, I could see the vicious burn across my palm. The skin was further callused from my digging; both hands were encrusted with blood, and soil had become ingrained in every line and cut. I rose, poured water from the earthenware jug and washed them, but at once I could feel the grime that clung to the rest of my being. I was not sure that mere water could slough it away, but I tried, and put on clean clothes, making sure that all was straight and smart; that I had at least the appearance of a civilised person.

Then I went to wake my wife.

Helena lay with her hair spread upon the pillow, her pale features transformed by repose into the image of peaceful calm. Her heavy eyelids were smooth and her lips were sweet; I was reminded of when we had first been married; for a moment, I almost wanted to kiss them. Then she stirred, as if she knew what I had been thinking, and she muttered something I could not make out.

I did not touch her, but put my hand upon the bedsheet, gently shaking her shoulder. The effect was startling; she awoke at once, her expression turning to one of alarm. It made me want to shrink from her, but I did not allow myself to show it; instead I met her eye.

"Helena," I said, my voice as gentle as I could make it, "pray, let us be reconciled. I am sorry—for all. Please know that I will always endeavour to do what I hope to be right; and to that end, I have decided that we should depart as soon as we can ready ourselves. Would that make you content, dearest?" I forced myself to take her hand, which she had raised to rub her eyes, and I gently squeezed her fingers. My burnt hand I kept at my side.

"I—I hardly know," she replied, and her voice was soft; she was half in a daze herself.

"I will bring something for you to eat." I smiled at her softly, and it felt more like an old smile, a ghost of the way we had used to be. "Will you like to be back at our own home?"

She gave a slight nod.

"Then let us prepare ourselves, my love. We should leave soon. I will hurry to the inn and have their man come for us. If you cannot pack everything, do not worry."

"Will you send for the rest, Albie?" She sounded full of sleep.

I squeezed her hand and smiled at her and stood. "I will make everything ready."

I brought bread and butter to her room, and tea, and fresh warm water for washing. She was already engaged in removing her dresses from the wardrobe and folding them for the journey. She looked brighter, and she smiled at me, though she did not speak. This was how it would be, I decided. We could still be as man and wife. We would find our way back to one another again; our wounds would heal. And then there would be three of us, and in that great moment, all would be forgotten.

I threw several of my own possessions into a bag, leaving some of the clothing and the heavier items where they lay. And then I knocked upon her door and called out that I would go to the Three Horseshoes and that I would return with all haste so that we could depart.

I hurried along the white road. The day was already warm, though the sun had barely risen. The people of Halfoak had been at their work in the fields for some time. I had thought once that when I left this place I should miss it, but now there was a new darkness at my back; it was still there, on Pudding Pye Hill, although for the moment I had pushed it from my thoughts. I had sworn to myself that I would first take care of Helena, and so I would.

The inn door was open, but no one was in the taproom at this hour and I gave up waiting. I went outside and let myself in at the wicket which led to the outhouses, stables and wash house—it seemed an age ago that I had witnessed its sorry contents—and I saw a boy there, filling pails from the pump. Upon hearing my enquiry he went chasing off inside, shouting, "There's someone 'ere!," and soon the ceiling was a-creak with footsteps, the landlord's heavy tread was heard upon the stairs and then the man appeared, blinking as if he had just risen, though his rolled-up sleeves and the crumbs of bread in his whiskers suggested otherwise.

I explained my need of a cart and he listened, nodding. He was attentive, but his manner was subdued and he barely met my eye. I remembered my sorry conduct since I had come to the village: my protestations over how he had managed the funeral; my wandering about the fields, tearing my clothes to rags. No doubt, in his position at his hatch, he had heard of it all. I had the opportunity to repent my behaviour now, but I said nothing of it; just pressed a remembrance into his hand as he gave his promise to have his man at our door in a trice.

I hurried back more quickly than I had come. Pudding Pye Hill loomed in my vision and yet I contrived not to look at it directly. When I opened the cottage door Helena was just placing a light bag in the passage. I told her I would bring down the rest, that the cart should not be long, and she smiled.

I hurried upstairs to collect my own things, and to carry out one final task. I hastily dashed off a note to Constable Barraclough, giving what details I felt necessary, and signed it. I slipped it into an envelope and as I did, my gaze fell upon the other papers I had left in the room: the pages of my wife's novel, scattered about the floor. I did not like to leave it looking as it did, all chaos and disorder, so I put down my envelope and bent to pick them up, reaching for those that had slipped partially under the bed. There was one that defied my reach and I kneeled upon the floor and peered after it. I was about to retrieve it when I noticed something else: pages other than from my wife's book, and not discarded upon the floor but jutting from the bottom of the bed-frame. I blinked. Was it only stuffing poking through a hole in the mattress? But I knew that it was not.

I lay down upon the floor and stretched beneath the bed until I could feel the rasp of paper under my fingers. I pulled it free, then remembered to collect the last page of *Wuthering Heights* before I stood once more.

I set aside the novel's printed sheets, then stood there, struck dumb, clutching the others against my chest. I knew at once what they were and I wanted almost to laugh, or to cry, to do anything that would steady my racing pulse. These were the pages of my cousin's journal that had been torn free; the ones I had so desperately sought to read. I knew not why they had been secreted there— had Lizzie known, somehow? Had she simply wished to hide them as best she could, in the event that one day, she may need to show them to somebody?

I had thought never to see her hand again. Some of the letters were cramped, some bleeding away across the page as if the pen had been a living thing trying to escape her. The rustic style: had I once taken such for charm? It did not seem so now, nor its opposite. It was more as if I held a foreign object, one I could barely identify but that could reveal untold secrets to my eye—and I had no time in which to read it.

I flattened out the sheets, catching brief lines.

They said the bairn could not say its name and so they held its nose and poured cure straight down its throat. It coughed and then it swallowed. It didn't seem to do no harm, but it didn't do no good neither.

I saw Essie again to-day. She said they told her it isn't working and they had to try summat else. She was scared, I think, they had her scared she would never hold her real baby in her arms. I asked what else and she wouldn't tell me and then she said you take a spade and heat it up over the fire and then you put the baby . . .

I closed my eyes. Then I opened them and scanned further down the page.

I told Jem all about it and I said they was mad but he didn't say owt, he just looked into the fire like he was thinking on it, putting a fairy to the hot metal, and I said aren't you going to say nowt to your cousin, he's Essie's father, some-one has to say summat, but he shook his head. And I said I wouldn't have anything to do with it and neither should he and he gave me this look, like he didn't rightly know who I was.

. . . what they did. I can't think on it. Jem said it'd all come back and it all went like it should but I don't reckon it and I tried to tell him, but I just cried. I was thinking what I'd do if it was my own baby. Then I said one of us should tell, and the look he gave me . . .

I folded the sad pages. It was a tale too sorrowful to be told. I did not wish to look upon their secrets; I knew them already. I took up the note I had written to the constable and pushed the sheets inside the envelope just as the stamp of a horse sounded in the lane and a knock rang out upon the door.

Helena and I rode in silence, but it was a calm silence, accompanied only by the endless clopping of the stolid bay mare. How often a journey seems shorter when one is going home! The fields were almost denuded of their crops, the little that remained so dry it might crumble in the first strong breeze. And still the labourers cut and bundled and raked and stacked, tireless as engines, or so it appeared from this distance, each man and woman and child knowing their part as surely as the fox knows its den and the rabbit its burrow. I turned and looked into the distance and made out the scarecrow I had seen before, though now its jacket had been taken. From here, it barely resembled a man, or indeed, any living form.

Soon we reached the town, and the bustle and the looming buildings felt strange to me. We stopped briefly at the inn for some refreshment and I put the envelope into the landlord's hand, pressing upon him the urgency of it reaching the constable before morning. He was a little surprised—if I had stepped out, I could no doubt have discovered the man myself—but I had no wish to be caught up in questions and explanations. For too long my priority had wandered from the requirements of my own family and on this day, I would set all else aside.

Soon afterwards, the shriek and rumble of the steam engine carried us away from it all, and I was glad to leave it behind me. I did not look out of the windows, but from the corner of my eye I could see the green and gold of the land slipping away behind us. Soon we would reach all the monochrome crowds and hard streets of the City, and I was glad of it: that was where I belonged; it was what I understood. And yet something tugged at my insides, a bond that was being stretched thin but somehow refusing to break.

I shifted in my seat, remembering something. I caught Helena's eye and smiled. "I brought this for you," I said, pulling the reassembled copy of *Wuthering Heights* from my pocket and passing it to her. "I thought you might like to read it."

She stared down at the sorry thing I offered her, with its cover broken and pages hanging from it, and I thought I would have done better to leave it behind us in Halfoak. I expected harsh words, but she simply reached out her hand, very slowly, and took it from me. She held it in her lap, careful not to rub the dusty cover against her clothing.

"I am sorry," I said, my voice low, but this time she did not answer.

It did not seem long until we were crammed into a hansom cab with our bags and racing along, its wheels smooth against the paved road as we passed all manner of city folk: sellers of pies; urchins; ladies with ostrich feathers adorning their hats; hawkers of penny bloods. The weather had turned all to dullness long before we had reached London, but here the sky hung more heavily than ever, the gloom sapping all colour from what lay beneath. Only a sharp chill in the air told that here summer had passed and autumn had come, though without its show of colour or fruitfulness. Before much longer, winter would be breathing down our shirt collars.

We made good progress, now that the end of our journey was almost within our reach, until we were delayed by a dreadful sight: a dray horse, in trying to turn, had come up against a wooden pavement and slipped. The pitiful creature had broken its knees, and I thought of the bay mare, so sure-footed on the country lanes, but I did not speak of it. Helena kept her silence also, staring down at her gloved hands, though she clenched them tightly around her wretched book.

Finally, we alighted at the door of my father's house. Before we had gathered ourselves, the housekeeper emerged to exclaim and wonder over our sudden appearance. My father was at his desk at this hour and would not be home until later; it was better so, since we could settle ourselves and rest from the journey before he demanded an account of everything that had passed since he last laid eyes on us.

At least he would have the happy news to distract him and I smiled at that thought as I went with Helena through the wide hall and up the stairs, so smooth and solid after what we had been used to these last days, the shining mahogany neatly topped with its scarlet runner and brass fittings, not creaking at all.

We walked into our rooms and I turned and took her hand. She was still wearing her gloves; I could not tell if her fingers were warm or cool, and her face was empty of expression. "My dear, it will all be better now, I promise you," I said. "Soon I will become my father's assistant. We can set up our own establishment. I shall think of nothing else—whatever hard work can achieve, I shall provide it. All will be for you—you and our child!"

I squeezed her fingers, drawing her to me, but she would not be drawn. She was suddenly stiff and motionless as a statue.

"Helena, will that not make you happy? Is it not what you desire? That is my only concern now—please be assured of it. I will show you every mark of affection. I will take care of you and the baby, as long as I draw breath—"

She snatched her fingers from my grasp. Her eyes flashed. "You are not to return to Halfoak?"

I gathered myself. I could not hide that I had been unprepared for her words—for her insight—even though I had known I must tell her.

"I have to go back, Helena, though it shall only be for a single day, if my own wishes prevail. It is a matter of the law, my dear, and so I must. It is nothing to do with my own preference."

She pressed her lips tightly together, so that they almost could not be seen. It made her look older; different.

"Helena, please. When you are like this, why, I could almost believe—" I sighed.

"What do you believe, Albie?" she sneered.

"I simply do not know you," I said, softly. I passed a hand across my face. She did not speak, and so I forced myself to go on. "I simply do not know. You must admit, Helena, that your conduct has been at times so very strange—"

"Strange!" Her eyes flashed with sudden passion. "Strange! You think it strange?" Her tone turned to mockery. "Do you think me a *fairy*, Albie? Do you think me a stock of wood and your true wife— your dear, sweet, obedient wife—is residing beneath a hollow hill? Is that what you imagine?"

"I—"

"My conduct was not *strange*, Husband. Do you not see why I conducted myself as I did? Why I sometimes barely *knew* what I did? You took me away from all the comforts of my home, from our acquaintances, from all the life I had known, and you placed me among the most barbaric of strangers. You did not even appear to care about my condition. And you had me live in that dreadful rough cottage, in a land more strange to me than any I have ever known, with no one to help me—"

I shook my head, unable to believe her onslaught. All I could think of were the words spoken to me by the parson: *As for those who seek them out—those who go looking to find evil—why, they shall find it, sir, and only harm shall come to them!*

It was true—it had always been true. But I had to endeavour to make our peace. "Helena, please. I did not ask you to be there, you know that. You did not have to follow me."

"Oh, but I did!" she replied. "Of course I did! For it was plain to me that something had begun to take hold of you. I could see it from the first moment your father spoke to us of your cousin, of that—that *fairy*! The way you looked, the way you grieved—and I did not wish it to continue, Albie. I did not wish to lose you."

It was my turn to be silenced.

"I married you for love, Albie," she said. "Do you not know that? Did you not *see*? I had thought ours a marriage of affection, like—like our good queen and her husband! And now Prince Albert is dead, and you are—*you*. You quit me at the first mention of *her*, flying out of the door as if you could not go quickly enough, and you barely even looked behind you."

I could only stare. I had not suspected my wife of such feeling—of such raw emotion. I had always imagined her to be cool, sensible, controlled, not powerfully affected by anything: a woman after my father's heart. I had not thought her capable of this. *An island*, I had thought, *an island, surrounded by cool, deep waters*. How could I have been so mistaken? And yet, if I had known her so little, how could I ever truly know her at all? How could I ever be certain what she *was*?

I think she saw something of what I thought in my eyes, for she stepped back from me and straightened. "I am your wife, Albie," she said, "in the name of God. And I will be your wife, for that is what I promised to be. But I do not think that I can look at you, not now. Not since—"

I reached out and touched her arm. "I tried, Helena," I said. "I wanted to do what I thought to be right. I wanted to do a good thing. Now I feel as if I am drowning. I do not know what I should do; perhaps I never did. But I will love you, Helena. I—" I voiced the thought that had come to me. "You ever steered me aright, my dear. I always trusted you to do that. You were always the one who was so calm, so clear. I am sorry that I forgot it for a time."

I took a deep breath and met her gaze. "I promised to take care of you, and I shall. I shall take care of you and I *shall* love you, Helena; I hope I can do it as you deserve to be loved. I am sorry for all my errors—there have been many, I am certain, and I am ashamed of them. I can only say I shall do better, for you and for the little one."

Before my eyes, her face began to change. Emotions gathered in her eyes; they darkened as I watched; her cheeks paled. Anger was there, and fear, and bitterness; and finally all gave way to the most exquisite pain.

"Helena?" A remnant of fear twisted inside me, and my heart went cold. I felt as if I were standing atop a precipice, with no firm step to be found anywhere, and I did not want her to speak or to move or to look at me that way any longer, but then her face screwed up into the semblance of an infant's, an angry, furious infant, and I thought of Lizzie's words in her journal—*I couldn't help but think it were old, older than the hills*—and I stepped away from her. I knew it was not her: this could never be her.

She spoke and the spell was broken. "There is no child, Albie."

I was frozen. I did not know how to look at her, how to respond.

She glared at me, unblinking, unrelenting, her eyes bright with tears that had yet to fall. I could not fathom her words. Had she lied to me? Had there never—

"Oh, there was a child," she said, as if reading my thoughts. "When I went to Halfoak, there was a child." Her voice slowed, lowering an octave as a dreadful calm came over her. "That was another reason I followed you, Albie. I wanted you to know. I thought we should be together: husband and wife and their baby—what could be sweeter? But it did not wish to be, Albie. It did not wish to stay!"

Fairies are barren. The words rose unbidden into my mind. I stepped forward, placing my hands on both her shoulders. "It—went away?"

She shrugged free of me. "I lost it," she said. "There was blood—"

A thought struck me and I turned cold. "I pushed you," I whispered, "against the bed, and you fell—was that—?"

She smiled bitterly and shook her head. "It was not your fault, Albie, if that is your chief concern. It simply happened. Perhaps it was not meant to be: we were not a fit family to raise it, and so it left us." She met my eye with a glare so icy it almost stopped my heart. "There was no love between us," she said, "and the child should never have been. And so it *died*, Albie—and you did not even notice it go!"

I opened and closed my mouth. "But I couldn't—I didn't—"

"You couldn't? You didn't? Get out!" She pushed me, beating her hands against my chest. "Get *out*, Albie!"

I fell back, driven less by her blows than by her fury, and at last the tears fell, streaming down her face, but I could not cry; not then. I backed away from her, doing at last what she wanted me to do, and all I could feel was a terrible numbness that started somewhere deep within and spread, cold and deadening, through the very heart of my being. I must have stepped over the threshold, for she slammed the door in my face before I even knew I had left her, and I stood quite still, staring at the blank polished wood, hearing not a single sound from within.

I felt eyes on me then and I turned to see the housekeeper standing at the top of the stairs, a bundle of towels in her hands, her eyes wide. I do not know what it was she saw, but I could not bear it a moment longer and I rushed past her. She cringed back, pressing herself against the wall, and I felt her turn to watch my passing, but I did not look at her; I had to get *out*. I strode across the tiled floor and reached the front door and spilled through it into the populous, tireless street, where no one would trouble to look at me or even know who I was.

Chapter Thirty-Six

I wandered without pattern or intention. I did not see anything before me, only the images whirling through my mind. I could not fix on anything clearly. There was a man with red hair biting into a yellow plum; a woman's hands, weaving stems of straw into a little doll; dandelion seeds floating through the air; an iron knife stuck into the ground, concealing—

But no, I could not think of that. Then I heard in my mind the raucous laughter of the wise woman; I could almost see her pulling at her skirts, and I shook my head—

—and saw that a woman was standing before me. She was rouged and painted, her hair piled high on her head, her neckline shameless and her skirt tucked up to show her petticoats. She was a harlot; she leered at me through reddened lips—she was a grotesquerie. I heard sounds I knew were not there: discordant music; the excited cries of costermongers spilling from a cheap show; I saw the flash of mottled skin beneath tumbled skirts. I shook my head, backing away. I did not want any of it. I only wanted . . . And I thought of a little hand slipping into my arm, of nut-brown eyes peeping shyly from beneath a faded bonnet.

I closed my eyes. I only wanted what was gone from me: what could never be within my reach. Was that all it was, really? Was that all *I* was?

I turned and made my way through the streets, their high brick walls stained irrevocably with soot, as somewhere a church bell began to chime the hour. Soon my father would leave his place of business and return home. What would he find there? I imagined Helena at the table, composed once again, her calm, pale face the image of decorum, and quite, quite silent. I pushed the thought away. It was not fair to her. I felt now that I had always been unfair.

I had believed I had acted for the good, but all was as a quicksand beneath my feet. There was no step I felt sure of taking without causing more harm, and yet I had to go somewhere. I could not bear the thought of my father seeing the chasm that had opened between husband and wife. I could not bear to look upon his disappointment.

I realised I was making my way back, slowly, in the direction of the station. The realisation did not slow my step nor change my mind. I had nowhere else to go. There was only Halfoak and the thing that I had to do, and so I kept going until a cab appeared at the corner and I hailed it. I hurried to step aboard and it swept me away, the rushing movement providing some small comfort. I felt in my pocket, ensuring I had the means to pay my way: I did, and so it was decided. I would not return to my father's home tonight. I would allow Helena a little time to gather herself—it was better she be without me for a while, before we could be reconciled. I would finish my business in the country, and then I could return, when it was done at last; when I could truly say to her that we were to begin again. Perhaps then I could find a way to deserve her.

I found a lodging-house close to the station. The landlady was uncouth, and so tall she might have been stretched to fit her mean, narrow establishment. She led me up the stair, indicated the dingy room I was to occupy, and looked me up and down as if to enquire as to the whereabouts of my luggage. I did not explain.

That night I slept upon a mattress stuffed with straw, and all too soon my little companions for the darkest hours emerged and crept in close. My arms and legs and back crawled at their touch; I burned with their bites. Whenever I searched for them upon my skin, I could not see them; but I knew that they were there.

Chapter Thirty-Seven

The next day passed in a blur once again, a reverse of the last, as the filth of the City gave way to all the green and gold of the country-side. The sky was of mixed character, one moment innocently blue and scuffed with sheep-like clouds, the next darkening with the promise of rain. It put me in mind of another day, long ago, that had not been able to make up its mind, and yet I knew that when I saw Halfoak once more, it would still be summer.

London felt far behind me, but my wife did not; she was con-stantly at my side, her face contorted with despair, yet so distant that she could not speak to me. I was determined that I would make all things right between us, though I could not see how to do so. Still, I tried to concentrate on what I must do before I returned to her. And here was my duty already: Constable Barraclough was waiting for me as I alighted from the train, his chest puffed out and his fore-head creased. I noticed that he had a new button on his jacket; was that in honour of the occasion? He also held an envelope in his hand which I recognised as the one I had left for him the day before—so long ago. I had not known if he would treat my missive seriously; to judge by his expression, he had.

I approached and said good day, but he only frowned more deeply. He waved the envelope before my face before staring at it with a gaze so penetrating he could surely read its contents through the paper.

"I am bewildered, sir," he began. "Whatever did you mean by it? Is it make-believe? I had not heard of there being such an infant in Halfoak, let alone one treated in such a fashion."

A twinge cut through me as I thought of another lost child, but I forced the thought from my mind. Now I must dwell only upon matters in Halfoak, just for one more day. Then, only then, could I leave it far behind me.

The constable went on: "Of course, they keep theirselves to theirselves in Halfoak. They do not welcome my visits; they are reticent of tongue. The farmhands hereabouts have a saying: that a Halfoak man should prefer to speak to his pig than his neighbour if he were divided from him by the boundary of the village; and I cannot admit that there is not some truth in it."

"Well, that may have been part of the difficulty," I said. "To answer your question: first, yes, there was such a child, and that was what they did to it, before the same thing was done to my cousin. It was the start of it all, you see. Well—not quite the start, perhaps. And no, there was no hue and cry; nothing came of it at all. Nobody knew of it because nobody cared—or perhaps they knew a little; the parson knew enough to preach against the child since it was born of sin. He turned his back upon it. I doubt he knows what became of it, nor that he wishes to know. And the father knew of it, of course; but how much easier for him if it had never existed!"

"And where is it?"

I thought of the little grave, unmarked with any name, on the green hillside. It was a few moments before I could gather myself enough to explain its whereabouts. I had wrapped the tiny body once again, after I had looked upon it, and replaced it. I think I had covered it with a fine layer of tilth; I thought I remembered doing so; but the evening had become unclear to me, as so much else.

"It lies beneath the oaks there," I said. "It will be quite plain where the sward has been disturbed and stacked a little to one side . . ." My voice cracked; I could not speak. Helena's stricken face was before me, so real that I could almost touch her. There would be no grave for our child, nowhere she could visit, to take flowers, to shed her tears. There was nothing left but emptiness and hollowness and it stretched out before me, a gaping chasm at my feet.

"Sir?" I realised the constable had asked me a question. He repeated, "How did you know where to find it? How did you know all of this?"

"I will tell you," I said, "but first, I think we should set out for Halfoak. I can explain everything to your satisfaction, I believe, along the road."

He nodded, his brows still lowered, and informed me that a horse and cart was waiting. We turned to leave, and he reached out and seized my arm, his fingers gripping vice-like as if I were some common criminal who might at any moment bolt and make my escape.

The cart was waiting for us outside the station. I had half expected to see Widdop's bay mare, but a smart chestnut with a clean white blaze down its nose stood in the traces. It harrumphed and stamped one foot as we approached, impatient at standing still. A driver stood by its shoulder and another constable—I had not seen him before— was already seated. We climbed aboard, the driver hastily gathering the reins, and we were soon on our way. The road was as dry as ever; the sky was blameless; there was not a single cloud. The sun glared down, ready to burn us all to cinders. Perhaps we deserved no less.

It was not long until the town lay at our backs and the fields were all around us, full of golden-brown stubble where wheat and corn had been harvested.

"You see," I said after a while, "the people here work so hard. I had not thought it so when I first saw Halfoak; I thought all was peaceful repose, when in reality there is as much difficulty and tribulation as in the city—possibly even more so." I was lost in reverie, thinking of the labourers' hardscrabble existence, until I realised the constable was waiting for me to go on.

'Mrs. Gomersal complained to me once that her son was a child of the fairies. She tried to impress upon me what a trial that was to her, but afterwards, I could not help but think she had come out of it rather well: she did not have to slave in the fields as others did. She has a decent cottage and well-dressed children and everything about her is comfortable and neat.

'Her child was not the son of a fairy, Constable Barraclough. Ah—you raise your eyebrows as if to say, *of course he is not*. But many in these parts believe it, or at least in the possibility of it.

"You see, her son—how odd that I find I am uncertain of his name—he is in appearance quite fairy-like, and he barely says two words together. He is practically a wordless child of nature, and so why should people not think him strange? And he was born, after all, long after the death of her husband. How much easier must it have been, particularly in a village with such a thunderous parson, to say she had been bewitched by a fairy, rather than admit what he was?"

"And what was he?"

"He was not the son of a fairy, for certain. He was born of the squire's son: of Edmund Calthorn."

The constable raised his eyebrows, all astonishment.

"He lay with her on the fairy hill, most likely—he goes riding there, and she wanders there often. It was most convenient, then, for her to think of the fairies when she found she was with child. And how fortunate a child! They say the old squire's time is near, and there is no doubt the family has been brought lower by the father's illness and subsequent mismanagement, and yet the son manages quite well to keep Mary Gomersal in her cottage, and to meet her every requirement. He takes care of the boy, though he may well be disappointed to see how he turned out—" Again, an image stopped my words: my father's face, his eyes turned upon me, the tightness of his lips expressing his coldest severity.

I shook my head to dispel the image. 'And if anyone should ask how it is that she lives so well, and her a widow—why, then, the fairies provide! For who does not know the stories of fairy gold? You see how neatly it is all explained. And such has been the way of it for seven years, while the boy grows more silent and the mother fades, until the present—and then what happens? Why, another comes along, younger and more comely, her blonde hair all in curls and her cheeks all blushes: Essie Aikin, who needed a position, and found one most readily at Throstle Grange, under the watchful eyes of the squire's son. His fondness for female company is no closely guarded secret. All laugh at it; they sing of him when they are in their cups.

"His mother, Mrs. Calthorn, would naturally have the management of the servants, but her every moment is presently occupied with her husband's care. So the most natural outcome ensued: Essie Aikin, despoiled and swelling by the day, cast out of her position and unlikely to find another—and what do you suppose might have happened then? An ageing mother and a surly boy giving way to a pretty maid with a laughing baby, and Edmund Calthorn's shrinking purse unable to keep them both."

The constable grunted; I did not know if it were in understanding or doubt.

"Mrs. Gomersal's fine cottage, her upkeep—all might have devolved to another, if Calthorn's purse had proved as fickle as his eye."

He frowned. "But the pages from Lizzie Higgs' journal, enclosed with your letter—I trust that is what these are—speak of 'they.' I know not who 'they' are, sir, and begging your pardon, it could have referred to anyone, could it not?"

"Ah—it was not anyone, constable. But I am running ahead." I glanced around me, lulled by the steady plod of the horse, its ears flicking at a cloud of flies about its head; by the heat; the somnolence of the day. The driver had not once turned, though his back was stiff, and I wondered what he made of it all.

"Mary Gomersal did not wish to change places with another," I said. "She had grown rather fond of her situation in life. And so, after the baby came into the world, she wasted no time in accusing it of being a changeling. She told its mother that the fairies had stolen her real child away, and after all, Mary knew all about the fairies, did she not?"

"But they surely would not believe her."

"Ah, but they did! And circumstances supported her claims. The parson, full of disgust at its parentage, would have refused to christen it. The girl had not yet even named it, which meant the child was not protected from the fairies by God nor by man. Mrs. Gomersal found a way to have at it." My voice turned bitter, and I endeavoured to speak calmly.

"I have spoken to the mother. She was quite convinced her own child would be returned to her after they disposed of the changeling in the way you have read of already in those pages. I even saw her one night, upon the fairy hill, waiting for it. I believe her to have been entirely taken in; her father, also. It says little for their credulity, but—well, such is the way of Halfoak. And people have believed in stranger things, I suppose."

Another image came to me: my own hands tearing pages from a book and stuffing them into a keyhole. I swallowed down my shame and went on steadily, "It was all in my cousin's journal, but I fear the rest of it is burned now. It was destroyed in an accident, you know. It is a pity. I had read from it, but I had passed over what might have been the most important matters of all: not of the belief in fairies, but about everyday things. Lizzie had written there about Mary's home and situation, and of her own, and of her neighbours'. I did not dwell on the detail; there was nothing of magic in it, you see—"

Suddenly I buried my face in my hands. "How would you know?" I asked. "If someone told you that your wife was not your wife, that your child was not your child—how could you ever really look into their eyes again and be certain? Every strange word, every infant temper, everything you had not seen before would raise its own doubts. We are born to wonder, are we not, we human beings? If we did not, if we had no wonder, no curiosity, no . . . imagination, what would we be then? We would be no better than beasts in the field."

The constable made another sound in the back of his throat, balanced exactly between assent and denial. I did not answer it, but roused myself and continued, "Mary Gomersal once said to me that in offering her treatments—her *cures*—to the little changeling, she was only trying to be kind. She said she was trying to spare its mother from what *she* had. I thought at the time she was speaking of her own fairy child, but now I think she was not. I think she was mocking me. She *did* wish to spare Essie Aikin what she had—but what did she have? A good home and a steady income. You see, I had thought it was all truly about the fairies. Halfoak is a place particularly lent to dreaming, is it not? 'Alfoak—*our folk*. There have been tales told about the hidden people of its hills and dells for centuries."

I paused. "I had thought it a story as old as time," I said, "and you see, it *was*—but a story of a different kind. It was about love, and jealousy, and passion, and about the material conditions of life. What was one little baby in the face of all their comforts? I wonder, after all, how much its mother, and poor Essie's father, actually *wished* to believe. It would have been so much easier, so . . . but that is a question I cannot answer. I only know they were sincere enough for me to be convinced of them as the dupes of Mary Gomersal."

"We shall know soon enough," the constable said.

He was right; there ahead of me was the road leading into Halfoak. There was the inn, its rusty horseshoes still nailed above its doors. There was the church, the grey spire with the clock still dragging its too many hands around its face. There was the green, and there, in the middle of it all, the cloven tree from whence the village had gained its name: the blasted thing, half living and half dead, still holding a misshapen crown aloft, trailing ragged ribbons and ancient withered flowers in its wake.

Chapter Thirty-Eight

I directed the driver towards the little cottage where I had last seen Mary Gomersal and her brood sitting by the door. I realised these might be my last peaceful moments before we reached it, but I felt too much turmoil within to find any comfort in exterior things.

We turned our back on the green and followed the lane. I did not shout when we reached the little gate but reached out and tapped the driver's arm. He pulled up the horse at once and all of us got down save him. We did not speak to one another. I looked towards the cottage and there they were: Mrs. Gomersal, sitting there with her weaving, golden corn stalks flashing in her hands, and both her daughters were beside her, just as if nothing terrible had happened; as if nothing had changed. The boy was there, too. He had caught a bright green cricket, and was engaged in trying to stuff blades of grass down the little creature's throat.

Mary stood the moment I set my hand upon the gate. Her brows drew down in anger, and then she saw the constables at my back and her expression changed. She turned to the girls and ushered them inside at once, her voice shrill. They left their work scattered upon the step and went in, casting sharp little glances towards us. The boy, as before, stayed where he was; he did not even look up.

I did not know where I should begin, but I realised I did not have to. The constable stepped in front of me. "A most interesting tale has come to my ear, Mrs. Gomersal," he began. "Most interesting indeed. It concerns a baby born to one Essie Aikin—you do know her, I take it?"

If he had expected her to pale at this revelation, he had been mistaken. She raised her head and jutted forth her chin. "I 'eard tell of it. What's it to me?"

"I think you have done more than hear tell of it, madam. I think you had a hand in its death, did you not?"

Her eyes flashed, with fury or fear, I could not tell. She shot a look at me so full of malignity it made me shudder.

"I should like to hear it from your own lips," the constable went on. His colleague stood back, waiting. "It would be far better so— about how it was not wanted, and taken for a changeling, and what was done with it thereafter."

Mary tossed her head. "It's not for me to meddle," she said. "They only asked for my 'elp, an' I'm not one to refuse a neighbour. They knew it was a wrong 'un, that bairn. They wanted to do summat forrit, so I went to t' wise woman, an' I told 'em what she told me. That's all. I might 'ave brung a cure for 'em to give it—only a few 'erbs an' such, to put t' fairy out on it. Nowt really. But I din't give 'em to t' bairn, an' I din't do nowt else to it neither, when t' cure din't do what they wanted."

"And what was that?"

"Why, send it back, o' course. They thowt it were a fairy, an' so they wanted rid on it, an' to get their own bairn back again."

The constable cleared his throat. I felt his gaze on my cheek and turned to him. "Wise woman?" he asked.

I nodded. "She is a mad woman who lives in a shack in a field— they call it the leys. She is quite deluded. She claims to have lived among the fairies—she even imagines that she can see them."

"And is it true it was she who supplied the child's cure? You did not speak of this."

"I had no time. Yes, it is true. She is a wild creature, unreclaimed, and I dare say does much harm to those foolish enough to visit her. The woman sells charms for her living. She finds lost items, turns off the evil eye, makes little potions and such like. She is poor, but she earns her bread by putting it about that she's 'failproof.' That is why men go to her who should have more sense than to listen to such nonsense. It would never be in her own interest to fail at sending back a changeling—she, who claims to know the fairies better than anyone. She would never intend to effect so hard a cure that the child was sent beyond the very boundaries of this world."

I turned to Mary, whose face had reddened with fury. "But it was in your interest, was it not, Mrs. Gomersal? It was you who persuaded Miss Aikin that her child was not her own. It was you who convinced her to try your cures—you did it for his sake." I gestured towards her boy, who still sat playing with his little captive upon the ground. At last the child felt our presence and raised his tousled head and gave a sudden broad grin, flashing his white teeth and tossing his curls. In that moment, there could be no doubt of his parentage.

"He is the child of Edmund Calthorn, and it is Calthorn who provides this cottage and his bread, is it not? He paid for the boots upon the boy's feet. Such matters are easily proved. You may turn your face away if you wish; we do not need your answer. We shall ask Calthorn himself."

"Tha'll do no such thing," Mrs. Gomersal cried. "'Tis madness— what's t' squire's lad to me?"

"Less, perhaps, than he was to Essie Aikin."

Her eyes flashed with vicious fury.

"Your dalliance was first, but her child was his also," I went on, "and with her so young and fresh and pretty—the baby was a threat to your existence, and so you removed it."

She stepped towards me, hissing like a snake. "Tha's got no proof o' that. I'd do no such thing, no such—" She reached out her hands;

they curled into claws. I did nothing to prevent her. Let her do what she would; let all see what she was.

But the constable was in her path and he waved something before his face. "No proof?" he said. "None? You see, certain papers have come into my possession, Mrs. Gomersal. They give a very different account."

He began to read from the pages I had glanced over, but had not had the time to finish:

> They said the bairn could not say its name and so they held its nose and poured cure straight down its throat. It coughed and then it swallowed. It didn't seem to do no harm, but it didn't do no good neither.
>
> Essie were happy with that, she said it was done and it were her bairn after all, but Mary said no. She said you could tell by looking in the eyes and she had Essie do it too, longer than enough, until she saw what she meant. I don't know what it was she saw. I said it were Mary's ideas reflected there, and that they were nowt, but Essie said she knew all about it, since Mary had been with a fairy herself, and she wouldn't hear nowt against her.

He looked up. "It seems this wise woman is not the only one to claim acquaintance with the fairies, is that not so?"

At first, Mrs. Gomersal did not answer; her lip trembled. When she spoke, her voice was a growl. "Whose hand is that? Who is it that accuses me?"

The constable opened his mouth to answer, but I burst in, "It was written by my cousin—by Lizzie Higgs! Her voice accuses you from the grave, Mrs. Gomersal—she cries from the ground."

"Mr. Mirralls." The constable grasped my arm and drew me back.

"Look at her—you know what she did next—you see it in her face!" I endeavoured to gather myself. "She burned the child, so badly that it could not live long enough to take *her* living from her. And then my cousin came to know it. She was in Essie Aikin's confidence, but she saw things too; I believe she always knew more of Mary Gomersal than the woman would allow. Lizzie saw their

comings and goings on the hill—Mary's, and Edmund Calthorn's.
She could hardly fail, her cottage being where it is—ah, they always
said it was an unlucky house! And they were right, though not for
the reasons they imagined. My cousin knew too much altogether,
did she not, Mary? And when she learned of what you did to the
child, she wanted to tell. You heard of it—probably her husband
told his cousin Thomas Aikin, Essie's father, and thus it came to your
ear, and so you turned on her also. What was it you said to her—to
her husband? That she was an unnatural wife, to wish to turn her
back on you all—so unnatural, in fact, that she could not really *be*
his wife?"

Mrs. Gomersal stared at me with hatred in her eyes. "I said nowt!
Jem came to me—he teld me Lizzie 'ad been taken too, that she'd
gone wandering on t' 'ill, only it were never 'is Lizzie what came
back—"

"And so you helped him get rid of her, just as you helped Essie
Aikin kill her child!"

"It *weren't* 'er child. It weren't *anything*."

"You accused my Lizzie before she could accuse you. You got
rid of her before she could harm you. She would have seen you in
prison for what you did. Such would have been right; but instead,
you stuffed your poisons down her throat and forced her to swallow
them. You pushed her down before the fire and held her to it, did
you not? Did you not pity her as she burned? Had you no mercy
in you?"

At first Mrs. Gomersal said nothing, but then she flew at me.
The constable caught her and held her back. "An' what o' that?"
she shrieked. "What o' that? It's only 'is word. There's nowt to say
it were true! Nowt! What did I do? I asked a mam to look into her
babby's eyes an' see what she would. I teld Jem Higgs 'is wife weren't
actin' nat'ral, an' 'e saw she weren't. What else is there? Prove to me
I've done summat wrong an' I'll walk to gaol mesel'—I'll weave t'
rope about me own neck!"

I was frozen. I could do nothing more. I waited for the constable
to march her towards the cart; to put her in irons; for something to

happen. Nothing did. The day stretched on, the sun kept shining; all was soundless and weighted with heat, and nobody moved at all.

Then came a sound: the boy, whispering his nonsense to the insect he gripped so cruelly. I knew that all would come to nothing: Mary Gomersal would go free and I would return home having failed my cousin as well as my wife. The constable would speak of the madman who had once come to Halfoak with his lunatic accusations and his derangement, and no one in this place would ever contradict him.

The boy went on with his little whispers and I heard another sound below that, a small clicking made by his captive, exactly like the winding of a watch counting down the passing seconds. Slowly, I turned to the constable. "I have proof," I said.

Mary's gaze darted to me. "There can be none. No proof can exist against them who is innocent!"

I edged around her and the constable and knelt at the little boy's side. He did not turn to me, nor appear to notice I was there. The insect went on with its clicking and he went on with his whispering, and I began to whisper with him. Encouraged, he spoke louder until he began to sing, as I had once heard his sisters do:

> *Tell-pie-tit*
> *Thy tongue'll split*
> *An' ev'ry dog in the town'll get a little bit!*

I looked up at Mary Gomersal. The constable was gripping her arm, preventing her from flying at me. Softly, so as not to disturb the boy, I said, "Did my cousin die because she was a changeling, as you insist? Or was it because she was a tattle-tale—because she wanted everybody to know what you had done?"

I reached out and stroked the boy's curls and he turned his head towards me. "Child," I said, "do you sing of the magpie?"

His mother cried out in protest and attempted to lunge towards me, but the constable's grip held.

The boy shook his head. His smile was like sunshine.

"What, then?"

He screwed up his face as if he did not like to speak. Then he brought his hand down—*smack!*—upon the cricket, and he raised it again, laughing in delight at the sticky mess he had made. "Lizzie Higgs!" he said. "Lizzie tell-tale!"

"It means nowt—he dun't understand!" Mary struggled. "He's simple as simple—he dun't know anythin'! You think that's proof of owt at all? It in't!"

Constable Barraclough cleared his throat. I knew him to be thinking the same. "But it is," I said. "Others in the village sing about the fairy maid, do they not? You might have heard them. '*O there I met with a bonny maid, as bright as any fairy.*' They would not admit of it, but I believe they sing of Lizzie Higgs. And yet in this house, they sing of the tell-pie-tit and talk of tattle-tales. Why should they do so unless what was uppermost in their minds was the fear that my cousin would tell what they had done? And Mary Gomersal saw her dead—because she was afraid of her!"

Mary shrieked, twisting in the constable's arms like a very devil, so that his colleague had to come forward and assist him in restraining her. "No—no! It's all lies—she were a fairy! A *fairy*, an' she 'witched us all!"

At my side, the boy at last realised there was a problem and began to cry, his face crumpling as he looked from his mother to the constables and back again. In another moment the girls spilled from the door, all bewilderment and concern. Flora came and took the boy's hand and pulled him to her side.

My gaze dropped to her feet, to the dolls they had been engaged in weaving, and I thought of something else. I stepped forward and picked one up, and spoke as if musing. "You say you believe in them," I said. "You believe that they live, hidden and secret, inside Pudding Pye Hill; in the land where it is always summer."

"I do."

"And the doorway stands open, does it not? Held open by an iron blade, placed there by Jem Higgs in the hope it would allow his true wife to return to him."

"I said so!"

"And that is why this summer is interminable—why the sun will not stop smiling on Halfoak. Because the door stands open and it will not stop spilling out. Why, if that blade is not removed, it could be summer for ever."

Her eyes blazed, as if it had just occurred to her that here was set before her a trap.

I turned to Flora and Ivy. I held up the corn doll. "What is this?"

"A kern-baby, sir," Flora answered.

"And its purpose?"

"It's to give an 'ome to t' spirit of the 'arvest." She frowned in confusion. "It lives in t' doll. It 'as to, see, when all t' corn's cut down. Where else would it go? So it lives in there, till t' land's ploughed again, an' they plough that doll into t' soil, an' t' spirit goes back into t' land an' makes new corn grow."

For a moment, there was silence. "You believe, then, that the summer will end. The autumn will come and the men will plough."

The girl frowned, wondering why I should even ask; but she saw the eyes all looking at her and she said nothing.

Mary hissed, "Fairies. All of it, the fairies—!"

I turned to her and slowly smiled. "You see how it is," I said to the constable. "The wise woman must practise her charms because if she does not, she would not eat. And Mary Gomersal believes in the fairies because she must."

"Must! Of course I must! Someone 'ad ter do it—if I din't, they'd be all over t' place! They'd 'ave our lives—our souls—our 'omes—" She faltered.

"I believe I have heard enough," the constable said, "and from your own lips, Mrs. Gomersal. I dare say this wise woman will confirm your part in it."

Her eyes narrowed to slits and she fairly spat with fury. "The wise woman? *Her!* Why, if 'er cures 'ad done what they ought to, I'd 'ave been set up in t' first place. If them 'erbs 'ad worked afore it were ever born, none o' this would 'ave been! There'd 'ave been no bairn, she'd never 'ave 'ad nowt to tell, I wouldn't 'ave 'ad to—"

I did not know how to answer. It was the constable who said, "What's that—you gave it a cure for being a changeling before it ever came into the world? How so?"

"Fool!" she answered. And then she turned her gaze upon me. "Aye, I did, or she thowt I did. She were a simpleton, that lass! I told 'er it were sure to be such a pretty child, it were at risk from bein' stole afore it were even out of 'er belly. An' she took it right enough, drained it straight off in a mouthful."

I frowned. "But it didn't work—you didn't even want it to work. You needed it to be a changeling—"

"Oh, you dolt!" she said. "She thowt them 'erbs were for a changeling, but it weren't no fairy them 'erbs was meant to cure. It were meant to bring it off!"

I stared at her, my whole being suddenly frozen. Nothing moved. The world stood still; no time passed. The constable said something, I knew not what. The girls had begun to cry too. I could not fathom her words; I could not think straight.

At last I stammered, "But—herbs meant to take a child's life while it still grew? They were not the same herbs you gave to my cousin—to Lizzie?"

"O' course!" she spat. "What I gave to one, I gave t' other. It were all for t' same thing, to send a changeling away. It 'ad to look right, an' it made no diff'rence. Besides, Mother Crow'll not cure owt for nowt, even for me! And anyway, it were only one of 'em that were havin' a bairn."

I stared at her. She looked back at me and I watched as the defiance in her eyes gave way to something else. She had realised the truth.

And so had I.

Her lips began moving once more. I caught the words, "Aye, well, I'm sorry for it, but—" and, "No matter, it changed nowt in the end—" but I heard none of it, not really. I was barely even present. I was in the cottage, half in a dream, standing cold-footed in the pantry. I was feeling my way along a shelf. I was reaching down a little jug I found where it had been concealed. I was mixing the residue that lay within with water, making it into a paste so that it could mingle with the tea. I closed my eyes and Helena's face was waiting for me there. I heard her low voice—*not your fault* . . .

I could not conceive of the kindness she had found within herself to utter those words to me, after all that I had done. Leading her from her home, alone and friendless, and bringing her—where? Among whom? I barely knew. She had never suspected, as she spoke those words, that they were anything but the truth.

I covered my face and saw only darkness. It was formless and empty and vast, and yet not endless enough to encompass all that I had lost; all that I had done.

Someone shook my shoulder, but I did not respond. I knew that Helena was still there, in my father's house. She would be waiting when I returned. For her, perhaps what had happened between us could still be mended. Perhaps she might one day find it within herself to look me in the eyes. But I knew I would never be able to look into hers again.

At last, I returned to the world. The first thing I saw was Mary Gomersal: her set features and sharp eyes. "Oh," she said softly. Her gaze was fixed on my own; she stared into me; she knew everything, saw it all. "*Oh.*"

And she began to laugh as the constables led her away, twisting in their arms to look at me, not at her children or her house but at *me*, and her laughter rose, encompassing everything, becoming everything, and I heard it and I despaired. I knew there would never be a time when I would *not* hear it, echoing always in my ears.

Constable Barraclough did not ask what her laughter meant. Possibly he thought her mad, but it did not matter. He placed her in the cart, his colleague on one side of her, and he settled himself on the other. I began to walk past them, my steps unsteady.

His voice followed me. "Where do you go—wait! Sir—do you not return with us?"

I did not reply.

"Wait!" he called again, and he made some sound of exaspera-tion. "If you must go, be sure to come to see me when you are next in Kelthorpe. I shall wish to speak to you!"

I waved his words aside, a single gesture, and I continued to walk. It must have been enough; I heard the clop of the horse beginning its journey. I looked up into the blameless sky before I continued walking along the road. It was still such a beautiful day.

Chapter Thirty-Nine

I came to the little stream that bounded the edge of Pudding Pye Hill and leaned out over the cold, clear water. There was nothing special about it, but I wished it the River Lethe, so I could lay down and drink of it and forget everything that had passed: my very self; even my own name. I stared into it for a long time, lost in its endless dream, and then I turned. I knew where I must go, and my hand went to my pocket. The key to the door was still there, as if I had known I would need it again.

The cottage stood abandoned once more, alone in the world, with only flowers and birds for company. I let myself in, moving like a marionette; the hands that held the key and turned it barely looked like my own; it scarcely felt like my own feet that carried me over the threshold.

I did not look into the parlour. I feared that if I did, I should see Lizzie's ghost at last, blackened and cracked and smiling upon the hearth. Instead I went up the stairs, the sound of my steps too steady and too solid to my ear. I did not enter the room I had called my own, but Helena's. Everything was too still and silent; surely everything should be raging, in a tumult, united in outrage at all that had passed . . . but there was only me and the empty room.

I sat upon the bed, my hands resting on the coverlet, staring at nothing. Then I rose and went to the wardrobe and opened it. Helena had not had time to pack all of her belongings. Her dresses were still there, folded neatly upon the shelves, empty of her form and character. I plunged my hands in among them, as if I could seize hold of all that we once had and bring it back to me, and I bent my head and I wept, pressing my face into the cottons and silks and brocades.

At last, even tears must cease. I drew back, staring at the water-spotted garments—had I ruined them also?—then it came to me that Lizzie had left her clothes behind her too; that I did not even know to whom these belonged, and I stumbled away from them.

I made my way into the room where I had slept. There was the window where I had stood and listened to a violin, its tripping airs stirring my soul so that I yearned to follow after it. There was the place I had lain my head upon a borrowed pillow, reading the book I had taken from my wife, and another, from my cousin. I did not feel now that I had understood either of them.

Here was the place I had pushed Helena away from me. I could not look at it. I turned and went back down the stairs, the sound of my steps once more too loud, too ordinary. There was the door I had locked against my wife, fearing what she might do; fearing what she might *be*. There was where I had torn the pages from her book to block up the chinks. That was another life; it surely could have no connection to me.

I went into the parlour. It too was still and empty and I stood at its centre. I had stood here before, staring at the ceiling, listening to little feet tapping across the floor above. I had listened to a mouse, and taken it for—what?

I turned and went to the kitchen door and saw, beyond it, the one that led to the pantry. I had meant to look in upon it too, to see everything, but I could move no closer. I knew what I had done there and I could not face it again.

Instead I went back into the parlour and crouched before the fireplace, now cold and dead. I ran a finger across the hearth. This was the home which I had provided for my wife; here the fire by which I had bade her to sit. Here, where a young woman had burned; and I had burned there too, mourning a cousin I had met only once in my life; a woman I had never really known at all.

I slumped into the chair where Helena had been wont to sit, her back so straight, and distantly, I heard a sound.

I went to the window and threw open the casement. My heart beat painfully within my chest. It was music—and such music as I had never before heard. It rose to meet me, the violins weeping and dying before rising again from the ash, a plaintive air so full of joy and sorrow that I yearned after it. In that moment, I knew that I would break; indeed, that I had already broken.

I turned aside and found myself facing the wide, spotted mirror hanging upon the wall. I did not recognise my own reflection; I leaned in closer and stared, unblinking, at the pale-faced, withered creature before me. It stared back; I wondered that it did not flinch from the sight. The features were mine, albeit thinner than they had been, but they were strange to me. The lips were whiter, the cheeks more sharply carved into hollows, the shadows lying deeper than they once had. The eyes, though, were the most peculiar thing of all; they met my own with the look of a stranger.

I swayed as a wave of dizziness took me, and the figure in the mirror swayed also, but I knew it to be a sham. It was something I did not—could not—understand, and then it came to me, I suddenly saw it all, and I felt sickened.

The hands that had pushed my wife away were not *my* hands. The ones that stole her book from her, that left her miserable—surely not mine. The being who crept into a pantry in the dead of night and took up a jug of old, dried herbs and mixed them into a paste—those hands had not been mine; they could never have been mine.

I caught my breath, started back from the mirror and peered at my fingers, spread before me. I saw it all. I had thought my wife a stranger to me; I had thought her changed, and she had been: she had changed as was *natural*, as should be expected. But I? I had changed also, and I had had no reason for it. My wife should have ever been as dear to me as she once was, but I had been a man possessed: a stranger even to myself. The one who had truly changed was me.

I rushed back to the mirror, seizing the frame and pushing my face up close to the glass, staring into the dimness. The face inside it was wild; elemental; *different*. I did not understand how I had failed to see it before, and yet—the old stories told of this too, didn't they? Some changelings forgot they were changelings, burying the knowledge so deeply that they could stay with their human families for ever.

In the next moment, I had torn the mirror from its hook on the wall and thrown it into the fireplace. It shattered; my image was fragmented into a hundred pieces and all of them stared back at me with *those* eyes! I could not bear it. Did a changeling not *know* itself to be a changeling? Why could they not be brought to understand what they were before they could do harm?

I looked at my hands once more, knowing what they had done— that they had stolen the life from my unborn child. All doubt drained from me. I was an unnatural creature; indeed, I know not how I could ever have considered myself to be a man.

I fell to my knees upon the hearth and snatched up a shard of glass, pointed and wickedly sharp, and stared into it. There appeared once more before me that familiar form: an illusion; a spectre. And then something strange happened, because as I watched, the form's expression changed; knowledge passed across its features— understanding, even an awful kind of acceptance. And then, slowly, the figure which looked just like me shifted and turned its back upon me.

I stared for one brief moment at the back of its head, and then I hurled it into the fireplace and rushed from the house. This time, I left the key in the door behind me.

Chapter Forty

I hurried up the slope of Pudding Pye Hill, seeing everything anew, and yet remembering the first time I had taken this path. The sunshine lent the grass an almost unnatural brilliancy and the sky above me was the most vivid and peerless blue. Buttercups shone like glass amidst the viridian, and I saw that something had changed after all: the dandelions were reduced to stalks, denuded of their seeds. There were no more clocks. The hours, minutes and seconds had all blown away.

I turned to see Halfoak, still somnolent, still peaceful, a thousand miles or more from the possibility of wickedness or tribulation. There, all went on as they always had—all, save perhaps for one.

I did not wish to dwell upon it. I remembered the way I had once climbed this hill, unused, then, to the endless glare of summer, and I had sat upon the barrow. There, sleep had overtaken me, rising out of the earth until I had been enveloped by it. She had warned me, had she not, that it was dangerous to sleep in such a place; that the fairies would come and steal my soul away. Perhaps even then, they already had.

I stumbled onward, not towards the crown of the hill but towards the little oaken grove. All was more vivid to my eye than it had ever been: enchanter's nightshade nodded in the sunshine; self-heal pushed its purple flowers up from the verdure whilst henbane bent beneath my feet. I knew all their names at last; they had been revealed to me. And then, with a start, I saw them.

It was so brief it might never have happened. I saw eyes, eyes peeping at me from behind a blade of grass, and then gone. Something fluttered at the edge of my vision and I whirled to see wings of the most brilliant blue, there in a moment and then vanished. As I stared, a little face emerged from the bell of a foxglove. It was sly and grinning, the eyes shaped like a cat's and as black as sloes, and I realised that I could no longer hear their music; that in its place there was only the faintest tinkling of laughter.

When I tried to look at them directly, they hid from me. I smiled at them but they would not greet me—that, perhaps, was as it should be. And yet I felt them watching, their eyes upon me, all around and everywhere. As I went on they were lost to sight, but I knew that they were there still, all of them, so bright and so beautiful; I saw their glowing colours; I glimpsed their tiny wings; and my smile broadened as I went, feeling all of their splendour, their *presence*, the magic that had been hidden and was revealed to me at last. And I saw that everything was more wonderful with them in the world. I did not sing the words that were in my heart, but the whole of my being expanded at the idea of them so that I felt it must burst for the joy and the madness of it.

The grass was soft under my feet. Thorn bushes did not scratch or hinder my way. It was not long before I was standing once again before the fairy ring, marked out so plainly in the grass. I did not enter it, not now; there was no need.

I stood beneath the first trees—they had not ceased their whispering; perhaps they never did. Perhaps now they would whisper to me. And it occurred to me then that they might all be waiting for me within the hill: my true wife, my true child. They would become the music I could almost hear, swelling and rising with the flowing of my blood and the beating of my heart, so filled with joy and sorrow and yearning. I would take them in my arms; they would cleave to me, and their smiles would have love in them; there would be nothing between us, no broken trust, no blackened promises, nothing to mar our perfect happiness. My heart, of a sudden, felt light, as if I were nothing but a dandelion seed, ready to blow away on the air.

There was but one thing remaining to be done. I forced myself to walk to the little grave. It was just as I had described it, in another world entirely. The sward was cut and stacked, the topmost layers yellowing in the sun. The earth, which had been so dark beneath its covering, had dried to a dull, lifeless grey. I had, as I had thought, covered it once more; the sad contents were gratefully hidden. At its head, still in its place in the ground, was the iron blade, keeping the door open.

I stood there for a time, looking down at the grave with its nameless occupant, returned to the hollow hill by the people of Halfoak. I did not know how long I lingered, but the air grew cooler and the breeze gained in strength, wrapping itself about me, and after a time its caress became interspersed with stronger gusts that presaged rain. The shadows lengthened, those of branches and twigs stretching inwards like fingers towards the cleft that lay on the other side of the grove. They pointed the way.

The light grew lurid with the hues of sunset, but still I did not turn. Instead I bent, seizing the knife by its leather handle, and without touching the iron, I pulled it from the earth. There was no reluctance; it slid out easily, the blade clean. The metal did not look as if it could burn my skin; it was cold and indifferent.

I walked towards the door in the hill, taking the knife with me. How long I had pondered the secrets of what might lie within, and still I had no inkling of what they may be; I knew only that its mysteries, held so close, were now upon me; and that soon I should know them all. I knew also that I would never tell. There were things of this world—and not of this world—that each man must discover for himself.

I did not look back. From somewhere behind me came the first distant intimations of thunder. It was the end of summer; the end of all things. It appeared, at last, that we were going to have a storm.

Out-worn heart, in a time out-worn,
Come clear of the nets of wrong and right;
Laugh, heart, again in the gray twilight;
Sigh, heart, again in the dew of the morn.

Come, heart, where hill is heaped upon hill:
For there the mystical brotherhood
Of sun and moon and hollow and wood
And river and stream work out their will;

And God stands winding His lonely horn,
And time and the world are ever in flight;
And love is less kind than the gray twilight,
And hope is less dear than the dew of the morn.

William Butler Yeats

Black and chill are Their nights on the wold;
And They live so long and They feel no pain:
I shall grow up, but never grow old,
I shall always, always be very cold,
I shall never come back again!

Charlotte Mary Mew

Acknowledgments

A couple of years ago, a fellow writer called Simon Clark asked me to write a short story for an anthology he was editing, called *The Mammoth Book of Sherlock Holmes Abroad*. I'll confess, the idea terrified me. I knew very little of Sherlock Holmes, and furthermore, the story would clearly need to be set not just in the past but overseas. It looked rather like a research-heavy nightmare, but the concept intrigued me, so I did what I often do with short story requests that sound like there might be an adventure attached: I said yes and figured I'd work it all out later. I followed up that "yes" with a month of immersion in Sir Arthur Conan Doyle's stories. Actually, I got lost in them. I watched all the re-runs of Sherlock adaptations on television that I could. I loved it all: not just the characters, but the author's wonderful use of language. And then I wrote my story, and found I loved doing that too.

This long-winded introduction is my way of thanking Simon Clark for giving me a nudge to try something, without which I'm not sure I'd have set out on the voyage that became *The Hidden People*. It not only gave me an interest in the era but a little confidence in writing a historical novel. So thank you, Simon, and indeed all the other independent press editors and publishers who have, from time to time, led me down new creative roads.

Massive thanks are due as ever to my beloved editor, Jo Fletcher, along with the team at Jo Fletcher Books and Quercus. Your enthusiasm made it a whole lot easier, and once again, I have benefited from Jo's editing magic (despite those darlings I couldn't quite kill). Thank you too to my agent Oli Munson, who has been hugely supportive of this project. I am also grateful to Leo Nickolls for an amazing cover design and to Wayne McManus for taking care of my website.

It may sound a little odd to thank a whole county in the acknowledgements, but this book owes so much to Yorkshire, as do I. It is a place full of richness and beauty and bluffness and odd words and wonderful sayings, even if, as Albie discovers, it may sometimes be a little short on consonants. Thanks in particular to Julie Law and the Meadowcroft girls for helping me collect Yorkshire-isms. I will try harder in future to "put t' wood in t' oyle."

Finally, for putting up with my odd and bookish ways, thanks are due as ever to Fergus, and to my parents Ann and Trevor. Love always.

Author's Note

The idea for this novel began, somewhat sadly, with the rather unpleasant case of Bridget Cleary, an Irish woman who was burned as a fairy changeling in 1895. Hers wasn't an isolated case, though it was one of the most recent and shocking deaths connected with the idea of changelings. Of course, fairy beliefs are perhaps rooted deepest and linger longest in the Celtic countries. The word "Celtic" comes from the Greek "keltoi," with "kel" meaning hidden—so they were the original "hidden people." The name Kelthorpe in this book is a little nod in that direction.

Yorkshire has its own tales of the folk, however. The name Pudding Pye Hill is borrowed from an ancient barrow near Thirsk, a mound which was said to have been raised by the fairies. Legend has it that if you run around it nine times, climb to the top and stick a knife in the ground, you will be able to hear their revelry within. Maybe one day I'll try it. There are also ancient tales of farm labourers stepping into fairy rings and being stolen by the folk; probably a grand excuse for an unexplained absence.

Several of my sources tell of the railways sweeping such beliefs away, and yet they persisted in forgotten corners of the land, or even not so forgotten: as late as 1917, Sir Arthur Conan Doyle proclaimed his belief in the fairies said to have been caught on camera at Cottingley, near Bradford in West Yorkshire. In his treatise *The Coming of the Fairies* he included several accounts of people's sightings of the little folk.

It may surprise many that cunning folk such as the wise woman were operating as late as the first half of the twentieth century. They did indeed gain much of their income from simple charms, herbal remedies or finding lost things; using iron goggles to view the fairies or staring into a bird's yellow eye to draw out the jaundice are based on real examples of their art.

And now to sources. The lines from William Butler Yeats in the epigraph are from a lesser-known version of his poem "The Stolen Child," as published in his book *Fairy and Folk Tales of the Irish Peasantry*. I preferred the mention of woodland to the more usual "waters and the wild" for the contrast with Charlotte Mary Mew's rather more terrifying wood in the extract from her poem "The Changeling." The lines at the end of the novel are taken from the same poem by Mew, whilst the verses from Yeats are from "Into the Twilight." *All Things Bright and Beautiful* was written by Cecil Frances Alexander.

The sharp-eyed will spot that Helena's "Look, Lizzie" song in chapter twenty-eight is from Christina Rossetti's poem "Goblin Market." I have of course quoted in several places from *Wuthering Heights* by Emily Brontë, and from the traditional folk songs *A Beautiful Boy*, *My Bonny Yorkshire Lass* and *The Poor Old Weaver's Daughter*. The Yorkshire Garland website at www.yorkshirefolksong.net was invaluable for setting me on their trail.

For those who would like to delve more deeply into some of the subjects touched on in the novel, here are some of the books or websites I found particularly interesting during my research:

The Burning of Bridget Cleary: A True Story, Angela Bourke
The Science of Fairy Tales: An Enquiry into Fairy Mythology,
    Edwin Sidney Hartland
The Coming of the Fairies, Sir Arthur Conan Doyle
The Edge of the Unknown, Sir Arthur Conan Doyle

The Celtic Twilight, W. B. Yeats

The Wind Among the Reeds, W. B. Yeat

Fairy and Folk Tales of the Irish Peasantry, W. B. Yeats

Grimm's Fairy Stories, Jacob and Wilhelm Grimm

Fairy Tales: Their Origin and Meaning, With Some Account of Dwellers in Fairyland, John Thackray Bunce

The Secret Commonwealth of Elves, Fauns & Fairies: A Study In Folk-lore & Psychical Research, Robert Kirk

Once Upon a Time, Marina Warner

www.fairyist.com

http://plover.net/~agarvin/faerie/poems/

The Old Straight Track: Its Mounds, Beacons, Moats, Sites and Mark Stones, Alfred Watkins

County Folklore Vol 2—The Folklore Society, 1899, Mrs. Gutch

Wit, Character, Folklore and Customs of the North Riding of Yorkshire, Richard Blakeborough

Yorkshire Folk-Talk, Marmaduke Charles Frederick Morris

Folklore Myths and Legends of Britain, Russell Ash and Katherine Briggs

Popular Magic: Cunning-folk in English History, Owen Davies

Daily Life in Victorian London: An Extraordinary Anthology, Lee Jackson

The Victorian House: Domestic Life from Childbirth to Deathbed, Judith Flanders

The Real Lark Rise to Candleford: Life in the Victorian Countryside, Pamela Horn

How to be a Victorian, Ruth Goodman

Victorian Country Life, Janet Sacks

Victorian London: The Life of a City 1840–1870, Liza Picard

Victorian Farm, Alex Langlands, Peter Ginn and Ruth Goodman

Houdini and Conan Doyle, Christopher Sandford

What Jane Austen Ate and Charles Dickens Knew, Daniel Pool

Forms of Speech in Victorian Fiction, Raymond Chapman

Hedingham Harvest: Victorian Family Life in Rural England,
   Geoffrey Robinson
www.ephemera-society.org.uk
www.crystalpalacefoundation.org.uk
http://ballads.bodleian.ox.ac.uk

About the Type

Typeset in Bembo at 11.5/15 pt.

Created by the Monotype Corporation around 1928, the modern interpretation of Bembo is based on an original design by Francesco Griffo that dates back as far as 1495. The modern version has since been a popular choice for publications due to its attractive and legible design.

Typeset by Scribe Inc., Philadelphia, Pennsylvania.